HOMA

Valerie Blumenth
and was educated
She worked in th ... for eight years
while writing for her own pleasure, but is now
writing full-time. *Homage to Sarah* is her third
novel, following *'To Anna' – about whom
nothing is known* and *The Colours of her Days.*

Valerie Blumenthal lives in Oxfordshire.

By the same author

'TO ANNA' – ABOUT WHOM NOTHING IS KNOWN
THE COLOURS OF HER DAYS

VALERIE BLUMENTHAL

Homage to Sarah

Fontana
An Imprint of HarperCollins*Publishers*

First published in 1990
by Collins

This edition first issued in 1991 by Fontana,
an imprint of Harper Collins Publishers,
77–85 Fulham Palace Road,
Hammersmith, London W6 8JB

9 8 7 6 5 4 3 2 1

Printed and bound in Great Britain by
Harper Collins Book Manufacturing, Glasgow

To Ingrid, a much loved daughter

CONTENTS

PROLOGUE

Dawn was just beginning to break, and in a small farmhouse in Dorset a woman sat working in her study. The gaslight illuminated the weariness of her face and the silver threads in her hair. It was New Year's Day, but there had been no party for her the previous night, no celebrations, no husband with whom to usher in the future. It was on his behalf that she was at her writing table, having worked through the night.

She put down her pen. It was over. This dawn, 1898, saw the culmination of three years' work to which she had devoted her energies, her love and her grief. And during that time, when she had immersed herself in his soul, had lived his life in its various stages, and been absorbed by his writings, he was alive and with her constantly: a child, a youth, a young man, then an older one – in all his guises. She had wept with him and rejoiced with him, and now, with the completion of her work, she had lost him – more thoroughly than when she had buried him.

She wiped her eyes and took control of herself once more – she was a strong woman – and added a footnote:

> These diaries of Adam Gilmour reveal the many aspects of his life. I have tampered with them as little as possible, and tried only to condense them into a more readable form. I have spent the past three years editing them in order to share with others the remarkable man to whom I had the great privilege to be married . . .

Chapter One

THE BOY

Tuesday, January 1st, 1861

'New Year's Day, and appropriately it is snowing. The flakes stick momentarily to the dark windowpanes in my room before melting and running down in rivulets. The house still sleeps, heavy after last night's revelry; but soon there will be the sounds of the servants going about their business, each with his allotted tasks, and the house will be purged of soot and cinders and dust and stains, and the fires will crackle away.

'New Year's Day! How I longed to write my name, Adam Gilmour, in this book as soon as Mrs Fitzgerald, our housekeeper, gave it to me for Christmas. It tempted me so, with its tan leather cover and blank, buff-coloured pages, but I knew that I must save it; I decided then that it would be my diary. I am going to keep a diary all my life. Everything I feel, everything I think and see and hear, will be recorded. What escape it offers. How private it will be.

'Jonathan received a box of candies from Mrs Fitzgerald. I do not remember what she gave Leah. I noticed only her gift to Jonathan, and was reassured that she favoured me. That is uncharitable, I know, but Jonathan is favoured in so many ways, and I am a poor comparison to him, as my mother continually reminds me. In the company of my brother and Mama, my stammer is at its worst. With Papa and Leah and Mrs Fitzgerald, I scarcely stammer at all.'

Brambleden was four miles from the riverside town of Henley-on-Thames, where Oxfordshire and Buckinghamshire met. Hidden in a lower fold of the Chilterns, and forming an irregular horseshoe, it was a village of about twenty-five houses and cottages, a provisions shop, a butcher's – to which people from nearby villages and even from Henley itself would flock for its game – St Margaret's Church, the Royal Oak Inn, where farmworkers and squires mingled, and a school, which also served the neighbouring hamlets.

It was a pretty village, with its brick and flint buildings and, meandering round its perimeter, a stream in which children and dogs would play; a happy place in which to grow up. Nobody who lived there had come from more than a few miles away; it was an untroubled place where one could not imagine any unpleasantness.

The little green by the sixteenth-century church was dominated by an ancient oak, beneath which stood an ornate water pump; and it was here that women gathered and gossiped as they waited to fill their pails. Here, too, the milk cart stopped to unload its churns, and dogs would bark excitedly at its arrival, fighting over spilt drops.

Set back from the rest of the village, surrounded by farmland, was Brambleden Manor, where old Lord and Lady Brambleden lived in lonely splendour. To its right, a steep track led to two more houses: one the Rectory – home to kindly Reverend Hibbert, with his passion for chess, and his wife who taught at the school – the other, higher on the rise of the hill so that its views encompassed the village, farmland and wooded valleys, Brambleden Hall. This was neither as large nor as stately as the Manor, and the land belonging to it amounted at most to twenty-five acres; however it was a Queen Anne house of great mellowness and dignity, and natural light flooded into the gracious rooms through well-proportioned windows. It was here that Sir Felix Gilmour and his family lived.

Sir Felix was a tall, genial man of forty-five. He was rather vain of his appearance – of his full head of hair, only just greying, his lean and fit body, his luxuriant whiskers and healthy complexion. But the blue eyes and humorous mouth belonged to a man who did not take himself – or others – too seriously; a man unworried by life, which was as well, since his spasmodic business dealings had resulted in serious financial problems.

'I have just conceived an excellent idea,' he would say to his wife, who would roll her eyes, having long ago become disillusioned with him.

'They are all excellent ideas,' she would comment witheringly. 'And look where they have got you.'

He never took offence. 'This one *really* is.'

His enthusiasm was difficult to suppress, and bordered on eccentricity. Even Lady Elizabeth's disdain could not quash his ebullience, and Adam would sometimes wonder how his father could retain his good humour. Occasionally Adam caught a distant and gentle look in Sir Felix's eye, and he wondered at that, too.

Lady Elizabeth had been beautiful once, with that fair colouring and refined, high-cheekboned beauty that was so English. Her large grey eyes, like her son Adam's, had perhaps held the same softness as his when she was young; but they had grown hard, and her face sharp, her body too thin and unyielding. Nowadays she concentrated her energies on her handsome younger son, Jonathan. And if she had any ability to love, this love she lavished on him; and any ambitions she had were also for him.

Jonathan, although always deferential towards his mother, was dismissive of her attentions, only reciprocating when it was to his advantage. Convinced of his own superiority, there was little he did if no rewards were to be reaped.

Eleven-year-old Leah elicited love from everyone who met her. People noticed her rich brown curls and lively grey eyes, but her real allure lay in her character. Leah made no concessions to anyone; she was not coquettish like so many girls of her age, and her gaze was disconcertingly direct. Spirited and artistic by nature, there were few things that intimidated her, and she faithfully followed her own instincts. Leah was wise beyond her years. She also understood her brother Adam – he of the introspective moods and quiet humour; stubborn, gentle Adam with his elfin features, bouts of ill health, and his obsessions . . .

And apart from the Gilmour family itself, there were numerous servants, the most senior of whom was Mrs Fitzgerald.

'How old are you?' Adam had once asked her.

'One hundred and ninety-nine,' she had answered without hesitation, laughing her fat laugh, as she folded and sorted laundry, before putting it in the linen press on the landing.

Adam had challenged her mischievously. 'Then tell me of life a hundred and ninety-nine years ago.'

'I saw the restoration of Charles the Second, and can remember the Great Plague of London; and a year later, every germ in the air was destroyed by the Great Fire . . . I remember learning verses of

Milton's *Paradise Lost* – and if you are not in bed as your mother requested, I shall threaten to recite them to you and put you to sleep on the spot.'

She was possibly in her early thirties, a childless widow whose life for the past decade had centred around Brambleden Hall and its occupants; in particular Adam. However, in her position she could only convey her fondness in small ways. But he knew of it, and it helped compensate for the knowledge that his mother disliked him.

He could recall her kissing him only once, on his seventh birthday. He remembered his arms around her neck and the longing to be close to her, the fleeting smell of her skin, the touch of her lips – then she had recoiled immediately, with a look of repugnance he had never forgotten.

'I almost died when I gave birth to Adam,' Lady Elizabeth would tell female acquaintances. It was one of her favourite tales, and she told it often, in front of him if he happened to be present. The story gained her sympathy and therefore popularity. 'Never have I known such agony,' she would continue, her hand pressed fervently to her breast. 'And afterwards – never did a baby scream so relentlessly for the first year of his life.'

Once, in the midst of this tale, Sir Felix had entered the parlour where she was entertaining a couple of new friends.

'Oh you're not still harping on about poor young Adam's birth, are you?' he had said brightly, impervious to his wife's glare, and the fact that her 'moment' was destroyed. When he had gone she had tried to recapture it by saying, 'Men cannot comprehend these things. They are so insensitive . . .'

Her companions had instantly rallied with her, and the morning had passed pleasantly, as husbands were torn to shreds.

Sir Felix Gilmour's attempts at business had taken him on travels not only in Britain, but all over the world: a stud farm in Berkshire, a tannery in Spain, a railway in Italy, imported spices from the East, ethnic jewellery from Greece . . . He was a glutton for adventure, and no sooner had one idea failed than he was hit by some new inspiration, and he would be off again – ploughing through the Bay of Biscay on a steamship, sailing peacefully in the Mediterranean, or rocking back and forth to the motion of a train along a ridge of

Tuscan hills. Sometimes he was gone for months – returning in high spirits with gifts and stories and mementoes; refreshed and content, for a while at least, to resume his life as country squire. But Sir Felix's wealth was all inherited, and during the years it dwindled away, lost to the allure of exotic places and outlandish ideas. Reluctantly he decided that those days must end.

But his friends remained loyal, and they frequently visited. They came from all over the place – an eclectic bunch of businessmen and writers, artists and politicians. It was a strange fact that under Sir Felix's roof the most unlikely people mingled – as on that New Year's Eve . . .

From the galleried landing, Adam, kneeling, had peered down into the large hall where guests gathered. He had seen one of his father's ballooning cronies talking to a banker, and a hot-headed radical conversing earnestly with a wealthy landowner. Then his gaze had fixed on the rumpled face of Edward Lear, whom his father had met in Corfu eight years previously. The colour rushed to Adam's cheeks and he longed to go down and speak with him; he remembered the summer, many years ago, when Lear had stayed for a week and told him stories. Since then the visits, in between Lear's voyages, had been rare and more fleeting, but Adam often thought of him and recalled that summer when they had sung ditties and recited nonsense rhymes and roared with laughter together; for Lear liked nothing better than to hear children's laughter.

Adam remained upstairs – and wondered on what pretext his brother had managed, with his mother's approval, to join the adults. Beside him his sister kept up a commentary.

'Look how *huge* Mrs Baxter's skirts are, Addi. How uncomfortable she must be! And Reverend Hibbert's eyes are popping out at the sight of Mrs Ellis's cleavage – it's like two mountains meeting in the middle! Oh I hope I don't have a great bosom like that when I grow up. I should be so ashamed.'

'She looks proud enough! And I think they look more like comfortable cushions than mountains . . . But don't you mind that we're not permitted to go down, Leah?'

She shrugged – a habit for which she was often reprimanded. 'I'm not bothered. It's more fun up here, watching.'

'When I am amongst them I'm lost for words anyway,' Adam consoled himself; and added dismally, 'and then I stammer.'

'You will outgrow it.' She laid her hand on his. 'I overheard Mrs Hibbert tell Mama that, when she visited.'

'They don't discuss me!' He stared at her, horrified.

'I'm sure Mrs Hibbert only meant it kindly.'

'I shall practise my speech,' he said firmly. 'Every night I shall practise in secret. I'll not be laughed at or talked about.'

Carriages lined the driveway to Brambleden Hall and the lane beyond, as guests continued to arrive. They filtered into the ballroom, from where the rugs had been removed ready for dancing later. In this room, as in the others, the chandeliers had been lowered and were lit with candles; oil lamps, too, were strategically placed, as no gas was provided to the village.

From their niche on the landing the brother and sister recognized local people: the president of Henley rowing club and his wife; Mr and Mrs Mackenzie of Fawley Court, who also owned nearby Phyllis Court; Lord and Lady Camoys of Stonor; the artist Jules Hollingham, who lived in a gaudily decorated houseboat, and whom shocked local moralists referred to as 'a bit that way'; the Marjoribanks from Greenlands; the Lanes of Badgemore; Lord and Lady Brambleden . . .

'I don't know where Papa meets so many people,' Leah said.

'Certainly it isn't Mama's influence,' observed Adam drily.

'Addi, don't be gloomy because of Mama.'

'I can't help it. The more I try to please, the more irritated she becomes.'

'I think Mama is sad.'

At that moment Jonathan returned, clutching a pie he had taken from the magnificent buffet laid out in the dining-hall, and the conversation between Adam and Leah came to a halt.

'D-did you s-s-steal it?' Adam asked admiringly.

'Of c-c-course,' Jonathan replied.

'D-don't copy me.'

Jonathan looked unconcerned and took a large bite from the pie.

'You might share it,' Leah complained.

Smiling, Jonathan put the remainder in his mouth and dusted his hands on his trousers. 'You will have to steal your own,' he said, his mouth oozing pie. 'Or get him to do it for you.' He gestured with his head towards his older brother, and his blond curls shook.

Adam felt that surge of heat in his body which happened whenever his brother antagonized him; a useless wave of anger that remained in him sometimes for hours, while in his mind he invented the replies he would have made, if only he did not stutter.

'I *shall* master my speech.' With those words Adam finished writing the entry in his diary. He had written five pages in a neat, forward-slanting style. Neat handwriting did not come naturally to him, and he had a headache from the effort of maintaining it. He had a headache anyway – partly from the noise of the party the night before which had long kept him awake, and partly because he was still weakened after a bad bout of bronchitis. But at least he was excused from having to hunt this New Year's Day; he hated hunting. He had been blooded his first time, and had almost fainted from revulsion – and sorrow for the fox, who only moments earlier had been streaking gloriously across a field.

'The fox is the sinner of the animal kingdom,' George Lundy, the head groom, had told him once. 'The very incarnate of the devil, is that wily creature. I snared one once that'd picked off the head of every chicken I owned. I tell 'ee, Master Adam, I ain't got no pity for a fox.'

Adam had argued with the old man for half an hour. He had stuttered, and his face had become contorted, but eventually George had clapped him warmly on the shoulder and smiled broadly. 'Well, I can't say as I agree with 'ee, but I'll say one thing – you've a stubborn 'ead on 'ee nothin'll sway . . .'

. . . And so, while Jonathan and his father joined a hundred others on horseback to chase a single creature through plough and mud, and trample on crops, half-blinded by falling snow, Adam would remain snug in front of a fire and occupy himself.

The house was alive now, with its own particular sounds – the servants were already busy. Outside, the sky was lightening, revealing a brown and white landscape. Suddenly he realized he was cold, and began to shiver, hugging his arms about himself. He returned to bed and surveyed his room, which was spacious and painted a dark green. He found this colour rather depressing; but who had consulted him?

'When I have children I shall make sure I consider their needs,' he thought. He lay back against several pillows, his face shadowed, and his long-lashed eyes pensive as he looked at familiar objects. Beneath the window, which provided a constant source of inspiration, was his mahogany pedestal desk, and upon it lay different writing implements and an inkstand and blotter. Next to the desk was a chest of drawers, and on top of this were a pitcher and basin, toilet mirror, and a few personal things. An ugly wardrobe occupied half of one wall, and beside this was an occasional chair – presumably for a friend to sit on. But he could not remember the last time he had had a friend to visit. There was only one picture – a grim etching of the Battle of Trafalgar.

His gaze wandered over to the fireplace, and lingered on the shelves in the alcove to one side. They were crammed with books; more than anything Adam liked to read. His taste was wide and varied: Dickens and Thackeray; George Eliot and Charles Kingsley; Shakespeare, Tennyson . . . These volumes rested against texts on Eastern teachings, manuals on ballooning, books on nature and anthropology, mythology and art . . . And as well as all these were magazines and journals he had collected over the years. Reading provided him with a world into which he could escape – and with knowledge and facts, often of little use, but of endless fascination to him. Just to see the irregular spines of all his books on the shelves made him happy.

There came a light knock on the door, and without waiting for his answer, Leah entered, barefooted and wearing only her nightgown. Her hair was in a long thick plait which had partly come undone during the night.

'I knew you would be awake.'

'It's freezing. Come under the eiderdown at least.'

She snuggled under, pulling it up to her chin. 'Yours is the coldest room in the house. And you've a bad chest.'

'Mama believes it will toughen me.' He smiled wryly.

'Phooee!'

'I heard them come upstairs at the end of the party. Guess who was reprimanded for having drunk too much, and for having told

Lord Brambleden that the Manor couldn't hold a torch against Brambleden Hall?'

'Oh Addi, he *didn't* say that, did he?'

'Well he denied it, but Mama insisted.'

'And she is always right. Oh dear. And he *will* suffer from a bad head today.'

'She will make him, if he doesn't already!'

'You *are* hard.'

'*She* is. *She* is hard.' He shook his head vehemently.

Leah didn't reply for a moment, but stared out of the window as he had done earlier, at the lightening sky and the wintry countryside. Under the layers of bedclothes Adam shifted his position so that her weight no longer pressed on his knees. He sat up and hugged her impulsively.

'Sweet Leah.'

'I often think about us all,' she said, 'what a funny family we are.'

'Funny laughable, or funny strange?'

'Strange, I suppose . . .' She frowned. 'Loving seems to go in pairs. All separate. Mama dotes on Jonathan, and perhaps loves me a *little* –'

'And me, not at all.'

'I haven't got to you yet, Addi!'

'Sorry.'

'And Grandmama also dotes on Jonathan. You – Papa loves you and Mrs Fitzgerald too –'

'What, Papa loves Mrs Fitzgerald?' Adam interrupted, deliberately misunderstanding her, and smiling when she became exasperated.

'No . . . You know *exactly* what I mean.'

'All right, and so I do. But what of yourself? Who loves little Leah then?'

'Papa and Grandmama.'

'And everybody else who knows you, and all those who will come to know you. You are annoyingly lovable.'

'But you see what I mean,' she said, ignoring his compliment. 'It's all so disjointed.'

'Well I daresay other households are the same – and at least there aren't a dozen of us vying for affection!'

'You're cheerful this morning.'

'It's the prospect of Bible reading later.'

'No really – something has made you cheerful.'

He looked at her doubtfully. 'You'll not tell?'

'Of course not.' She reached over to flatten his brown hair which had been standing up in spikes.

He let her toy with his hair. 'I'm keeping a diary – the book Mrs Fitzgerald gave me for Christmas. I'm going to keep a diary until I die. I can write down all my thoughts besides everything that happens . . . I shall be a writer when I grow up.' As he made this pronouncement he was as surprised as his sister.

She sat with her knees huddled to her chin, reflective.

'What are you thinking?'

'That all I shall have to do when I grow up will be to smile prettily, and embroider, and play the piano passably. And I shall be *bored*.'

'You? You'll never be bored. There is so much that interests you.'

'Yes. But those things stop as soon as you grow up. Look at Mama – what does she do? She pours tea and talks to boring women in the boudoir, as she calls that silly room she has just had decorated. And the only book she reads is the Bible. It is all religion, embroidery and *boredom*. Phooee!'

'But Leah, you are not Mama. It need not be like that for you.'

He thought for the first time of the tedium – as he saw it – of his mother's life, and felt a stirring of pity for her; and then thought that maybe his pity was misplaced, and she was happy as she was. 'Anyway,' he said, 'it's all a long way ahead.'

'You know what I should love to do more than anything?' she said. 'I should love to get my hands really filthy. I should like to bury them in the earth and make things from it.' She studied her pale hands, which were soft and spotlessly clean, and imagined them encrusted, with dirt beneath the fingernails.

'Do you mean you would like to be a sculptor?'

'Yes. I'd forgotten the word. Yes, that's what I'd like to be.'

'You'd have to use clay then, not earth.'

'Oh. Well, I'll use clay then. But I'd still like to dig my hands in the earth.'

They mulled over their separate futures. Through the thick door could be heard the sounds of feet and brushes, and the muted whisperings of two maidservants.

'They must be so tired,' Adam remarked.

'Who?' Leah asked.

'The servants. They had barely finished clearing up after the party and were in bed, before they must rise again. And they worked so hard yesterday. You can be sure nobody thanked them.'

'You always notice things, don't you? I love that about you – you always care about things.'

The church clock could be heard chiming eight o'clock, and Leah started. 'Goodness, I must leave your room.'

'Why?' He smiled at her anxiety. 'Am I about to become a wicked giant who will cut you into pieces and eat you for breakfast?'

'Silly! No. It is because Miss Baldwin says that it isn't proper at our age to visit each other's rooms in our nightclothes.'

Leah had passed on the governess's remark in innocence, but Adam understood the innuendo. On his fourteenth birthday his father, after several whiskies, had taken him aside and explained some simple facts to him. Now he blushed with shame and anger, and his good mood was destroyed.

Why did they have to ruin the sweetest, most harmless moments with their tarnished thoughts? He heard their scandalized voices – his mother's, his mother's friends', his aunt's, Miss Baldwin's – thought of their prim bodies and pursed lips, and could not tally these things with the things his father had told him.

He said gently to his sister: 'You mustn't get into trouble with long-nosed Baldwin.'

'You are funny, Addi.' As she slid from under the eiderdown her nightdress became ruched up, revealing part of her thigh, and unconcerned, Leah smoothed it down.

Adam watched her – and felt only fraternal fondness.

'You're much funnier than Jonathan, or even Papa.'

'Funny laughable, or funny strange?' he asked, as he had done before, and pulled an ogre's face at her.

'Laughable. You make me laugh. But you're not like it with anyone else.'

'I stutter with anyone else . . .'

When he was alone he lay thinking: of another time when his

innocent pleasure had been similarly tainted. He had often used to sit on his father's knee while Sir Felix told him anecdotes, until one day, when he was about ten, his mother had looked up from her needlework and said sharply, 'It is the height of absurdity – and quite disgusting apart from that – to see a boy of Adam's age sitting on his father's lap.'

He remembered his father's intake of breath, and how his knee and thigh had tensed and become rigid; the arm which had been casually and lovingly draped around Adam's neck had fallen away, and instead a hand was on the small of his back, pushing him gently but firmly away. They had looked into each other's eyes afterwards, regretfully.

'I don't understand,' he thought, as he got up and went over to the chest of drawers. 'I *cannot* understand the way they are. But at least in our house we don't cover the chair legs and table legs as Grandmama and Aunt Mary do in their dismal tomb of a place in London . . .'

He dressed and hurried downstairs for breakfast in the parlour, where he found Leah, Miss Baldwin and Edward Lear.

'Ah – young Adam!' Lear, who had been in the middle of relating a tale to his small audience, broke off and clapped his hands in pleasure when he saw the boy. 'I would have you know I declined breakfast in my room in the hope we would have a chance to speak! Are you well, lad?'

'F-f-fine, s-sir.' He sat down, blushing, but once seated felt more comfortable. 'I-I'm glad t-to see you,' he added, looking into the bespectacled man's kindly face.

'It has been a couple of years, and you're considerably grown.'

'N-not as much as I would wish, sir.' He smiled gaily, but Lear saw through the flippancy.

'Height is of no consequence,' he said solemnly. 'It is all up here.' And he tapped first his own, rounded forehead, and then Adam's. 'Let me see your feet a moment.'

Adam caught Miss Baldwin's eye: she was frowning, and her chin was tucked in disapprovingly to her neck. He suppressed a laugh, and stretched out both legs.

'You see!' exclaimed Lear – also noticing the governess's expression, and relishing her discomfort. 'Big feet! You will grow to be tall, anyway. Now put them away, lad! This is extremely bad manners at the breakfast table, isn't it, Miss Baldwin?'

A maidservant brought plates of broiled sheep's kidneys, poached eggs, ham, muffins and toast. Behind her a footman fussed around the sideboard, and arranged cutlery. Leah and Miss Baldwin departed – the former casting a rueful glance at her brother – and Adam was left alone with Edward Lear.

'A-are you remaining in England l-long, s-sir? Is Mr Lushington w-with you?'

Frank Lushington was Lear's close friend. There had been some gossip about the nature of their friendship, but Adam did not know this; nor could he know that recently there had been a rift between the two.

Lear hesitated. 'I grew weary of Rome and have taken rooms on my own. I thought I'd return to England for a while – and have somehow, so far, survived the cold spell, working out of doors a great deal. Now I'm back in London, nearer to my favourite sister, and am very busy working – particularly on a huge canvas called *The Cedars of Lebanon*, which, frankly, I wish I'd never started. Sometimes I am carried away by my own enthusiasms, Adam.'

'That is how I am, sir!' Adam said delightedly. 'I know that I'm too impetuous . . . But you are famous.'

'I wish I were as famous for my paintings as I am as the author of Nonsense.'

'But you have taught the Queen!'

'There lies no merit – only prestige. And do you know, when my book of Nonsense first came out everyone was convinced it had political innuendo, and was in reality written by Lord Derby or Lord Brougham . . . How incapable of lightheartedness adults are. Anyway, I must write some more, or I shall be in danger of losing *my* sense of humour.'

'I-I should like to write when I g-grow up, sir. My st-stutter will be blessedly silent on paper.'

Lear chuckled. 'I like your wit, lad. But you must start writing now. Why wait? And I sympathize with you for your stammer, particularly as I have an affliction myself. Try and relax when you speak.'

'It is so hard.' He prodded a kidney with his fork and studied it. 'It's as though something blocks my words and prevents my lips from releasing them.'

'You see – you didn't stutter then!'

'It's when I am di-discomforted that I am worst.'

'Well, you must not be discomforted with me. You will begin writing, won't you?'

'I have already, in a way.'

'How is that?'

'The only person wh-who knows is my s-sis-sister. If I tell you, you'll not s-s-say anything?'

Lear leaned forward and patted Adam's arm. 'You can trust me.' He nodded reassuringly.

'It's a journal. I'm keeping a j-journal.' Blushing, he looked down at his plate.

'Why, that is following in a great tradition,' the other said, retaining his hand on the boy's arm. 'I'm most impressed. But don't be stuffy in it! Too many journals are stuffy.'

Adam looked up again, eagerly. 'Oh, mine is not . . . Well, actually I only s-started it this morning.'

'It is an ideal day to commence. And have you made any resolutions?'

'One.'

'I shall not pry.' Casually, Lear took a bite of toast.

'I should like to tell you –' Adam, so shy, felt a compulsion to confide in this man. 'I have r-resolved to m-mas-master m-my s-s-speech.' The words came out in awkward bursts, and his cheeks were suffused with pink.

'Then you will, lad. You surely will. And tell me – what of your painting?'

'Oh I am still doing it. But it's been too cold to do my watercolours outside, and before that I was ill . . .'

Lear's expression was sympathetic. 'We share the problem of bronchitis. It's not a pleasant thing.'

'No. But now I am recovered, and in the spring I'll paint out of doors again.'

'Could you not work indoors now? I do.'

'I w-wish I were you, sir,' Adam said passionately.

'No, Adam, that you most certainly must not,' Lear answered. 'You must be foremost yourself.'

Across the table from this renowned man, Adam's eyes shone; he felt flattered that Lear should treat him so seriously. He was about to ask him about the 'affliction' he had referred to, when his father approached.

Lear would not, anyway, have said. He guarded his epilepsy to himself.

Sir Felix, despite having drunk so much the previous night and slept so little, was in a cheerful mood: his head was remarkably clear, he had a day's hunting to look forward to, his house was full of guests. He was already dressed in his riding breeches, and his shirt without the stock, but over these he wore a silk dressing-gown.

'Good day, Edward. 'Morning, Addi.' He ruffled his son's thick brown hair. He felt an empathy with his first-born child he did not have with his second. This imbalance in his affections bothered him, and he could not understand the reason for it. But although he respected Jonathan's courage and honesty, and appreciated his charm and handsome appearance, there was something chilling in the boy's nature which did not appeal to him. He tried to treat his children equally, but found it so much easier to love Adam.

It was Adam whom he took ballooning; Adam who accompanied him on walks, when they would each take their easels and watercolours and paint different views; Adam to whom he read aloud his favourite passages of literature, and with whom he discussed his opinions; Adam to whom he showed his fuchsias and orchids and rare lilies. He offered to share all these things with his other son, but Jonathan was unresponsive. He preferred to hunt, shoot or fish; although he showed an early interest in his father's wine cellar, which Adam did not, and sometimes Sir Felix took him down the stone steps, the butler lighting their way with an oil lamp.

With his arm deliberately around the boy's shoulders, he would explain about the different wines, as the butler took bottles from the racks to demonstrate a point; and sometimes they would have tasting sessions. Afterwards, Jonathan would shake his father's hand politely and thank him, and Sir Felix would pat him genially on the back, inwardly glad that it was over. He had tried – made an effort. He was a good father, and a fair man, and prided himself on these things.

Adam was thin and pale after his illness; his eyes seemed huge. Every time he was ill, Sir Felix worried that he would die, and now he checked his son's face anxiously, his fingers still threaded through his hair.

'I heard you last night, Papa!' Adam leaned back and looked up to see his father's reaction.

'Never!'

'I did! And you were lectured for your behaviour.'

'Enough of that.' His father feigned sternness. 'Well, Edward – such respect from the young, eh? So tell me – we scarcely had a chance to speak last night – what news with you?'

Adam listened to them with interest – could not help noticing the adroitness with which his father steered the conversation away from politics, and redirected it towards Darwin's controversial book, *The Origin of Species*, published two years previously. He thought, 'Papa's so confident. I'll never be like that. And he's so handsome . . . Please God, make me like Papa. Make me not stammer. Make me grow . . .'

God awaited him. At eleven o'clock exactly, when the church clock chimed, and hounds bayed in the grounds of Brambleden Manor, in Lady Elizabeth Gilmour's pink boudoir Bible reading was about to take place. The swagged and tasselled curtains were half-pulled to exclude the pale winter light; but instead of the sombre atmosphere intended, the rosy glow was, ironically, reminiscent of a brothel. Above the freshly-made fire an ornate mantel-mirror reflected the heads of the small group seated before it. Grandmama Georgina, small and plump, her thin hair in a tight, grey bun, reclined in a soft armchair, with her swollen feet resting on an embroidered stool. A faint smell emanated from her; Adam always noticed it: a mixture of stale fish and lavender water. Leah sat on her left, her head bent; but Adam knew the corners of her lips would be quivering with suppressed nervous laughter. On Grandmama's right, in the middle of the group, was her daughter, Lady Elizabeth, whose face had already assumed its 'devout' look. In her hands, tenderly poised, was her Bible, open at Chapter 8 of *St Luke*. Beside Lady Elizabeth, very upright in her chair, was her older sister, Mary, whose eyes were pink-rimmed and lashless. 'Like a rabbit's,' Adam, next to her, thought, casting surreptitious looks at her tight-lipped profile. She was a spinster, and her dark brown dress and frown proclaimed her strict morality to the world.

Lady Elizabeth stared at them each in turn, her gaze resting longest and most severely on her son, then, in a stern voice, she began to read. 'As if we have each just committed some dreadful sin, even Grandmama,' thought Leah. And the laughter she had been suppressing burst out in a snort she quickly turned into a cough. Adam glanced at her and winked. Their mother glared at them both and continued to read:

' ". . . And the twelve *were* with him; and certain women, which had been healed of evil spirits and infirmities, Mary called Magdalene, out of whom went seven devils . . ." '

. . . They were setting off. Adam could hear the clattering of hooves, and above them, the master's horn and cries of hounds. Amongst them were his father and brother, the former, no doubt, already merry from port. He smiled at the thought – and was only glad he was not with them. He preferred to hack quietly along the lanes and tracks into the hills, on his cob, closely followed by the English setter.

Lady Elizabeth had once liked to ride, and hunting had been her passion, until a couple of years previously, when a back problem had ended such pleasures. Adam watched her to see what she might be thinking; but her face showed no emotion. It was as if she were deaf to the sounds outside, which had once brought a light of excitement to her eyes. Her voice droned on:

' "Those by the wayside are they that hear; then cometh the devil, and taketh away the word out of their hearts, lest they should believe and be saved . . ." '

'I don't believe in the devil . . .' Did she know he didn't listen? Would she care? Was he blasphemous? Did God care? Was there a God?

The three women's forbidding faces – and his sister's vibrant, tender one: where was the link between them? He wondered whether they had ever been like her, and whether it was the constraints imposed upon their lives, as women, and upon their joy, which had changed them.

Leah noticed his abstractedness. 'He's away again,' she thought; 'in his own world. Poor Addi. He's always so bothered by things . . . And all I'm bothered about is that it will be mutton for lunch, and I'll have to eat it alone with Miss Baldwin . . .'

The day passed, and just before teatime, when the light was failing, Sir Felix and Jonathan returned. The latter was blood-splattered, his face distorted with bruising and swelling.

Lady Elizabeth raised her hands to her mouth when she greeted them in the hallway. 'Oh, my darling boy! What has happened?'

'He was very brave,' Sir Felix answered on his son's behalf, laying a hand on his shoulder. 'He grabbed a riderless horse that was galloping off, fell off himself, held fast to both horses, and was dragged along.'

'Oh my poor child, oh my darling boy . . . let me bathe those wounds.'

'I shouldn't have fallen off,' mumbled Jonathan through cut lips. 'It was stupid. I could have stayed on.' And he shrugged his father's hand from his shoulder and went upstairs, followed by his mother.

Adam had never seen her like it; so natural and anguished. He yearned, with a fierce longing, to have her fret over him in such a way, and felt suddenly alone. He should have been sorry for his brother's discomfort, but he wished it were his own, so that he could be a hero. He, too, went upstairs, to his room, breathing heavily from a pain in his chest. He could not be sure if it was the remnants of his illness, or sadness.

The fire had gone out, and it was cold again, but to relight it was an effort, and instead he went over to his desk where he took his diary from a drawer, and sat down. It was almost dark already, and he lit the oil lamp and a couple of candles. Then he dipped his pen in black ink and began to write:

'January 1st, continued . . .'

Chapter Two

AWAKENING

'There was a Young Lady whose chin
  Resembled the point of a pin;
So she had it made sharp,
  And purchased a harp,
And played several tunes with her chin.'

Adam stood by the chest of drawers in his room, reciting Edward Lear's limerick and looking into the toilet mirror. His face gazed back at him in the failing light – pinched but triumphant.

'I *have* it. I *know* Mama could enter this moment – and Jonathan too – and I wouldn't stammer.'

True to his New Year's resolution he had practised his speech every day. After reading out loud his 'ten commandments', a list of valuable hints he'd compiled, he always rehearsed one of Lear's Nonsense rhymes. Slowly, he progressed.

Only his sister knew what he was doing, and sometimes listened to him. Lying on his bed she willed him on, as his mirrored reflection looked now at her, now at himself, running anxious hands through his hair, twisting his mouth round awkward syllables. At first she had cried inwardly for him – that he should have to endure all this in order, such a tiny thing surely, to be able to speak like anyone else; and she had felt increasing admiration for him as she saw the strength of his determination. Then, gradually she noticed an improvement. Perhaps it started the day he realized his trousers were now too short . . .

Leah had immediately measured him against his wardrobe: 'Five feet five.'

'I don't *believe* you.'

'It's true. I promise.'

'Oh, but that's too, too good!'

. . . Or the day his voice cracked in the middle of a sentence and altered its cadence, so that he knew he was on his way to becoming a man . . . Or perhaps both these things were merely coincidental, and the improvement was due solely to his own perseverance.

'Oh – "There was a young lady whose chin Resembled the point of a pin . . .'

He began to laugh, and danced demonically round the room. Today had been a good day.

Friday, March 19th, 1861

'Leah's birthday. Before I went to school this morning I gave her the book on sculpture I had managed to find in Oxford last week – and which cost me almost all my money. She was washing in her room, and was tousled in that sweet way she is when she is newly woken.

' "Which hand?" I teased. But the book was too large to hide, and, laughing, she grabbed it from me.

' "It's the best present of my life," she told me, when she saw what it was.

'Who knows? Perhaps my present will set her on her path.

'The second good thing to happen was that I have discovered a unique way of coping with my worst lessons: I imagine the masters as animals! Before my eyes Mr Tackley, the maths master, becomes a pig, and Mr Atkinson is transformed into a crocodile as he snaps his jaws open and shut around endless Latin verse! I sit in the front row, under their constant scrutiny, envisaging them in their different guises, while pretending to concentrate. Oh, if they *knew* how demeaned they had become!'

Wrokfield College was in Wrokfield village, which straddled the Reading Road, where the countryside was at its flattest, and dark with woodland. It had developed as an extension to Henley during the last twenty years, and incorporated in its small area some of the worst architecture in Europe, according to Sir Felix Gilmour – who was a lover of all things past. The school itself was no better. Home to six hundred boys, some who boarded and others, like Adam and

Jonathan, who attended daily, it was a depressing Gothic-styled creation which nevertheless had quickly established a reputation both for sports and educational standards.

When his sons were barely toddlers, Sir Felix had put their names down for Eton, his own old school. But even as he filled in the form, his wife knew that he was fooling himself, and would change his mind when the time approached . . .

'It is so much more *convenient* to have them at Wrokfield,' he told her predictably, a year before Adam was due to go. 'And really, what purpose is there in sending them to Eton where as a bonus they might learn to become snobs, but academically be no better off?'

But the truth was that the fees at Wrokfield College were a fraction of those at Eton.

Each day the coachman drove them the six miles to school. They sat side by side in the Clarence, drawn by one of the pair of Cleveland bays, and only rarely would any conversation be exchanged between the two. When Jonathan was alone with Adam, and there was nobody around to impress, he did not find it worthwhile baiting his brother, and would stare through the window of the carriage, sometimes idly picking his nose. Occasionally he surprised Adam with an impulsive gesture – the offer of a toffee, a word of encouragement about a master or fellow pupil – and Adam would feel stupidly grateful for this morsel of normal brotherly generosity that should have been taken for granted. Sometimes Jonathan even told a joke, at which Adam would laugh loudly to show his appreciation – knowing that Jonathan was only testing it on him before relating it to his friends. He wished he did not crave his younger brother's good opinion.

The moments of rapport between them ended as soon as they reached the school gates and entered the forbidding building. They were in the same class, despite their eleven-month age difference, for Jonathan was an exceptional student, excelling at Greek, Latin, mathematics and physics – all subjects on which the school had founded its reputation. Adam could not understand the reason for learning a dead language, and detested both mathematics and physics. His brother also shone at sports – which Adam disliked. Graceful and neat in his body and its movements, compared to his brother's muscular aggressiveness, Adam had no desire to tumble in mud, or to haul his arms back and forth to the shrieks of a cox; to scrape his flesh, or expose his lungs to the bitter cold and his limbs to possible breakages . . . Adam could have spent his entire school day absorbing literature, history and French. These were his subjects, but they were not taken seriously at Wrokfield.

He was not popular at school; but because of his brother he was largely left in peace. He was not comfortable with children his own age; he thought they were laughing at him, and found them intimidating with their boisterousness and their interests which were not his. And his stammer always intruded. It was easier on his own – nobody to blush on his account, or finish sentences for him. It was simpler to be an observer.

Later, at home, he would transfer his reflections on to paper. It was becoming a vital thing for him – to write; and when his thoughts were confused, transposed into written words they became lucid.

'Master Adam, supper is served.' The tiny maid, who looked younger than him, knocked and peeped round his door as the grandfather clock on the landing struck the half-hour.

'I'm coming, thank you.'

He scrawled a final note: '. . . And tomorrow I am going ballooning with Papa, and in the afternoon Mrs Fitzgerald has promised us we may help her gather the rhubarb and prepare it for wine. I must close now, as it is supper time, and it is to be a special birthday dinner for Leah.'

The curtains to one of the windows in Adam's room were not fully closed, and through the gap the sun wormed its way – blocks of pale yellow which glanced off the walls and furniture. Adam, just awake, lay watching them, nursing his excitement. Then he could no longer stay in bed and got up, padding towards the windows and pulling the curtains open fully, to reveal a fine spring morning. He could see their own sleek-coated Jersey cows grazing and hear the occasional, muted, low. He hummed to himself as he washed and dressed, and went downstairs to join his father for breakfast.

Afterwards they set off on foot together to the cricket pitch on Lord Brambleden's estate. Sir Felix's arm swung wide with each long stride, and he whistled tunefully. Adam, struggling to keep up, glanced at his father.

'What are you smiling at then?' his father asked fondly.

'You. Your whistling. Everything. This morning feels good.'

'It *is* good. What a life, eh Addi? Riches indeed. Who could want for more than a day like this? And having worked up an appetite, we shall return to a hearty lunch. What say you – is it beef or pork today?'

'I'll bet neither. I'll bet lamb.'

'Of course. Lamb. What a treat. Accompanied by a fine claret. Ah, happiness is really too simple. Listen – a cuckoo.' He craned his neck, stroking his bushy dundrearies. Beside him Adam was silent, and they both listened to the distinct calls coming from a mysterious source. When they had stopped, Adam cupped his hands to his mouth and mimicked them perfectly. Immediately the cuckoo responded.

'Where did you learn to do that?' his father asked, impressed.

'I practised last year. I can do an owl too, and a gull . . .' And so saying, he went through his repertoire, looking up at Sir Felix for approval when he had finished.

They came to the cricket pitch, and there, three-quarters inflated from the gas cylinders, and held down firmly by weights, was the balloon. A crowd was gathered, some people as spectators, others to help. Sir Felix's two gardeners and two stable lads had been there for several hours already, pumping in the gas, and now that the balloon had risen from the ground they were able to attach the passenger basket to the circular load ring. From all sides came the murmur of conversation. Children were lifted on to shoulders, and their delighted cries resounded as they pointed fat fingers: 'Look! Look!'

'Here they come!' People gestured to one another as the pair arrived. Everyone knew and liked Sir Felix.

Amidst the crowd, Adam saw Mr Hibbert, the Rector; the Brambledens' estate manager; a group of farm labourers; several village girls and youths; and Mr Mason the sherry merchant, with his wife and one of their daughters. Adam felt mingled fear and excitement, and he began to perspire. His shirt itched him around the collar and armpits. Now he wanted only to climb into the basket and be up there; away.

Alice Mason waved boldly to him, and he wondered what he should do, whether or not to wave in return. He could tell from the way she looked at him that she had built a certain image of him: young Adam Gilmour – the *Honour*able Adam Gilmour – aeronaut! Instead of waving he blushed and averted his face; but the little boost to his morale made him proud. He remembered Alice Mason had visited once with her mother – a precocious dark-eyed girl of his own age; and now as he recalled that visit, he thought that, after all, he would wave. He turned back towards her and belatedly lifted his hand. But she was no longer watching him.

The balloon itself, made by the famous firm C. G. Spencer and Sons, and measuring about fifty-six cubic feet, was made of varnished red silk, and encased by netting which extended to the basket. Adam helped the men attach a pipe to a new gas cylinder and link it to the opening of the balloon. He was conscious of trying to look efficient, of people's eyes upon him . . . and of the itchy warmth of his collar. Eventually everything was ready, and volunteers held the ropes down as the weights were removed.

'Come on then, Addi.' Sir Felix's bright gaze met his son's.

Adam climbed in afterwards and sat opposite him, a pair of binoculars in his hands, and the barometer at his feet. He tried to appear nonchalant but he was tense with anticipation. Any minute now they would release the ropes . . .

'Right!' Sir Felix called.

At his cry they let go, and the balloon lifted gently from the ground. Together they leaned out to coil in the rope, and when this was done, without being asked, Adam released ballast – a handful of sand at a time, to enable them to ascend smoothly.

Higher they sailed, soundlessly and diagonally, the light wind behind them. The only sounds came from below, drifting upwards with extraordinary clarity: voices, the bleating of sheep, lowing of cows, a dog barking, the rustling of trees, carriage wheels. Higher still – and they were above a thin layer of cloud. Father and son exchanged a deep look; and on both their faces was the same expression of supreme happiness.

From the barometer they could tell that they had climbed to over five thousand feet, and they drifted smoothly in air currents while beneath them the countryside unfolded, map-like. Lush and cultivated, it exemplified a way of life; fields were well-rotated, boundaries well-defined, and villages tidy. Nobody starved.

Around them the sky was an arc, and they were minuscule within it. Elated, Adam raised his arms. At that moment he felt close to God in a way he never did when he said his prayers, or when, with his brother and sister, he sat in his mother's pink boudoir for Bible reading.

Tiny figures stopped to point; carriages came to a standstill, and as they neared Ibstone and began their descent, dogs barked frenziedly, and horses in fields shied. Sir Felix instructed Adam how much gas to release from the valve. There was a hissing noise as he did so. A little more – and they dropped another few feet. Adam, in charge of the valve-line, looked about him to assess their position.

'*Now*,' his father said. 'Before we drift any further. Release more, *now*.'

The balloon, in his control, descended smoothly and arrow-straight. Just before landing Sir Felix deployed the trail rope – and they touched down, the rope dragging behind them, serving as a rudder.

'Well done, Addi. Well *done*.'

They were surrounded by onlookers – some of whom had followed their passage from Brambleden cricket pitch; and in front of them all, still in the basket, Sir Felix hugged his son, to loud applause.

They left the balloon in the care of Sir Felix's gardeners, and were given a lift back by the farmer in whose field they had landed. With his dog between them, they sat in his large cart amongst the clutter of feed sacks and root vegetables, answering his endless questions. Adam, listening to the warmth in his father's tone, thought: 'That's what I like about him: he's the same with everyone. He gives himself no airs.'

Instead of going directly home they were dropped off at the Royal Oak, where they were instantly surrounded anew. Sir Felix bought ale for everyone, and Adam gulped his thirstily, feeling its warmth dispersing inside him. Around him – the cheery conversation, bawdy jokes, congratulations, the burr of country voices; the smells of ale and smoke and manure from boots, mingling with the drifting odours of roasting from the kitchen . . . He thought: 'I'll look back on this day and remember it as special.'

Over lunch his exhilaration was still with him, and he kept saying, 'There's nothing to compare with it. And *I* landed it' – forgetting to stammer in his enthusiasm. He was even impervious to his mother's rebuke for eating too ravenously, and the accompanying look of malice that Jonathan shot him. Then for some reason an image flashed before him of Alice Mason, the sherry merchant's daughter, with her black eyes and bold wave.

He saw her again the following morning in church. He was on the outside of his row, next to Jonathan, and she on the end of the corresponding row, beside one of her sisters. She was wearing an outfit of purple velvet which was far too elaborate for an ordinary parish church service. 'Flashy people,' Adam had heard his mother say once. 'Everything about them shrieks new wealth . . . Although Mrs Mason is a God-fearing woman.'

Now, Alice Mason kept turning her head and staring at him, almost with a look of conspiracy, her small mouth pouting. Once she licked her lips.

Embarrassed at first, then increasingly flattered as he caught her glance several times, he did not know how to react. First he avoided her stare, and then, furtively, he began to respond, so that it became a kind of game. In this way the service passed. But before it was over came Reverend Hibbert's sermon.

In a voice quivering with emotion he told the congregation how he had visited the East End of London earlier that week, and been horrified by what he had seen: the squalor, the terrible conditions in which people lived; the cholera or typhoid amongst entire families; starvation; children working in factories. Dickens's characters lived on, he said.

Once, during this address, Alice Mason had tried again to attract Adam's attention, but he was engrossed, stricken by what he was hearing, so that when she caught his eye, he scowled at her without meaning to. He reverted his attention to the rector, and as he listened to him speaking of the plight of the underprivileged, of children his age who were already old, but would die young, tears came to his eyes. Without taking his gaze from the Reverend Hibbert, he wiped them away. The sermon that morning, in a small church in a Chiltern village, was to have a profound influence on the rest of Adam Gilmour's life.

Afterwards people could be heard discussing it amongst themselves, or they went up to Reverend Hibbert: 'Congratulations . . . Excellent sermon – makes one think . . . Makes you feel humble . . . Looking forward to that game of chess with you tomorrow evening . . .'

'How could anyone think of chess,' Adam wondered, sickened.

Alice Mason, with her family, was only a few feet from him, and she smiled, licking her lips again, provocatively, so she imagined. But he ignored her – which he didn't realize further tantalized her. His mind was elsewhere; and as soon as they returned home he ran up to his room, and counted out his remaining money, for he had spent most on his sister's present.

Immediately after lunch he rushed to the Rectory, and breathlessly handed Reverend Hibbert his savings.

'I-it's f-for the p-p-people y-you told u-us about in y-your s-ser-ser-mon,' he explained, stammering worse than he had for a long time, and becoming red.

Reverend Hibbert looked at him with surprisingly moist eyes and said, 'You're a *good* boy, Adam. A *truly* good boy. God bless you.'

So, with God's blessing conveyed by the rector ringing in his ears, he dashed back to his own house, hoping he had not been missed.

Later the whole family went to visit relatives in Henley. They drove down New Street, past elegant Georgian houses, and the brewery with its lingering aromas; and then their pleasant little journey was marred by one of the horses shying at a heap of rubble in the road: the remains of a Tudor cottage. There was an ugly space where it had once stood, and as the coachman calmed the horse, within the carriage Sir Felix fumed at the sacrilege being committed by architects. He was only just simmering down when moments later they stopped outside a fine eighteenth-century building on the edge of Waterside. Lady Elizabeth always feared rats when she called on her husband's sister.

'Addi! Addi!' All five children clamoured round him when he arrived, tugging at his sleeve, begging to be hugged in turn.

Laughingly, he obliged, swinging the smallest in the air. 'Oh, but how heavy you've become,' he told the delighted toddler. 'Oh, but you're almost too heavy for me now.'

They were a harmonious, informal family, and Adam always envied this sense of ease, and the affection openly displayed between them. Every time he visited he was made freshly aware of the contrast, which Leah had pointed out, with his own home.

Jennifer Robinson, who was several years younger than Sir Felix, resembled him in many ways – both in her easy-going nature and in her appearance: similar blue eyes, a strapping build, black hair, and humour in the sensuous mouth – the 'Gilmour' mouth, as she referred to it, which was also Adam's.

He had not wanted to visit this afternoon, to be part of their joyfulness and hospitality. After the sermon and his subsequent visit to the Rectory, he had wanted to be on his own; to dwell on his thoughts. But as always he was swept along by their contagious gaiety.

His cousins' ages were between three and ten, the two oldest being girls; and because they were younger than him, Adam felt no awkwardness, and joined energetically in their games. If he was weary with them, then he never showed it, but threw himself wholeheartedly into their activities, deliberately making them laugh at his antics. They rewarded him with their affection; it was, and would always be, the only reward he wanted.

This afternoon, he immersed himself in charades and Blindman's Buff, a puppet show – and finally he told them a story about an old man who reverted to childhood. This had Leah, and even Jonathan, enthralled, and the little ones in such howls of laughter that the nanny came to investigate the uproar in the nursery.

Tea was muffins and fruitcake – and port for the men, who afterwards played billiards, watched by Adam and Jonathan, the latter hoping he would get a chance to play. Sir Felix had drunk too much port, which tended to make him irritable, and his thoughts were not on the game. He remembered the fate of the cottage in New Street and latched on to his pet topic.

'Do you know, on the way to you I saw that that delightful Tudor cottage in New Street has been demolished. What in the name of God has got into everybody? No doubt some monstrosity will go up in its place . . . Missed. Your shot.'

'It was uninhabitable, Felix,' his brother-in-law said reasonably, taking the cue and aiming it carefully at the red ball. His bushy eyebrows knotted in concentration. 'Got it! You really *can't* berate modern architecture *and* play billiards, Felix.'

'But they're ruining Henley! All along Duke Street they're taking down perfectly satisfactory buildings and putting up new things with as much style as a dung heap. I cannot stand to watch it.'

'Well move house then, dear man – and let me have first option at a reduced price!'

'But I'm serious, David. Perhaps we should start a petition, you and I.' He brightened at the thought of doing something positive, for life was definitely duller now he no longer travelled. But his idea was instantly quashed.

'You know that wouldn't work,' argued the grain merchant, setting down his cue, and sighing because the conversation was a waste of time, and the game was being spoiled. He should not have been so generous with the port; he knew it had this effect on Sir Felix. 'You can't prevent progress.'

'Progress!' Sir Felix gave a derisive snort. 'It's desecration, not progress. Why, I was reading the other day . . .'

Adam, who had been listening to them amused, no longer heard. He had also been flicking through a newspaper on the chair beside him – the radical *Daily News*, originally edited by Charles Dickens, and now by his friend, the biographer John Forster. In it was an article entitled, 'They are forgetting the flock'.

The article strongly attacked the Church, in particular Evangelism, for turning its back on the poor, unless they became religious converts – which was little more than blackmail. It described the combined strength of all the factions in the Church, and stated that with the full support of its leading members, much more could be done to raise money to help. The article then went on to cite examples of deprivation that made Adam silently cry.

Jonathan nudged him. 'Stop it,' he whispered harshly, as the two men argued and played their game of billiards, oblivious;

the balls hitting one another made soft clicking sounds.

'I c-c-can't help it,' he whispered back, struggling with his tears. 'It's so sa-sad.'

Jonathan clicked his teeth impatiently. 'What is?'

Adam pointed to the column in the newspaper, and Jonathan said without reading it, 'Lots of things are sad, aren't they? And stop snivelling. It's babyish.'

'What are you two whispering about?' asked Sir Felix, who had lost the game and also interest in the discussion.

'Nothing, Papa,' both brothers answered simultaneously.

Later that week, at school, Adam was birched for the first time in his life. It had happened that during the maths lesson Mr Tackley had continually found fault with him. Then, after a particularly scathing attack, he had asked Adam the answer to a problem, and despite all his hours of speech practice, Adam had stammered like an imbecile. Standing in the front row, for all to see, he had felt excruciatingly embarrassed as he struggled amidst their sniggering to speak, to give what he knew anyway to be an incorrect answer. Afterwards, when he sat down, sinking with relief on to the bench, he knew a burning rage within him that seemed to occupy his whole body, and a sense of shame so strong that he could not bear to look at any of the boys; he did not want to see their mockery, or the satisfaction on Mr Tackley's face.

During break-time he had to remain in the classroom to revise his maths, but instead, still seething, he had drawn a cartoon of Mr Tackley as a pig. He had forgotten time as he sketched hairs on the ears and coming out of the snout. With skilful strokes – beginning to giggle now – he perfectly captured the irascible master. And then, when he was putting the finishing touches to the bow-tie, the other boys came in, in groups, and he was caught. Guiltily, he tried to whisk the drawing away, but someone snatched it from his hands – and burst out laughing. 'Why – it's brilliant,' he spluttered. 'Look, everybody!'

They gathered round, exclaiming and laughing, slapping Adam on the back heartily.

'Do one for me! Oh, I must have one . . .'

'You must do one of old Atkinson.'

'I wish we could pin it on the wall.'

Adam barely had time to bask in his new-found glory, when the object of their mirth entered the room, and the laughter died away. Mr Tackley was also their housemaster, and passing the door had heard too much noise for his liking. He ordered the boys to return to their seats, and, reluctantly, they moved, unwilling to expose the drawing. Adam took it, trying to hide it behind his back, but it was done on art paper and was too large to conceal.

'I should like that, please.'

The teacher could not fail to recognize himself, and his reaction was first to become silent, then to grow pinker than usual. He was storing up the fury, when one of the boys gave a choked laugh, which caused him to release it.

The torrent was over. Adam followed Mr Tackley out of the room towards his study, fearful yet exultant: several of the class winked at him encouragingly as he left, and even as the door shut behind them he heard their support for him. He would bear what was about to happen, because he knew it would bring him popularity. His eyes fastened on to the scarlet backs of his teacher's ears . . .

By the end of the next week Adam could sit down again without wincing; each of the class had his own cartoon; and, most important of all, he had been accepted. It was a useful lesson for life: that in order to ensure popularity, one had only to keep people amused.

Wet spring merged into early summer. The weather changed abruptly to become fine, and the cough which had threatened Adam disappeared. Everyone seemed possessed of time: to smile, to linger and chat, to pass a piece of advice, to do a job for someone else . . . The hayfields turned yellow, and the lambs looked as big as the shorn ewes; puddles in the lanes dried, and muddy tracks became hardened; keen walkers appeared from London at weekends, and houses were full of guests . . .

'Like a hotel,' protested Lady Elizabeth in despair one day, flinging her arms upwards. 'It's like owning a hotel, with everyone coming and going all day long, and no time to oneself.'

'It's the penalty you have to pay for living in this beautiful part of the country, my dear,' said Sir Felix equably.

'It's the penalty I have to pay for having a husband who picks up strays from all areas of England and Europe,' she snapped.

A month of croquet and tea parties, fêtes and boating outings . . . Adam would go for walks along the river, sometimes alone except for the setter, which always went with him. He would walk to the mill, on the main road about a mile away, and follow the towpath to nearby Medmenham. On the way he would stop to throw sticks into the river for the dog, loving to watch it swim – the way its muzzle stuck above the water, and its paws, visible in the clearness, moved back and forth rapidly. Afterwards the dog would shake itself vigorously, and then leap up, twisting in the air until Adam threw the stick once more. When both grew tired of this, the dog would come to lie, panting, by Adam's feet, and the boy would sit, his hand resting on its silky head, simply absorbing the beauty about him. He noticed everything – the active sky and changing lights on the sloping fields of the opposite bank; picturesque barges lived in by whole families; skiffs skimming past; lovers rowing by, the woman shaded by a dainty parasol. Cows might stroll to the river edge to drink, and ducks alight dramatically on the water.

'I'd like to be a duck,' he said once to Leah, when she came with him and they were lying on the bank, Leah threading buttercups. 'An inedible kind, for I'd not want to be shot. What bird would you be?'

'A gull,' she replied without hesitation. 'A pure white gull.'

Summer was Ascot and Wimbledon, and in early July, Henley Regatta: three days of picnics and parties and bunting; river-craft of every description, bedecked with flowers and flags; houseboats and steamers forming a line from the bridge to Regatta Island, where the course commenced. The bridge was packed with carriages and spectators, and hordes of jostling pedestrians; more coaches stretched along the Berkshire-side pastures; while the grandstand spilled over with men in flannel trousers and women in organdie dresses and elaborate hats. The place was a riot of colour, and forming a backcloth to it all were the wooded Chilterns – hazy in the sun. The cries of the crowds and honking from craft drowned the shouting of coxes as sweating teams flashed past in skiffs, almost unnoticed; for there were few amongst the thousands present who watched the rowing.

During the spring and summer months of activity and socializing, Adam became aware that wherever he went, so, it seemed, did Alice Mason. And wherever it was – at someone's house, in church, out walking, riding, flying a kite on the cricket pitch, at the Regatta – her black eyes lanced into his with their signals. These signals in turn confused and thrilled him, so that he began to look out for her and think about her at nights, worrying about what he would say if he had to speak to her. And then one rainy day, in mid-July, he returned from school with his brother to find her there, in his home. She was with her mother, visiting. Demurely dressed in white, her knowing expression and developing body, pushing at the seams of her bodice, belied her modest apparel.

They were having tea in the parlour, and the door was open into the hallway. Adam could not believe it when he spotted them, and hovered nervously, without entering. Jonathan, as usual, went in to greet his mother, and Adam heard her welcome him, 'as though he's a lap-dog,' he thought bitterly. He was about to enter, poised behind the shield of the door, when his mother's voice drifted out:

'This is my dearest son, Jonathan. I am very proud of him. Jonathan – this is Mrs Mason and her daughter, Alice. Mr Mason is a sherry merchant, dear, you know, and I was earlier saying of your interest in wines.'

He heard Jonathan's civil reply, and through the crack in the door watched his brother shake hands and smile charmingly. He thought Jonathan's eyes lingered on Alice Mason.

'Would you like some tea, dear? You must be hungry.'

'Yes please.'

'A hard day?'

'Not too bad. I got top marks for my maths and Latin homework.'

'That is excellent, dear. He is very conscientious,' she said to the mother and daughter seated together on the chaise-longue, and they both smiled politely. Jonathan had the grace to look embarrassed, Adam noticed.

He was on the point of creeping away and going upstairs, both relieved he would not have to speak to Alice Mason and despondent, when she asked in a purposeful tone, 'What of your other son, Lady Gilmour? Does he not come in to greet you?'

He looked through the crack again, and saw that his mother was astonished at the girl's impertinence, and that the question had flustered her, making her aware how it must seem not to have welcomed her 'other son'.

'Oh, he must have forgotten,' she said, laughing artificially to cover her awkwardness. 'I shall ring for the maid to fetch him. Really, it's too much that he cannot be troubled to say good afternoon to his own mother.'

As she rang for the maid Adam disappeared up the stairs in bounds – quickly reappearing in the hall upon being summoned. He tried to induce calm. 'Slowly,' he reminded himself, as he went in. 'Speak *slowly*.'

He greeted his mother and her guests, noting Lady Elizabeth's feigned affection, and sat on a chair beside his brother, opposite the women. For something to do, and to avoid talking, he helped himself to a cucumber sandwich. His mouth was full of bread when Alice asked him in her direct way, 'Have you been ballooning recently, Adam?'

And caught by surprise, he could only chew self-consciously until his mouth was empty, his embarrassment making him forget all his careful practice. His voice jerked out: 'N-not s-since a m-m-mo-nth a-go.'

She stared at him, briefly shocked, and he smiled, half miserably, half defiantly, aware of her disappointment, and momentarily hating her for it. This antagonism gave him strength, and after a pause, during which she seemed reluctant to pose further questions, he composed himself.

'Are you in-terested in ballooning, Miss Mason?'

'Oh yes. And do call me Alice . . .'

From then conversation progressed, as far as possible with the two mothers and Jonathan present. But later, when they stood in the hallway and Mrs Mason prepared to leave, her daughter hung back close to Adam and surreptitiously pressed a note into his hand.

Afterwards he rushed to his room to read it. It said: 'Meet me Saturday, midday, in the disused barn at the back of the Royal Oak. A.' And beside the initial was a tiny 'x'.

The barn behind the Royal Oak was rarely used; it belonged to the Brambleden Manor estate, but was too isolated from the rest of the farm to be of much use. Surplus hay and straw were stored in it, and some rusting farm machinery, long forgotten; also mouldy sacks of pheasant feed. The barn was left unpadlocked simply because there was nothing in it of value to anyone, but over the last few years it had been witness to more than one clandestine love affair.

Adam dressed with especial care that Saturday morning, but he was disgruntled with the contents of his wardrobe; suddenly his clothes seemed drab. In the end he settled on the only pair of trousers which weren't too short, a dark-beige pair more suited to winter, and a semi-fitted jacket in maroon. It was the same outfit he always wore to church. For the first time he was truly aware of his own appearance, and peered closely at himself in the toilet mirror. His thin face looked back, anguished. He gave an experimental smile and noticed that a dimple appeared in his right cheek. But the smile vanished as, peering closer, he saw two spots on his chin, which turned white as he pressed them, and then red, the skin around them swelling.

'Oh no . . .' He dabbed cold water on the area and the irritation subsided. 'At least it's dark in the barn,' he thought. He took his watercolours with him and told Mrs Fitzgerald he was going to paint – crossing his fingers because of the lie – and then he was away, walking briskly down the stony track towards the barn and his assignment with Alice Mason.

It seemed, that morning, that everyone was out and about, and as he greeted yet another person he knew, his nervousness became so intense that he considered turning back. Customers from the Royal Oak gathered outside and he thought, 'It was madness to meet here.' But then, miraculously, the lane cleared, and with a furtive glance Adam pushed open the creaking barn door and was inside, blinking in the darkness, inhaling the musty odour.

The church clock chimed for midday, and she was not there. Adam thought, 'She's decided against it . . . Or maybe she couldn't get away.' Fleetingly he was glad, but following this came disappointment, and he wandered about desultorily, touching dusty machinery, pulling out wads of hay from a half undone sheaf. There came the creak of the door, and for a moment light flooded in, and Alice Mason stood haloed in it – hand on hip, assured; so unlike

Adam, who at the sight of her was again consumed by shyness. He made himself go up to her, and was about to shake her hand when he decided it was too formal, and let his arm drop to his side. He was aware of it dangling, feeling too long.

'Hallo. I th-thought you weren't going t-to come.'

'Why not?' Was she laughing at him? Now with the door shut and in semi-darkness again, her tilted face appeared mocking.

'I don't know. I just – thought.' His awkwardness was such that he felt almost in pain. He began to regret the whole idea, longingly pictured his bedroom and its safety. And then she smiled and took her bonnet off – tossing it into a corner – and sat down on a heap of sacks. Her conspiratorial smile and relaxed attitude put him at his ease, and he smiled back and sat tentatively beside her.

'I thought you might have changed your mind.' He wanted to explain to her how he had felt. But she leaned toward him and said, 'Your teeth are really white in the gloom.'

'So are yours.'

'No. Yours are whiter.'

He began to laugh.

'What are you laughing at?'

'Us. Having a c-conversation about teeth. It's s-such a funny thing to talk about.'

'Well, we have to talk about something.' She leaned back, and the edge of her dress brushed his ankle. 'You're shy, aren't you?' Her gaze was disconcerting and he looked away.

'Yes.'

'Is that why you stammer?'

'Probably. But it's b-better than it was. It also depends whom I am with.'

'Oh well . . .' Alice became quickly bored and moved restlessly from one topic to another. 'Do you want to know what excuse I made so I could meet you?'

'Yes.'

'I said I was going to collect wild flowers to press.'

'So you must return with some.'

'I'll say I gave them away to that dreadful old deaf woman in the cottage next to the forge, and Mama will say how generous I am.'

'Mrs Blackthorne isn't dreadful.'

'She looks as if she should be burned at the stake. She looks as if she mixes potions in a cauldron and eats small children.'

Adam, who liked and was sorry for the old lady, was mildly shocked by Alice's callousness, but despite himself he laughed, because this was what she obviously wanted. Compared to him she was sophisticated, and he was immensely flattered she should be bothering with him. He was prepared to laugh or be serious accordingly, simply to please her.

For the next half-hour Alice Mason did most of the talking, and Adam was content to listen and to watch her, impressed by her malicious, frivolous chatter, which seemed to him defiant and brave. By the time they parted – emerging separately and cautiously once more into the light – he was smitten.

School finished for the summer, and their snatched meetings continued for a couple of weeks; Adam was always amazed at her resourcefulness at being able to escape unnoticed. It was easier for him, as a boy. She was so sure of herself, and he marvelled at this, too: the effortless way she could maintain a conversation.

And then she told him she was going to Brighton with her parents.

'So I should like you to kiss me,' she said, matter-of factly. 'As I shan't see you for a fortnight.'

Dumbfounded, he stared at her. He had no idea how to kiss a girl, nor was he sure that he even wanted to. Alice had not done it before, either, but was more imaginative than he.

'*Well?* Won't you move closer to me?'

He did so, apprehensively, and she took his hands in hers. 'You've nice hands,' she observed in that same matter-of-fact tone. 'Now, put them round my neck, and I'll put mine round yours . . . Then you have to put your lips on mine, and then –' Here she faltered uncertainly, '– then I think you have to press.'

All this while, Adam was compliant yet nervous, but as she placed his arms about her neck, and he felt hers around his, as he touched the softness of her hair, a delightful warmth and sense of happiness pervaded him, and without waiting for further instructions, he pressed his lips to hers and gently forced them apart . . .

He thought about Alice Mason the entire fortnight she was

away, recalling the mysterious blackness of her eyes, and the sweetness of her lips . . . He wrote poems for her, pages in his diary about her, and stories inspired by her. He became lofty in his passion, aloof from everyone; and Leah, not understanding this sudden distance in her brother, was hurt.

Then she returned, and for a week or so things continued as before, with a little advancement – a squeeze, a fumbling hand placed on her breast – until the party.

The party, in nearby Skirmett, was to celebrate a boy's fifteenth birthday, and his parents – who belonged to the 'new rich' – had planned everything on a grand scale. It was held on a Saturday evening, and there was a buffet, and negus to drink, a small orchestra for dancing, and fireworks planned for later. Adam, Jonathan and Leah were all invited, arriving at the same time as a crowd of other children, amongst whom was Alice Mason with her two sisters.

'Hallo –'

Adam tried to get her on her own, but whenever he thought he had succeeded, she seemed to turn away to somebody new. He thought it must be chance; that he imagined the coolness in her attitude and hostility in her expression. And when, at the buffet, he tried to join her and her sisters, and she immediately turned to someone and began chatting vivaciously, he thought, 'She has to be polite to them. Why should she ignore everyone on my account?'

Leah noticed he was becoming increasingly downcast. She noticed, too, the way he kept following Alice Mason, at first confidently and proprietorially, then hesitantly and dismally.

'So, that's what's been wrong with him. Oh Addi. Oh poor Addi . . . And can't he see how *horrid* she is?'

She tried to talk to her brother, divert his attention, but he would not risk losing a moment's opportunity. He moved away when he feared she would detain him, answering her sharply.

He asked Alice Mason to dance.

'I'm booked,' she answered, tossing her head. 'For every one of them.'

He was left standing, rooted to the spot, feeling as though he had been robbed. All his recently acquired confidence ebbed. He felt it going from him, and could almost imagine it as a slimy mass. The secret joy he had hugged to himself for the past few weeks, and which had made him feel so manly, was crushed.

'Addi?' Leah approached him and took his limp hand. 'I have a spare dance. Will you dance it with me?'

'I don't feel like dancing,' he answered, aching. He clenched his jaw.

'Addi –' she pressed, longing for him to confide in her.

'Please leave me alone, Leah.' He walked away from her, head lowered, wondering what had happened; why it had happened.

Glumly he watched Alice Mason twirling with different boys; in particular one with whom she danced several times. He was seventeen or eighteen – strapping and fair – and his eyes never left hers, which were coal bright.

'What did I do wrong?' he repeatedly asked himself, gazing at the pair until they merged into one in his imagination.

'You're too young,' she explained to him, when he managed finally to corner her and ask her outright. She was breathless from her dancing, and there were spots of colour in her cheeks. 'And really, Adam, you're not my *type*. It was useful practice, though,' she added on a note of innuendo, and gave a little tweak to his chin.

The humiliation and pain remained with him for a while; and the fragile sense of his own manhood, the temporary superiority, withered and were replaced by fresh doubts. But school started again, and with it came its own problems.

Chapter Three

THE ACCIDENT

Sunday, September 28th, 1861

'This morning, in the *Reading Mercury* there was an article which greatly upset me. It told how an elderly Reading street trader, crippled with rheumatism, was evicted from the room he had lived in for ten years. This basement room, which he rented for a pittance, was rat-infested and damp – but it was his home; now he has nowhere to go. He was found shuffling about Whiteknight's Park in a daze, and was taken to the police station. No doubt he will eke out his days – and they are surely not many – in a workhouse.

'Is there really nothing that can be done for such people? Should there not be a law protecting tenants? Apparently the landlord needed to have the room vacant so he could renovate and sell the property and move abroad . . . I am confused, because obviously I can see his point, too. But he would not suffer to the same degree as the old man, would he, by *not* selling the building?

'I wrote immediately to the newspaper with my views, and said I thought money from taxes should be paid to the poor. I don't expect they'll publish the letter. But I also sent them a postal order for a shilling and sixpence (all I had), for them to refer to him. I hope he gets it. He'll know at least that somebody cares.'

Adam closed his diary and changed into his riding clothes. He had been intending to exercise his cob an hour ago, while the weather was still fine, but now it was drizzling outside and past three o'clock, and the afternoon was drawing to a premature close. He hurried downstairs, calling the setter – which pirouetted alongside him as Adam ran to the yard. From the stables appeared old George Lundy, leading the cob.

He gave an extra polish to its round hindquarters. 'You might be in a hurry,' he said, as the boy hopped from foot to foot impatiently, 'but that ain't the right mood to set off in. An 'orse must be done proper. B'sides – I think it's too late for you to be going.'

'I shan't have a long ride. I need to get out.'

'Well, you be careful then. I shouldn't be gone for no more'n half an hour, if I was you.' He tightened the girth before the gelding had a chance to puff itself out. 'And tomorrow's your birthday, I was hearing from Miss Leah.' He gave one of his broad, toothless smiles.

'I'm going to be fifteen.' Even to his ears it sounded adult.

'Fif*teen*, mind! . . . Now you goes easy,' he called, as Adam set off briskly.

After a few moments Adam relaxed and slackened the little horse's pace, sitting deep in the saddle. The hedgerows were still laden with blackberries, and he stopped every so often to pick and eat them.

'No one to tell me to wash them first,' he thought, popping several into his mouth – then leaned forward to give one to the horse who, he had discovered, had a penchant for them. He crossed the road and joined a track in the woods which wound from behind a pink cottage. A thin coil of smoke came from its chimney.

Overhead the leaves, dull green to amber, formed a roof, and he was barely aware that the drizzle had become heavier. He felt invigorated, noticing little details about him, listening to sounds, and breathing in the mixed odours of the sweet conifers, damp leaves and burned smells of autumn. The dog ran back and forth, its nose close to the ground, giving chase to a squirrel or rabbit, and making Adam laugh with its fruitless attempts.

'Daft creature. You'll not catch them.'

The track opened out, and when Adam pressed the cob into a canter it responded eagerly. Exhilarated, he patted its neck. This was the way he enjoyed riding; to hack amidst familiar countryside, spot wildlife, and listen to the woodland sounds . . . And now, walking once more, he saw a small herd of deer just a few yards away – roe deer with a stag amongst them, feet pointing, noses quivering; then they were fleeing, springing over tangled branches and fallen timber. He heard them after they had disappeared from view – the cracking of branches. Disturbed pheasants broke out of their hiding places.

'Not to chase,' Adam told the trembling dog. '*Not* to.'

It was raining hard now, and growing dark, but Adam was oblivious. The sight of the deer had thrilled him, and as always when he rode he was preoccupied. Occasionally, as they jumped a fallen log or broke into a canter, he remembered that next Saturday he was going hunting; but it seemed remote. More important and imminent was his birthday. Surely when he was fifteen all his problems and anxieties would disappear?

'. . . My speech is definitely coming along . . . Perhaps Mama will learn to care for me . . . And Jonathan's a bit better since my cartoons at school – how furious he'd be to know I've done one of him as a dog on Mama's lap . . . Perhaps one day I'll do a cartoon for *Punch* . . . I wonder if they'll print my letter in the *Reading Mercury* . . . I hope they give the man the money . . . How lovely to see those deer. Of course – it's the rutting season . . .'

Too late, he saw the fallen tree in their path. Instinctively, the cob jumped and cleared it, but Adam was thrown into the air, his head striking wood as he fell.

He knew fleeting pain, and lost consciousness. He could not know, therefore, that his loyal horse made no attempt to bolt, or that the setter, after a few moments of whimpering, dashed back purposefully to Brambleden Hall, tail between its legs. Nor was he aware of the rain beating down, penetrating his clothes and drenching him. He lay still, his face pressed to the muddy track, his body surrounded by sodden leaves, and blood coming from the wound on the left side of his head.

Led by the dog, they found him a couple of hours later, by which time dark had fallen and a strong wind had come up. The four lanterns bobbed in the blackness.

''Ere,' called George Lundy. 'Lad's over 'ere.' He stooped beside the boy. 'I told 'im to go easy,' he said sorrowfully. 'Oh, but 'e's in poor shape.'

Sir Felix ran to join the groom, stumbling over undergrowth. 'Addi, Addi . . .'

''E's unconscious, sir.'

Crouching over his motionless son, Sir Felix saw the blood seeping from his head. 'Oh God. Oh God . . .' He raised his voice: 'Help me, someone. We must carry him back to the carriage.'

The valet and butler bent simultaneously, and Sir Felix snapped, 'Not both of you. One of you . . . You, Burton. Right? Gently . . . gently.' With his valet he lifted the boy. He was surprisingly long and heavy.

'He's grown,' murmured Sir Felix. 'It was all he wanted – to grow. And I didn't notice.'

Adam was unconscious for three days. The hired nurse slid gruel and medicines down his throat with a long spoon, and the physician bled him – an incision into his thin pale arm which looked as though it could not possibly contain any blood to be released. His father went mournfully up- and downstairs all day, as did Leah, who had no one to speak to of her terror that her brother might die. Lady Elizabeth visited from obligation a few times, and Jonathan just once. Illness frightened him. Besides – what use was it visiting someone more dead than alive, who was unaware of your presence? He wondered if he would be sad if his brother died – and decided that it would make little difference.

And then, on the fourth morning, Adam awoke, clammy with sweat, coughing – and delirious. Voices dwelt in his head, shouting and echoing and fading. They threatened him; they commanded him; they entreated and muttered and discussed amongst themselves. And while the voices possessed his brain, people came and sat on his body, squeezing the breath from him and constraining his limbs, pinioning them so he could not move. Then suddenly he would be released, and there would be a wonderful lightness in his body. He soared over the county as a duck or a gull. But the gull became a crow pecking at his head, puncturing his right eye.

'Addi, do you remember picking mushrooms, peeling them to make sure they weren't toadstools . . . and making the rhubarb wine?' A stout woman who was not his mother was crying over him, loving him, plumping his pillows.

'*Mama!* Where is she?'

'Hush – I shall get her, babe, my babe. I shall get her.' And Mrs Fitzgerald vanished, and replacing her was a huge pig.

'Addi, get well, well, well . . . Well, what have you to say for yourself, Gilmour? If it takes three men two and a quarter hours to pull a cart five miles, how long would it take them to pull it seven miles?'

'I don't *know*. It's a stupid question. How could I know . . .'

Alice Mason was strangling him, and as her eyes bored into his, their blackness became opaque pools concealing poisonous eels which wound round his lungs.

'Repent of your sins.'

'What sins? How must I repent? I can't breathe.'

'I know. I'll get some water.'

'Addi, I love you. Addi? *Addi?*'

His name was constantly repeated. People spoke to him of love. But *she* never said the word. She could not, because it was untrue. He was repulsive to her. In between his periods of delirium he knew this.

'Oh Mama. Oh Mama.'

'Hush babe.'

There were others who cared instead. They would have to suffice. For a fortnight Adam was critically ill, and alternated between reality and fantasy. The physician bled him again.

'Severe concussion,' he said, 'as a result of the blow to the head. And bronchial pneumonia. However, it is likely he will survive now.'

He spoke these words, while standing at the foot of Adam's bed, to Lady Gilmour, and Adam's thought before he drifted back to sleep was, 'I am a nuisance to her. Nothing but a nuisance.'

He lay in bed for a further three weeks, sleeping and waking and being fed like a child, his bottom raw from lying for so long. His father or Leah would visit him, and sit with him, watching him with worried faces. His mother's visits were rare, and she would stand by him tensely, longing to be away again, not knowing what to say. He almost felt sorry for her: at having to offer compassion to someone she despised.

However, there was something else wrong that was far more serious, and finally he had to acknowledge it: he could not see out of his right eye.

When it registered – truly registered – that he was half blind, Adam knew a feeling of utter despair. He wanted to scream; to vent his rage, terror and disbelief that this could happen to him. The screams remained locked in him, and he lay there, silent, private and bitter. Nobody could appease him. Gentleness, cajoling, humour, affection, pity – none of these affected him or could penetrate the barrier of solitude he had constructed around himself. His inner pain could not be reached by anyone, nor released by him. It became part of him, and gradually he grew used to it.

'Unfair . . . unfair . . .' The words formed an incantation in his head. Each morning he awoke in the hope of finding that during the night some miracle had occurred to restore his sight, or that perhaps it had all been an atrocious dream; but this was not the case, and, inevitably, with the passing of time, he came to accept that the catastrophe which had befallen him was not, after all, ever going to disappear. With this acceptance, his anguish lessened, and one day he asked Leah for a mirror.

'I can hold it myself,' he said impatiently, when she held the silver hand-mirror up for him. 'I am not that feeble.' And taking it from her, he studied his reflection: wan and shadowed, it gazed seriously back at him. His right eye looked no different except for a dullness. He had not realized how frightened he had been about its appearance; he had not dared ask, or see himself, before – and perhaps confront a white marble.

He laid the mirror down on the counterpane. 'I'll get up tomorrow. I've stayed in bed long enough . . . Tell me, do you think she hoped I'd die?'

'Who, Addi?' Leah looked puzzled.

'Mama. Do you think she's disappointed?'

His sister was seated on his right, and he had to turn his head to see her fully. He would get used to that, to adjusting his position accordingly, to constantly swivelling his head. He realized he had shocked her.

'Addi, that's a dreadful thing to say.'

He gave a brittle laugh. 'Is the truth so dreadful?'

'Oh, Addi . . .' Her eyes filled with tears. Herself a child who badly needed affection, she had been pushed aside the past few weeks, and had been at the mercy of Miss Baldwin, who had seized the opportunity to display her power. Now she longed for some lightness of atmosphere in the house, for normality to be resumed, and for her brother to jest with her as he used to.

'She did wish it,' he continued dully. 'It would have been easier for her. I am her thorn. She dislikes herself for disliking me. But it doesn't matter. I don't think I care any more. I've other things to think of now . . .'

Life had its strange compensations; during his illness and long spell in bed Adam had grown a couple of inches. He was now five feet eight – only an inch shorter than his brother, but Adam took a size larger in shoes. The other strange thing was that Adam's stammer had almost disappeared. Mrs Fitzgerald reasoned that it was because after the shock with his eye, nothing else seemed important.

'And do you know,' she said, stoking the fire, then propping the cushions behind his neck as he sat in the morning-room, straining to read, 'all the time you were delirious you didn't stutter once. Oh, but you were proper pitiful, you were. I'm glad that's over and done with. And just think, Master Addi, there'll be no more hunting for you, at any rate.'

He laughed, his new, deep laugh; his voice, too, had changed and almost settled down to become a man's.

'That's good to hear you laugh,' she said, fussing with his blankets, then feeling his forehead briefly with the flat of her hand. 'You want to laugh a bit more, Master Addi. You've got one fine eye and two splendid ears, and I'll tell you a thing: I'd as soon have one good eye than two shortsighted ones. Now there's a thought for you!' She chuckled, and nudged him in his ribs. 'And you start to eat proper again and put some meat on your bones. You've brooded enough now, eh?'

Efficient and quick, despite her stoutness, she bustled about the room – then left him, to his book and his thoughts, with a smile on his lips and a light in his left eye.

A few days later he received two letters. The first, in a package, was from Edward Lear, and was brought to him by his father, who had recognized his friend's writing. He stayed with his son as he read it.

'What does Lear have to say?' he asked afterwards. 'Or is it too personal?' He always respected another's privacy.

'No . . . I'd like you to hear it.' He picked it up again, and, focusing with his good eye, began to read out loud:

Dear Adam,

I was so sorry to hear of your accident from your father, and the resultant problems with your sight, and I am writing now to offer you not only my sympathy, but also my encouragement; for, Adam, you must not be deterred. You must regard whatever befalls you in life as a challenge. In fact, it is these very things – so trying, so apparently monumental to overcome at the time – these things which help build us as men. We have more to combat, and therefore more strength is needed. Accordingly we develop this – and how wonderful is that new-found strength. Use your defects to your benefit, Adam; not to gain pity from others, but to benefit your soul . . .

At this point Sir Felix squeezed his son's hand tightly and blinked back tears.

Adam continued:

And now you will see I have enclosed a small gift for you. It is a watercolour I came across the other day, and which I did some years ago. I remembered a conversation we had last time we met, when you told me of your aversion to hunting, so that when I rediscovered this I immediately thought of you. It is entitled 'The One That Got Away', and I fancy the fox is smiling. Anyway, I hope you like the picture, and perhaps you will find a place for it somewhere on your bedroom wall.

As your dear father may have told you, I am now in Italy where I came shortly after my sister's death – a loss to which I cannot accustom myself; for Anne, who was twenty-two years older than me, was mother and friend to me, besides sister. She went down very rapidly. I had been painting her portrait, and then one day – March 4th – she could not come to her sitting because of a swelling on her neck, and nausea. In the early hours of March 12th she died. I felt very alone. I went briefly to Farringford, Isle of Wight, to visit my friends the Tennysons; but they were much preoccupied with other matters, and the visit was not therapeutic, as I had expected. More bad news followed: my sister Mary died also, and my painting, *The Cedars*, which I believe I told you about, did not sell – yet I was, and remain, convinced of its merits. How turn-face the public can be; yet they fuss that sentimentalist Millais (whom I used to admire) as if he were God's next of kin!

Now I am in Tuscany, and the healing process is underway. You see, Adam, one must persevere, and this is why I write to you in such a manner, because I believe we are alike in our determination to persevere against the odds. When one is born with an affliction one really has little option . . .

Here Adam stopped, because Edward Lear then admitted to being epileptic, and stressed that Adam must guard this knowledge to himself.

'What does he mean about an affliction?' his father asked. 'What affliction does Edward have?'

Adam made no reply. He rubbed his good eye, which was becoming sore from the strain of reading.

Sir Felix said gently, 'If it's a secret between you, then you must not reveal it. I am glad such a man has taken an interest in you. Does he have further news?'

'Not really. He only goes on to say he intends to remain in Italy for the rest of the winter.'

'He is fortunate,' said Sir Felix, sighing heavily, remembering his own days of travelling. 'It must be very pleasant to come and go as one pleases, and to live off one's creativity.'

Adam resisted saying: 'It's what I wish to do.' It was too early to tell his father this; first he must have some proof of his ability. He wanted his father to be proud, to reward him for his love and constancy.

So he did not read the last paragraph of Lear's letter, which said:

I should like to see something you have written and illustrated. It can be amusing or sad, but *do* send it to me without self-consciousness, as I am truly interested in you, and in your progress . . .

Adam was uplifted by this letter. He could hear Lear's voice speaking the words he had written, and their poignancy and wisdom stirred him; at that moment he could almost regard his shortcomings as privileges. He had been singled out in order to test his strength. It was as though he had sought something elusive and now found it.

'What a remarkable man he is,' thought Adam. 'I can see now that I've nothing to be morose about after all. And I have one perfect-sighted eye which I shall learn to control; nothing around me will go unobserved, and I shall listen to each sound – every creak and every squeak . . . This afternoon I'll write in my diary, and then look out one of my stories for Mr Lear . . . But my left eye aches so with strain, and my useless right one also . . . I'll not be disheartened. I'll not . . .'

'Addi,' his father said softly, 'there's another letter for you.'

Adam took it from his father. Its postmark bore a date three weeks earlier.

'It arrived ages ago,' Sir Felix said. 'When you were first ill, in fact . . . who is it from?' he asked, anxiously studying Adam as he read, noticing how his left eye watered, and the slight wheeze in his breathing.

Adam made a gesture with his hand for his father not to interrupt, and continued reading, then handed the letter to Sir Felix. It was from the editor of the *Reading Mercury*.

Dear Master Gilmour,

I am writing not only to thank you for your letter to our newspaper – which no doubt you saw published on Friday, October 4th – but also for your generous contribution to the welfare of the poor unfortunate concerned. Rest assured he will receive this, and be most touched by your consideration.

With regard to your letter itself, I noted with great interest your points, and hope we shall hear from you again on other matters which might attract your attention. You certainly have a talent for expressing yourself, especially as I noted you are only just fifteen years old. Indeed, were you not destined, no doubt, to a different kind of future, I should venture to suggest you pursue a career in journalism.

I am, sir, faithfully yours,

Patrick G. Best, Editor

Sir Felix folded the letter, his black eyebrows drawn together reflectively. 'I don't know what to say . . .' He swallowed. 'I had no idea about this. How dreadful that I should have missed my son's letter in the local paper. As you know, I never read the correspondence page; it's usually filled with waffle. But I shall straight away send the coachman to the *Reading Mercury* offices to ask for a back copy. My goodness, but I feel quite choked . . .'

That afternoon, amongst his piles of scribblings, Adam found a story he had written some months previously, called 'The Dragon-Governess'. It told of a formidable governess who became a dragon and persecuted children, but was ultimately slain. In Adam's intricate illustrations she bore the unmistakable features of Miss Baldwin.

He put this story in an envelope, enclosed a covering note, and sealed it with dark-red wax. The thought of the contents so officially dressed up made him laugh.

But he was tired. It had been his first full day; and his left eye was bloodshot. He lay down on his bed and pulled the counterpane over him; it was so tedious being ill, he thought – and such a waste of time. Over a month had gone by, without his being aware. He would grow old, and chunks of his life would be missing.

'. . . A challenge. He said it must be a challenge. I challenge you to a duel, life . . .' He gave a small half-giggle, and slept.

It was the week before Christmas. Prince Albert had died in Windsor of typhus, and those people who had scathingly spoken of 'that German', now spoke of the legacy he had left to culture.

Adam thought, 'They are so inconsistent. I hate that. You can't trust a person who is inconsistent . . .'

In St Margaret's Church a few days later, a full congregation gathered to lament the passing of the Queen's consort. From the building came the innocent tones of a girl singing 'I know that my Redeemer liveth'. Except that Alice Mason, who stood singing so sweetly, was not so innocent. She was three months pregnant, and unrepentant. Her mocking eyes settled on Adam, and he thought, 'No, she's not pretty at all. Her soul's ugly.'

After church the family sat together in the parlour pursuing their various activities. Christmas cards and decorations adorned the room. Through the open doorway, in the hall, part of a tall tree was visible. Lady Gilmour, seated at the small bureau, wrapping presents, remarked to nobody in particular, 'I hear the Masons are moving from the area. I must say it is all very sudden . . .'

When Adam heard this announcement he felt no sadness; it was as if he had never known Alice, nor trembled because of her, lain awake because of her, nor been inspired to write poetry because of her. He was glad she was going. The business was finished, and he would no more be reminded of his inadequacies, and that he had been used. His fear would go with her departure – that no girl would ever love him for himself.

The Gilmours celebrated the onset of 1862 with another party; but this time Edward Lear was unable to visit. Instead he wrote to Adam a couple of weeks later. He had returned from Italy and was back at his rooms in Stratford Place:

> My dear Adam,
>
> Happy New Year, and I trust it will prove a healthy and fruitful one in every way; indeed I can tell you it has already begun with a propitious start as far as you are concerned. Why is that? You must be wondering, and I shall enlighten you. I am happy to inform you that your 'Dragon-Governess' story has been accepted for publication by *Blackwood's Magazine*. This is no more than you deserve, for it is a most wickedly amusing little piece, and quite delightfully illustrated. I would welcome seeing anything else you may do in the future, so keep at it. *Blackwood's* will write directly to you, enclosing payment, and telling you when your story is to be published, so you have something to which to look forward.
>
> I myself am in the throes of working on a third edition of my *Book of Nonsense*, and deriving much enjoyment from dreaming up limericks. It is a rather different occupation to painting landscapes and birds, but equally rewarding in its way, and helps me to retain my humour.
>
> Meanwhile, young Adam, keep fighting your battles and winning. You will be a finer person for them . . .

And he was fighting. Every day there was a new fight: with physical pain; with fluctuating emotions; with the daunting task of overcoming his disability. At first he would constantly bump into things positioned on his blind side, and become frustrated and short-tempered – both with himself and others. He also became frustrated at not being able to read or draw for long periods without his left eye streaming and almost closing. His concentration, too, was affected, so that he often felt a sense of detachment, as though he were not part of events.

'I wish I were a cyclops,' he joked to Leah one day. 'At least then I would have central vision.'

But joking was an effort. It was all an effort, and his enemy was depression, which he tried to keep at bay – as he tried to keep his impatience checked, and to quell his overriding fear that a similar thing might happen to his other eye.

The weeks passed, and he refused to give in to his weaker impulses, the insidious aches and anxieties which would destroy his peace of mind. He learned to deal with his affliction, and eventually, almost to disregard it . . . And everywhere were signs of spring, and optimism in the air . . .

He would wander into the cowshed, where the cows stood protectively by their newly-born calves; chat to the earnest young cowman, whose hands were as pale as the milk he drew patiently twice a day from the docile animals. Adam watched him sometimes – the strength and rhythm of his fingers; and afterwards, when the cowman handed the full maplewood pails to the dairymaid, Adam knew from their gaze that they were in love. He was in awe of them because of it.

The idea of love, or more realistically, sex, interested and disturbed him nowadays. It bewildered and thrilled him. He could not help but be aware of his body's changes – the soft brown hair covering his limbs and sprouting on his chest; the broadening of his shoulders, and deepening of his voice. He could not help but acknowledge the involuntary stirring in his penis, so that sometimes for no apparent reason he grew hard . . . And yet he could not imagine that a woman would ever want to love him in that way; such a prospect was distant and intimidating. But his body continued to mortify him with its impromptu urges.

He wondered if his brother felt as he did. But he never saw Jonathan blush, as Adam did if a pretty girl approached. Nor, as Adam did, would Jonathan avert his eyes in shame, nor perspire under the arms, nor revert to the old habit of stuttering.

It was not only thoughts of love and sex which preoccupied him, but also of beauty; and as his soul became increasingly romantic, he searched for it everywhere, gratified that he could find it in such unexpected sources, and not only in the obviousness of a perfect face. But whilst his appreciation of aestheticism developed, so did his doubts about his own appearance, and he would examine himself critically in the mirror, comparing his fine-boned, olive-skinned features to his brother's ruddy and vigorous looks.

'How do others perceive me?' he wrote in his diary one night, when he was particularly plagued by uncertainties. 'Are people pleasant to me because they like me, or because they pity me? Am I tricking myself that my blindness does not notice, when really it is the first thing people *do* notice? But even then, I should be able to be dismissive; for if others feel awkward on my behalf, that is because of *their* limitations. But I have a horror of ugliness. Am I ugly? Is that why Mama dislikes me? Did Alice Mason think me ugly? And must I go through life trying to be amusing, in order to divert people from my defects?. . .

'But you are *not* ugly,' Leah assured him when, a few days later, he asked her to tell him truthfully. 'And I don't notice your eye, I promise. I wish you wouldn't be so self-conscious. I don't care in the least about my appearance, and I'm a girl.'

'I think you're very pretty.'

She gave one of her elaborate shrugs, and he laughed. 'Well – I shall change the subject. I've something to show you. Look.'

He handed her a copy of *Blackwood's Magazine*, and she almost snatched it from him. 'You're in it! Oh, where?'

'Page eleven.'

He watched her fumble through the pages until she came to his story. 'Here it is! Oh, I don't believe it – it's Miss Baldwin! It *is* her! How clever you are, Addi. Have you shown Mama and Papa yet?'

'No.'

'And Miss Baldwin – but she must surely see it . . . Have they paid you?'

'Yes. But not very much.' He flushed slightly, and his sister smiled and touched his cheek.

'Tell.'

'Ten shillings.'

'But that's a lot. What will you do with it, Addi?'

'I've not decided yet.' But he had. He was intending to buy her a birthday present with it.

When he saw the copy of *Blackwood's*, Sir Felix Gilmour roared with laughter and slapped his son repeatedly on the back – then, thoughtlessly, and perhaps a little maliciously, he left the magazine lying in a prominent position on the hall table. The following day a grim-faced Miss Baldwin, her lips a straight line in her face, handed in her resignation without explanation.

'I am appalled,' scolded Lady Elizabeth to both father and son, when she realized what had happened. 'It was an unspeakable thing to do. And Adam, I will not permit you to write such rubbish. Mr Lear is also to blame for having it published. Certainly he'll not be welcome here again. Well really! And now we are without a governess, and I shall have to waste valuable time engaging a new one. Such offensive, disrespectful behaviour I have never come across.'

Wednesday, March 26th

'Today has been the worst day of my life. I am so upset I can hardly think.

'The morning started normally – breakfast with Leah and Jonathan and Papa. Papa seemed particularly cheerful, and asked each of us how we were going to spend the day, it being the school holidays. I was about to tell him I was going to Reading when Mr Burton called him away about something. I did not see him again before he left the house. Oh I wish I had. If he had known where I was going, then it would not have happened. I would not have seen them together. It would all be the same. I would not *know*. And now I cannot look him in the eye, or smile at his jokes, or bear his hand on my head. It feels false. He is false. I am let down.

'This evening he looked at me with bewilderment at my coldness, as if to say, "What have I done to you? What have I done wrong?" But I could not behave otherwise. At least with my mother I know where I stand. Now who do I look to for guidance and encouragement? My father gave me these things, and because I respected him I was proud. But I no longer respect him, and therefore do not trust his pride in me.

'I must start at the beginning: At about midday our coachman drove me to Henley station and I caught the train to Reading. This is one of my "privileges" now I am fifteen, that I may make unaccompanied trips. So this day – for the first time – I made use of my "privilege". What a strange treat fate had stored for me.

'It was a mild day, and I wandered around the town feeling really rather happy – along Broad Street, up St Mary's Butts, and past the almshouses, towards Market Place with its bright stalls and live animals and hoarse shouts from marketeers. A young flowergirl handed me a flower. I offered to pay her for it.

'"It's for free, pretty boy," she said, and I felt myself blush, as that embarrassing swelling started in my crotch.

'In St Mary's Butts is the art shop I have been to several times with my father (I can scarcely bring myself to refer to him as "Papa"), and this was the reason for my trip to Reading. I went inside to buy some modelling clay for Leah's birthday.

'"It's heavy," Mr Goodfellow said as he handed it to me. "I heard you've been in poor health. Why don't you get your father to take it?"

'"My father's not with me."

'"But I only saw him a couple of hours ago. He came in to buy a new watercolour box."

'How stupidly excited I was that he was also here in Reading, and at the prospect I might bump into him. Carrying the heavy bag of clay, I walked back to Broad Street and, hesitantly, ventured into the Post Office Tavern. I did not see them immediately, for the place was, as usual, packed; and then, as I stood waiting to be served, I spotted them. Huddled as close together as they could be, at a small round table in the corner of the room, were my father and a young woman.

'I stared, thinking I must be mistaken, and my father became a stranger, a virile-looking, infatuated man whose whole body keened towards the woman beside him. I was, briefly, relieved. It had, after all, been a mistake; a play of light. I was about to turn away when the man glanced in my direction, not to look at me, but to smile into space with an unseeing expression. Then I knew for sure, and ran from the tavern, quite forgetting the bag of clay, so that another customer ran after me in the street, brandishing it and yelling . . .'

It was almost midnight and he was unutterably tired. He could no longer write. Dismally, he climbed into bed and blew out the candle and extinguished the lamp. There was no sense anywhere; no one to trust; nobody by whom to judge right or wrong. Nothing was as it seemed. Even little Leah, who longed to muddy her hands, would one day become like their mother and forget that she had ever craved other things.

'What's it all for? What are *we* for? Why did my father – the one person I looked up to in all the world – why did he have to let me down? The thought of him touching that woman . . . He's a lecherous old fool. Does Mama know? Perhaps that's why she's so hateful . . . I can't understand . . . I'll not confide in him again. I have Leah, and Mrs Fitzgerald. And my diary. I have myself, Adam Gilmour. Adam's a good name. No one shall call me Addi again.'

Chapter Four

MATURITY

During the past two years there had been several changes in the Gilmour household: Miss Baldwin had been replaced by Miss Sweeby, a young and pretty governess who adored Leah and filled Adam's nights with erotic dreams; Mrs Fitzgerald had unexpectedly remarried and moved to Skirmett, leaving Adam bereft and aggrieved: she seldom visited now that she had five stepchildren of her own; Jonathan had become even more arrogant and had decided to go 'into the City'; and Sir Felix was a sad and chastened man. He could not understand why his son Adam was so changed in his attitude towards him.

The more reticent the boy was, the more garrulous the father became in his efforts to joke and to please. There were no balloon trips, no outings together, painting sessions or walks, or visits to the greenhouse to view Sir Felix's prize orchids. Stricken, Sir Felix spent an increasing amount of time away from home, and when he was there, all the spirit seemed gone from him. Without his joviality Brambleden Hall was a cheerless place – even regular callers stopped coming, and Lady Elizabeth became the unbridled force of the house.

Leah asked Adam: 'What's happened between you? Papa seems a broken man.'

But he couldn't tell her, and was unyielding. He missed his father desperately – their close rapport, their confidences – but because he believed he had been betrayed, he could not forgive. At nights he would remember the many happy times they'd shared – small episodes, intimacies, which despite everything he still treasured. He remembered how his father had whistled when he walked beside him.

'I shall make everything all right again,' he sometimes mused.

'How easy it would be to take his hand, and clasp his fingers . . . and the house would be alive again . . . But I can't. I can't do it.'

Other worries kept him awake at night: he worried about articles he'd read, highlighting the problems of the poor; about his mathematics homework; about the plight of the blacks in war-torn America – and of the Lancashire cotton-workers with no cotton; about his own future; about the fact that he was so unlovable that even Mrs Fitzgerald had deserted him, and that Leah would one day marry and he would have no one; that he would die young, and have done nothing with his life.

But his days were full. Outside school hours he painted, wrote and collected – antique writing implements which cluttered his room. He walked for miles into the hills above Turville, where he would sit by the windmill and reflect. Or he would read. He read more avidly than ever nowadays, and took an active interest in the newspapers, and himself often contributed to the correspondence pages. Newspapers excited him – the way they reached out to thousands of people, expressing their views freely. Freedom: freedom to speak one's mind; freedom to *do* was another issue entirely. That was the privilege of the comfortably-off.

Adam's latest letter had been accepted by *The Times*, and shyly he had shown it to his mother.

'I don't know why you bother,' she had said, barely glancing at the open page, and his letter in print there. 'It serves no purpose. As far as I'm concerned it's all a waste of time.'

His pride withered. 'Everything's a waste of time,' he protested heatedly. 'Don't you see that? It's all only a matter of passing time until we eventually die.'

'I see that your remark is ill-considered, Adam, and that perhaps you should find other gainful ways of employing your time.' Her mouth gave a fierce, distorting twitch.

Whatever he did was insufficient for his mother; for her there was only Jonathan. If he made a friend he did not invite him home because his mother would humiliate Adam in front of his guest; and eventually friends would weary of one-sided invitations, and give him up.

He would not admit to being lonely, for loneliness was tantamount to being pathetic, weak, unattractive. He dreaded that he should be regarded in such a light, and consciously created an image for himself, wearing his hair unusually long and parted at the side, and dressing rather like a latterday Byron.

Jonathan mocked his brother's romantic appearance, but nowadays Adam would quickly answer back, so that a quarrel would start, and sometimes a fight.

'I shall blind your other eye,' Jonathan had shouted at him once, and in terror Adam had hit him first. Their mother had entered at the moment Adam's fist shot into Jonathan's mouth, and, horrified, she'd shrieked and hauled her older son away with surprising strength.

'He said – he said –' His breath came in short bursts. His fists were still clenched.

'I am not interested,' his mother told him furiously. 'Come straight to my boudoir.'

'. . . Said a spider to a fly . . .' He smiled fleetingly, and followed her, casting an unrepentant look at his brother. It was absurd, he thought, that at his age he was about to endure such a demeaning punishment.

Upstairs, in the pink room – slightly faded – he held out his hand to take his mother's wrath, and remembered an occasion when as a child of ten or eleven he had been punished for stealing black-currants from the bushes outside the kitchen door. Lady Gilmour's knee had been raised to give her arm greater force as it lifted the birch; but as she brought down her arm he had instinctively moved away his outstretched hand, and the birch had hit her own knee instead. How she had howled in rage and pain! And how he had suffered for it after, when she recovered.

Saturday, September 26th, 1863

'Why is it that I cannot talk to women? I even have a problem with Leah's friends. I become a bumbling buffoon and cannot help myself.

'This morning when I went to the village post office and stores to send a letter (another to the *Reading Mercury*), I was served not by Miss Tinley as usual, who always complains about the weather no matter what it does, but by a much younger woman, in her mid-twenties. She turned out to be her niece, and is standing in for her aunt, who is ill.

' "I'm Ethel Brown," she told me. "You must call me Ethel."

'And of course I was, at once, struck dumb. But she herself talked so freely that she put me at my ease and I was able to look directly at her: a round freckled face, and a chin that quivers when she laughs, hazel eyes – an unremarkable face, except for its liveliness; and her hair is a pretty wheaten colour. She wore a ring on her left hand, and I dared to ask, "Is your husband helping you?"

' "My husband isn't with me," she answered, and looked at me in a way that made my heart quicken.

'When I left she said, "I hope I'll see you again soon."

'Surely I was mistaken that there was an invitation in her tone? But I shall find an excuse to call again next week. By then I shall be seventeen.

'This afternoon when I went into Leah's room she had no time to hide her present: a clay sculpture of our setter. She has never done anything like it before, and it would be good for an adult, let alone a self-taught girl of fourteen and a half.

' "You must take it up seriously," I told her, as proud as if I had made the model myself.

' "Oh yes," she said, raising her eyebrow in that sceptical way she has. "And do you think Mama would permit it?"

'Why does Mama defeat us both? Why do we let ourselves be defeated by her?

' "She cannot dictate our lives for ever," I answered. But is that true? One continually wants to appease Mama and gain her approval, to see even a glimmer of tenderness, and hang on to it.

'When I was younger I used to perform solitary plays in front of the mirror, and in one of them my mother was dead. I felt an enormous sense of freedom as I acted and pulled faces at myself, believing her to be gone from my life. May God – if He exists, although I confess to my doubts – forgive me . . .'

After school on the Monday he visited Ethel Brown again at the village post office just as she was about to close. The following day he feigned illness, and instead of going to school met her secretly, in the barn where he had used to meet Alice Mason.

From the onset Ethel Brown had had a single intention: to seduce Adam Gilmour. She had been instantly attracted to him: he was handsome, in a rather languid way; refined and young; and obviously still a virgin. But from the way he'd gazed at her with that mixture of gaucheness and pent-up sexual longing, she could tell he would be passionate.

And now Ethel was enveloping Adam in her strong arms by way of a greeting.

He was taken aback. He had been going to enquire politely about her, her life, her husband, where she lived, and perhaps discuss her political views – he had stood in front of his mirror practising various facial expressions. But she was there before him – waiting in a shadowy corner with cobwebs overhead, and barely gave him a chance to speak before pushing herself at him, thrusting her lips and tongue hard against his, pressing her pelvis to him.

Her hands were all over him, clumsy and rather rough. But she was warm, and smelled good – of rosewater cologne, she told him later – and her loosened hair thick and soft between his fingers. Her hands explored him in parts he had never imagined a woman's daring to do . . . He succumbed to her with relief, and, fumbling with her complicated clothing, was vaguely aware of her unbuttoning his trousers.

'I love you.'

'No my darling – you *need* me.'

'*Yes* . . .'

'Not yet. Put your hand here, my darling . . . my darling . . .'

Later, he asked her what he had intended to ask beforehand, and learned that her husband was in prison for killing a man he believed had poisoned his sheep.

'And he *did* poison them. We know he did. Only John took the law into his own hands. He didn't intend to kill him, though. He's just rough when he's heated . . . We've no money, and it's John's word 'gainst a dead man's. Mr Flannagan was a big farmer and wanted us off our land so he could buy it, as it cut into his. We lost more than fifty sheep . . . We can't afford a good lawyer . . . He was a bad man, was Mr Flannagan.'

'It's unfair – I'm so sorry for you.' He shook his head, distressed for her.

'My darling – don't take on so. I'm beyond it now. I'm prepared for the worst.'

'But you *shouldn't* be.'

'But I am, and that's the way it is. Your heart's too soft.'

'I love you, Ethel,' he said again.

'No you don't. It's only 'cause I'm the first.'

He thought about her a lot – her problems and the realism with which she faced them; her body which was always welcoming. She was a heavily built young woman, unimaginative to make love to, but he didn't know otherwise. She sighed a great deal, and stroked him, and Adam felt cosseted and satiated. The sexual act became entirely natural to him, and he couldn't think of this joining of flesh, which set in motion sequences of nerve-tingling reactions, as shameful. He rejoiced guiltlessly in feeling himself drawn ever deeper into her, and would always remember Ethel with gratitude.

Once or twice a week – into the winter months and New Year, while Miss Tinley remained obligingly ill – he blissfully emptied his inhibitions into Ethel's lazy body, and he began to think of himself as a man of the world. However, as such, with a mistress whose background was less than respectable, he was forced to reconsider his relationship with his father.

'Was I wrong in my judgement of him?' he wondered one night, and the thought kept him awake, branching into myriad other thoughts. Despite the coldness of the room he grew hot, and kicked off the bedclothes.

The following morning when Adam saw his father at breakfast, he initiated a conversation for the first time since that fateful day.

'I heard yesterday at school from Thomas Milroy – you know he's Lord Brambleden's great-nephew – that Lord Brambleden has just bought a Holman Hunt painting for four hundred guineas.'

It was pitiful to see the way Sir Felix's eyes lit up; the way, like a glad hound, he leapt at this unsubtle offering.

'Holman Hunt is a friend of Edward Lear,' Sir Felix said. 'I know Edward's always admired him – and had lessons from him in fact.'

They continued, haltingly, to discuss the merits of Pre-Raphaelite art, but neither was really concerned with the subject. Painfully, each was trying to reach out to the other. Their gaze held, and Adam attempted to smile. His mouth was trembling, and he noticed his father's was, too.

Appalled, he realized, 'I've hurt him so. Oh God – and I loved, – *love*, him. What right did I have? . . . All these years he's suffered.'

He took his father's hand which rested on the table. 'Papa –' He swallowed to relieve the lump in his throat.

'Addi.' His father reverted to the old pet name, and tightly squeezed his hand in return. Then he gave a dry sob, and unwilling to weep before his son, rushed from the room.

Adam sat on, shocked by the suffering he had caused his father, by his own shortcomings. Then he thought, 'But it's going to be all right.' He brushed away his tears. 'I must be honest, explain what happened, bring everything into the open. I should have spoken about it at the time . . . but I was too young. I didn't understand such things . . . But shouldn't I have forgiven him without the need to understand? How could I have judged my own father, whom I care for more than anyone in the world? I'll make amends. I shall, I shall . . .'

He began to brood on his own faults – his obsessiveness and stubbornness, his impulsive and inflexible nature.

'Adam, are you going to dream all morning, or are you coming to school?'

Jonathan had been standing in the doorway to the parlour, watching his brother for a minute or so. His voice held exasperation, but also a new note of tolerance which, increasingly, he had been showing. Perhaps he sensed and respected the change in Adam; whatever the reason, it seemed that the worst of their conflict was over.

Jonathan was sixteen years old, and at six foot, just half an inch taller than Adam. Athletic and broad-shouldered, he moved with confidence – as he spoke with confidence, in a rather clipped tenor. His manner was dour, and he was still fiercely competitive, but his bullying streak had become a more normal assertiveness, and his aggression was now channelled into ambition. Jonathan was going to be a City banker; of that he was as certain as Adam was that he was going to be a writer, and Leah that she was going to be a sculptor . . .

'The doves have still not been fed,' Adam said, absently staring out of the window towards the dovecot where about thirty doves waited, jerking their heads impatiently. It was Sir Felix's job to feed them; he loved to watch them swoop and alight on the lawn as of one, in a flurry of flapping. 'I must remind him.'

'Adam, I refuse to be late for school because of the doves. Disgusting birds, anyway. They make such a mess.'

'So do humans.' Adam got up, and went into the hall. He called upstairs, 'Papa, don't forget the doves' – knowing his father hadn't forgotten; it was an excuse to extend their contact before he left for school.

His father's face appeared over the galleried banister. 'Thank you, Addi – Adam. Take care,' he called back, his voice tender.

Adam looked upwards at him, and saw he had aged. He thought, 'It's my fault . . . But I'll make everything well.'

'You have a good day too, Papa,' he said softly – and left with his brother, who was clicking his teeth in annoyance and glancing at his watch.

That March morning there was a light breeze and a stinging freshness to the air; an ideal ballooning day, Sir Felix Gilmour thought as he walked to the cricket pitch. He felt rejuvenated, and whistled as he strode out like a young man.

The balloon was ready, and his helpers welcomed him enthusiastically. A friend had been due to join him, but his valet had sent word that he was ill; on such a day, in such excellent spirits, Sir Felix had decided not to cancel his own plans. He climbed into the basket and settled himself.

'Right,' he called as usual, and the balloon rose slowly as they let go of the ropes. He coiled them in, released some ballast, and sat back. He'd forgotten to bring binoculars, which he liked to have with him, but this morning he was content to give himself up to his thoughts, and to let the silence wash over him. He was glad to be alone, at one with his surroundings, and aware of everything about him with a rare acuteness. Into the silence filtered those stray sounds of the world below – and of the air itself, for nothing was ever truly silent.

He had released all his ballast and was as high as he'd ever been. The balloon, in his control, had become a falcon from which he surveyed the span of his kingdom. His son, Adam, occupied his thoughts. He didn't know what had caused the rift, or what had brought about the sudden mellowing of mood, but he would ask no questions; it was enough that his son still loved him. That he knew, and the knowledge made him a contented man again.

It was time to start descending – he was over Fingest and Sir Felix pulled at the valve line to release gas. Nothing happened; it seemed to have stuck; and he gave a harder tug, not unduly worried. There was a massive noise, a roar, as the gas escaped in a single burst and the balloon began to deflate about him, and then he felt a dreadful fear as he realized he was going to crash.

Half-way through the afternoon Adam and Jonathan were both told to report to the headmaster. He faced them across his wide desk, his expression sombre.

'I have some sad news,' he said heavily, looking at them each in turn. 'You must both be strong . . . your father is dead. I'm terribly sorry.'

'Papa? *Papa?* It cannot be.' White-lipped, Adam felt a wave of dizziness overtake him. Next to him, Jonathan, fists clenched, was rigid.

'I'm afraid it is. He was killed in a ballooning accident this morning.'

The world reverberated and came to a halt about him . . . And so much had been left unsaid; there had been years of damage he was intending to repair . . . 'Papa, don't forget to feed the doves.' 'Thank you, Addi – Adam. Take care, care, care . . .'

Sir Felix bequeathed his estate and thirteen thousand pounds of debts to his wife and three children. The financial chaos was sorted out between the family's solicitor – an elderly, shambling man – and Jonathan, who proved himself precociously shrewd at handling such matters. But even after all his efforts and mounds of paperwork, which kept him in his father's study until late at night, it had to be faced:

'We must sell up and go to London,' the sixteen-year-old calmly informed his mother, brother and sister, one Sunday afternoon in late summer. 'There is no option.'

They were sitting on the terrace looking out on to the wide lawn which was irregularly striped with the grey shadows of trees – blue fir, pine and cedar. Adam and Leah were playing chess. Lady Gilmour, in black, was reading and inhaling snuff in between, her mouth twitching.

The three of them looked at him with different expressions: Adam, aghast, Leah, disbelieving . . . Their mother, with a slow smile of satisfaction.

Jonathan pulled a chair up so that he sat facing them, in the shadow of the umbrella. He covered his mother's hand with his own in a rare gesture of affection – contrived, Adam immediately realized.

'Papa shouldn't have done this to you, Mama,' he said to her. 'Really – it's not good form.'

'There must be a way of staying,' Adam burst out, staring at their hands fondling one another and finding the little act repulsive.

'There is not,' Jonathan stated, unperturbed.

'It is all very well for you,' Adam said. 'It suits you fine – you want to go into the City after University. What about us? If we *have* to sell up, we could remain in the area. What reason is there to live in London, other than for *your* gain?'

'Adam –' Lady Elizabeth began. But Jonathan interrupted her:

'I was not thinking of myself –' He turned and looked lovingly at his mother. 'I was thinking of dearest Mama; she will have Aunt Mary and Grandmama Georgina close at hand.'

He had worked everything out, and turned the situation to his advantage. There was nothing Adam could say without sounding churlish. Wordlessly, he got up and strode across the lawn, which was springy beneath his feet. Tears started to his eyes, and he wiped them away viciously.

Leah caught up with him; he looked up to see her running down the garden, her hair flying, her body graceful. As she came closer he saw that she was crying, and his pity for her overshadowed his own sorrow. 'Poor Leah – I must look after her.'

He put his arm around her. 'We have each other.'

'I came to tell *you* that.'

'And it is true.'

'It's only that we're leaving so much behind.'

'It may not be bad. There will be the theatre, opera – and music halls! I should love to go to a music hall.'

'Halls of depravity, Mama calls them. And you do not trick me for a moment, Adam Gilmour.'

'*Sir* Adam Gilmour, do you realize that?'

'Oh Adam . . .' She gave a juddering sigh, and he tightened his arm about her.

'Shall you use your title?' she asked after a moment, sitting down beneath a wide-boughed cherry tree, fiddling with the ribbon in her hair.

'Not until I earn it in my own right,' he answered firmly. He lay beside her, staring up at the irregular shapes of sunlight between the leaves, and wondered how he would ever be at home in London. He saw, too, the demolition of his hopes; for he had planned to train as a reporter on the *Reading Mercury*.

Chapter Five

CHANGES

October 19th, 1864
'. . . So, seven and a half months after Papa's death, his matters have been put to rest. We have left our home, our lovely home – voices of guests lingering in the hall, and images of Papa, the genial host; Brambleden, with its quaint cottages and swift stream – and in the summer, young village women sitting on its edge, provocatively bathing their white legs, and the local boys leering from a safe distance; Alice Mason's voice resounding sweetly, falsely, throughout St Margaret's Church; pensive, solitary walks; Henley, with its festive atmosphere – and rowing with Leah on the river; lying on the Thames's lush banks, or sitting sketching; Ethel enclosing me – now with her mother somewhere in Bedfordshire, her husband hanged. All gone; all left behind . . .'

The house in a Knightsbridge square had been recently constructed in red brick, with a shallow, grey slate roof. It was a solid, semi-detached and narrow building, the sort that the new middle class liked to buy as a symbol of respectability; and Sir Felix Gilmour would have loathed it. Lady Elizabeth spent three months decorating it – in twilight colours which merged, and heavy velvets which excluded the scant light coming through the north-facing windows. The kitchen had the newest type of range, and water flowed freely into the great enamel sink from an efficient brass tap, instead of having to be laboriously pumped. There was mains gas, too, so that instead of having to go round the entire house lighting candles and oil lamps, one had only to turn a central knob to switch on all the lights. Their glow was rather orange, and did nothing to enhance one's complexion, but vanity had to be sacrificed when it came to practicality and moving with the times. It was a house of curious shadows, ugly pipework, and many smallish rooms which led one to the other; and the reception rooms were crowded with furniture from Brambleden Hall.

Adam would walk around touching everything nostalgically, and recalling, 'This was in the corner of the library, by the fireplace', or, 'I remember this table standing by the french doors to the terrace, and how it used to catch great beams of light . . .'

At first he felt suffocated in London, where abysmal poverty and obscene opulence snuggled adjacent; he thought of himself as rather like their setter, pining for its old home. The darkness of the house and the waspish faces of his mother, aunt and grandmother pursued him, and he found every conceivable excuse to escape. When he shut the front door behind him relief swept through him so that he could have danced along the street. And then, as the days went by and he came to know the metropolis, he developed a grudging affection for it.

His bedroom overlooked the square – with its small mannerless dogs, and bold pigeons – and in between writing he would pause to stare out of the window. All around, building was going on: a new house here, another there – solid, red-brick and bourgeois like their own; a four-storey mansion encased in scaffolding, being converted into apartments; piles of ballast and heaps of bricks lying in odd corners and driveways; and the gutters yellow with mud and sand, littered with discarded rubbish from the workmen . . . But lining the pavements and in the square itself were chestnut trees with blackbirds and thrushes hidden in their frosty branches; the church on the corner was a perfect copy of the Romantic Italian style; from a room somewhere came the regular sounds of someone practising the violin, and from another, the piano . . .

From their house one could walk almost everywhere, to shops, museums and galleries, to Hyde Park with its odd assortment of humanity: tramps and prostitutes, nannies and children, lovers, gentlemen out for a brisk spot of exercise; brushing past one another, their lives never touching . . .

*

November 5th, 1864

'This evening, in Hyde Park, Leah, Miss Sweeby and I stood amongst a crowd of hundreds and watched the huge firework display. We queued for roasted chestnuts and spoke to strangers while we waited. Somebody gently pushed Leah forward so she had a better view of the bonfire with its flames licking the guy's sausage-like legs, and in the rather sinister leaping light the whites of her eyes shone, then went dim, then shone again. She seemed very vulnerable beside me, and I put my arm round her shoulder. She glanced up at me affectionately, then back at the bonfire, her face beneath the bonnet vital as I have not seen it for a long while, and suddenly everything seemed to reassert itself into order in my mind, and it was as if a weight was lifted from me.

'Mama had already retired when we returned, and I said good night to the others and came to my room. I had an urge for the evening to continue, and parted the curtains: as I write now there is a haze from the gaslights in the foggy air; the clipped outlines of the chestnuts are just discernible; the constant roll of carriage wheels along Knightsbridge is gradually becoming intermittent; stray voices carry; a pair of cats fight and yowl directly outside, scuffling on a pile of rubble . . .

'And on my desk, propped up, is Edward Lear's 'The One That Got Away'. How wistful it makes me as I remember the circumstances in which it was given, and then I think of Papa, and I miss him so. How dreadfully I repaid him for his devotion.

'But that is the past, and now is the present, and for the first time since we moved I am almost happy.

'When I saw Mr Lear the other day at Stratford Place, he said, "Why don't you accompany me on some of my travels?" I told him I wasn't brave enough for that yet.

' "Brave?" he said, looking surprised. "I think it is the opposite as far as I'm concerned. Travelling is my escape."

' "From what?" I asked.

'And his rumpled face fell on to his chest as he said, "From the reality of my failures, dear Adam. It has to be admitted that my oils will never be recognized. I have decided to marry instead."

'Poor Mr Lear. But I've digressed, and whilst he is happy to leave London, I have only just discovered it: its constant excitement, which one becomes part of, and is carried along by. Perhaps I'll not go to bed at all tonight, but shall listen instead to the London night sounds and spin stories around them. And not so very far from here the countryside is dormant.

'Although, certainly, there was nothing altruistic in Jonathan's motives for persuading Mama to move to London, perhaps he did us a favour, as he shuffled us about like a pack of cards . . .'

Jonathan had been accepted at Oxford a year early, on the strength of his brilliant academic record and sports ability. Their mother made sure her favourite child was not deprived of University because of financial hardship.

'No – even if we have to scrimp as a result, you must go,' she had insisted to Jonathan, who had not needed much persuasion.

'Since you are not academic there is no question of *you* going,' she had told her older son severely.

She had no idea that he was fluent in French, or that he could quote from any Shakespeare play or that Plato had often been his bed-companion. But Adam had no desire, anyway, to attend University. The idea of fellow students terrified him.

Leah was also happier than she had thought she would be; her room at the back of the house was on the third floor, and her mother, whose legs and back were increasingly causing her problems, rarely disturbed her. It was the largest and lightest bedroom in the house, and its view gave on to the small garden with its naked tangled rose-bushes, laurel and hydrangeas, now dried to a pale sepia colour. In this room she could make her models, encouraged by pretty Miss Sweeby who had become a friend to her.

They were a house depleted of servants, and Lady Elizabeth was bitterly conscious of her reduced circumstances and the fact that as a result they were in danger of meeting the 'wrong types'. Her gaunt face became gaunter, her tongue more acid, and her eyes sharper. She took larger and larger quantities of snuff, and secretly began drinking.

Meanwhile, Adam wrote to newspapers and journals, requesting a job. The replies came back – polite and negative. Increasingly despondent, he wrote new letters, calling himself by another name and enclosing articles he had written. But the replies to his box number were no more encouraging. He felt spurned and took the rejections personally.

'You cannot languish at home all day,' Lady Elizabeth complained one day, when he came into the morning-room where she sat embroidering. 'You are constantly under my feet. Why don't you look for a job? It is unenterprising that you do nothing.'

'I *have* been looking for a job.'

'Oh?' Why did she always sound as though she were sneering at him? He was eighteen and towered over her; yet she commanded him.

'Yes, as a journalist. But I have had no luck.'

'Journalists are riff-raff. I will not have you associating yourself with such people.'

'I have said – I have not been offered anything, in any case.'

'Good. I would suggest you apply yourself to some useful purpose, and start looking for work that befits your station.'

'Oh Mama – we can no longer afford to *choose*.'

His exasperation at her surprised them both, and she stared at him momentarily, her eyes narrowing, before pursing her lips and turning once more to her embroidery. Unflinchingly, he returned her look. What thoughts did she nurture? he wondered. What emotions and resentments?

Finally, he took a job as a clerk in a solicitor's practice in Bayswater: Butler and Baker, read the faded sign beside the front door; but Butler was long-since dead, and Baker – who was in his early thirties – rushed about agitatedly, lanky and tall, the extent of his halitosis depending on how stressed he became. He was an example of a boy from a working-class background who had managed to haul himself from it, and he was defiantly radical and uncompromising. Despite his irascibility, Adam liked him.

'I cannot be a specialist in everything,' he would storm at a client. 'Nor do I work exclusively for you.' And Adam would marvel at the docility with which the clients generally accepted his bad humour.

'Pass me that file, Mr Gilmour.' He did not know of Adam's title, and would have been unimpressed. 'No, not that one, you moron. The one next to it.'

'You asked for the brown one.'

'I meant the *grey* one. You should know that by now.'

He was amusing in a way, with his little eccentricities – the way he referred to both the wall-mounted clock and his pocket-watch for verification, correcting the latter minutely; the way he manipulated his mouth, as though it were elastic; his tendency to keep changing his crossed legs when he sat down; the sickly smell of his hair ointment . . . And under his irritability there was kindness.

'What's wrong with your left eye?' he asked, concerned, after Adam had been doing hours of close work and the strain had caused it to become rheumy.

'Nothing –' He smiled assessingly. 'It's my right one that is the problem.'

'Your right one looks fine.'

'It's blind.'

After that Baker seemed to warm to him. Occasionally they lunched together at a local tavern, but when his employer asked him about himself, Adam was evasive. He took home twenty-two shillings a week, half of which he gave to his mother, and half of which was his to do with as he pleased, and he did not wish to jeopardize his independence.

It was early in 1865, and the Gilmours had settled into London life and adjusted to their different routines. Memories of Brambleden were less acute, and the death of Sir Felix and its sordid aftermath slipped discreetly into the past. Lady Elizabeth was galvanized by a new sense of purpose; this was to introduce Leah into society. Cautiously, she began to entertain.

'It's time you started meeting people. You are almost sixteen now.'

'I think we have different kinds of people in mind, Mama,' Leah answered crisply, with that annoying lift of her eyebrow.

'Enough of that, young lady. *I*, and I alone, shall decide who is suitable for you to meet.'

To this end Lady Gilmour began to cultivate friends. She met them at charity functions or through acquaintances of acquaintances. Energetically, she escorted Leah to different houses, fund-raising events, church functions, the occasional ballet . . . Her plan was a two-year one, and she was determined: her daughter would be married by the time she was eighteen.

Leah began to be noticed. With her small, neat figure and heart-shaped face, her rich brown curls and lively grey eyes, she was certainly pretty. But she was also disarmingly frank, and when her mother's back was turned, was inclined to voice her opinions in a way some people found amusing, and others rather shocking.

Leah had no desire to marry at eighteen – or necessarily at any age; nor did she desire to enter society (what an absurd expression, she thought). Her only desire remained unchanged: she wanted to be a sculptor. She had just over five years to wait before she could do as she wished. For five years she must keep the peace and pretend to accord with her mother's wishes. It seemed an eternity.

Their first spring in London – and Adam tried not to yearn for Brambleden. Sometimes during a lunch-break he would listen to part of an outdoors concert; or he might attend a Liberal Party rally; or he would browse in local bookshops where he was already becoming known: a tall, aesthetic-featured youth who had a habit of turning his head completely to look over his left shoulder; a writer, apparently . . .

That was how Adam referred to himself – and by the end of June, in the true sense of the word, he was, for that month three of his pieces were accepted.

Punch agreed to print his little satire entitled 'Travels in a Fictitious Haven', which he himself had illustrated; and a more obscure journal, recently established, published another of his stories. But it was his success with the *Cornhill Magazine* which most thrilled him.

When he had posted his story 'The Late Arrival', about a sinister dinner guest, he had not dared hold out hope that it would be accepted, and his shoulders had slumped as he left the post office and returned to the tedium of his job. His disconsolate employer was on his knees searching angrily for a file.

'Where *have* you put the Old Hag's papers, Mr Gilmour?' he said, standing up and glaring at Adam.

The Old Hag was a rich widow who kept changing her will, and was driving Mr Baker more insane by the minute.

'On the top shelf, next to her nephew's, sir – where you instructed me to.'

'That will do, Mr Gilmour. You have no need to remind me of my failing memory. How I loathe the woman . . . Mr Gilmour, have you *any* idea what it's like to have to pander to the whims of people you loathe?'

And he had looked so wretched and ungainly with his drooping body, long face and greasy hair, that Adam had smiled sympathetically. He knew that despite all his outbursts, despite his absent-mindedness, Baker was an excellent solicitor.

But by the end of the afternoon, having spent hours amending a contract, perspiring in the heat of the airless room, he was again filled with a sense of hopelessness. He thought: 'I'm trapped. My life will be forever this – peppered from time to time with hopes falsely raised. Why should I believe myself to be talented at all?' He shuddered at his own audacity in sending his story to such a prestigious magazine as the *Cornhill* – which had originally been edited by Thackeray, and had Trollope and George Eliot amongst its impressive list of contributors.

Later, at home, he confided to Leah what he had done.

'Have you another copy?' she asked.

'Yes.'

'Let me read it.'

'I *could* not.'

'Don't be silly, Adam. Now go and fetch it,' she ordered him.

'You sound as though I were a dog retrieving a stick. Woof-woof.' He pretended to beg, and put his tongue out, panting.

'Exactly! Woof-woof to you.'

When she had read it in her room, she came to find him. He was lying on his bed, himself reading. He sat up when she entered, his expression uncertain.

'It's marvellous.' She hugged him, and laughed at his continued uncertainty.

'I wanted to show the hypocrisy of society.'

'You *have* done.'

'Does it stand a chance, do you think?'

'Why shouldn't it stand a chance? It's the sort of thing that is fashionable to read nowadays, it would seem. And it's very well written – or so it seems to me. I think you're terribly clever.'

'I felt so ashamed after I had posted it.'

'Ashamed? How could you have felt ashamed?'

'I continually doubt myself. I dread being ridiculed. It's all I want to do – to write.' He made a rueful clicking sound with his tongue against his teeth.

'It will happen,' she comforted him.

'They've accepted it!' he shouted that morning in June, from the hallway. His sister immediately appeared on the top landing, and ran down the stairs.

On the first floor their mother, hair tucked into a white cap, face shiny, blearily opened her door. 'What is all this noise? You have woken me, and I had a quite dreadful night's sleep.'

'Adam has had a story accepted by the *Cornhill*, Mama,' Leah said, not apologizing, or stopping in her flight.

'Well really – for that I am woken? Disgraceful behaviour. And Adam knows I do not in the least approve . . . Riff-raff,' Lady Elizabeth added, before shutting the door decisively once more and returning to bed.

In her room the smell of stale sherry mixed with that of lavender water. Lady Elizabeth had awoken with one of her headaches. She had barely slept at all; dissatisfaction made her listless. She missed her son Jonathan; how selfless she had been in sending him away. What did he do at University? she wondered. With whom did he associate? And with what riff-raff was that wastrel Adam involving himself now?

Lady Elizabeth had never loved her husband. When she had first met him there had been something about him she found repulsive. Later, she realized it was the obviousness of his sexuality, worn as overtly as his smile. But he was rich as well as titled, and the two did not always go together; there was nothing so tempting as wealth to sway a young woman anxious to leave home, and escape the influence of an autocratic and violent father . . .

Adam was conceived a year after her unconsummated marriage when, one evening, her husband's patience with her snapped, and he raped her.

The week before the baby was due she asked her sister in a panic, 'Mary, how does it get out?'

Her sister had not a clue, but offered the possibility that it might make its exit through the navel.

Five days later, after wave upon wave of agony, hour upon hour, Lady Elizabeth discovered how babies were born.

All her resentment against Sir Felix, she transferred to her first son. She hated him. Bald, sickly, and the colour of glacé cherries, he cried continuously and tried to make her guilty with his tears . . .

By the time Jonathan was conceived, Lady Elizabeth was used to her husband's obscene demands, and had begun to long for a son to be proud of. She envisaged him – a beautiful child devoted to his mother; and later – grown into a handsome, respectful young man. *Her* son.

He emerged from her after an easy birth; with his flaxen downy head and creamy complexion, his placid temperament and robust health, this second baby was the culmination of her hopes. She was ready to adore him.

When her third baby was born Lady Elizabeth regarded her as superfluous. She could not be disliked, as was her eldest child, and sometimes she even felt a fondness for the pretty, vivacious girl, but little Leah became increasingly wilful as she grew older, and now – what comfort was she to her mother?

Sleep would not return to Lady Gilmour, and she reached for the bottle of sherry next to the bed.

'Let me see!' Leah snatched the letter from her brother's hands.

'Careful.'

' "Dear Mr Gilmour," ' she read out loud,

> I have pleasure in acknowledging receipt of your story, 'The Late Arrival', and would like to congratulate you on a sharply observed and excellent piece of writing. We are happy to accept this for publication in our September issue, and enclose a cheque as payment for the sum of two pounds.
>
> Assuring you of our attention at all times, I am, sir,
>
> Yours,
>
> Anthony Osborne, Assistant Editor

'I told you! I told you! Aren't you *proud*?'

'I wish Papa were alive,' he said, by way of answer.

During the summer there was a heatwave, and Jonathan, down from Oxford, would sprawl on a rug in the garden and talk in a low voice to the latest in a series of pretty girls he had been escorting. In the shade of a parasol, never more than a few feet away, Lady Gilmour would sit scrutinizing them, her mouth twitching.

From a distance Adam and Leah whispered about their brother and his friend. Leah was cynical. Her introduction into society had done little to curb this trait. Adam noticed how Jonathan's thigh muscles bulged beneath his trousers; how broad and strong his face was; how blond his hair in the sun. He noticed the way the girl listened, enraptured, to his every word, and gazed at him with admiration, and he could not blame her.

'He looks like a Norse god,' thought Adam. 'It would never be believed that we are brothers.'

He wrote prolifically that summer, and at weekends he took his watercolours to Hyde Park and painted by the Serpentine where the coolness from the water reflected on his hot face. His complexion was tanned; his hands, too, were brown. People stopped to watch him paint, bending to pat the setter lying calm and panting at his side, and Adam would glance up self-consciously, then continue. He was happy painting – the birds, the river, boats; subjects which evoked memories, so that a pang would start and settle for a while within him, before shifting gently, and leaving him with a sense of deprivation.

They went for a few days to Bognor, where Jonathan was irritable at having to leave London, and Lady Gilmour so weak from the heat she could not even lift the Bible.

Adam and Leah strolled along the crowded shingle beach, shuffling stones, their heads bent towards one another; dogs ran to the water's edge, barking as the thick white rim of the tide rolled over their paws; children flew kites, or waded waist-high into the sea and threw balls; men and women swam – strange, out-of-place fish, the women's costumes swirling about them. There were donkeys, and pet monkeys; cockles and ice-creams; side-shows and brass bands . . . And amongst all the colourful jollity Adam made plans to change his life.

Chapter Six

THE RADICAL

Wednesday, November 2nd, 1865

'From my window I watch the shy beginnings of day: impenetrable greyness suspended over the square; and the piles of pipes, the rubble, the mounds of damp sand all indistinguishable shapes. Isolated sounds reach my ears: a carriage – no, a cart, it rumbles too clumsily for a carriage; a tentative bird, and another; the barking of a dog; but otherwise there is silence outside. It hangs in the air, just as the greyness hangs. Autumnal silence.

'I imagine my mother's reaction when I tell her I am not going to work today:

' "Oh?" she will answer in her superior tone. "And might I know why?" (She does not say "*mite*", but "*meet*").

'And with great pleasure I shall tell her that finally Mr Baker has found a replacement for me, one who is unperturbed by his new employer's bizarre ways and sour breath.

'But I mustn't be disloyal. Yesterday evening Mr Baker invited me to join him in a beer at the Rose and Crown, and we talked, not as employer and employee, but as colleagues. Since the day I told him my plans he has been most supportive, and when we went our separate ways last night he seemed flatteringly sorry to see me go – as in that moment I was sorry to leave him.

'He said, "Journalists have a curious habit of courting trouble. If ever you need a lawyer, you know where I am."

'He shook my hand and held it a moment, and so we parted. As I walked home in the drizzle I could still feel the dampness of his palm in mine, and see his fingernails, bitten to the quick.

'Now I am free to begin my new career. But first there is Mama to mollify . . .'

*

She would not be mollified, and for ten minutes, without pause, berated her elder son, who stood before her, leaning against the upright piano in the morning-room, his tolerant expression further infuriating her.

When the tirade was over, he said softly, 'Mama – there are now more than one *thousand* newspapers in Britain. Surely that must make you believe in the s-ser-seriousness of what they have to say. The ma-majority of these are liberal in outlook. N-n-newspapers voice important opinions which the individual in the street needs to know, and wishes to know – and indeed *m-must* know. In the provinces the p-press is equally important. In Yorkshire alone there are *eighty-six* local newspapers –'

'I am not interested, Adam.' How silly he was, with his stammer and boring opinions.

'Mama, there are ma-matters which concern me deeply –' He looked at her, pleading with her to understand, '– which I need to write about. There is s-so much to write about.'

But she remained impervious – straight-backed and matriarchal in her chair, and did not, as he longed for her to do, and as most other mothers would have done, ask with love in her voice: 'Please tell me about these matters.'

Instead she said scornfully, 'You do not truly imagine that people will be interested in what a nonentity like *you* has to say. Really, Adam, you try my patience.'

'That is abundantly clear, Mama.' A hardness came into his eyes, and he altered his position and moved away from the piano. Everything about his stance became defiant – the arrogant tilt to his head, the lofty expression, the hand in his pocket . . .

Lady Elizabeth's mouth began to twitch ferociously. 'I must tell you, I find that huge – foreign-looking – bow-tie you wear absolutely distasteful.'

'And I must tell you, Mama, that from today your opinions cease to bother me.'

Taken aback, she started in her chair, and seemed momentarily a shrunken figure beside him. He smiled gently at her, the indifference in his eyes condemning her utterly.

'Adam,' she called imperiously after him as he was leaving the room.

'Yes, Mama?' As was his custom, he turned fully round.

'I would like you gone from this house.'

'No, Mama. Legally the house is mine. But don't trouble yourself. I shall not bother you.'

He gave a tiny bow, and closed the door quietly.

On her own, Lady Elizabeth began to tremble. Indignation and anger possessed her – and shock at the recognition that she no longer wore the mantle of power. Stiffly, she got up and went to the sideboard where the sherry was kept, and a supply of snuff. Later her sister and mother would be arriving, and she would pour out her story to them, of her son's ingratitude . . .

'So much to write about,' he thought. 'But what have I to say that men such as John Ruskin or John Stuart Mill haven't already said? But Ruskin is motivated by God, and antipathetic towards science, and his ideals are sometimes too intellectual, however fine. Mill: his views are realistic and important, but *laisser-faire* isn't *always* applicable . . . What about the *un*skilled for example? And while free trade is worthy and essential, it lures men away from their villages and into towns. This is short-sighted, for what then is to befall agriculture? . . . But one thing's certain: whatever I write will be true, as I see it.'

He put on his coat, and left the house to visit Edward Lear who, having failed so far to marry, was in London in amorous pursuit of a girl named Gussie.

In October Lord Palmerston had died and Lord Russell had taken his seat; but so far there had been few changes, and few promises, and those who had accused Palmerston of complacence, now accused Russell of the same. Adam, cautiously edging his way into a circle of passionate young radicals, attended meetings where all but blood was shed . . .

'The reason for their smug attitude is simple,' the principal speaker addressed the small gathering at a rally in Hyde Park. 'They are assured of their seats and know they need not bother to alter their policies.'

'But alter them they must,' another cried.

'But in what *way*?' Adam asked his neighbour softly. Yet they all seemed to hear; as in a game of Chinese Whispers, his words were carried around, and everyone turned to look at him.

Running his hands through his hair in a flustered manner, he smiled nervously. 'I m-mean I know there are cha-cha-changes to be made, but what changes spe-specifically do *you* mean?'

The main speaker was a huge, copper-bearded, lion-maned young man with extraordinary light-blue eyes. His gaze fell piercingly on Adam.

'For a start there should be a stronger division between Liberalism and Conservatism,' he said in his enormous, ringing voice. 'I could then perhaps mention Poor Relief, which is too haphazard, complex and unstructured – and overshadowed by private charities. Do you know that last year only £6,420 in official Poor Relief was spent? That's less than a single rich man's debts . . . I could go on for ever. But sadly, there is no for ever.'

He scowled, then looked more leniently at Adam. 'You'll learn soon enough,' he said. His name was Claud Chambers, and that moment marked the beginning of their friendship.

Late that afternoon, in Claud's spartan attic room in Notting Hill, they sat on the floor before a stove, drinking wine and talking. It was already dark outside, and Claud had lit the pair of candles on his desk, illuminating the papers, books and journals heaped there in disarray. Apart from the desk, a bed and chair – and a magnificent samovar on a wooden crate – there was nothing else in the way of furniture. His clothes spilled untidily from a trunk, beside which lay a lute and a backgammon board.

'I'm not bothered about material comforts,' he said, bounding up and pouring more wine into Adam's glass. 'But that's not to say I'd reject them if I could afford them!'

He took a swig of wine directly from the bottle which he held, and sat down again, rocking to and fro on his haunches.

'I was brought up to them,' Adam mused. 'But I always thought that if my surroundings weren't too dismal I could live in a slum.'

'Hark at the boy!' Claud laughed loudly, but not unkindly. 'I'd say you need a lesson in reality. You don't *select* your slums. I doubt you could live in a slum anywhere. You don't know what it means.'

Adam was silent, humiliated. Thinking he would leave, yet reluctant to do so.

'I'll take you on trips that will make you want to vomit,' Claud said.

'All right.'

Claud thought, 'He talks like a pampered young boy . . . but there's something about him. And he's sincere . . .'

His eyes softened. 'How old are you?'

'Nineteen,' Adam said defensively.

'And enamoured of causes you don't know or understand . . . And I tell you, when you do know them, in the end you want to leave them all behind and settle down. You've done your part.' His old-young face looked weary. 'There's always someone to replace you . . . I tell you I've just about had enough now. My mother was French – from the Dordogne region. One day I'll live there – play *boules* with the old men in a square lined with plane trees . . . Maybe I'll own an *auberge* . . .' He took another swig from the bottle and smiled sheepishly. 'And meanwhile I can offer you nothing but wine. I forget about things like having to eat.'

Adam looked pointedly at the great hulk close to him. 'I can see you're starved.'

The other laughed and punched his shoulder lightly. 'Do you like music, my friend?'

. . . My friend, my friend . . . A glow spread through Adam. He remembered how, when he was very young, he had approached other small children and stammered, 'W-will you b-be my fr-friend?' He recalled himself – lonely and scrawny.

'I don't know much about it,' he answered. 'But I enjoy listening.'

Claud jumped up, surprisingly light on his feet, and fetched the lute. He sat down with it on the edge of the creaking iron bed, and began to strum and sing quietly: 'There was a lover and his lass, with a heigh-ho, heigh-nonny-no . . .'

From his position on the floor Adam watched him. The candle-light caught his wild, orange hair, and the gold hairs on his wrists and the backs of his hands.

He was twenty-five, the uncontrollable atheist son of an Evangelist schoolteacher, and as the only surviving child, a bitter disappointment. The more he was beaten, the more unruly he became, and at sixteen, when his mother died, he had left his modest Hertfordshire home, the endless rules and the tedium of religious doctrine, to make his way in London. Within his first week he had lost his virginity and knew most of the prostitutes' names in the Tottenham Court Road.

'I earned my living playing my lute and singing,' Claud said. 'I thought of myself as a troubadour, whereas in reality I was simply another beggar. I slept in the street or in a workhouse – where another inmate taught me to play backgammon; he had no possessions – just this old backgammon set. I spent a fortnight at that particular workhouse, and at the end was a proficient player . . . There was nothing else to do.

'I dreamed every night, wherever I was, of my mother; her sloe eyes and black hair. When I was no more than five, she took me to where she was brought up, about three miles from the ancient town of Sarlat. In my dreams I was there with her . . . That was her samovar on the crate . . . *Tant pis* . . .

'Like you, I began to write articles, which were published. I wrote a book of rather angry poetry, and that was also accepted; and then I found this place through a friend of a friend. It was a relief, I can tell you. Sleeping rough quickly loses its appeal. And a workhouse is a repellent place. I have a fetish now about personal cleanliness. The smell of an unwashed body revolts me! I've become respectable now – almost bourgeois! I teach French to private pupils, continue my writing, and am half-way through a biography which I've been commissioned to write. I still play too much backgammon – we must play, you and I. I continue to fight for causes, but –' he grinned disarmingly, 'my voice is growing smaller.'

He fell silent, a Samson of a man, suddenly awkward, hugging his bulky knees.

The mood between them had changed subtly and the suspicion had gone. Each recognized in the other his direct opposite – the ideal foil – and instinctively edged towards establishing a relationship.

Adam said, 'When I was fourteen and a half our local rector gave a sermon in church . . . What he said shattered me. Before that I'd never thought about social injustices . . .'

There was something else he had to tell Claud.

'At the rally you mentioned a "rich man's debts". My f-father had debts. He owed a fortune and left chaos behind him when he died.'

'You can't be held responsible for your father's faults.'

'But I *loved* my father,' stated Adam quietly, seeing his father vividly before him – and a bolt of pain shot through him.

Claud looked tolerantly at the young man beside him. 'I like him,' he thought. 'I like him extraordinarily well.' He was a man of instant judgements and few half-measures. He either took to someone or not; and beneath the explosive veneer, the drinking, the womanizing, he was fiercely loyal and tender-hearted.

Adam stretched his hands towards the stove. The ring of his father's that he wore on his little finger glinted. He wondered how he could describe Sir Felix. He turned once more to Claud, his tongue loosened by the wine, and by the intimacy of the moment.

'My father was shallow and selfish,' he said, his love undiminished as he acknowledged these imperfections. 'But he was also kind, and had an unquenchable zest for life. He actually wanted to be erudite . . . He believed himself to be a Liberal – though it was an easy thing to play at, from where he sat. No one disliked him – except Mama, and I daresay she had reason. But I'm sure that's why his debts ran so high: nobody had the heart to demand money from him, he was too popular. I envied him – everything aout him. I longed to be like him and revelled in his affection for me . . . Later on, I judged him harshly, and I had no right. He was a truly caring man, who would not have knowingly hurt anyone's feelings.'

'Did he know you loved him when he died?'

'Thank God, yes.'

'I don't disapprove of wealth . . .' Reflectively, Claud fingered the rim of his glass. 'There will always be inequality. *Unfairness* is another thing. What I dislike are dishonour and hypocrisy.'

Adam was still trying to justify his father. 'Papa gave a great deal to different charities,' he said, then laughed. 'Even though it all came vicariously via his tailor, the corn merchant, his wine merchant, his club, various gambling friends . . . I shouldn't mock really.'

'Of course you should.' Claud's cheeks were as red as a gnome's. He was feeling happy and benevolent.

'Do you know, at his funeral were several hundred people, and probably half of them were people to whom he owed money. They all wept.'

'I envy you your father.'

'I envy you your mother!'

'What an unlikely couple my parents were,' Claud said. 'He, so strict – my backside was constantly raw from some beating or other – and my mother, so free-spirited, so *French*. But he was once handsome, and she was easily impressed. He soon took the joy from her, and she died bound to him, giving birth to her seventh dead child . . . How I loathe the pious sod,' he said with contained vehemence, bringing down his fist heavily on his thigh. 'And I had no friends. Who wants to be friends with a boy who has an Evangelist schoolteacher for a father, who each day deprives you of something different because it's good for your soul?'

For a while neither spoke, each dwelling on his own thoughts.

Adam broke the silence. 'Tell me, Claud, what do you notice about my right eye?'

And Claud, who had realized a few minutes earlier, asked, 'Is it blind?'

'Yes.'

Claud got up and stretched. 'We have much – *much* – to talk about. Let's go and eat. There's a café down the road where the wine is cheap, and the food reasonable.'

The café was crowded with intense young men and a few pale-faced young women, muffled against the cold in scarves, mittens, overcoats and hats. People kept coming up to Claud, slapping him on the back by way of greeting, inviting him to join them at their tables. No, Claud answered in his firm way, he was with someone – and introduced Adam to his colleagues, who looked at the new-comer with curiosity, immediately friendly towards him because he was with Claud.

At last they sat down at a table by the window, and over more wine, and a supper of steak pie and boiled cabbage, they discussed the issues of the day and discovered more about each other – becoming increasingly voluble and noisy as the evening wore on. The café buzzed with animated voices, laughter and, from a hidden corner, the strains of a Hungarian dance, played on a violin. Behind the bar the jolly-faced proprietor polished glasses and stroked the waitress's bottom.

Much later, joined by a small group, they left the café arm in arm, singing Christmas carols, their breath forming cold clouds in the freezing air.

It was past two in the morning when eventually Adam returned home. Leah greeted him distractedly in the hall. 'Where have you been? I was frantic –'

'What's happened?' His evening, his whole wonderful day, toppled. Now that he was back in the house with its gloom, it had the usual effect of deflating him.

'Mama's unconscious in the morning-room,' she whispered, pulling urgently at his sleeve.

'But you must get a doctor – why are you whispering?' Stubbornly, he resisted her tugging.

'For goodness' sake, Adam, she's *drunk*.'

'Oh, bother her.'

His sister looked at him in amazement, but he made no further comment, and reluctantly followed her.

Lady Elizabeth lay sprawled across the Persian rug, a smell of vomit hanging over her.

'You should have seen the mess,' Leah said, wrinkling her nose. 'She was lying in it. She was still clutching the sherry bottle, and her glass was broken and strewn all over the place. I cleaned her up – everything up – as best I could, but I couldn't lift her on my own, and I couldn't leave her here for the servants to find.'

'Oh I don't know – it might have been amusing: "My lady" stripped of her pretensions.'

He surveyed his mother detachedly, remembering how all he had ever wanted was the touch of her lips on his cheeks. 'Bother her,' he said again, and without preamble hoisted her like a sack of meal over his shoulder, and transported her upstairs.

When they laid her on the bed, Lady Elizabeth half woke momentarily and groaned once, before lapsing again.

'She looks terrible, poor thing,' said Leah. 'Adam, you must help me undress her.'

'Leah, I *can't*,' he protested, appalled. 'She's my *mother*.'

'Exactly,' she said tersely. 'Now, help me, please. I'm not strong enough on my own. And then I must wash her. With luck, tomorrow she'll not know of her humiliation.'

'But we shall,' Adam thought, staring at her scrawny loose-fleshed body in dismay. And the love for her which had uselessly consumed him as a child now became a rush of pity. Under her stiff, plain clothes, this was all she was.

'Oh Mama, poor Mama,' he whispered, compelled to touch her wrinkled white belly with butterfly fingers, before Leah covered her decently with the counterpane, and her shrunken breasts and sparse grey-gold pubic hair were banished from his sight.

Business-like, the girl washed her mother – her face, neck and shoulders, sponged her fine hair and rubbed it dry. She dusted the tired skin with powder, and dabbed cologne on her neck and forehead. When all this was accomplished, she said tiredly, 'Hoist her up again. We must put on her chemise and nightgown. Careful . . .'

As they dressed her, Lady Elizabeth lolled forwards and backwards, grunting and muttering in her half-comatose state, a drooping, rather obscene puppet, Adam thought. But when they finally pulled the bedclothes over her, she was respectably clad, powdered, perfumed – and snoring.

The following day she would treat her two children, but in particular, Adam, with her usual contempt, unencumbered by the awful knowledge of her own degradation.

Almost three years had passed. Adam sat by Edwin Landseer's controversial lions in Trafalgar Square and, chuckling to himself, read again a column in the *Telegraph*, headed: 'Unrepentant Baron Arrested'.

> Yesterday afternoon, having spent the night bound over at Chelsea police station, 21-year-old Sir Adam Gilmour – masquerading as plain *Mr* Gilmour – was released, defiant and uncontrite. He had been arrested the previous afternoon for disturbing the peace by distributing radical pamphlets likely to incite public anger. He himself was responsible for the printing of the said pamphlets, which showed photographs of families in slum areas, in which one woman, about to feed her baby, had her breast bared. Another photograph showed human excreta in the gutter, and a tiny child playing amidst it. The caption beneath both these photographs read: 'These pictures speak for themselves.'

They did indeed, and *Sir* Adam Gilmour was smartly whisked off the King's Road by a patrolling policeman after one outraged matron, upon seeing the photographs, became hysterical.

His night in a cell has done little to diminish Sir Adam's zeal for his cause. 'Only by shocking the public from its complacency,' declared the dashing young baron, his flamboyant silk bow rather rumpled after his experience, 'will anything be done about the terrible – and terrifying – poverty in certain areas of London where cholera is rife.' Amen to that, Sir Adam.

Thursday, August 8th, 1868
'My companions that night, two nights ago, were an imbecile who the following day would be admitted to an asylum, a drunken cripple, a child pick-pocket, and a male prostitute who kept eyeing the latter. It had been an unusually busy day, according to the warden – who rubbed his hands gleefully as he imparted this to me. In fact he looked as though he should have been where I was.

'When I returned home yesterday, Mama asked disinterestedly where I had spent the night. In a police cell, I answered; whereupon she rebuked me for my facetious and juvenile humour. Fortunately, since she never reads the papers, she will not have seen this morning's *Telegraph*.'

As he sat by Landseer's lions, he thought a great deal about freedom, and about life in general; then, more specifically, about his own life. It came to him with a jolt that he was bound to die young, because of his poor health. He thought of his changed existence from just a couple of years before, when he ran between grey and brown files in Baker's office and dreamed of other things.

Now there were articles to write, rallies to attend, people to meet. On one day he would visit a match factory, where yellow-faced women worked in shameful, airless conditions for twelve hours a day (it was officially ten hours, but their 'breaks' were excluded); another, a candle factory; the next, a textile factory . . . In all, children and women bore the brunt of toil. He trudged the slum areas – saw for himself the destitution, disease; the inhuman suffering people had to contend with and could not hope to escape. The only escape was death – cholera, typhus and childbirth being the most common causes. These people were ignorant of the precautionary measures which could have prevented the hardship of the latter – but who would tell them? Who amongst this moralistic lot who claimed to run the country, wondered Adam, would venture forth and say, 'Here, this is how you prevent babies. Here is how *we* shall help you to prevent them'? Oh yes – *Laisser-faire* was all very well, indeed.

After his visits he returned home to write. He felt enraged and helpless. Words jangled in his head. Money did not jangle in his pocket; most of his earnings went to charities.

'God! How I wish I had more to give. How I wish there were more I could do,' he said to Claud – who had watched the metamorphosis of Adam from idealistic boy to committed man. 'I write articles. I lose my voice shouting at rallies. I speak to editors, write to the Prime Minister . . . I talk to as many of the destitute as I can, but mostly they're wary and resentful. When I ask them to come with me to stand outside No. 10 Downing Street, they either laugh, or look at me fearfully, or threaten me. They don't *want* to be helped . . .'

Gradually, however, he sensed a growing trust, as he became a familiar figure to some of them. He brought parcels of food and clothing gathered from different sources. He spoke to them of hygiene and of various charities they should approach for help; of unskilled jobs he'd heard of; and, slowly, they began to listen. He dreamed of standing with a hundred of them, a bedraggled, filthy bunch, outside the Prime Minister's house: emaciated ragged men; barefoot coughing children; hollow-cheeked pregnant women with babies in their arms; they would gather together, shuffling and silent; the shame of Britain . . .

Monday, August 12th, 1868

'Claud confided this afternoon that he is in love with my sister. Claud, that mighty Samson, brought to heel by little Leah – who sculpts his head secretly in her room. Little Leah – who takes French lessons from him, but simultaneously tames him and inspires his devotion, while our mother sits as unsuspecting chaperone, ignorant of their glances, picking at her eternal embroidery; minute stitches, as minute as her life.'

Adam hunched over his desk, clutching handfuls of his hair, then releasing it. Lately he had become obsessed by the idea of writing a novel, and this morning the bones of a plot had occurred to him. Now, as he tried to work on an article commissioned by *Punch* on the need for balloting, he couldn't concentrate. A sentence, like a refrain, kept recurring in his mind; '. . . And the farmer's son left the village of Little Lee, lured by the false promises of city life . . .'

He took a loose piece of paper and wrote down the words. They stared back at him in a spidery black hand, gathering importance.

'*The Farmer's Son* . . . It should be the title. How well it sounds.'

As he pondered over the obscure sentence, a pencil of light fell, arrow-straight, across his page, and without thought, the words spilling from him of their own accord, he wrote:

> They called him John, because it was a simple, honest name, and they were simple, honest people. He was born to them when they had both given up hope of ever having a child, and Emily Higgs, at forty-four, had believed herself to be barren and her age of conceiving past her. It was difficult not to spoil such a long-awaited child, particularly one endowed with such beauty . . .

Impelled by his imaginings, Adam wrote until the church clock struck seven and jarred him from his fictitious world. He was sweating profusely; and looking through the sash window, it was not the square with its newly completed red-brick buildings he saw, or the tidy pavements, or the pollarded trees, gilded by the lowering sun; he saw instead a small, close-knit village – somewhere in Wiltshire perhaps? – called Little Lee, and in particular an impoverished farmer – a gruff, stooping man, with a new sense of purpose since the birth of his son.

He was quite wrought with excitement as he envisaged an entire plot: a story of good and bad, of love and ambition, of family relationships, and the influence of the city upon a rural village . . .

He stretched, and yawned several times, then went over to the washstand to refresh himself. He bent his head and doused it in water, and when he raised it the water streamed from his hair, down his forehead and cheeks, into his reddened eyes. His face broke into a slow smile, and he began to laugh.

He was late. Claud was already at the Circle Club restaurant – a literary club in Carlton Terrace – and the contents of a bottle of claret were considerably reduced. His eyes alighted on Adam, weaving his way between occupied tables, and he beamed expansively.

'You're in time for breakfast,' he said as Adam sat down.

Adam took in Claud's waistcoat unbuttoned over his girth. 'You look as though you've had several,' he retaliated, helping himself to some wine.

Claud chuckled and scratched his chin through the tangle of his beard. 'Well we can't all be as "dashing" as you, my friend!'

'Oh be quiet,' Adam said good-naturedly, stretching out his legs under the table, and coming into contact with Claud's lute. A footman appeared and took his hat – he wore no coat over his loose-fitting jacket.

Claud attracted the attention of a passing waiter and ordered another bottle of claret; he had just been commissioned to write a biography of Cyrano de Bergerac, and was in funds at present. 'So?' he enquired. 'How have you been getting on with your article for *Punch*?'

'I've barely started it.'

'But it's supposed to be in by tomorrow . . . *Tant pis* . . . You're smiling like a child with a secret.' His blue gaze fixed on his friend. 'And by the by, speaking of *Punch*, John Tenniel is over there in the corner with old Bulwer-Lytton, and wishes us to join him for a brandy after dinner. You and Bulwer-Lytton can compete on fashion,' he added snidely.

'That's underhand – he's a renowned fop.' Adam turned fully to look at the table where the pair sat: well-known as a cartoonist and illustrator of *Alice in Wonderland*, John Tenniel was a serious-faced man, whose drooping, dark moustache made him appear even more so. Opposite him the elderly baron – who was at constant war with Tennyson – was loudly attired, his cheeks suspiciously pink.

'He's wearing rouge,' said Adam, shocked, raising his hand in greeting to John Tenniel, who had caught his eye and was smiling.

'It's probably blood pressure,' said Claud. 'Anyway, you must admit he's an excellent writer. I'm not talking about *The Caxtons*, which is mundane, but *Eugene Aram*, for example. Funnily enough, it was one of my father's favourite books. That should have deterred me, I suppose.'

'He's a provocative writer,' agreed Adam, who had read *Eugene Aram*, about a repentant murderer, several years previously.

He looked round the gracious room with its dark brocaded walls. He enjoyed coming to the Circle Club; there were always people to 'spot': writers such as Dickens or Mary Ann Evans, alias George Eliot; Swinburne and Rossetti; the editor of the *Telegraph*, Thornton Leigh Hunt; John Stuart Mill . . . and many more, some better known than others, but all members of the writing fraternity in one way or another. Sometimes there were quarrels and undertones of scandal – Mary Ann Evans's unorthodox relationship with George Lewes was a constant source of interest to everyone, and the subject of much gossip; but this evening there were few well-known names, and Adam was impatient to tell Claud his own news . . .

'I'm writing a novel.' He leaned forward, elbows on the edge of the table, and related the rough outline of *The Farmer's Son*.

He barely noticed when the waiter brought their food. Claud listened, his fingers pressed together to form a steeple. From time to time he nodded.

'It's splendid!' he exclaimed, when Adam had finished telling him. 'An excellent plot. It only remains for you to write it!'

'I can progress then, with the Claud Chambers seal of approval?'

'You would have done so without it, you stubborn sod.' Claud sawed energetically at his steak. His napkin was tied round his neck, under his beard.

'I've just realized you look like Neptune,' Adam said, and before Claud could comment, continued, 'You know – I've never known such a compulsion as I have to write this book.'

'The test is whether the compulsion remains in you. I wonder how many brilliant unfinished novels there are lying around in attics.'

'Well I'll not be deterred.'

'No, my friend, I'm sure of that.' Their eyes met in a moment of empathy. Then Claud said, 'And by the way, I think I'd rather look like Bacchus than Neptune.'

Adam laughed. 'You'll have plenty of opportunity for that in France.' Claud was off there early the following morning – but he was not looking forward to going.

'Old Cyrano will keep me busy,' he said, fiddling with his fork. 'I'll resurrect a few childhood ghosts . . . And I shall try to reclaim my soul, which your sister has so shattered.'

He pretended to joke, to make light of the fact that Leah continually rejected his marriage proposals, but he couldn't mask his despondency.

'The stupid thing is I should be longing to go to France. I've thought of it often enough. Now I'm not even tempted by the possibility of dark eyes and silken thighs – ah, it rhymes – you see how she's subdued me. She should come with me. I need her. I've asked her repeatedly, but she's so obstinate – it must run in the family.'

'It's only that she's so young,' Adam consoled him, although he found the whole idea of Claud's infatuation with his sister amusing. Even more amusing was their mother's lack of suspicion. Claud had elaborate plans to elope with Leah, and Lady Elizabeth innocently paid him money at the end of each French 'lesson', which was put aside for the future.

'A rejection is always a rejection.' Claud was increasingly morose. 'And I must listen to her witter on about the dreadfulness of society, how false the people are; and for all I know this might be a pretext, and she is only playing a game. Perhaps she feels I'm not good enough for her.'

'You know that's not so. She loves you. She only wants to wait a while. She wants to become apprenticed to a sculptor –'

'But I wouldn't *stop* her. I *want* her to do her sculpting. If she came with me she could be immediately apprenticed. It pains me – do you know that? I have to hear about these horrific society visits, and balls she attends and claims to dislike so – and imagine her dancing with some trussed-up dandy who gropes at her afterwards on an ivy-decked veranda . . . I meet her for snatched moments; she won't let me kiss or touch her below the neck; I starve myself of other women, and end up having to pleasure myself in bed . . . You're laughing! Adam – you're *laughing* at me!'

'I'm sorry,' Adam said, his shoulders still shaking. 'Only you are so funny. The situation is so funny.' His foot accidentally caught the lute under the table, and it twanged.

'I can't see why,' Claud said, with offended dignity. 'Oh, you may kill yourself laughing. You wait until *you* are in love – and I shall just laugh at you.'

And Adam was instantly sombre. Increasingly he longed for love, and his body craved to be joined with a woman's again, and his nostrils to inhale the smell of that woman.

'It'll never happen,' he thought, staring at the tiny, untouched quails on the white plate in front of him. 'No woman will ever love me.'

His high spirits crashed; and looking down at his paisley silk waistcoat he saw that it was stained with wine. Claud was still sulking. Adam poured more claret into both their glasses, and thought about the only two women with whom he had been romantically entangled: Alice Mason, and Ethel Brown.

Chapter Seven

THE TAILOR

Two weeks had passed, and downstairs in the shadowy parlour Lady Elizabeth Gilmour, whose hands were never still, restlessly inhaled snuff and fought against the urge to have a sherry; pink-eyed Aunt Mary berated modern society and glared at the old setter who lay snoring and passing wind by her feet; and Grandmama Georgina, half bald now, and smelling more strongly than ever of stale fish and lavender water, reminisced about events of fifty years earlier – while things which had happened only the day before, or even that same day, she could not remember at all. Nobody listened to her anyway.

On the third floor, in her bedroom, Leah lifted the damp protective cloth from her sculpture and she and Adam looked at it together.

'It's extremely good.' Adam carefully turned the leonine head. 'Even unfinished it could only be him.' He chuckled at the thought of his friend, and ran his index finger lightly over the line of the cheeks.

'I miss him terribly,' his sister said. 'His voice, his swaggering walk, those piercing eyes . . . Even his huffing and puffing. I always laugh at him when he loses his temper – it makes him so annoyed: and under it all he's as gentle as a lamb.'

'I miss him too. Everything about him is larger than life . . . He's mortified you'll not elope with him, you know.'

'It's not that I don't want to be with him – I just don't believe in dramatic gestures.'

'I don't see that it need be in the least dramatic. It would only be a case of going.'

'I told you, Adam, I want to have time on my own before I marry – if I marry.'

'But it's still two years before you come of age.'

'Mama will weary of me before then. She's already tiring in her efforts to introduce me. And she knows that behind my back people discuss me unfavourably. My outspokenness intimidates them; and I've even heard our background questioned. Imagine Mama's horror – she who wishes to be thought so impeccable! You see – soon she'll be glad to let me do what I want. Her affection for me wanes daily.'

'For everyone except her beloved banker. He'll be her saviour and halt the degeneration of the family.'

Jonathan had left Oxford, having attained a first class honours degree, and had recently joined a merchant bank in the City.

'Of course, he can do no wrong,' continued Adam. 'Does he know about you and Claud, do you think?'

'I am certain of it. But he'll not tell.'

'No,' agreed Adam. 'Whatever my opinion of my brother, I know he's not a sneak. Besides, he's fond of you in his way.'

'He used to be. I think I rather baffle him now.'

'You know – I don't envy him any more. Of our two lives, I'd rather have mine. But what about Claud – poor man, you've driven him to France,' he teased.

'Nonsense,' she said defensively. 'He's gone to research his biography.'

'Naïve little Leah – that's only part of it.' He reached over to stroke her cheek, and she resisted him.

'I hate it when you're patronizing. And I am *not* naïve.'

'I apologize for being patronizing. That, I've no right to be. However, you are naïve. And so am I. Compared to Claud we are both sheltered and naïve.'

Inexplicably, she blushed. She moved away from her brother and sat on the gilt French-style stool in front of her frilled dressing-table.

'What have I said?' he asked, bewildered.

'Nothing . . . It's what *I* wish to say. Adam – I know nothing about – about –' She couldn't continue, and he looked at her tenderly and finished for her: 'You know nothing about physical love.'

Her eyes wouldn't meet his; her face was crimson. 'I know – I mean, I know about *kissing*.'

He came over to where she sat; her silky brown head was bent, and the centre parting showed as a thin pale line. Her neck was slender and pale, with a small knob at its base. He mourned the passing of her curls – all scraped back now and wound out of sight, save for a few tendrils around her forehead and ears. Crouching at her side, he took her hand and told her without shyness of the most pleasurable act a man and woman could share.

The weeks passed. He had his twenty-second birthday which his mother either forgot or chose to ignore, and which Jonathan marked by giving him a new dictionary as a present, a gesture which Adam could interpret only as a thaw in their relations. Bulwer-Lytton had invited him to join a group at the Royal Italian Opera to see Wagner's *Rienzi*, based on his own novel; and for the first time he met a man he had long admired – George Smith, the founder of the *Cornhill Magazine*.

He had been in the recreation room of the Circle Club trying his hand at Patience, when Bulwer-Lytton had plucked him from his lone table amongst the whist players.

'There is someone you *must* meet,' he said in his forceful way, and led him to the other room where there was a heavily carved bar and panelled area, and a surfeit of mirrors; it was a rather grand club for such an ungrand breed as writers.

George Smith was pacing in small circles as he waited for Mary Ann Evans to arrive, and drily commented on women's inability to be punctual. When they were introduced, Mr Smith frowned and said, 'I think I know you. I have seen you here perhaps.'

'Yes, that's probably it,' Adam agreed.

'But I know the *name* – Adam Gilmour,' he insisted.

Bulwer-Lytton corrected him: 'Sir Adam Gilmour.'

And he was quick to say he didn't use the title. Then Smith's brow cleared. 'Of course, you have written for the *Cornhill*, and there was an article about you in the *Telegraph* which I actually cut out. Congratulations on the good work. I'm delighted to meet you.'

Adam thought, '*Me*? He's delighted to meet *me*?'

'You must dine with us at our offices – we must fix a date,' Smith added eagerly, to Adam's enduring surprise.

*

Who would have believed, Adam mused, when, as a lowly solicitor's clerk, he timorously submitted his 'Late Arrival' to the *Cornhill Magazine*, that he would one day be walking nonchalantly into their offices? But that was the way of things, so that before long you took for granted familiarities which you had barely dared contemplate before, and you found yourself fraternizing with great men who yesterday had struck awe into your heart . . . And then, one day – perhaps *you* would become the great man before whom others quaked and gawped; and yet you were no different. Inside you dwelled still, the uncertain boy.

And meanwhile, he was becoming more immersed in the world of *The Farmer's Son* – the growing boy, and the father putting himself in debt to upgrade his farm and buy machinery he couldn't afford, in order that his son might inherit a place to be proud of . . .

Adam could see them all: his people – his creations; his village, Little Lee.

Monday, October 15th, 1868

'It has happened. I have mustered together a tribe of a hundred – the motleyest, most heartbreaking bunch you ever saw – to gather outside No. 10 Downing Street a week today. I have explained to every one of the adults what the purpose of this demonstration is to be, and what points we have to make; and those who before were resigned to their lot are actually becoming inspired – and angry. They *should* feel angry. They have every right to be.

'Out of the seventy adults, thirty-eight are unemployed, and of the thirty-eight, thirty-two lost their jobs through illness, and no fault of their own. What frightful world is this, that a man is too ill to work, and then recovers, only to find that during his indisposition his job has gone to someone else? As a result of this there are *dying* people working, simply so they can provide for their families.

'What kind of democracy is this which cannot create new and subsidized housing for its people? Such housing would mean construction, roads, other projects. Projects mean employment. Employment means pride, self-respect, but most importantly, money. Money to improve sanitation, schooling, hospitals, welfare. We send envoys to India who feast like princes, while their wives sit languishing in the heat at an eternal round of tea-parties; send them to the slums of London and see how far their feasts would go! Give the scraps to the rats: there are plenty of them around.'

On Wednesday, October 24th, two days after the demonstration took place, the following article appeared in the *Daily Telegraph*:

> BARON IN TROUBLE AGAIN
>
> For the second time in two months, young Sir Adam Gilmour, that reluctant shining Knight, spent the night in detention – this time at Westminster police station.
>
> Once again he was arrested for disturbing the peace, and detained with him were three less fashionable-looking appendages: ragged destitutes – some with dead rats draped round their necks – from the East End, who had formed part of the hundred-strong crowd of protesters demonstrating outside Number 10, Downing Street on Monday.
>
> The bedraggled march, which ended in such disorder, was master-minded by none other than our aristocratic hero, who, upon his release yesterday afternoon, was as unrepentant as on that earlier occasion, and said that his only regret regarding the throwing of eggs and tomatoes at government officials who would not take notice of their plight, was that the food would have been better off in a starving man's stomach. 'They should consider themselves lucky,' he added, breaking into his rather quaint stammer, 'that the dead rats were not thrown.' And he gave a glimmer of a smile.
>
> We shall follow your career with much interest, Sir Adam.

It happened, that mild and sunny Wednesday morning, that Lady Elizabeth decided to walk to her sister Mary's instead of taking a hansom. Together with Leah, she set off at her brisk pace, which slowed fairly soon as her rheumatic stiffness took over. It happened every time: she would start out, full of vigour, impelled by a rare brightness of mood, and then the stiffness would possess her limbs and she would increasingly regret her decision to walk with each step she took. But she would not give in. Walking – or the idea of it – was one of her few remaining pleasures, and so, suffering, she continued, complaining all the way.

They passed a newspaper stand, and although she would not normally stop, she was attracted by the bold headline emblazoned on the seller's board: 'Baron In Trouble Again'.

Always interested in anything pertaining to the aristocracy, she said to Leah, 'I wonder what that is about.'

And Leah, who knew exactly, took hold of her mother's arm and tried to steer her away. 'I'm sure it is nothing,' she said.

But Lady Elizabeth was glad of a chance to rest, and would not be deflected. 'I shall buy a copy.'

'No, Mama.'

'What do you mean, "No", my girl? If I wish to buy a newspaper, I shall. How much is that, young man?' she asked the vendor, and noticing him properly for the first time, saw that he was an amputee.

'A penny to you, Ma'am.'

'And I shall give you *two* pennies,' she said, feeling charitable on account of the terrible sight of him, unable to look at his trousers gathered up beneath his stumps.

He only smiled knowingly at her; they all reacted that way. He was twice as well off as had he had legs.

She took the paper, folding it, and tucked it firmly under her arm. 'I shall read it when we arrive at Aunt Mary's.'

As always, in tense moments, the nervous laughter bubbled to Leah's throat. She could imagine her mother's reaction. 'I wish Adam were here,' she thought. 'He'd appreciate the joke. How we would set each other off! Oh dear, poor Mama. What a shock she will have . . . Don't laugh, Leah . . . Do *not*.'

Aunt Mary's house, where Grandmama Georgina also lived, was a sombre, grey, semi-detached villa in a small road linking Knightsbridge and the outskirts of Kensington. The two women lived in this place with a handful of elderly servants, and Leah detested going there.

'It's the most dismal house in England, if not the world,' she thought, entering the dim hallway, whose only natural light was through the stained-glass 'fan' above the front door, and from a small 'porthole' window.

She followed her mother into the library, and greeted her aunt and her grandmother, who kissed Leah affectionately, hugging her to her lumpy, dark-clad body with its own immediately identifiable smells. Grandmama Georgina, if she had not been so subjugated, first by her father, then by her husband, then by her two daughters, might have been a very different woman. The vitality of her youth had been ground out of her, and now she was simply another old woman of her time, who had long forgotten the meaning of repression.

'I have brought with me a newspaper,' announced Lady Elizabeth, when they were all settled in the 'library' – a room of few books. 'There is an article I thought might interest us.'

'Oh dear . . .' Leah watched her mother unfold the newspaper and smooth it. She was unable to contain herself any longer, and gave a splutter.

They all turned to her, startled, and her aunt's disapproving pink-rimmed eyes were more than Leah could stand. She bent double, and the laughter pealed from her. Helplessly she listened to herself.

Grandmama Georgina enquired kindly, 'What is it, my dear? What is it that is so funny?'

'It's not funny, it's –' Leah's gasped reply was curtailed by her mother's cry.

'The wicked girl! She *knew*! She's laughing at *this*. Laughing at it, I tell you. Oh the wicked, evil boy, how could he do it? Oh how *could* he?'

'Wicked girl, wicked boy, what is all this?' enquired Aunt Mary.

Her sister handed her the newspaper limply. 'Take it –' Lady Elizabeth was sobbing now. 'I cannot, *cannot* bear to look at it further. He must leave the house. I do not want him within my sight, the wastrel. Such disgrace to his family – think how people will talk! And you, young lady – you're no better than your brother.'

The nervous fit of laughter had exhausted her, and Leah began to tremble; she could almost feel herself growing pale, as the consequences of her mother's anger impressed themselves on her.

'If Adam leaves I'll be on my own with Mama and Jonathan. I'll go mad. I'll simply have to elope with Claud . . . But I'm not ready for marriage yet . . . Oh what a trap; oh how unfair it is being a woman.'

After several sherries, use of smelling salts and some snuff, Lady Elizabeth recovered herself. She became cold and composed, and newly purposeful. As her purpose had been to marry off her daughter by the age of eighteen (a failed cause), her purpose now was to banish her elder son. She *would* be in charge again; she would not have him behaving as he wished and taking no notice of her, whilst living under her roof.

That same morning Adam sat working in his room, ignorant of the rumpus he had caused. Another matter occupied him: his novel. He was beginning to realize its full potential, and his excitement grew as he thought about all the twists and turns it might take. He would show how, after the death of a villager's son who followed John to London, the close-knit community changed, and people ceased to be civil to one another; he would show how easy it was for a community to fall apart, and petty vendettas begin . . .

He ran his hands through his hair and rubbed his burning cheeks. He knew, with a momentous jolt, that he was writing a great book.

'I wish Claud were here. He'd understand how I feel.'

He slid down in the chair and laced his hands together behind his neck. Papers were scattered all over his desk with his scrawled notes on them. Illegible writing, crossings-out, asterisks, arrows and numbers made them a nightmare to read. Articles for newspapers, stories and cartoons were jumbled with ideas for *The Farmer's Son*. And vying for space amongst the confusion were text books and dictionaries and magazines.

'Chaos . . . it's utter chaos. I need more space. I need more cupboards or drawers . . . I need my *own* place. It's high time . . .'

He ran his hands through his hair again several times. He was intoxicated by the prospect of having his own place to live; somewhere to be as he wished, do as he pleased, entertain at will. He could no longer sit, and went to wash his face and brush his teeth and rinse his mouth – which was suddenly dry and sour-tasting. He combed his hair, examined his bloodshot left eye, retied his bow and went downstairs to request tea from the housemaid. Soon he would be making his own tea.

Leah ran in to warn Adam in advance. She found him in the morning-room, lying on the sofa, his legs draped elegantly over the end, staring, apparently, into space.

'Addi – Adam – Mama is in the most awful state.'

'That is nothing new,' he said laconically, annoyingly unconcerned, after all she had been through.

She became riled. 'She knows, for goodness' sake.'

'Knows what?' He thought that he would buy a samovar, although he couldn't afford a solid silver one; and that he would have to buy a bookcase, and possibly a secretaire . . . After meetings and rallies people would be able to come back to his lodgings; he would invite them in – offer them wine . . . Women could come back . . .

'Adam, Mama knows you were in prison.'

'I was not in *prison*!' Jarred unpleasantly from his thoughts, he corrected her indignantly.

'A police cell, then.'

'Oh bother, how did she find out?'

'She actually bought the paper.'

'Oh bother her.'

'You always say that.'

'And you always say "phooee".'

'What will you tell her?'

'That I am moving out.' And then he saw her expression; that of an abandoned child. He had not meant to tell her like that. He had meant to tell her quietly and gently.

'Oh Leah – dearest Leah – don't be sad.'

'I'm not. I'm ecstatic.' She ran from the room, just as their mother came in.

'Adam, I wish to speak with you.'

'Speak, Mama. I'm here.' Carelessly, he readjusted his position so that he was sitting, instead of lying.

'Stand up when I enter, please.'

He obeyed – but he seemed so tall, and wore such a supercilious smile, that she felt disadvantaged, and instructed him to sit again.

'I have read about you in the newspaper today, Adam, and I am too horrified for words. You should be ashamed of yourself.'

But it quickly became clear that he was not. Moreover, before he gave her the chance to banish him from the house (which she knew she could not legally do), he told her he wished to leave and go into lodgings – so that instead she found herself saying, 'Is this house not good enough for you, then?'

He looked at her kindly, seeing her as an embittered woman who had lost her beauty, wealth, love, and finally her power, and he said softly, 'It's a necessary thing for both of us, Mama. I have no wish to offend or antagonize you, which my presence here does. Perhaps one day you will respect my views and my work.'

'*Never.*'

'That is a shame. But I shall visit you, even though you may not wish it, because it is my duty as your son.'

The next day Leah, reconciled to her brother's decision, helped him to find lodgings. She was bossy with him, and assertive with prospective landlords or landladies. They traipsed from place to place, so that in the end Adam would have agreed to anything, simply to be done with the whole procedure.

'It is too small,' she would say decisively, or, 'Too dark, you will find it depressing.' Or, 'Too noisy . . . too damp . . . too dirty . . . I don't trust the landlord . . . it is not grand enough . . .'

'I can't afford anything grand, Leah,' he protested. 'I thought this would be simple.' But he was amused by the role she had assumed. 'It *is* simple. We'll find you something. We've been concentrating on central London. It is a question of moving slightly further out.'

He was sceptical. 'Where for instance?'

'Hampstead. How about Hampstead?'

'But that's miles away!'

'What twaddle you do talk, Adam. Why are you always so negative?'

'I'm not,' he replied, hurt. 'Anyway, how do you know Hampstead?' He himself had never been there, although he had heard much about it.

'Claud took me there when Mama was out visiting one day.'

'Claud has a lot to answer for.' He gave an exaggerated sigh. 'Very well, show me where Keats lived. Perhaps that will sway me.'

They took a two-horse stagecoach shared by two elderly gentlemen, and headed north – out of London, along the Finchley Road, then leaving it to follow a small lane cut between fields and farmsteads which were gradually being eroded by urban sprawl. Half an hour after they had set off they were put down in the Bird In Hand Yard, off the High Street.

'It is so pretty,' Adam marvelled. 'And rural – close to London, yet rural. And what joy to have heathland all round.'

'I told you. And I gather there is quite a community of artists and writers here.'

'Well, we have yet to find something.'

Leah gave him her most withering glare, and laughing, he tilted her red hat forward so that it tipped on to her nose. They chased each other down the busy street with its assortment of shops and tea-rooms, laughing and shrieking, startling pedestrians, who turned to look – then smile – at the undisciplined pair . . .

'Upper floor to let. Very reasonable.' The sign was nailed to the door of a tailor's bow-fronted shop on the corner of the High Street and Downshire Hill, and they stopped outside to peer through the window. A shadowy face peered back at them.

'We have to go in now,' Adam said.

'May I help you?' the small, dark-haired and immaculately-groomed man enquired politely of them both, bowing slightly.

'You have an upper floor to let,' said Adam hesitantly, looking round the shop with its shelves of rolled and folded fabrics, and tailor's dummies with half-completed suits pinned on to them.

'At a very reasonable rate,' added Leah.

'*Leah*,' chided her brother.

The man smiled. He had sad dark eyes. 'Your wife is a good businesswoman.'

'My sister, actually. It is for myself that I am looking.'

He decided it was time to assert himself, and Leah meekly accepted this; she had done her engineering and was satisfied.

'Let me show you.' The man locked the front door, led them through a back entrance and up two flights of stairs. 'I live on the first floor,' he murmured in his lightly accented voice. He took a key from his jacket pocket and unlocked a freshly painted door on the top landing, flinging it wide for them to go in. It opened on to a large, light and double-aspected room with another doorway to a corridor.

'It leads to a small bedroom,' the tailor explained, 'and also to a wash place with a pail closet. The secondary staircase is to the attic. But I don't wish to rent that; it is full of –' He broke off, and for a moment Adam thought he was going to cry, '– full of books and albums and suchlike.'

Adam stared out of the rear window. Beyond the secluded tree-fringed garden, with its glimpses of other houses and irregular roofs, was the heath, just visible, like the separated pieces of a jigsaw. He could visualize himself walking there with the setter – wrapped against the cold, the long grass whipping around his ankles.

'I'll never be able to afford this,' he thought despondently.

'Do you wish to view the bedroom, sir?' the tailor asked gently.

'How much is the rental, sir?' Adam turned to face him fully, and the tailor, a perceptive man, realized then he was half blind.

He had been going to ask five shillings a week, which was the accepted rate; but he was drawn to this cultured-looking young man with the proud stance and troubled expression. He liked the outspoken little sister, too.

'Four shillings and sixpence a week,' he said. 'But with one small condition.'

'I'll take it.' Adam smiled broadly in relief, and he shook the man's hand firmly.

The landlord held himself aloof. 'My name is Levy, Karl Levy,' he said softly, studying Adam as he waited for his reaction.

'And mine is Gilmour,' Adam replied. 'Adam Gilmour. I am so *delighted* to have found this place.'

And Levy's hand returned his clasp firmly.

'By the way, what is the "small condition"?' Adam asked, belatedly.

His new landlord smiled. 'That every so often you take tea with me. I should greatly value your company.'

The following day he moved in with his dog, his desk, 'The One

That Got Away', his clothes, books, and his expanding collection of antique writing implements. A bed and wardrobe were provided, and in the twenty-four hours since they had viewed the place the kind-hearted tailor had organized a carpenter to erect shelving either side of the fireplace in the sitting-room.

'It is perfect,' Adam kept saying, overwhelmed with gratitude towards the little man, who was helping him with his things – transporting them up the three short flights of stairs, and running nimbly down again to fetch the next load.

'And you are sure you don't mind the dog?' Adam asked, when everything had been carried upstairs, taking off his coat finally, and brushing the rain from it, while the setter sniffed about the place.

'I like animals. I had a dog as a young child. My wife – she sneezed whenever she was near a dog or cat, so we had no pets except for a canary.'

'But you have children?'

'No. Sadly, no children.' Mr Levy's small red mouth flickered at the corners, and he made a show of looking at Adam's books – quickly becoming genuinely interested.

'Such a collection. You told me you had many, but not how varied.'

'I am a wr-writer myself,' Adam said.

'Ah yes. I could see from your face you were some kind of artist. It is a face which denotes creativity. But now I must leave you. I'll not interfere in the least. Only call me if you require anything. And don't forget our little pact: I shall look forward greatly to entertaining you to tea.'

Tuesday, December 3rd, 1868

'From the north end of Downshire Hill runs a fast-flowing stream, green with watercress, winding its way – above and below ground – to Fleet Street. It makes me think of Brambleden, and the village girls' white legs, blurred and distorted as they dangled them in the rushing water.

'I still cannot believe my good fortune in finding this place – the most perfect place for me to be at the moment. Only down the road, in Flask Walk, is the *Punch* cartoonist, Charles Keene; Thornton

Leigh Hunt – editor of the *Daily Telegraph* – also lives in Flask Walk, and is the butt of much local gossip as his mistress is George Lewes's wife, Agnes, by whom he has four children. At 14, Well Walk, lives that keen Socialist, Henry Hyndman, and there are many others – writers, artists, musicians – in the locality. We are a community, and I am part of that community. At nights I fall asleep, filled with well-being, and I awaken in the morning brimful of energy and eagerness such as I have never known. Even my health, usually so poor at this time of year, feels robust, and in fact I have heard that Hampstead was once famed for its pure air.

'We meet at cafés or taverns – The Freemason's Arms in Downshire Hill, or Jack Straw's Castle, just past the Whitestone pond – which froze solid the other day, and was as picturesque as a Jan Breughel painting, with its brightly attired ice-skaters. When I first came here, there was an old man selling donkey rides to children at weekends. He would wait with his tattered assistant – his grandson, I later heard – on the hillock by the pond, his three sleepy-looking donkeys tethered to a tree. At about ten o'clock the children would flock to him, breaking free from their parents or nannies, and the old man would remember the name of every child, and lift him or her tenderly on to the donkey . . . But now it is vicious winter, and there is no custom for the old man. I often wonder about him; what he does for half the year and where he hides himself: in the Hampstead workhouse more than likely, where, despite its fair reputation, men have to crush stones for road repairs before they are allowed their breakfast . . .

'Or, we will go further afield, towards Golders Green, where at the Bull and Bush we are always made welcome by Harry Humphries, the licensee. He has just obtained a music licence, and plans, in the spring, to hold concerts and 'sing-songs' in the pleasure gardens. But for the moment we shelter within the cosy little snuggery, sitting on the narrow window seats, roasting our feet by the smouldering fire and drinking Harry's excellent beer – getting up at regular intervals and making room as newcomers arrive.

'I am so enamoured of everything, I cannot believe I could be happier than I am at present. I am earning a reasonable, though not vast, sum for my articles, cartoons and stories; my novel is progressing well; I have no debts, many friends, a dog, glorious surroundings; and lodgings where I am free to do as I please and entertain as I wish. The other day a young lady I met at the tavern came home with me and stayed the night – a thing which could not have been contemplated in Knightsbridge!

'Poor Leah, stuck there. I visited on Sunday to have lunch with everyone – Mama, Grandmama, Aunt Mary, Leah and Jonathan – and even on the journey I felt myself becoming tense in anticipation. The disapproving faces, the dark house, the rigid rules and gloom of it all oppress me; and I am forced to sit with them exchanging banalities whilst my mother stares at me with barely disguised dislike.

'And Leah – what of Leah? Twice a week she visits her sculptor master, so in this she has her own way at last; but there are no other concessions, and Leah told me she feels as though she is "rotting" in the house as surely as an ancient timber beam.'

It was mid-December and Adam was invited to join Mr Levy for dinner.

'It's Chanukah,' the little man explained. 'The festival of the light. It is a time to be with family, but I have none . . .'

The apartment was bigger than Adam's. It had two bedrooms and a small, spotlessly clean kitchen with a modern range. From the sitting-room one could see the tumbledown stable with the grey pony's head and neck over the door. Next to the stable was the outside privy built in red brick.

He had been to Mr Levy's on several occasions before – for tea, or simply for a chat, but his landlord had a way of eliciting confidences so that each time, when Adam came away, he realized he had spoken freely about himself, and in return knew nothing about the Jewish tailor.

'Mr Gilmour, I am so pleased to see you.'

Mr Levy came into the sitting-room from the kitchen, an apron tied around his portly midriff. He shook Adam's hand and smiled at his surprise. 'Cooking is my hobby. I learned after my wife died, before I found a Jewish cook. You see, our dietary laws are awkward for a gentile to understand.'

'I confess I know nothing about them,' Adam apologized.

'Why should you? but I shall tell you a little – perhaps you would be interested. Would you like some sweet red wine? It's very good indeed. I have finished in the kitchen now. The rest I can leave to my housekeeper.'

He showed Adam some of his 'treasures' – silver and enamelled boxes, candlesticks, book-ends, ancient Hebrew prayer books, other ornaments, encrusted with semi-precious stones.

'My wife – she was the collector,' he said, bending his head in dejection.

They sat beside each other on the brocade-covered chaise-longue, sipping the wine from small silver goblets.

'When did she die?' Adam asked, hesitant to broach such a sensitive subject.

'Two years ago today.'

'How very sad.'

'Yes.' The word stretched out in a sigh. 'Chanukah and Yahrtzeit on one day. Celebration and grief.'

'Yahrtzeit?'

'It is the anniversary of a loved-one's death. One attends a memorial service at the synagogue, and at home lights a candle in honour of the departed one. See – it is over there beside the menorah; that is the Chanukah candelabra with all the prongs.' He pointed, and Adam's gaze followed his finger.

The tailor shrugged – a small, helpless lift of the shoulders. 'These things happen.'

There was a photograph of a laughing-faced middle-aged woman on the table beside them. Adam picked it up. 'This is her?'

'Yes. That is my Herta. Always laughing. I shall remember her as always laughing, despite the terrible events of her life . . . Now, dinner is ready. I shall tell you more as we eat. Come.'

At the far end of the room an oval table was laid for two, with as much care as if it had been laid for a dozen princes: a white damask cloth, upon which the cut glass, silver and china sparkled. A plaited loaf rested on a salver and in the middle of the table was a tureen of steaming clear broth with small dumplings in it.

'It is a traditional dinner,' Karl Levy explained. 'I hope you will enjoy it.'

So saying, he put a small cap on his head, incanted a short blessing, and cut into the bread.

*

'I was born in Kiev,' he told Adam, 'and my surname then was Levandovsky. My earliest memory was of a hand ploughing through the glass of a lower floor window, and pulling objects off the table in front of it. I remember my father fighting with the hand, trying to push it back, through the gap of the pane. But, bloodied from broken glass, it clasped Papa's necktie and hauled him towards the jagged edge. And then the tie was wrenched in two; Papa fell back, and the hand retreated. I returned to sleep, and when I awoke thought I had dreamed the incident. But the window was boarded up, and I heard my mother weeping. My father, also, was a tailor – an excellent and fashionable tailor, and there were constant raids on his shop. His fault was that he was a Jew, and it was not the right of a Jew to exist, let alone be prosperous. When a close friend of his was murdered, there was nobody prosecuted, no trial, nobody charged, even.

'My father brought us – my mother, my much older sister, and myself – to England. I was ten at the time. We came on a cargo boat, no better than cargo ourselves, with no possessions except a few items of jewellery my mother was able to conceal on her person. But we were together, and alive. My father immediately sold the jewellery, and with the money rented a shop with accommodation over it, in the East End. He then set up in business again. He – none of us – spoke a word of English.

'I grew up and learned my father's trade, and we expanded, and moved to larger premises. And then I met Herta. She was from a small village in the Ukraine, and had only recently arrived in England with her widowed mother. They had both been raped by drunken soldiers . . . All the Jews knew each other in the part of London where we lived, and so it was we were introduced – and fell in love. Her hair was a burnished black.

'One Sunday – I remember the exact day, it was July 11th, 1834 – we took the mail coach – it was cheaper that way – to Hampstead, and we walked on the heath. The sun poured down, and we sat beneath a tree, and I proposed to her. We both vowed there and then that one day we would live in Hampstead.

'As a result of the terrible violation which had been done to Herta in her village, she had become with child, and then miscarried badly. She was unable to bear further children . . . During the course of the years, our parents and my older sister passed away. But we had each other. We finally came to Hampstead about eleven years ago, but Herta had much illness in one way or another. I lived in constant fear of her dying – I doubted I could survive without her – you see, my happiness was completely dependent on her.

'One day, she began to vomit, and it was diagnosed that she had a tumour. I spent all my money on treatment by physicians. One physician after another. But God's will was greater than their knowledge. She died . . . And somehow I survive. I am so sorry,' Levy said, averting his wet eyes from Adam, taking a gulp of wine, and choking a little on it. 'I am so sorry to have bored you.'

'But you have *not* bored me,' Adam said. 'How could you think it?' Briefly, he touched the other man's arm.

'It has helped me to talk. Thank you.' Levy gave a small emphatic gesture with his elbows as though to show he intended now to be bright, and his mood changed to one of forced jollity.

But after dinner he led Adam up to the attic, and by the light of a couple of oil lamps, showed him boxes of daguerreotypes and photographs, letters and newspaper cuttings: years of memories and tributes to another long-ago life . . . And a lock of his Herta's hair, when it was still a 'burnished black'.

Chapter Eight

THE NOVELIST

'... The village of Little Lee was steeped in the stillness of dusk; and its inhabitants went about the evening as they had always done, their faces closed and wary.'

This last sentence, written in a frenzy, was barely legible; and then came the final full-stop. Adam lingered over it, reluctant to leave it, before replacing his pen slowly on its stand. He got up stiffly, rested his chin on the window ledge, and looked out without seeing.

He had envisaged this moment so often, imagined himself exultant; but now in reality, he was possessed by a sense of isolation.

The garden came into focus again, and beyond it, scraps of the heath. The isolation lifted – and then more. A smile crept to his lips. 'I've done it . . . I've *done* it!' He rushed from his room.

It was July 5th, 1870, and *The Farmer's Son* was finished.

Claud was back in England, and had abandoned a garret existence for a first-floor apartment in Chelsea, claiming that as a respected biographer a grander residence was more befitting – his *Portrait of Cyrano de Bergerac* had been widely praised. But Adam knew Claud was trying to impress Leah; as was the case when he increased his tuition charges, and accepted a weekly post in Oxford, lecturing on French literature.

'I'm making myself into more marriageable material,' he joked. 'What else can I do?'

Adam ran up the stairs to his friend's room, aware of his own breathing – faster than it should have been, a faint break coming with each intake. There was no reply to his impatient knocking.

'Damnation,' he muttered, and ran down once more – tripping on the bottom step where the carpet had rucked up. 'Damnation,' he muttered again – and then was out in the sunlight and afternoon heat, striding along the avenue. He knew where he would find Claud.

He was sitting on a particular bench in Kensington Gardens, looking out towards Holland House. His sheer size, and the way he had appropriated the entire seat with his lute and other bits and pieces, deterred anyone else from sharing it. Adam found him sprawled there, his beatific face upturned to the sun and his massive beard blazing gold. He stood silently in front of him, deliberately blocking out the light, and Claud's head slowly lowered.

'Hah! It's you! Move to the left will you, there's a good man.'

'Lazy so-and-so,' Adam said. 'Well, at least make some room, will you?'

'What do you mean, lazy?' Claud replied, not moving. 'I was up half the night playing backgammon with my landlord! I lost half a week's rent.'

'No commiserations. Now move up, or I'll stand here for ever and block the sun.'

'The concessions I do make.' Claud picked up the lute and various books beside him, and put them by his feet. He moved himself further over and patted the empty space. Adam sat down and took off his jacket.

'How is the police cells' favourite inmate, then?'

During the past six months Adam had been detained overnight three times, and on the most recent occasion, when he had protested about the continuing scandal of child labour, *Punch* had carried a cartoon depicting him as Tom from Charles Kingsley's *Water Babies* – standing waist deep in a police cell. The caption read, 'W-why do I k-keep t-treading water?'

'I've finished it.' Adam ignored the jibe, and thrust the manuscript on to Claud's lap.

Claud was instantly serious. 'How do you feel about it?'

'Strange.'

Claud nodded. As another writer he appreciated what it meant to devote oneself to such a labour for an intense and prolonged period – and that where creativity had dwelt was now a fallow place.

'Do you want me to read the last chapter?'

He had read the others enthusiastically. The odd time he had ventured a criticism Adam had pounced on him like a possessive mother cat. But then as he calmed down he became more dispassionate, and would alter accordingly.

'I'm not changing anything. It's done, finished,' Adam told him aggressively. 'Whatever you say.'

'*Reste tranquille*, my friend.' Claud stretched hugely. 'Now, do you want me to read it or not?'

'Well, I'd like to submit it to the *Cornhill* offices this afternoon. I suppose it ought to be checked.' He looked contrite, and Claud picked up the manuscript from his lap . . .

As Adam walked away from Claud he was assailed by his usual doubts. 'I shouldn't have digressed from journalism. As a freelance journalist I'm respected . . . But I've moved on from that – progressed to different things . . . But it's taken me so long to earn respect, and now to risk it all again. Be laughed at. Rejected . . .'

He watched a group of children flying their kites – geometric flashes of colour dancing in a clear sky. A father stood close to a tiny girl, protective, adoring, his hand on hers clasping the string. Further away a small crowd gathered around an organ grinder to watch the squirrel monkey – dressed in red pantaloons and waistcoat – dance and perform tricks.

Adam thought, 'Poor thing having to endure such indignity to amuse us.' He looked around him as though at a stage set. 'Everything has changed. *I* am changed . . .'

He sat down on a bench beside a uniformed nanny feeding scraps to the pigeons, and looked morosely towards Claud on his bench; the leonine head was still bent, sunk into the beard, as he engrossed himself in Adam's last chapter. The nanny, stiff in her corsets, glanced suspiciously at the young man who had come to sit beside her.

'Beautiful afternoon again, isn't it?' he offered.

But she fixed her eyes fiercely on him without replying. Why were nannies always so ferocious? he wondered – and then looked again towards Claud. He was standing up, scanning the area for Adam, and spotting him, waved. Reluctantly Adam got up, murmuring a polite 'good day' to the granite-faced nanny.

Claud immediately clasped him in that Gallic way he had

acquired during his year in France. 'It's wonderful.' His light-blue eyes were moist. He released Adam from his embrace and sat on the grass, the manuscript on his knees. 'I'm proud of you and envious, for having written such a work . . . And I am disturbed.'

'Why?' Adam sat down, too, relieved. He flexed his neck to relax himself. He had depended on his friend's good opinion.

'I am closer to you than I've ever been with another man. I thought I knew you. And then I read this, and realize I do not. I feel – excluded.'

He looked so petulant that Adam laughed. 'That is absurd. It's a work of the imagination. Nothing more.'

'But such imagination. *Such* imagination.' Claud shook his head. 'I feel so mundane.'

The *Cornhill Magazine* had moved its offices to Waterloo Place, and Adam took a hansom there to meet the new editor – Leslie Stephen, a fit-looking man in his late thirties who was a noted mountaineer.

'I have followed your career with interest,' Stephen said, gesturing for Adam to take a chair.

'I w-wonder which career that would be, sir,' Adam commented with a wry smile.

'You do seem to make a habit of spending the night in places most of us would prefer to avoid,' Stephen conceded tactfully, and paused, wary of being over-familiar.

But he was an intuitive man. He took Adam's manuscript, glanced at the title and the first page, heard Adam's stammering account of the story, and knew that this was going to be a good book . . .

Leah was now twenty-one, and at last independent of her mother. She still lived at home, as did Jonathan, but her small personal allowance meant that she was not beholden to Lady Gilmour; she could do as she pleased. She had been apprenticed for several months to an up-and-coming sculptor called Joshua Blackwell who lived and had his studio in Flood Street, close to the Embankment. Nearby were Dante Gabriel Rossetti, James McNeill Whistler, and Holman Hunt; and Blackwell, a handsome, moody man who was only happy when surrounded by people, cultivated their friendship. They and others of the Pre-Raphaelites frequently visited, and inevitably Leah was drawn into this enlightened circle – with its confused relationships and tempestuous affairs. She herself was always serene and equable, and she observed the impassioned goings-on around her with amusement.

Claud was jealous of her life, of the people she met; in particular he was jealous of Joshua Blackwell. Poor Claud – so in love, so tamed and besotted: he had not glanced at another woman since he had known Leah – he who had used to boast that he had a woman for every day of the week. But although she adored Claud as much as he did her, she was not about to abandon that which she had waited for patiently: her right to be herself.

'You *can* be yourself. I wish *only* for you to be yourself,' he shouted at her, stamping his foot in his frustration.

And then, one afternoon, curled within the protective curve of his great body, the rumpled sheets kicked from the bed, she had sleepily murmured, 'When I am twenty-five. On my twenty-fifth birthday.'

'What about it, my littlest mouse? What about your twenty-fifth birthday?'

'I'll marry you.'

'You're forcing me to wish the passing of time – I who have always valued each minute of each day.'

'I thought you would be happy.'

'I am,' he said thickly, and buried his face in the back of her neck and tumbled hair.

'Good.' Her voice became fainter. 'So we are engaged then, I suppose.'

'Yes, my littlest mouse. We are engaged.' He felt her sag into sleep against him, and himself scarcely dared breathe for fear of disturbing her, and making her move away from him – so that he would be alone.

He gave her his mother's ring, which in turn had been her mother's, and Leah wore it on her wedding finger. Lady Elizabeth noticed, but said nothing: there was no point. The acknowledgement would not have brought any happiness to the bitter widow whose mother had just died, whose oldest son was a wastrel, and whose only daughter was – she said the words in horror to herself – nothing more than a slut.

It was not yet half-past four when Adam left the *Cornhill* offices. He was suddenly very weary, and the pain in his chest could no longer go ignored; but he could not return to Hampstead without first visiting his sister.

The cab left him by Chelsea Bridge, on the Embankment, and he walked the rest of the way thinking it would do him good. But it was unbearably hot, and the river smelt, and when he arrived he was perspiring and lightheaded.

He could see Leah through the glass of the studio – which was a converted conservatory. She was wearing a stained smock, and her hair was scraped back. There was an incomparable loveliness in her simplicity, he thought – noticing her graceful assured movements as she worked on a model, unaware she was being watched. He remembered their conversation as children, when she had told him of her longing to bury her hands in the earth.

Perhaps Leah finally sensed his presence: she glanced up, and her mouth parted in delight. She said something to the tall, fair-haired man beside her, who nodded – and then rushed out to meet her brother as he was coming in.

'Dearest Adam!' She flung her arms around him – her hands leaving dusty clay stains on his neck – then pulled back and pouted. 'I haven't seen you for almost two weeks.'

'I'm sorry. It has been a busy time.' He would tell her about the book in private. 'Good afternoon, Joshua.'

'I was just about to have a whisky,' Joshua said by way of greeting. 'Join me?' He was always just about to have a whisky.

'Thanks.' Adam flopped into an armchair from which the horse-hair stuffing oozed out – like an obscene wound, he thought.

Leah noticed the flushed spots on his cheekbones, the unevenness of his breathing. 'You're ill,' she said, concerned.

'Nothing Joshua's excellent whisky won't cure.' He took the generously filled glass from the artist and winked at him.

'Oh how annoying you are when you're trying to be funny about something which is patently not.'

'She is a bossy little thing, isn't she?' Joshua observed in his laconic drawl.

'Always was,' said Adam, smiling at Leah's irritation and catching her hand as she was about to brush angrily past him. It relaxed in his, and he squeezed it fondly.

'I loathe it when you adopt that pose of male superiority,' she said.

'You know I was only teasing. I love to tease you.' He stroked her fingers, which felt rough.

'But men *are* superior,' Joshua said into his glass. 'I didn't speak – I didn't speak!' he protested as Leah turned furiously to him.

Adam got up and wandered round the studio – with its dust and disarray and workmanlike efficiency: vicious-looking tools strewn amongst bags of plaster and clay; half-finished busts on shelves or in corners beside frameworks of wood and skeletons of wire; the kiln – unlit – with its door part open, to reveal a fired model of a ram. Large chunks of Tournai marble stood between the wide work-benches which lined the room, and on these were pots of beeswax and brushes and models in various stages of being cast.

Leah had explained the different techniques to Adam, the ancient *cire-perdue*, or 'lost-wax', process of hollow casting in bronze which Joshua used, and the even older method, used in sixth-century Greece, of sand-casting. Once he had visited when they were in the middle of the lengthy procedure, and he had watched for a while as the model was covered by wax moulded on to its form, and left to set. This was then surrounded by plaster, and much later – but he did not have time to wait – the wax would be melted out and liquid metal poured in in its place.

'Years,' Leah told him that afternoon, her anger forgotten as she toured the studio with him. 'It will be years before I can call myself a sculptor.'

Joshua, swigging whisky while working on a clay model of a rearing horse, glanced up briefly. 'But you will be good. Show your brother the nude you're doing.'

'I couldn't.' She blushed.

'Why not?' Adam asked. 'Are you afraid of corrupting me?' and then he saw it anyway, and realized the reason for her embarrassment. It was of herself, reclining in an abandoned position, one arm lifted upward behind her head.

'It's superb,' he said softly.

'I told you.' Joshua sniffed and wiped his nose on his sleeve. 'And you know why she is so good? Because she is always honest, always bold.' Humming, he went back to work.

Leah laughed nervously. 'It's for Claud. I hope he likes it.'

Adam said, 'He'll treasure it. Though I daresay he'll prefer the real article.'

He touched the sculpture carefully: his naked sister – luscious and wonderfully feminine. He marvelled that she could have seen herself with such objectivity.

'Imagine Mama's reaction!' He chortled at the thought.

'Poor Mama,' she answered. 'What a burden to have us as children.'

Outside the studio he told her, 'I've finished the book.'

'You haven't! How marvellous. Why didn't you tell me earlier? Oh I *am* so thrilled.'

'I wanted to tell you alone. I showed the last chapter to Claud and then –'

'Did he like it?'

'Yes.'

'You are so clever . . . And are *you* happy about it, dearest?'

'Oh I don't know. One minute I think I am, the next I am besieged by doubts. Anyhow, it is with Leslie Stephen of the *Cornhill* now, so it's beyond my control; a matter of waiting.'

'Poor you – you will just have to put it from your mind for a bit. How difficult it will be for you.'

'Yes it will be . . . But *you*, little Leah – you are clever, and I am proud of you.'

'Phooee.'

They parted, and as she watched him walk away with his long easy gait, a peacock of a figure amongst the other people in the street, she remembered her earlier anxieties about his health, and called out, 'Adam, please look after yourself.' Others turned, but he did not, and she consoled herself, 'He's probably just in one of his dreams.'

That night, back in his Hampstead lodgings, Adam could not sleep. He was alternately hot and cold, and was unnaturally conscious of his own breathing – the rise and fall of his chest, the sound it made. The more aware he became, the harder it was to breathe normally; it was as if he were incapable of inhaling sufficient air. He would drift into the beginnings of a nightmare, then be jolted into wakefulness, the surreal figures of his subconscious mind vivid still, then wavering and disintegrating . . .

On its mat beside him lay the old setter, shuddering a little in its sleep. Adam reached downwards and found its sleek head. Immediately awake, the dog's warm nose met his hand and a dry tongue licked his fingers.

'Dear old thing. You've not long to go, have you?' Every day he expected it – to find his dog, whose hind legs now dragged, dead; but the expectation didn't ease the prospect. He stroked the animal's head till it dropped once more on to its paws, and the heavy breathing recommenced. Adam's hand remained dangling outside the bedclothes, the tips of his fingers just touching the silky fur, and eventually in the small hours, he slept.

The morning was oppressively hot, the sky having that thick greenish tinge which pre-empts a storm. The setter's whines and thrusting nose woke his master, who, groggy and aching, rolled over and pushed his face into the pillow. The continuing whines could not be ignored, and Adam sat up and rubbed his eyes. His throat felt raw.

'What is it, old thing?' He fumbled for his pocket watch amongst the heap of his clothes on the floor, and peered closely at it. 'Five past ten – poor lad. Who's a poor neglected lad?'

He hauled himself from the bed, his limbs as heavy as meal-sacks, went to the wash room, then hurriedly dressed.

The morning wrapped its cloying greenness around him. There were few people about on the heath as he walked, lethargically, with his dog along a well-trodden track amidst the dry, bleached grass. This area was hilly, and usually the dog, despite his frail back legs, would somehow scramble up and down, but this morning it showed no inclination other than to perform its duty and return home . . . Until it saw the hare. Impelled by old instincts, the dog was gone – up and down the hill and out of sight, fired by the energy of youthful memories.

Vainly, Adam called it back, at the same time chasing in the direction it had gone. His chest rasped as he ran.

He found his pet a couple of hundred yards away by a clump of trees; his brief and ecstatic sprint had proved too much for him. As Adam crouched over his body and fought back tears, the first drops of rain fell; pulling the body gently into the copse, he made his way back as fast as he could – up Downshire Hill and to the tailor's shop.

Mr Levy was with a customer, pinning him into the sleeve of an unfinished jacket. There were pins in Levy's mouth. He removed them when he saw Adam. 'What has happened?'

'M-my dog has d-died. Could I b-borrow a s-s-spade?'

By the time he returned to the spot the rain was driving down and thunder rumbling, and Adam was reminded of another storm nine years previously. He dug frantically, avoiding tree roots, becoming drenched – and then the rain changed to hail; stones the size of peas hurling from a blackened sky and bounding off him; driving into the grave . . . He lined the pit with bracken and lovingly laid his dog on top, covering him with more bracken and then soil, marking the place finally with a heavy stone.

'Poor old lad.' But it was he who was poor. The animal was dead and knew nothing – had died ecstatically. Adam was left, ridiculously bereft and missing him already, his childhood rushing back in convoluted memories, making him yearn for it – when at the time it had not seemed to bring him much pleasure. An attack of giddiness overcame him, and the space around him was an immense vacuum in which he floated.

At his lodgings Mr Levy knocked on the door. 'May I come in?'

He found Adam lying on top of his bed, his rain-soaked shirt unbuttoned to the waist and disclosing a hairy chest, shoes pulled off, and trousers half undone. A sound like a bow drawing faintly across a violin's strings came from his chest.

Levy knelt by him, alarmed. 'Mr Gilmour – you are as white as a ghost. And look how wet. Let me help you change and get you to bed.'

Adam's teeth were chattering together like nibbling mice. He tried to speak, but instead a fit of coughing took hold of him. One minute he was burning, the next icy; and he was sad – so very sad with his childhood dog gone; and his father.

'Papa . . .'

Then he was aware of what he had said and shook his head to disentangle his thoughts. Gratefully he submitted himself to Levy's care – the drying of his hair, the change of clothes into his nightshirt, and the meaningless guttural language soothing him all the while. He slid between the sheets with relief and slept – to dream he was in prison alone with the setter, who was lying on the painstakingly written pages of his book, muddying it, so that the writing became indecipherable.

Leah stayed with him for a fortnight, sleeping on a mattress beside him at night, and keeping constant vigil by day. Sometimes Claud kept her company, terrified by the sight of his friend. Levy would nip upstairs at the slightest opportunity, creeping into the room, whispering to Leah, asking yet again, 'Any improvement?' He made the young man soup and dumplings which went to waste, but was afraid that if he ceased to make them Adam would die. The soup and dumplings became for him symbolic of Adam's life. One day he would sit up and eat.

'Why did it happen?' he asked Leah – a young woman whose inner fortitude he marvelled at. She had come straight round that first day, still in her stained artist's smock, plainer yet more beautiful than he remembered her.

'He has had poor health since childhood,' she said. 'He will not admit to it because he thinks it makes him appear pathetic. He has a horror of that – of seeming feeble; of being mocked – or pitied.'

Levy was amazed. 'But who would mock him? He is such a fine young man in every way.'

'Of course he is –' they were speaking quietly outside Adam's bedroom, 'but he cannot think that of himself, and constantly drives himself, to prove his worth. He has always been the same.'

'And you, young lady?'

'Me?' Leah, weary, frightened for her brother, yet not believing in her heart that anything would happen to him, suddenly seemed to sag.

'Yes. What about you?'

'Oh, I am straightforward.' She gave one of her shrugs and laughed lightly.

'And single-minded.'

'Yes, that too.'

The doctor came and went, his expression non-committal.

'I've seen him like this before, Doctor,' Leah said, wanting his reassurance, for him to say, 'And you have seen him emerge safely each time.' But instead, refusing to be led, he told her, 'His lungs are not strong. With each attack they weaken.'

'I just thought –'

'Young lady, I am not a soothsayer. I do my humble best as a doctor, and it is not always enough.'

But Adam rallied. And as with those other times he regarded everything around him with incredulity.

'In a way I am fortunate,' he told Claud, who was visiting and had been reading out loud to him from an adaptation of *The Hunchback of Notre Dame*.

'Why is that?' Claud's relief at his friend's recovery was considerable. Seeing Adam now, propped against three pillows, with his hair brushed, and his clean-shaven face lively, one could not suspect that days earlier he'd been close to death; that during his illness he had cried for his father and pleaded with his mother, and held conversations with a woman called Mrs Fitzgerald and someone else called Alice. Now that the period of anxiety was over Claud felt exhausted from it, shaken within himself, still horrified at the thought that a person he dearly loved might have died.

Adam answered, 'I value life in a way that no one who hasn't been close to dying could possibly do. After each bout of illness I'm given this superb gift: life. All my senses become newly aware. And perhaps because I have been so near it, death holds no terrors.'

Claud could not bear to contemplate the subject, so afraid was he of the ceasing of his own existence. Sometimes he was frightened to sleep, in case he didn't awaken.

'I am immortal. I feel it. Dying is an impossibility.' He waved his hand dismissively.

'It is not only a possibility, it's a certainty,' Adam said, shifting his feet into a more comfortable position. 'But once we were not here, so why is it any different? Besides, there may be an after-life – no, don't interrupt, I know you don't believe in God. But maybe after-life is unconnected with a superior being.'

'How is that?' Grudgingly, Claud leaned forward in his chair and rested his elbows on the edge of the bed.

'Take Buddhism, for example. The Buddhist belief is that you re-circulate, if you like. There is no mention of a creator, but you undergo different karmas, following a code of existence based on acceptance and truth, and pursue the Eightfold Path of Morality, the aim being Perfect Enlightenment –' He saw that Claud's eyes were glazing over, and hurried on, 'And then you attain Nirvana, and all your bodily and mental cravings will be no more!'

'How ghastly! I thoroughly enjoy my bodily and mental cravings!'

'I've simplified it, of course.'

'I'm glad you didn't preach this shit when you were delirious. You would have been locked away.'

'It's easy to be dismissive about what is beyond our comprehension.'

'Something I *can* comprehend is my very great thirst.'

'There's some wine in the cupboard,' Adam told him, laughing and pushing him off the bed.

'That's a great relief. Having spent a life-time repelling the clutches of Christianity, I'm not about to embrace another religion. In fact my opinion of *all* religion could be summed up neatly with that most eloquent of Leah's little idioms: "Phooee".'

The Circle Club was just recovering from the sudden death in June of Charles Dickens. As one of its founders, he had been its most respected figurehead, and had been held in awe by everyone, even those who believed his work to be 'sensationalist'. But now, this Tuesday lunchtime, in the first week of August, things were back to normal; it was a quiet time of year anyway, with people holidaying.

In the dining-room, which overlooked the rear courtyard and was adorned with green plants, Adam sat opposite Leslie Stephen. The lunch was Stephen's treat, and the reason for it, the acceptance of *The Farmer's Son*.

'One of the reasons I so enjoyed your book,' he said, 'apart from the sensitive portrayal of your characters, is the moral issue of the story. I mean, one can blame the father as much as the son: he spoiled his child, and then stretched himself financially beyond his means in order to make his farm "the best in the county". By building the boy up as a prince, it had to be expected that the lad would have princely ambitions – but not necessarily the intellect to follow them through. I also liked the way everyone in the village had a secret somewhere to be exposed. It works very well indeed.'

'Thank you.' Adam quietly basked in his praise. He was unable to prevent the corners of his mouth from quivering, and had an urge to laugh. He was still disbelieving. He broke the roll on his side-plate, buttered and bit into it.

'You must have realized you had written something exceptional.'

'I was not sure.'

'Well, we shall print the first two chapters in October's issue, and thereafter monthly,' Stephen said, businesslike. Then he saw that the young author seemed dazed, and asked, 'Is that agreeable to you?'

'Yes, yes . . . I suppose I'm overwhelmed.' He could barely restrain himself from leaping up and shouting with joy. It was what he had hoped for, yet never believed would happen. He was truly a writer – not merely a journalist, but a writer. He would mix with other novelists he admired. He was no longer just another keen amateur.

He cleared his throat. 'Thank you for accepting my novel.' It was all he could think of to say. His eyes became embarrassingly moist. He thought, 'People will be reading my story each month . . . I'll become known . . . It's incredible.'

Stephen, who had invested his faith in the young man's future, thought, 'It's a shame – in a year he'll be used to it all.' To Adam he said, 'You'd better get on with your next book now. Your public will expect it of you.'

And whose pride would not have been a little inflated at such words?

Christmas was approaching, and the Hampstead streets were a hive of activity. Street traders banged their hands together in their fingerless gloves, and proclaimed their wares: 'Chestnuts!' 'Hot pies!' 'Knives sharpened!' One man set himself up on the corner of Heath Street and High Street with an elaborate canopy, selling miracle cures for Christmas gluttony . . . Shops were packed and the pavements crowded with people carrying parcels.

Adam returned from a walk on the heath – still unused to being without his dog. He had been trying to think of a plot for another novel, but his mind was occupied by *The Farmer's Son*, and no new characters came to usurp the old. He could not seem to relinquish that first book – which was enjoying considerable success in the *Cornhill Magazine*: the correspondence page was full of letters praising it.

He stamped the snow from his boots and brushed his coat; unravelled the woollen scarf.

'You had a visitor,' Levy told him, cutting a length of dark material. 'She is returning in about half an hour.'

'*She*? Not Leah?'

'No. I've not seen her before.'

Curious, he ran upstairs to wash, and change. His cheeks tingled from the cold. *She*? He thought of the women he knew, with whom he had spent a night or at most a week; there had not been many, and he could not think they would call on him, unless . . .

'Oh no, that would be too much!' The possibility of unwanted fatherhood occurred to him and he blanched, stood rigid in the midst of tying his bow.

He finished dressing quickly; he paced the room and waited and looked at his watch. The triple knocking was bold, and when he went to open the door he did not, at first, recognize the young woman with the scar across her face. Then something in her eyes became familiar.

'Alice Mason!'

'Adam Gilmour. May I come in?'

Chapter Nine

THE AFFAIR

'Well, I certainly succeeded in surprising you,' she said, sitting down in the balloon-back chair in her old assured manner.

'That you did,' he said, trying not to stare at the livid scar disfiguring the left side of her face.

'Oh dear.' She laughed – a high trill. 'You are so polite. You are desperately trying to avoid riveting your eyes – no, your eye, isn't it? – on my scar.'

The mocking tone, the bold, disconcerting gaze, were unchanged. She removed her fussy little hat and laid it on the bed, and he noticed it had a veil which she had chosen deliberately not to use. Perhaps she had wanted to shock him.

He didn't question her about the scar; it was not his business. He sat at his desk – he felt safer there – and turned the chair towards her; his forward position with his fist propping up his chin was aggressive.

'Why did you come? How did you know where I lived?'

'A whim. Curiosity. I obtained your address from the *Cornhill* offices.'

What right did she have to come and invade his privacy? 'Resourceful,' he commented drily.

'Oh come now, Adam, why don't you admit – you find my visit an imposition.'

'Excuse me.' He got up abruptly and took the kettle to the wash-room to fill it with water; her skirts brushed his ankles as he passed her chair, and he was aware of her eyes following him. Everything about her seemed to be calculating, he thought, as he pumped water into the copper vessel. 'She's motivated by sudden whims which must be satisfied even if it means disturbing lives . . .'

And he was disturbed; far more than he pretended – seeing her standing there with her ruined face, ten years on. Ten whole years. And with her presence, memories of his childhood assailed him; Brambleden Hall rang with voices in his ears, and he was Addi again.

But he was not. He lit the paraffin burner and set the kettle on the top, arranged two cups and saucers and put some gingerbread he happened to have on a plate.

'I am most impressed by your domesticity.' She sounded sarcastic, as she had always used to, but then she had had beauty, and it had made her seem challenging, and added to her attractions.

He said defensively, 'Why shouldn't a man be as capable of domesticity as a woman?'

'No reason, I suppose.' She curled her lips.

'Besides, I couldn't have not offered you tea.'

'No, that would have been churlish,' she agreed.

He sighed in exasperation, and intertwined his hands behind his head. The chair rocked precariously then righted again. They were each waiting for the other to begin asking the questions; it had become a game. And meanwhile they sipped tea and ate the gingerbread, and Alice made trivial conversation.

'You're still the same – still silent,' she said after a while.

It annoyed him that she assumed him unchanged. What did she know about him or his life? He wouldn't chat merely to please her. But he was interested to know what had happened to her, and only perversity held him back. He examined her through narrowed eyes – her elegant clothes and tall slim figure, her thick hair which was more auburn than he remembered, the smallish plum-toned mouth, the purple ridge marring the whiteness of her skin. He remembered he had once decided her soul was ugly, but then, what did he know of her soul, any more than she knew of his?

'I've been following your novel,' she said suddenly – and blushed unexpectedly, holding her hand to her bad cheek as if it burned. One could only see the right-hand side of her face then, unblemished and seductive, and he felt a rush of pity for her.

'Are you enjoying it?' he asked, bracing himself for the quip he was sure would follow.

'I think it's beautiful.'

And he was so taken aback that he could only make an exhalation of surprise and look astonished.

'– And so I thought I would come and see you – what had become of you; how it was the first boy that I kissed became a writer; what he was like as a man.' She glanced at him coquettishly.

'What *am* I like as a man?' he asked, adopting her teasing tone, and she tipped her head to one side and pursed her lips.

Smiling, he observed her observing him. He couldn't help admiring her apparent lack of concern over her disfigurement, and found that he himself was no longer disturbed by it.

'You are quite handsome,' she stated matter-of-factly, so that he gave a burst of laughter. A glimmer of reciprocal laughter came into her eyes. 'What you are *like*, as a man, I must waive judgement on.' There was no mistaking the innuendo in her words, and she stared at him frankly.

An erotic warmth flooded his body . . . But he wanted to ask her so much. He wanted to stoke up places and people and memories – the common denominator of their youth. Yet he was not sure he liked her; he was confused by her – the more so, now that he was sexually aroused.

Rather brutally he asked, 'So what did happen to your face?'

'Halleluja!' She clapped her hands lightly together. 'He's dared broach it.'

And he was immediately antagonized again by her goading manner. But her finger was tracing the scar, and he thought it trembled slightly.

'My husband did it,' she said.

'So you're married.'

'God, not now! Not after *this*,' she said passionately, leaping briefly to her feet, pacing a few steps, then sitting down again and regaining her composure. It was the first time he had seen her show emotion.

'Well, technically I'm still married, I suppose, but I've petitioned for a divorce.'

'When did it happen?' Adam asked, pouring them both more tea. Her eyes followed his hand resentfully.

'Six months ago. No, seven. It'll fade a bit more, the physician says. Sometimes I put powder on it, and it helps to hide it – but something in me likes to horrify people.'

'I've noticed.' He smiled, and she smiled back.

'When we left Brambleden the whole village was alight with talk about me.'

'Why?'

'Didn't you know? I was pregnant.'

'No I didn't. I remember my mother said it was rather sudden – your family moving. What happened, then?'

'I was sent to stay with a family in Somerset – cousin of our housemaid, can you believe – and my mother told everyone I was convalescing in Switzerland after an illness. Such lies! Such stupid lies! All this fuss about a woman doing what she wants with her body . . . I wouldn't have the baby – a girl – adopted, so in the end I married the father when I was sixteen.'

'And?'

'You are like a child saying, one more page, just one more page.'

'I'm intrigued.' She had made him defensive again, and she laughed and laid her hand on his arm. The feel of it made his skin singe.

Her face became serious, and her voice flat. 'My husband repented his lost youth – I think you saw him once. He was the boy I danced with that night at the party in Skirmett, when you were so miserable. Anyhow, Alexandra died at eight months old, and my husband claimed I'd tricked him. Perhaps I did . . . Who knows? Who cares? Everything's an elaborate trick, after all.'

He looked at her keenly, thinking this the most profound remark he had heard her make – yet she threw it away without dwelling on it.

'The only thing that bound us was our sexual needs,' she continued, brandishing the words without embarrassment.

Adam interrupted, 'The baby – Alexandra – were you sad about her?'

She stared at him as if he were mad. 'Of course. What do you think? Why did you think I didn't want her adopted?'

He was instantly ashamed, and more bewildered than ever by her.

'We became sexually daring, I suppose you would call it. It

relieved the monotony of our quarrels. It was fun. Not harmful, just imaginative –'

Adam was stunned. He had never heard a woman speak like this – openly about such a prohibited topic . . .

'He would tie me up, smack me a bit – nothing serious – until a year or so ago. He had always had affairs – so had I, before you offer me wasted sympathy. But in between his affairs he was restless, and he became quite violent. We would scream at each other so loudly that neighbours would complain, and that would make us laugh, united against them: puritan busibodies . . . Anyway, I was expecting a baby again, and he didn't want me to have it. Child that he was, he could not cope with the prospect of fatherhood again. He denied the baby was his. He yelled. He hit me. Then, that night he bound me to the bed – I was not unwilling at first – until he brought out a knife. He said he would mutilate me unless I did something to get rid of the baby. I refused. I could not believe he would do it; I longed for a baby . . . So that is it. Grisly it. Oh, and I lost the baby.'

The emotionless way she told her tale made the horror of it all the more vivid. Adam was dumbfounded. 'W-where are you l-living now?' he finally asked.

'How quaint! You still stammer! I am in our own rented house in Hill Street, off Park Lane. Paul has hidden himself away. He sends me money. He doesn't dare put a foot wrong.'

'What does he do for a living?'

'He's in banking. Don't shed tears over him.'

'I had no intention of it. My brother – you remember Jonathan? – is in banking, too.'

'It is the thing to be in,' she said. 'Except for all the Jews.'

'What do you mean by that, "Except for all the Jews"?' he flared.

'Dear me, we are touchy,' she said mockingly. She added, 'I didn't mean anything really. I never do,' and regarded him levelly. He said nothing.

'Ah!' She gave a knowing exclamation. 'I've just remembered – that little man – your landlord – he is a Jew, isn't he?'

'What of it?' Above all things Adam despised prejudice. And as for Levy – he had grown fond of him during the last couple of years. He was a friend, an uncle figure, someone whose kindness he could rely on. Sometimes he went with him to buy cloth from the factory

– sitting beside him in the trap, pulled by the grey pony which the tailor treated like a friend. Adam often had an evening meal with him, and afterwards Levy would bring out the chocolates . . .

Alice said, 'Don't look so mortified. I have nothing particularly against Jews.'

'That is magnanimous of you.'

She pulled a bored expression and gazed round the room at different things. His things; which he prized in one way or another and did not want criticized. He wished she would go – and yet also wanted her to stay. He wanted to quarrel with her, understand her, make love to her. 'Would you like me to show you Hampstead?'

'Yes, why not?'

But first she reached into her little bag and carefully applied some concealing cream to her wound, covering it finally with powder. When she was finished, she stood before him as a beautiful unblemished woman – unless one looked closely. She smiled a funny, twisted little grin which he took to mean that for him she had laid herself bare, but now she wanted to see, not be seen; and they went out into the cold.

They saw each other several times a week, dependent on one another for the wrong reasons, and coming no closer to a mutual discovery. But at nights she sometimes cried in her sleep, and then Adam almost loved her. Her vulnerability made her accessible. He stroked her back – its bony spine, and the twin hollows above her buttocks; she might waken, and turn to him, wrapping her strong legs around him, and he would roll her on to her stomach, submissive, to play with as he wished.

She was uninhibited about eroticism; her own body pleased her, and she gave herself up entirely to the sensations it offered. He loved the way she arched herself upwards sinuously when he stroked her bottom; and he would substitute his tongue for his fingers, and her muted groans would fill his ears. When she tried to lift herself up, he would immediately pinion her down with his hands firmly on her shoulders, and her cries would become so loud he feared the tailor would hear. Gently he would put his hand in front of her mouth, and she would taste herself on him, and bite his hand; then with all her force, roll over and free, slide downwards in the bed and take his penis in her mouth . . .

Yet throughout all this intimacy no word of affection ever passed between them, and when they were finished with one another, they would turn away, leaving a void between them.

He said to her one morning, 'Did you know you cry in your sleep?' She refused to believe him, and when he insisted, wanting to find some weak spot in her he could touch and learn to cherish, she became angry, and lit a cigarette, which she knew he hated. The smoke hurt his eyes and irritated his throat; he disliked the smell on his clothes. But at nights the plaintive sobbing continued to wake him, as her subconscious sought a refuge her conscious mind denied.

Their relationship limped into 1871. She had few interests of her own, though she liked to walk. She never spoke about his work and scorned the causes to which he was so committed – regarding the people who attended rallies as 'bunches of turnips dressed as tramps'; and he hadn't dared introduce her to Claud, or tell Leah whom he was seeing. Yet she followed his novel in the *Cornhill*, and when he interrupted her once, said with a scowl, 'Be quiet, I'm reading' – and engrossed herself again.

One blustery March morning Adam left her languishing in his bed in a particularly infuriating and incomprehensible mood – which made him wonder for the hundredth time, 'Why on earth do I stand it?' But she had already answered that question for him when, in that flippant voice which sometimes belied her seriousness, she had said, 'We are using one another.' Did she mean that her scarred face precluded her from having other men? Did she mean that he was so insecure that he would only take what conveniently offered itself? He questioned her, and she laughed away his earnestness, refusing to elaborate.

'Don't let it trouble you.' She touched his forehead lightly. 'You are a truly excellent lover.' And later that day she had bought him a present – an old quill to add to his writing collection. She mystified him.

He arrived at Morley's Hotel in Trafalgar Square just after twenty minutes to twelve. Flustered as always by his own unpunctuality, he hurried into the lounge. A stocky, bespectacled man stood up to greet him. From a nearby seat a fair, fox-faced man watched the pair.

Gray-Courtney Publishers had been established by Algernon Gray-Courtney in 1840, and had become known since the advent of his son, Geoffrey, as a selective house with a forward outlook. It was Geoffrey whom Adam was meeting this morning, to discuss *The Farmer's Son*, which they had agreed to publish.

He was an intense man of great energy, with a habit of banging his hands together for emphasis, clenching his lips and jerking his square jaw simultaneously. In his own way he was as much an innovator as the authors he represented; he had no fear of being controversial, saw talent where others did not, and was as excited by it as had he possessed it himself. If he could be the discoverer, the nursemaid, the mentor, then he was well-satisfied.

Adam Gilmour's reputation was already established; he had been discovered – but as yet in a small way. Geoffrey Gray-Courtney was confident he could make him into a household name – cultivate Adam's romantic image. For a book was no different from any other commodity which had to be marketed.

He had met Adam once before – at their offices in Albemarle Street, W1, and had recognized him immediately as a solitary person. He was encouraged; in his opinion the best writers were, at heart, solitary, tending to be self-immersed. Nobody comprehended more than he did the loneliness of writing a novel. He had attempted two, but could not cope with the isolated self-discipline entailed, the sapping of energy as one had to reach continually into one's own head for inspiration. He realized he was better equipped to help other authors than be an author himself, and put his works aside. It was not sufficient to be intellectual. It was, as Adam was now explaining, a matter of compulsion.

'You are, I think, a young man of great determination,' Geoffrey Gray-Courtney said.

'Some people would call it stubbornness.' Adam smiled – and caught the eye of the fair-haired man nearby. He was staring in a way that disquieted him.

'How do you feel about your own writing, Mr Gilmour?'

He turned back to the publisher. 'What do you m-mean?' His coffee was cold, but he swallowed a mouthful. He disliked talking about himself.

'I mean, what kind of novelist do you regard yourself as? Are you influenced by other writers?' He gave one of his emphatic jaw-jerks.

'Oh Lord!' Adam rubbed his hands over his hair and face self-consciously. 'As I have written only one novel perhaps it is too soon yet to say if I fit into any mould . . .'

'Surely, Mr Gray-Courtney, you do not perceive *Mr* Gilmour as a serious writer? Would not that be an insult to writers such as Trollope, or George Eliot, or Bulwer-Lytton?'

'Mr Chesterfield.' Gray-Courtney rose to his feet to acknowledge rather than greet the fair-haired man who had earlier been staring at them.

Chesterfield inclined his head slightly, and Gray-Courtney introduced him to Adam, who also stood up.

'Mr Chesterfield is the assistant editor of the *Quarterly Review*, and an arts critic,' the publisher said.

'Ah.' He did not shake the newcomer's hand, and prepared himself for the next attack. The *Quarterly Review* – A Tory journal – represented the church, monarchy, and order, and had once printed an article denouncing Adam Gilmour as a dangerous radical who incited violence and unrest, using his privileged birth to attract followers and publicity. In the correspondence page of the following issue, he was accused by many of anarchism, and he had no doubt that any letters which spoke in his favour had been discarded.

'I have to say I regard your book as purely sentimental,' Chesterfield said. 'I regard it as anti-Christian, too.'

'Oh? Why is that?' Adam asked pleasantly.

'You have made your central characters non-believers, shown the parish vicar as corrupt –'

'But he *was*.'

'You *invented* him. You had no right.'

'I had *every* right,' Adam counteracted heatedly. 'I show life as I think it is, not as some might wish it to be.'

'So *that's* how he sees himself as a writer,' thought Gray-Courtney, satisfied, regarding the two combatants with new keenness.

'It is blasphemous to misrepresent the Church.' Chesterfield was almost shouting, and several guests of the hotel turned to look. He was an Evangelist who had converted his wife, father-in-law and brother-in-law to his way of thinking, and although he gave his money away, he gave it only to the 'deserving', as he saw them. He was frugal and reactionary, a harsh disciplinarian and moralist, and this spoiled young aristocrat incensed him with his foreign-styled clothes, radical writing, and irresponsible public behaviour. He was self-indulgent in his exercises, attempting to rid himself of his guilt for having been born in a privileged family. Chesterfield had seen it before. But in Gilmour's case it was all the more dangerous because it was accompanied by charm and conviction.

'Well, he'll find me in his path,' Chesterfield thought. 'I'll not let him get away with things. Upstart . . .'

Adam said, 'I have misrepresented nothing. And I have to tell you I consider the selectiveness of Christian charity appalling.' He clenched his fists. 'And as for the c-c-character of the vicar portrayed in my st-story – a vicar is as susceptible as anyone. He is an ordinary mortal. I have created imperfect people.'

His heart was beating fast. Within him was a similar anger to that which he had once felt with Mr Tackley, his maths master who had deliberately misunderstood him. He was disturbed that he had an enemy in Chesterfield – an influential man.

'There are three kinds of people I dislike, *Mr* Gilmour –' Chesterfield began, laying his pink hands with their buffed nails on the back of the chair.

And Adam cut in sharply, 'Yes, sir – men, women and children!' He gave a short derisive laugh and sat down, so proclaiming their conversation at an end.

The other spluttered, became red in the face, then, with a brief and furious nod, left them.

Not long after his departure, over a fresh pot of coffee and fruitcake infused with rum, Geoffrey Gray-Courtney offered Adam an advance against royalties of £500 for *The Farmer's Son*, to be published the following autumn, with an initial printing of four thousand copies.

Alice had returned to her own house in Hill Street, but his apartment smelt of her – the sharp tangy perfume she wore, the make-up which concealed her damaged face, the oils she massaged into her skin to keep it supple.

'Poor Alice . . .' He went over to the window and looked out. He could feel the approach of one of his 'bleak' moods – when he questioned the purpose of everything.

He thought of his brother, successful in his career, a dutiful son, still living in the gloomy house with their demanding mother who ceaselessly twitched, drank sherry and inhaled snuff. Jonathan seemed not to mind; but then he travelled extensively and went to parties and to the opera – which Leah said he slept through, and only attended for appearance's sake . . .

He thought of Leah and Claud, and their interminable engagement. Claud had decided that when they eventually married they would live in France.

'What will I do without you both?' Adam had asked, stunned at the thought of losing them.

'You will have a wife and child yourself by then,' Claud had replied. 'You will just have to come and stay – or better still, live in France with us. You speak excellent French, and the climate would suit your health.'

'No. I like England.'

'I can't think why.'

Adam tried to envisage the wife and child Claud had alluded to, but their faces were blank, and he couldn't believe that anything would change for him during the period of Leah and Claud's engagement. It was three years hence – but already he dreaded their departure.

Meanwhile he had just been offered £500 for one book, yet was morose because he had no idea of what to write next.

Alice had left a decorative hair-slide behind. He saw it lying on his chest of drawers. He fingered the long strand of hair caught in it. And then it occurred to him: he would write about a young woman with a scarred face who saw herself as a victim of men, whereas in fact she offered herself as a target. It would be a character study of an ambitious woman . . .

He sat down at his desk and began to make notes.

Chapter Ten

GOING BACK

Thursday, May 25th, 1871

'How strange it is to be back. It must be at least seven years since I was here, just before Papa's death. I find my little cousins, whom I entertained with stories and pranks, grown-up, my aunt's hair greying and coarse, and my uncle with the eyes of an anxious man. I notice that the house is in need of redecoration, and that the servants are few . . . And my uncle has already mentioned the tumbling grain prices three times. But they are still a boisterous bunch.

'I am haunted by the meaninglessness of time – see buildings which are unchanged and others which would have tortured my poor father to witness. The Market Place is the same; I recognize shopkeepers – but they frown at me, unsure. Time can be of consequence to one person, yet have no significance for another.

'I drove with Leah in the wagonette to Brambleden – and caught my breath at the sight of village girls sitting on the bank, dangling their legs in the stream; but I knew none of them. I saw our dairymaid at the pump with a child in her arms and another clinging to her hips as she chatted to a couple of other women. She had the full-blown look of a woman who will bear a dozen children. Did she marry our cowman? How their covert glances used to enflame me! Leah wanted to stop, to speak to her, but I could not bring myself to do so; after all, as children when did we ever exchange more than a few words with her? And I was loath to interrupt the three young women who presented such a pretty spectacle as they stood engrossed, clustered beneath the oak tree, their country faces speckled with shadows. Better to keep things as they were and as they are.

'Miss Tinley was in the post office, and she at least was

unchanged. Seven years on the face of an old woman makes no odds. She offered us tea, and I asked about Ethel.

' "How is your niece?" I enquired casually.

' "My niece?" she looked wary.

' "The one who took your place when you were ill, years ago. Ethel, I believe her name was."

' "Oh *her*. We don't talk 'bout *her* no more." She made a "hmph" sound, and poured the tea, muttering as she did so, "a bad girl . . ."

'Poor Ethel – did she seduce a lord? Or murder the judge who condemned her husband? Or is she walking the streets?

'Miss Tinley gave us a summary of the past few years. Lord Brambleden had died and the Manor was going to a nephew. "Your place was sold on 'gain some six months back," she said. "The land went separately. London people, the new owners be. Rich. Banking, they say. Lowenstein they be called – Jews, you know."

'Her tone of voice made me prickle. "And do they practise witchcraft?" I asked politely – whilst beside me Leah gave an explosive guffaw.

'Damn me if the woman didn't answer seriously, "Oh no, sir, nothing like that. Quiet, decent people they be. And the missus – well, she comes in with her daughter and they seem right regular. Ever so pretty the girl be."

' "Witchcraft indeed!" expostulated my sister when we were outside.'

They were visiting for their cousin Julia's twenty-first birthday. Jonathan was in Paris on business, and was unable to join them. Lady Elizabeth had declined to travel down, using rats, the damp and her rheumatism as her excuse. Unencumbered, Adam and Leah spent several days before the party, visiting people, drinking at the Red Lion in Hart Street, walking along the towpath by the river . . . Or to nearby Aston, where they painted side by side, and afterwards had tea at the Flower-Pot Hotel – a popular meeting place for keen boaters. In the evenings the whole family would gather to play cards, or charades, or David Robinson would challenge Adam to a game of billiards. He thought of his father then; remembered a particular afternoon when Sir Felix had drunk too much and lost his game to the perils of modern architecture.

His uncle finally confided in him: 'Business is desperate – non-existent. Grain is coming from America so cheaply that however much we lower the prices, we simply cannot compete. I have lost everything. It is desperate,' he repeated. 'I have colossal debts – they were not only the prerogative of your father, you know. I cannot see a way out of it, that is the terrible thing. I worry so much for all of them –' He motioned with his hand to the door which led to the family room where his wife and five children were at that moment playing 'rummy'. 'I love them all so much . . .' He put his head in his hands, and to Adam's horror began to sob.

Adam went immediately to his side, to comfort him. He heard the muffled words, 'I'd be better off dead. They would be better off . . . I have a life insurance policy which would keep them comfortably.'

'Don't talk like that,' Adam said harshly. 'They *need* you here to be with them, loving them.'

'But I would not be here. I would be in prison,' his uncle whispered despairingly.

Adam's grip tightened round his bent shoulders. 'I'll not let it happen.'

The man looked up, his face ravaged. He attempted a smile. 'You're very kind – but then you always were. "An exceptional boy", your aunt used to say. I am sorry to have involved you. Please forget this conversation.'

'I can't. I want to help.'

'You can help by being here. By staying on for a while after the party. Just a little while, eh?'

The night of the party was fine, and the house was resplendent: flower displays, candles, gleaming silver, starched damask cloths, tables laden with tempting fare, all detracted from its shabbiness; and then, when the guests began to arrive, the women beautiful in evening gowns, the shabbiness retreated further. Nobody noticed a patch of damp on the wall, or yellowing paintwork or peeling paper. The small orchestra struck up, champagne was served, and canapés passed round on salvers. Everyone was happy; and the host, smiling, touching an arm here or a shoulder there as he flitted between guests, seemed the happiest of them all.

Leah was talking to an old friend she had met. Adam, on his own, watched his uncle, unconvinced by his gaiety. His resolve to help strengthened. '. . . I'll speak to Jonathan. Surely a loan could be arranged . . . The low prices can't last.' He looked round the crowded room – his cousin Julia was approaching him, weaving her way laughingly, large and plain. She was leading another girl, also laughing, by the hand. Adam stared.

'Adam,' Julia said when she reached him. 'This is Sarah Lowenstein – I've just told her all about you.'

'I have been reading your novel in the *Cornhill*,' the girl said. 'I think it is marvellous. How long did it take you to write?' She had a low-pitched voice with a lively inflection.

'T-two years.' He could not take his eyes from her – the small fragile oval of her face, its paleness contrasted to the blackness of her hair, which was only partially held back, the rest left loose to ripple down her back in the style of the Pre-Raphaelite models; the intelligent, clear forehead with its widow's peak; the delicate narrow nose; and beneath it the short deep groove which lifted the full upper lip provocatively. Her eyes were thick-lashed and dark, but in their darkness were dazzling hazel flecks.

Adam thought he had never seen a more compelling face, and his gaze took in the rest of her: she was of average height, but exquisitely slender and smooth-skinned; the bodice of her cream silk dress was tight over the fullness of her breasts. He felt a sudden racing of the heart, joy, so that he was momentarily weak; and then he became aware that he must have been gaping at her like an imbecile, and composed himself.

She was apparently oblivious to the effect she had had, and was not similarly moved. She regarded him levelly.

'You must have breathed, eaten and slept with your characters –'

Julia slipped away, leaving the pair alone together, and the girl continued, '– I cannot believe they were born solely in your mind.'

'But they were,' he assured her, laughing.

And she shook her head disbelievingly, very serious. 'How wonderful it must be to have such a talent. I think I should never cease to be grateful for it.'

Her praise made him feel awkward. He wished she would speak

of herself, not of him, and said dismissively, 'There are many talented writers about, Miss Lowenstein.'

'But you write from the *soul*,' she insisted. 'You must know it. Your characters *live*. Why do you belittle yourself? – And please call me Sarah.'

He smiled in confusion, and rubbed his jaw. 'I suppose I have no confidence in myself,' he said quietly.

'But you must. Surely a writer *must* believe in himself . . . Perhaps it is only that it's all too new for you to accept.' She looked contemplative.

'Please tell me about you,' he said impulsively. He wondered that she couldn't see the impact she had made on him – that he was already smitten.

'Oh, but I am not nearly so interesting,' she protested.

'Now who is belittling herself?'

'But it's *true*. However, I shall tell you a little if you wish. Only, first I *must* tell you that we are living in your old house.'

'I know. I heard it from Miss Tinley at Brambleden post office.'

'Goodness, *she* is a gossip, if ever I met one! And the weather – how many aspects of the weather she manages to include in every sentence! I always have to prevent myself from laughing.'

'She said you were very pretty.' The words came out unbidden, and to soften them, he added, ' "Ever so pretty, she be," she said.'

'Oh dear – now I am embarrassed, and can feel myself reddening.' She held her hands to her cheeks, and he laughed – took her hands and held them from her face, and saw that she was in fact blushing. He kept her hands in his for a second before releasing them.

'I mustn't seem so enamoured,' he thought. 'It will only deter her.' He said lightly, 'It becomes you to blush. Now, speak to me of my old home. Are you happy there?'

'Oh yes –'

He felt a nudge in his ribs and turned to find his sister at his side. Briefly he resented her appearance, and then he was immediately guilty, and introduced them.

The three discussed Brambleden Hall and the changes which had been made; joked about its creaks and eerie noises, and the reputed ghost of an old man that nobody had seen.

'Papa fell in love with its lightness,' Sarah said. 'We stood in the centre of that wonderful drawing-room and the sun flooded in. Papa just looked at us.'

'Come now,' Adam said gravely. 'You know the real reason you bought it was the delightful pink boudoir.'

She gave a peal of laughter and Leah joined in.

'You mean your mother had it decorated like that?' Sarah asked. 'I thought the owners just before us did. But it looked like a brothel!'

'We had Bible-reading sessions in that room,' Leah said. 'Adam and I would fight back tears of mirth when we glanced at one another.'

'I confess Mama changed it as soon as we moved in,' Sarah told them. 'It's yellow and white striped now.'

They remained in their little group for dinner, and Adam was unaware of anyone else in the room. Somebody would come up to him and greet him, but later he would recall nothing of the meeting; he could not have said what he ate, or who made speeches . . . Then the room was cleared, and he danced with Sarah, held her narrow hands in his. Once, her hair brushed his cheek as she swung round, and he smelled its freshness. But he must hold her at a respectable distance, be aloof; while for him the most immense event had just taken place.

The following day at breakfast, which was a lengthy affair with various members of the family trickling down sleepily at intervals, the conversation between Adam, Leah and Julia centred on Sarah Lowenstein.

'She is so beautiful,' Leah said, 'and such a lovely person.'

'She's coming over this afternoon for tea,' Julia told them. 'She was certainly struck with both of you. They are not all the time at Brambleden, you know. They've a place in London also.'

'Tell me more about her.' Leah bit into her toast and nibbled at it, rabbit-like. Adam tried to look nonchalant.

At twenty-two Sarah Lowenstein was the oldest by seven years of three girls, the daughter of integrated Jewish parents whose ancestors had been in England for several generations. They were an enlightened family, and Samuel Lowenstein was a quiet, erudite, broad-thinking man for whom free trade and the rise of the middle-class had been his salvation. Once he might have been scorned, and socially outcast; as it was, he was respected in business and accepted in most company. Had it been possible he would have been an academic, a philosopher perhaps, but there was no inherited wealth for him, and he had bought his way into a banking partnership and was happy to conduct business during the day; but in the evenings and at weekends – then he was a family man; then he could read his books and write his theories and watch his children grow.

They were a cultured and close family, and each of them was artistic in one way or another: the father played the piano, the mother, Carlotta, painted, the youngest sister sang, the middle one was a violinist; and Sarah wrote poetry and played the harp.

They were not religious and adhered to few rules and traditions, attending synagogue for weddings, funerals, bar-mitzvahs and Yom-Kippur – that day when virtually every Jew in the world repented for his or her sins, remembered the dead, and fasted. These few concessions were all the Lowensteins practised, simply because Samuel believed that anything more would not be practical for the type of life they led; but in his convictions he was Jewish to the core and proud to be so, and he read a great deal on the subject. He would defend his race and history at the slightest provocation, and when on occasions he met with antagonism and prejudice, then he would argue with wisdom and knowledge – and weary patience born of experience of many similar debates.

It was in this unusually liberal environment that Sarah grew up and was encouraged to be independent and free-spirited. There was never any pressure upon her to behave in a particular way or adhere to a specific belief, and her education had been as intensive as had she been a boy. Their Belgravia home was a hospitable one, and there were nearly always guests for meals, when she was allowed to remain with the adults and be included in the conversation. She loved those conversations, which ranged from the arts to current affairs, and if she broached her opinion nobody ridiculed her, but took her views as seriously as anyone else's.

Because she was so much older than her sisters she had to look beyond her own family for friends; but there was nobody she met whose upbringing resembled hers, and she found other girls dull and superficial, with no excitement in their minds, no questions. She herself was brimful with questions – she required constant information, which she would digest and rarely forget. She was certain women had a role in society apart from that of wife and mother; and if they could not go out to work – then at least let them be interesting! On her own she was apt to dream; because despite her high and sometimes rather dogmatically expressed ideals, there was an aspect of her nature which depended on romance for its contentment. The idea of Romance, of Passion such as she read about in novels, thrilled her. She knew that when she came to fall in love there would be nothing prosaic about it; she would know it the instant she met someone . . . In this way, though she did not realize it, she differed not an iota from those girls to whom she felt superior, and indeed from thousands, even millions, of other young women.

She spent her time in a variety of ways according to her moods, which differed from day to day. One morning she might shut herself in her room and write poetry she wouldn't have shown to a soul, or on another the tinkling of the harp might drift from the drawing-room and it was accepted that nobody could enter or disturb her. It was a double-action pedal harp, and she could pass hours engrossed in playing the compositions of Berlioz or Delibes, Saint-Saëns or Haydn . . . But the next day she might awaken restless and full of energy, and then she would dress quickly and go out – to museums and galleries, or to obscure exhibitions.

In the evenings she often read – and could not have known that she shared her taste, apart from the romantic fiction, with a young man called Adam Gilmour. She read newspapers and magazines as avidly as she did books, and herself had had several letters published. Her parents followed everything she did with fond approval, and Carlotta Lowenstein was not bothered that her daughter could not knit or embroider, that she was often assertive, and showed no signs of marrying. This oldest of their girls continually rewarded them with her beauty, warmth of character, generosity and intelligence. She was a rare creature and if they could keep her for a little longer, and shelter her from some of the harsher realities of life, they would be happy to do so; they dreaded the day her enthusiasms might wane.

They bought Brambleden Hall in the autumn of 1870, intending to use it as a holiday home, but Mrs Lowenstein was so enamoured of it, and her husband made so light of the journey from London, that they spent an increasing amount of time there, and after three months sold their Belgravia house for an apartment in the same area.

Before the purchase of Brambleden Hall Sarah had been thinking vaguely of 'opening a business'; but with the new circumstances she saw it would be impossible. It didn't occur to her she might be toying with life, that maybe she was rather self-indulgent and pampered, or that she was not always as serious-minded as perhaps she considered herself. But she was constantly aware. Each day offered itself up to her personally, and she flung herself into it – whilst patiently awaiting her fictitious hero.

As Adam waited with the others for her arrival that afternoon, he thought despondently, 'How can I expect myself to be attractive to such a woman?' He stared out at the view – the river, and rowing boats tied to rings along the wharf; ducks and swans with their broods bobbing past; the traffic on the bridge; children queuing for Italian ice-cream . . .

The bell rang, and he leaped at the sound. Leah, perceptive, noticed his tension, his awkwardness as he stood to greet Sarah.

'He's fallen in love. At last!' she thought.

The girls saved him the effort of talking. Bright female chatter filled the room, and through it he learned more about Sarah. He studied her every inflection and mannerism, her mercurial changes of expression, the lines of her body, the shape of her hands. He noticed, too, her habit of sucking her finger when she concentrated. She was sensual and sexual, and he wanted to memorize every detail about her so that when he was on his own he would be able to capture her image perfectly.

Different people came and went from the room; conversation moved from one subject to another; and tea was served. David Robinson joined them, positioning himself on one side of Sarah so that she had to move her chair closer to Adam in order to make room.

'You must come and see us at Brambleden Hall,' she said. 'You and Leah. If you'd like to, that is.'

'I should love to. It will be strange to see it again.'

'Yes, I imagine you will feel quite nostalgic.'

'It was a happy place,' David Robinson reminisced. 'Old Felix – your father – certainly lived life to the full there. I still miss him, you know.'

'You were a good friend to him,' Adam said.

'More like brothers than brothers-in-law.' The grain merchant looked wistful. 'Ah well – it happens to us all. Sometimes it is a welcome release.' His mood became vague, morose, and Sarah looked startled.

Adam feared the turn of the conversation, and the morbidness in his uncle's eyes. He said to Sarah, 'You mentioned earlier you played the harp. I should like to hear you.'

'I'd be far too embarrassed to play in front of you!'

'Why?' he asked, hurt.

'You are talented and successful. Me – I am merely an amateur.'

'But that doesn't prevent you from being good. And even if you were not, I should still wish to listen to you. You told me last night to believe in myself, well so must you in yourself.'

His uncle said, 'You never need be embarrassed in front of Adam. He's quite the nicest person you could come across.'

'Oh come now, Uncle! So – it is m-my turn for em-b-barrassment now, is it?' He shuffled his feet and accidentally touched Sarah's. 'I'm sorry . . .'

'It's fine. It's nothing. And I'm sure what your uncle says is true,' she said warmly, smiling with a kindness which hurt him, because kindness was what one showed to a friend, but not a lover.

Leah came over and knelt between them, an arm resting on the back of each chair, symbolically linking them, he thought; and the discussion changed again. He looked round the large irregular-shaped sitting-room, and realized how the happiness of everyone in it was so dependent on a single weary man who was all too aware of his responsibilities.

'What a fragile plinth security sits upon,' he thought.

'So you will stay on for another week,' David Robinson said to him later that evening, stretching his arm across the snooker table as he aimed the cue.

'Just a week,' Adam agreed, following his uncle's aim. 'Then I must get back. I have work to do, people to meet – a book to write.'

This made him remember Alice Mason. He hadn't thought of her since his arrival in Henley. In bed that night, he contemplated their relationship with a new distaste. It seemed now to have been a decadent adventure: two people who cared little about each other, intent only on sexual gratification, becoming more and more daring, as though it could compensate for their mental disenchantment. He was disgusted with himself – and with her.

'I must end it as soon as I return,' he thought, rolling on to his stomach. But then he recalled how she had wanted babies; saw her ruined face. He reflected on the inconsistencies in her character which still disturbed him and made him think that there were depths to her she would not reveal.

'I can't help it. She decided to invade my life. I didn't ask for it. I don't love her. I'm weary of the whole thing.'

But at that very moment he was becoming aroused as an image of her nakedness flashed before him – Alice bending over, naked and supple . . .

'Oh bother her . . .' His hands reached beneath the bedclothes to touch himself. Afterwards he felt lonelier and more disgusted than ever, so that he did not dare think of Sarah, of whom he had been intending to dream.

Instead he dreamed of his uncle and his father. They were sitting in a rowing-boat talking about John Ruskin's influence on contemporary architecture, when his uncle complained that he had some grain in his eye. Sir Felix laughed. 'That new house in Duke Street is made of grain,' he said. 'It was built in America.' As he spoke his face changed and became that of a rat, and he shrank rapidly in size and moved on to the grain merchant's foot. David Robinson kicked the rat with his other foot, but it would not be dislodged and looked pitifully at the man – who was now Arnold Chesterfield – all the while it was kicked to death. As it died it vomited up a pile of grain which weighed down the boat to such an extent that it sank.

Adam awoke, struggling for breath.

Chapter Eleven

LOVE

Two days later Leah and Adam visited Brambleden Hall. The rain lashed down that Tuesday, whipping into the coachman's face – which wore a sour expression. His shoulders in the waterproof cape looked hunched and angry. Adam wondered, 'When was he last paid?' Beside him his sister was unusually quiet, as the wagonette rocked and rattled along the pitted road.

'Are you all right?' Adam asked, suddenly aware of her silence.

'Yes – I only feel anxious returning.'

'I know.' He covered her hand with his. 'And such a pity it has to rain.'

'Are you in love with her?' Leah asked unexpectedly.

'Eh?' Taken aback, he was unsure at first of what she meant.

'With Sarah, I mean.'

'Love?' he laughed scornfully. 'My dear Leah – *love*, after a couple of days?'

'After five minutes, Adam,' she said softly.

He was dismayed by his transparency. 'Oh blast . . . I suppose I must be,' he admitted, slumping against the brocade seat.

Leah's hand, still in his, twisted slightly and applied pressure. 'I really like her. And we've agreed to see plenty of each other – either in London or here.'

'Will you try to establish her feelings towards me?'

'Poor Adam.'

'Don't say that,' he snapped at her. 'I am not *poor* Adam.'

'Don't be wrought. I only meant well.'

They drove up the track whose furrows were filled with rain and mud, which sprayed the wagonette's windows . . . Past the Rectory. And between the curtains in a downstairs room a face peered out.

'Reverend Hibbert!' Adam exclaimed. 'He recognized us – he's waving. We must stop and say hallo on the way back . . . He's disappeared now.'

But the rector had rushed to the door and was standing shouting, 'Don't go by without calling in on us!'

The coachman stopped and Adam jumped out and ran to meet the man who had inadvertently influenced his life. In the pouring rain they pumped each other's hand delightedly.

'We were intending to visit you on the way back. We're on our way now to Brambleden Hall.'

'Please do. We'd love to see you both. Come to supper – we're having cold venison. Give my kind wishes to the Lowensteins. They are a charming family.' And, sheltering his bent head with his arm, he dashed inside.

'If only there were more people like him,' Adam commented as he climbed into the wagonette and the horse trudged once more up the remainder of track towards Brambleden Hall, urged on by the disgruntled coachman.

Leah took a handkerchief from her pouch bag and ruffled it over her brother's hair. 'You're drenched. You look just like a young boy.' And seeing his expression, she knew she had said the wrong thing again.

They pulled up outside the gracious front door, and, holding an umbrella over them, the coachman helped Leah as she climbed down from the carriage.

'It feels so peculiar,' she said. 'It's as if we never left; yet also as if we never lived here.'

And he who had been thinking only of Sarah was similarly overwhelmed as he confronted his childhood home.

A butler showed them in, and they stood for a moment like misplaced children gazing about them – at unfamiliar furniture and decorations in an otherwise unchanged reception hall; remembering. They exchanged looks and followed the butler into the drawing-room.

Mrs Lowenstein stood up to greet them, as did her three daughters. She was a tall stout woman with fine eyes and mousy hair. 'I am so *glad* to meet you both,' she said, shaking hands. I am only sorry my husband is in London today. Sarah has told me a great deal about you. And to meet the famous author himself – well, well!' She had the same low voice as her oldest daughter.

'Fame is some way off yet, Mrs Lowenstein,' Adam protested.

Sarah said, 'Mama, Adam is impossibly modest' – and linked her arm in his. She did it without self-consciousness, unaware of the reaction it triggered in him.

'Modest or not, I must tell you we are all thoroughly enjoying the serial in the *Cornhill*,' the mother said. 'And I shall be one of the first to purchase your novel in book form.'

'It will give me great pleasure to make you a gift of a copy, Mrs Lowenstein.' He glanced down at Sarah's arm so casually interwoven with his. How could she not know what he was feeling? Didn't she realize her own attractiveness?

The other sisters were introduced – pallid, giggling, shy creatures, a little awed by this romantic-looking man who was a writer, and who for the last couple of days had been the subject of much excited conversation in their home.

The youngest, who was eleven, asked, 'What is it like in a police cell, Mr Gilmour?'

'Faith – what will the child say next!' exclaimed Mrs Lowenstein. 'Felicity, that is most impolite. And the gentlemen is *not Mr* Gilmour; he is *Sir* Adam Gilmour.'

'No, really – I never use the title. It is something I feel I must earn. And her question isn't in the least rude, I assure you . . .' He told the child: 'A police cell is cold and smelly, and there are often people in it who ought not to be.'

Sarah asked, 'Tell me, Adam – how do you propose earning your title?' She removed her arm from his – so that he felt abruptly chilled – and regarded him intently.

'Truthfully I am not bothered by a title at all,' he answered. 'But *if* I were to earn it, it would be by helping others achieve their aims and by trying to bring some happiness to lives bereft of it.'

Sarah's eyes glowed. 'You see how nice he is. Did I not tell you all?'

'Ah – but at nightfall I become a vampire.' He curled both his index fingers at the sides of his mouth to resemble fangs, and pulled a ferocious face. Felicity gave a shrill cry, and the others laughed. He was relieved. He had a horror of conversation when it became personal.

Outside, the downpour continued, but within all was warm and convivial. Adam looked round him – at the discreet good taste of wallpaper and fabrics, the fresh flowers in vases everywhere. His sister was talking with Mrs Lowenstein; the two younger girls were lying on the rug on their stomachs, playing dominoes . . . Seeing the harp prominently displayed, he said quietly to Sarah, 'We have a pact, don't forget.'

'What is that?' she asked, puzzled.

'You agreed to play the harp for me.'

'I did not!'

Mrs Lowenstein stopped in the middle of a sentence to Leah. 'Why are you two arguing?'

'Sarah is reneging on her word,' Adam said, drumming his fingers on his chin.

'It's not true!' Laughing, she lightly slapped his shoulder.

She was persuaded to play, and they sat in a semi-circle round her. Her slender body was curved like a sapling, her arms tender, as she plucked the strings; her thick black hair fell forward over her shoulder, shielding her face – and the delicate music of Delibes rippled through the room.

Adam watched her with blurred eyes. Once, bravely, she glanced up to look at her little audience and smiled, at him in particular. Her expression was transported by the music, and he felt as though he had been wounded.

The afternoon passed pleasantly. Adam reeled off Edward Lear's Nonsense Rhymes, to the youngest child's delight; he played cards with the middle daughter . . . With half an ear he listened to his sister and Sarah discussing the suppression of women, while trying to seem attentive to Mrs Lowenstein who was relating their trip to Italy the previous year. He kept the smile fixed on his face.

'I am so happy that we've become friends,' were Sarah's words as they stood in their old hallway, ready to depart. And she kissed each of them on the cheek. They left, and his image of her, tall and exotic, haloed in the doorway, stayed with him.

In the carriage Leah consoled him, 'It's early days. It happens differently for everyone. For you love was instantaneous, but I certainly didn't love Claud directly. In fact I thought him rather frightful! I thought his outlook extreme and his morals shocking.

He has changed, and so have I. So you see, Sarah might *grow* to love you.'

'And how long must I wait while she makes up her mind and "grows"?' he asked angrily. 'Look – I've no wish to discuss it, Leah.'

'But you *asked* me to establish what she felt. And I was very careful not to reveal anything, I promise.'

'I *know* what she feels. I am already indispensable to her – as a friend.'

His sister sighed, and he glared at her, wanting her to suffer also.

They pulled up outside the Rectory, and Adam jumped out first, without waiting for Leah. At the front door he had a mental picture of himself standing there ten years previously, his heart thumping, his savings in his hand, that Sunday he first understood the meaning of 'conscience'.

'Leah, I'm sorry,' he whispered as she came to join him.

'What for?' she answered, shrugging.

It was still raining when they left the Rectory at past midnight, and a pair of owls hooted from nearby. Adam imitated their cries, and was rewarded by a prompt reply. He was replete with the Reverend Hibbert's port. They had parted emotionally, and the rector had hugged him.

'I read of your progress from time to time, and of your energetic campaigning on behalf of the poor. You have no notion of how proud it makes me. My sight is failing now, so my wife has been reading your *Farmer's Son* to me. I tell people I meet, "I know him. He grew up in my parish". And Adam – God bless you.'

He and Leah leaned sleepily towards each other in the wagonette, and in a drowsy voice she sang to him:

'John Anderson my jo, John, we clamb the hill thegither,
And mony a canty day, John, we've had wi' ane anither:
Now we maun totter down, John, but hand in hand we'll go,
And sleep thegither at the foot, John Anderson my jo.'

He said, 'That sounds nice . . . Robert Burns . . . You know – I should rather have her as a friend, than nothing. If it's a question of seeing her or not, then of course I shall have to content myself with merely being her friend. I value her too much to lose her . . . And you truly have not told her of my feelings?'

'Of course I wouldn't do that.'

'So if she doesn't know, I've lost nothing. And who knows – one day . . .' He let the sentence hang in the air, and dozed against her.

When they arrived back at Riverside House the front door was wide open, and a policeman hovered outside. In the hallway they could see another policeman, and several other people – all talking urgently. In the midst of them was a sobbing woman.

Filled with foreboding, Adam, followed by Leah, ran in.

'What's happened? What is it?'

'Adam dearest . . . Thank God you're back. There's been a terrible –' His aunt fell against him, breaking into sobs again. Beside her, Julia was red-eyed from earlier tears, but now calm, and from upstairs came other sounds of weeping.

Adam realized what had happened before Julia stated, 'Papa is dead. They found him an hour ago, drowned . . .'

'So you will stay another week . . .' the grain merchant had said, aiming his cue at the billiard ball. How innocuous the remark had seemed.

Appalled, Adam closed his eyes tightly. And it was up to him to make sure that nobody suspected the death was anything but an accident, least of all the widow.

He helped his aunt to the other room, and settled her in a large chair. She seemed diminished in stature, and sat huddled, shivering, her lips pale and shrivelled.

'He complained of a severe headache,' she said. 'He told me he was going out for some fresh air, and I tried to prevent him because of the rain. I thought he'd catch cold.' Her voice caught on a sob. 'If only he'd *listened*. He fell from the bridge . . .' She stared round vacantly. 'I cannot believe it.'

Julia, sitting at her side, gripped her hand, while her sister sniffled, coiled at her feet.

Adam, who knew so much they did not, imagined the inner torment of his uncle, the dreadful moment when he had made his irrevocable decision and literally sacrificed himself for his family. He recalled Sidney Carton's immortal lines in Dickens's *Tale of Two Cities*: 'It is a far, far better thing that I do, than I have ever done . . .' Then thought at once, 'But they wouldn't have *wished* it . . .'

Leah, looking in his direction, saw her brother shaking his head several times, and thought sadly, 'He'll take everything upon himself now.'

At the funeral he stood beside his aunt and supported her. Unlike the night of David Robinson's death, the weather was fine, so that after the service, in the small graveyard, the mourners shaded their eyes against the sun. Its pale brightness picked out the black garb of the widow in stark detail.

The Lowensteins were there – Mr and Mrs Lowenstein and Sarah. Adam noticed that the parents held hands, as though reassuring one another of their infallibility. He had seen them in church and been surprised – but then thought, 'Why should I be? Death is common to every religion, after all.'

They shook hands with him when it was all over, and Mr Lowenstein, a tall, intellectual-looking man, murmured, 'I hope to meet you again soon in happier circumstances.'

Sarah kissed his cheek again. A chaste, sisterly kiss, which he savoured, regardless.

Adam stayed on for more than a fortnight, and during it he found out the name of the family solicitor and met him several times to try to disentangle his uncle's finances, without raising the suspicions of his aunt. He contacted the Equitable Life Assurance Company, and had further meetings with one of their brokers – a dour man named Atkins – who insisted on visiting them in Henley, and interrogating Jennifer Robinson.

He kept saying, 'I am obliged to make these enquiries, you understand', and scratching the sparse grey hairs stretched carefully across the top of his speckled head. 'We are obliged to ascertain that death was not caused by suicide, for our policies rule out cover under such circumstances.'

'Suicide!' The new widow looked shaken. 'Why, my husband would never have considered such a thing. He was a happy family man.'

'Nevertheless, these possibilities have to be investigated. Did your husband have business problems?'

'We never discussed business. I have a poor head for such matters ... But I would have known. Oh yes, my husband would have confided such things to me. And if he'd had the worst business problems in the world, he would never have taken his life.' Her voice wavered, and she turned pleadingly to Adam.

He gave a barely perceptive nod, and addressed Atkins: 'I really think you have troubled Mrs Robinson enough. Can you not appreciate her distress?'

'Of course, I am only –'

'My husband had the most dreadful headache,' Jennifer Robinson interrupted, with new strength. 'I have told you that. Nothing else would have induced him to go out on such a night – oh such an awful night. I could see the pain in his eyes; why, his temples throbbed with it! The doctor now says he may have been suffering from a tumour.'

Eventually Atkins left, telling them he would let them know his decision within a week.

'Who is your doctor?' Adam asked his aunt.

'Henderson. He lives in Market Place. He is – was – a close friend of David's and mine.'

'I think I should meet him.'

He visited the physician that afternoon, a short, aquiline-featured man of about fifty, and they took an instant liking to one another. When Adam left, he was armed with a certificate stating that Doctor Henderson had been treating David Robinson for several weeks for severe headaches and spells of giddiness, and that a tumour was suspected.

Adam posted this certificate for the attention of Mr Atkins at Equitable Life, and at the end of a week heard the decision – that the widow, Mrs Robinson, was to be an immediate beneficiary from her husband's life insurance policy. This entitled her to a sum which would enable her to live securely for the rest of her years.

And meanwhile Leah had left a few days earlier, tearful and missing Claud. Sarah still visited regularly. She listened to reminiscences and looked at blurred photographs, never flinching from the conversation as so many people do when confronted by death and the bereaved. And if someone cried she didn't turn away in discomfort, but would hold a hand until the crying fit had passed. She was instinctive in her caring.

Alone with Adam, she talked easily and naturally, treating him sometimes to an impulsive hug. 'I feel I've known you for ever,' she said once.

'Maybe you have,' he answered.

They spoke of everything – poetry, which they quoted to each other; her liking for romantic novels, which he teased her about; other novels they had both enjoyed; they discussed music, religion, social injustices, his writing . . . She was the first woman he had met who wanted to know about him. And they could lapse into mutual silence without awkwardness; a companionable silence in which he was acutely aware of her. His love for her grew daily, and he knew it would remain for ever in him, an inseparable part of him.

It was a period of closeness and grief, interspersed by moments of personal happiness for Adam. But eventually, when a semblance of order had returned to the household, debts had been settled, servants taken aside and paid, and the business wound up, it was time for him to leave. Everything that needed to be done had been done, and his aunt could live her life with her illusions intact.

He said goodbye to them all, and his aunt – thinner, paler, greyer – held on to him and said, 'I cannot thank you enough, dearest boy. I think you have kept things from me. But perhaps it is best that way.'

She was beautiful in her sad composure, and he thought how changed her life would be now. Her relationship with her husband had been a commitment of love.

'I wish that one day I might have such a marriage as you and my uncle had,' he said.

'I wish it too, for you,' she replied.

He went to Brambleden Hall to make his farewells to the Lowensteins. Sarah came alone to the door to see him off. 'I shall come up in a couple of weeks' time. I haven't been to London for an age, and I'll not be able to survive for more than a fortnight without seeing my special friends. I feel quite, quite sad saying goodbye to you, you know, Adam.'

'I also.' He kissed her gently on her forehead, holding her narrow shoulders – his fingers pressing on the silk of her dress. He stood back and studied her – then tweaked her nose lightly and teased, 'No doubt you will go and immerse yourself in one of those awful books now.'

'No, I am not in the mood. Today is for walking. It is so beautiful. Or I might ride . . . Or write some poetry.'

'I should love to see your poems.'

'I should be embarrassed.'

'You always say that. And look how content you are now to let me hear you play the harp.'

'Yes, you are different from anyone I've ever met before. You make me feel capable of anything.'

'You *are* capable of anything.'

He was exhausted when he returned to Hampstead. The little tailor was away for a few days, and the place seemed empty and unhomely. Adam walked desultorily round his lodgings. His books lay untouched, messy and dusty on his desk. Everything felt strange. He decided to visit Alice at her house in Hill Street.

After barely greeting her, he roughly undressed her and thrust himself lovelessly into her without a thought for her pleasure or mood. Pinned beneath him, she lay like someone dead. Afterwards he was deeply ashamed, and, stammering, apologized.

For answer she slapped his face twice, and silently held up his clothes for him to dress. As he left she said, 'You are no better than any other man. You are worse, in fact, because you fool yourself you are better.'

He wrote in his diary that night, 'I must reassess my life and myself. There is truth in what she said.'

The following morning found him at his desk writing the third chapter of his novel in earnest. He had thought of a title. It would be called *The Struggle of Alicia Manson*.

Chapter Twelve

THWARTED

Adam was in a police cell the day Sarah arrived in London. He would have been further dismayed had he known that while he was being fed on dried bread and a cup of tasteless broth for his supper, his love was at that moment being introduced to his brother.

This time Adam had been detained for assaulting a policeman. He had stood outside No. 10 Downing Street, intending to see Mr Gladstone about his latest grievance – that despite the 1869 Irish Land Act whereby landlords must compensate tenants who had improved their farms, their repayments were raised so outrageously that they were obliged to leave anyway.

As an 'up-and-coming' author, Adam thought he had a better chance of obtaining an audience for his multitude of causes, and his confidence was boosted. He approached the formidable front door – and was stopped by the policeman on duty. He knew Adam of old, and would not allow him past.

'You again.'

'Yes. Me. I should like to see the Prime Minister. I have an appointment.'

The policeman looked sceptical and stood his ground. 'You're trying it on.'

'I assure you I am not.' He had in fact written, but hadn't received a reply.

'I'll check. You stay out here.'

Adam paced up and down under the hostile stare of a second policeman. The first reappeared a few moments later. 'No one knows anything about it. Like I said, you're trying it on. Skidaddle, or I'll give you one in the eye.'

'Don't you threaten me. I'm perfectly entitled –'

The policeman came at him, his fist raised in front of Adam's left eye, and Adam lashed out, aiming for the jaw. However, the other ducked, and the blow was only a glancing one on the chin.

'It was self-defence,' he shouted as he was marched, struggling, down the street, watched agog by passers-by. He couldn't tell them of the terror he had felt when he thought the policeman had been going to strike his one good eye.

The following afternoon he appeared before a stern-faced magistrate at Horseferry Road Magistrates' Court and, stammering, told his side of the story. The magistrate was unsympathetic. Adam was found guilty of assault, fined one guinea, and bound over to keep the peace. He felt shocked and humiliated that he should be standing there – he who was so unaggressive and opposed to violence.

Wearily, he left the building – to see Claud sitting on the low wall outside, gazing up into the sunlight, his lute resting on his lap. Adam's face broke into a smile, and he went to sit beside him. 'It's about time you assisted me on one of my missions.'

'Oh no – I told you. Those days are over. My God – but you stink to high heaven!' And he grinned like someone proud of his protégé. 'Word has it John Tenniel is depicting you in Saturday's *Punch*. Infamy if not fame is yours.'

'Perhaps it's preferable.' Adam got up. 'I can smell myself! I'm going to take myself off to the baths.'

'I'll come with you . . . I've some news.' He strummed a chord on his lute. 'Your lady-love is in town.'

Adam whirled round. 'Sarah? In London?'

'Leah told me this morning. Apparently Sarah dined last night *chez* Mama Gilmour. The latter was not amused.'

'What *are* you talking about?' Claud's jocularity was annoying him. He was tired, and impatient to see Sarah.

' "Lowenstein?" your mother asked. "That is a *foreign* name is it not?" Leah imitated her perfectly. She said that Sarah behaved impeccably.'

'She would do,' replied Adam. 'My mother is quite dreadful, and becomes worse as she grows older. Sometimes I think her mind quite twisted.'

'Anyhow – I've come to tell you we are all dining out this evening

– at the Cock Tavern. So it's not worth your returning to Hampstead.'

'They discourage women at the Cock Tavern.'

'Apparently that made lady-love all the more determined.'

'Will you stop calling her that.'

Claud accompanied Adam to the Chelsea baths. As they undressed, Claud said, 'My friend – go easy, eh?'

'What do you mean?'

'With Sarah.' Claud's face was concerned.

Adam clenched his teeth. 'Will you kindly let me direct my own life.'

'Very well . . . My God, but I envy you your lean belly.' He patted his own massive one which was liberally covered with golden hair. '. . . Adam, I think I should tell you, Jonathan is joining us tonight.'

'*Jon*athan? My brother Jonathan?'

Claud nodded. 'Leah said he invited himself.'

'Why?' Then he knew, and a sinking feeling took hold of him. Without another word he soaped himself quickly and got out of the pool.

The Cock Tavern, in Fleet Street, had once been the haunt of Pepys. Now it was renowned for its excellent chops and steaks, and for its reluctance to admit women. But when Sarah arrived on her own she was made much of.

'Sod it. No wonder you've lost your head. She is a stunner,' said Claud, watching her hand the waiter her cape.

'Enough of that. And I'll have you remember your philandering days are over, Claud.' He couldn't take his eyes from her as she approached their table, her head held erect, and the strength of his feelings shocked him.

Unusually, they had arrived early, and sat in one of the booths; the dining-room was divided by low partitions, like stalls in a stable block, and in each section was a rectangular table, simply laid with a white cloth and cruet set. Over the fireplace was a heavily carved mirror, while the floor was laid to boards. Around the walls were rails with hooks, and from these hung men's hats – and now Sarah's velvet cape.

He stood up to greet her, and kissed her in a brotherly way. 'It's good to see you,' he said, holding on to her wrists for a few seconds and feeling their smallness.

They sat down and settled themselves. Claud poured wine from the flask.

'I hear you spent the night in one of London's less prestigious boarding-houses,' Sarah said to Adam.

'Oh God – you know.'

'Of course I know, Adam! The whole of London knows. It was in this morning's *Telegraph*, for one thing. But Leah told me yesterday.'

'And while I dined at Her Majesty's expense last night, I gather you had the pleasure of dining with my mother.'

'Yes –' She hesitated, and gave a hurt little laugh. 'She didn't like me.'

'It's not *you*. It's *her*. My mother likes nobody,' she said vehemently, 'except for Jonathan.'

At the mention of Jonathan's name Sarah flushed. Her hand slid from under his, and her fingers picked at the tablecloth. Adam was suddenly cold; he drained his glass with a couple of gulps and refilled it. Claud watched him, frowning.

The dining-room filled, and arriving amongst a small crowd of people appeared Leah and Jonathan. Adam hadn't seen his brother for six weeks, and was struck anew by how handsome he was: the blond hair was offset by a faint tan – acquired from a week in Cannes, after Paris; his physique was muscular and athletic; and when he smiled there was a boyishness about him. He was smiling now, scanning the room for a particular person, and when he saw her, his smile broadened. He propelled Leah – who had copied her friend's hairstyle, so that it hung, thick, down her back – towards the table where the three sat.

Jonathan extended his hand. 'Hallo everyone . . . Do I detect prison pallor, Adam? . . . Miss Lowenstein – it is delightful to see you again.' And his gaze held hers.

She did not look away; neither, as she had done with Adam, did she tell him to use her first name. Instead she murmured something in return and became flustered. Adam watched them through narrowed eyes. He felt sick.

His brother was in sparkling form; Adam had never seen him like it – so genial, amusing and charming. He talked enthusiastically about his French trip, business affairs, an exhibition of Holman Hunt and Millais, and even managed to ask Adam and Claud about their respective books. He put his arm fondly around Leah from time to time and called her his 'little sister'. His performance was impeccable. And it was all for Sarah. She became more flushed and talkative, and soon it seemed that the pair spoke only amongst themselves. The others no longer existed; and he, Adam, was a spectator at the show.

He became increasingly withdrawn. He had not envisaged this – losing her so soon; and to his brother. Once Jonathan glanced at him – was there smugness in that glance? Under the table Leah's hand sought his. Her expression was compassionate, and it was more than he could stand.

'I'm sorry – I feel suddenly ill. Forgive me, will you . . .' Adam stumbled from the restaurant and inhaled the summer night air. He leaned against the wall, breathing deeply.

'Come with me, mister?' A girl of about fifteen sidled up to him, her eyes huge in a thin face; her breath smelt of sherbet.

He shook his head, and after fumbling in his pocket, gave her a florin. 'Now you go home to bed – on your own,' he mumbled, and hailed a passing cab. He took it all the way back to Hampstead, and later regretted his extravagance, just as he regretted his dramatic exit from the Cock Tavern.

The following afternoon when he was working – or at least trying to, for his mind was not on his novel – there came a knock on his door.

'Come in,' he called, thinking it would be Mr Levy.

And Sarah entered hesitantly, carrying a bunch of flowers. Adam jumped to his feet, knocking over his chair. 'What are you doing here? . . . But how lovely to see you . . . Oh sit down – anywhere you can find.'

He rushed about – first to her, then to plump up a cushion, next to gesture to a chair and sweep a pile of magazines from it. He was conscious of his dishevelled appearance, and of the untidiness of the room. His mouth tasted sour; when he'd returned home from the

Cock he had drunk an entire bottle of wine and fallen asleep in the armchair.

Sarah laughed gently. 'I didn't visit to throw you into confusion. I wanted to find out whether you were feeling better.' She held out the flowers. 'Now, if you stand still for more than half a second I can give these to you.'

He took them from her slowly and clicked his teeth. 'You shouldn't have. It was unnecessary.' He wanted to bring *her* flowers – bundles of them. He wanted to pamper her . . .

'Of course it was unnecessary – but I wished to.' She unpinned her hat and put it on his desk, on top of a book. He followed her movements; the graceful way she held her skirts to one side as she sat down.

He remained standing. 'I must put them in water. I have a jug somewhere.'

And while he hunted for it in his wardrobe, under a heap of other things, she looked round the room of the young bachelor writer, and saw it was just as she had expected it to be.

'So this is where it all happens,' she commented, when he returned from the wash-place, having filled the jug, and also the tea-kettle. 'This is where you invent your characters and manipulate them.'

'They manipulate me,' he said.

'Is that what happens?'

'More often than not.'

There was a short silence, then she said, 'I was worried about you last night. You didn't seem to be yourself.'

'I'm better now.' He was relaxed in his own environment, surrounded by his things. And when she was gone he would be able to picture her here, in his room. He watched her pour the tea. A stream of light caught the jug of flowers on the windowsill.

'It is such a pretty place,' she said. Then she told him she had been to Hampstead once before, to the fair – where a gypsy had said she would marry a farmer and live 'down west'.

And although she claimed to disbelieve such things, her scepticism was unconvincing.

He had grown a moustache, and she said, 'It really suits you – however, it doesn't disguise the fact that you're tired.'

'I am rather.'

'No doubt a police cell is not the most comfortable place.'

'They were intent on humiliating me this time . . .' And Adam related how the police had manhandled him into the cell, where he was the sole occupant. They had refused for hours to bring him a slop; refused his request for a mug of water, and deliberately given him a mattress that was split and lice-infested. For, to have 'assaulted' a policemen was unforgivable. Adam had traversed the border and entered different territory.

He explained his fear about his eye, and the events which had led to his arrest; how he had felt standing in the magistrates' court, charged with a violent crime . . . And she came to kneel by his side.

'Poor Addi – but it's finished with now.'

He started. 'What did you call me?'

'Addi. Do you mind?'

'No. It was just odd to hear it again after so long. I was called Addi all my childhood.'

'May I continue to use it?'

'If you like.'

Then she told him she was seeing Jonathan that evening; he was taking her to the theatre and for dinner afterwards.

'What are you going to see?' he heard himself ask politely.

'Molière's *Le Misanthrope* – translated, of course,' she replied.

Adam refrained from telling her his brother disliked the theatre; that he disliked anything profound. He listened to her chatter on about Jonathan, and the pain in him became like the blindness of his right eye: it became acceptable simply because it would not go away.

Before she left, she made him promise to get on with his writing. She called him Addi again, and kissed him goodbye. He heard her retreating footsteps down the stairs, and rushed to the window which overlooked the front of the house, from where he could watch her – tall, wearing pale yellow. A cab drew up, and she was gone.

'Silly man. Weak man,' he chided himself. He found her yellow hat on his desk, and setting it tenderly on the floor by his feet, he immersed himself in his writing.

*

Adam unfolded the July issue of the *Quarterly Review* and read his way steadily through the latest article by Arnold Chesterfield:

> It is disgraceful that this trouble-maker is repeatedly allowed to walk free from his 'skirmishes'. With a benevolent pat on the head, and a warning, this dangerous – yes, dangerous – young man is released from another night in another cell. He should be taught a lesson once and for all, that one cannot stir up discontent, or resort to violence to achieve one's aims. And what *are* his aims? He whinges interminably about what the country must do; when does he acknowledge what has been *done*?
>
> This time *Sir* Adam Gilmour has gone too far. He has shown himself to be an enemy of peace, law and order – as embodied by our excellent police – and is no better than that agitator, the shoemaker George Odger. He wastes everybody's time, and achieves nothing. He writes a frivolous, blasphemous novel – and expects praise for each move he makes. He should be taught a lesson. Next time, and be assured there will be a next time, he strays from his boundaries he should not be treated like an erring child, but as the threat to society that he is. I would recommend a six-month spell in prison for *Sir* Adam Gilmour. See if that does not quench his misguided enthusiasms.

He passed the magazine to Claud. It was a Saturday, and they were sitting in a quiet spot on Hampstead Heath, having stopped to buy the *Quarterly Review* on the way.

'He is certainly not enamoured,' Claud said, when he had read it.

'Would *you* say *The Farmer's Son* is frivolous?' Adam thought of the characters he had created and their interwoven lives and problems; of the village which had become so real to him. If the novel was frivolous, then *he* was frivolous.

'It's no more frivolous than it is blasphemous. The man is demented.'

But Adam was disturbed by Chesterfield's hostility to him, by the personal nature of his attacks.

Claud said, 'My friend, when you become a public figure, you become a candidate for abuse. Look at old John Ruskin. He's constantly in the midst of some controversy.'

Adam wasn't listening. 'Perhaps he's right. Perhaps I'm not achieving anything.' He leaned broodingly against a tree trunk.

'You know what I think?' Claud said, chewing on a blade of grass.

'What?'

'That you should stand back for a while. Stop all the protesting and – no, wait.' He held up his huge hand. 'You are the archetypal young agitator. Nobody takes you seriously; I think you should begin again, quietly. You've taken on too much, too quickly. It is not the poor you want on your side, but the rich.'

Adam felt the muscles of his jaw tighten. He had an absurd urge to cry. This was Claud speaking, whom he had met as the headstrong leader of a group of radicals. What had happened to all those people? Had they fallen by the wayside to become part of the bourgeoisie? Was there anything *wrong* with the bourgeoisie?

He thought of his trips to the East End, with food and clothing parcels for entire families; of his visits to factories to try to have employees reinstated, and conditions improved; the times he had, with a team of volunteers, helped clean the streets; or accompanied doctors he had persuaded to tour slum districts and offer medical advice. Did these efforts count for nothing?

Beside him, Claud shut his eyes, and his battered hat slid forward on to his nose, so that it appeared as though his beard was growing from it. The sight of him like that made Adam smile, and his anger dissipated.

'One day I'll run my own charity for underprivileged children. I'll take groups of them on trips, hear their laughter . . .'

Claud grunted and began to doze. The sun was sharp in Adam's eye. What had happened to make Claud a moderate? Was it Leah's influence? Adam could believe it. He would change every aspect of his life if it would please Sarah.

'. . . I used to think God spat on the earth, and everything grew out of His spit,' she had said once, giggling at her child's mind; and another time, in romantic mood, 'I'd like to live amongst fallen apples and herb bushes . . .' She told him of a widower she knew who had kept his wife's hair and pinned the tresses to a wigstand, combing them daily. And of the old woman who had had her dead Pekinese dog stuffed . . . He treasured all their conversations.

A while ago, he had told her he would be a brother to her, and she had said, 'There's no one I'd rather have as a brother.'

This was a true test of his character. He must wish for her happiness above his. And he felt virtuous.

Claud shouted, 'You cheated, you sod. That was a five and three. You just moved five and four.'

'I did not. Look –' Adam moved the pieces back into their last position. 'See?'

Defeated, Claud slumped in his chair. He was red-faced from a day in the sun, from too much wine, and from humiliation at losing two games of backgammon – and about to lose a third – to a newcomer like Adam. He muttered incoherently, hunched in a sulk. He would have sulked anyway. For Leah was at a sculpture exhibition that evening with Joshua, and had made it clear that he was not invited.

'I am invited as Joshua's guest. The guest of a guest cannot ask another guest,' she'd explained reasonably.

But he accused her of having an affair with Joshua, of being infatuated with him, of wanting to be with him in order to meet his 'fancy artist' friends. She had smiled at the other accusations, but this last made her livid. Never in her life had she been a person with ulterior motives, and she was both hurt and insulted. She raged back at him and stormed from his apartment. And now he was repentant, but would not see her until the following night. He knew his jealousy was at fault – but knew also that if she were his wife he would cease to be so insecure.

'Such a tiny mite to have me round her finger . . .' he mused, and his face softened at the thought of her.

He was with Adam sitting outside the Bull and Bush on this Monday evening, and three of his 'men' were still on the bar of the board, waiting to get back in. Adam had already started to take out, each of his men being safely covered. Then, as spaces became available, Claud moved two of his pieces in, and was beginning to feel hopeful that he would not be disgraced after all, when Adam threw a double six, and leaped up. The rickety table shook, and wine shot from the glasses.

'Backgammoned,' he yelled gleefully – so that everyone could hear, Claud thought resentfully. 'That makes three games to none.'

Claud glared into his glass – half the contents now being over the table. 'Well you know what they say: lucky in gambling – unlucky in love.' And was first mollified, and then full of contrition, at seeing the boyish pleasure go from his friend's eyes, and his face tumble.

He stayed with Adam that night, and was with him the following morning when he received his post. They were having coffee, and some cake which Mr Levy's cook had made over a week previously, which was now stale. Claud had been out to fetch the paper and was engrossed in it, when Adam exclaimed suddenly, 'I don't believe it.'

'What?' said Claud, glancing up. He had recovered his usual geniality – he would be seeing Leah later and would make everything well, and oughtn't he to be proud of Adam's prowess at backgammon, since it had been he who had taught him in the first place? In addition, he was about to start work on another commissioned biography: this time on Christopher Marlowe . . .

'Leslie Stephen has rejected the first half of *Alicia Manson*, on behalf of the *Cornhill*. I cannot believe it,' he said again.

'But *why*?'

'He says it is likely to upset public morals, and that sympathy towards a woman who leaves her husband would be limited . . . And just wait until you hear this: her ambitions are unfeminine, and her desire to be hurt could be construed as masochism – or worse, depravity!'

'The hypocrisy of it!' Claud said. 'It makes me want to retch.' And he made a gurgling noise in his throat.

Adam felt betrayed. He was astonished at Stephen's reaction. He wrapped his paisley robe tighter about him and, getting up, went over to the window to look out – towards the garden, where the grey pony had its head over the stable door as usual, and was munching hay; at the starlings and sparrows on the untidy lawn . . . and a cat on the fence watching for the right moment to pounce. Adam kept his back to Claud, so that the latter couldn't see his expression.

'He mitigates himself by saying that he recognizes the novel's merits and is judging it not by his own tastes, but his readers' . . . If that is the case, I can only say that the readers need educating. Well – tomorrow I shall visit Stephen at the *Cornhill* offices and, politely mind, tell him my views.'

The set of his shoulders was defiant, and Claud thought, 'At least he's angry, not unhappy. It is all part of the toughening-up process . . .'

But Stephen would not change his mind. He tried to dissuade Adam from continuing with the novel. 'Your reputation is just about to be made with *The Farmer's Son*. In another couple of months it will be out in book form. Your career is burgeoning. Why risk it?'

'I can't remain static. I must continually explore. If the public dislikes it, then it is too bad.'

'It is the wrong attitude.'

'I can't help it. I have to write from the heart, with honesty.'

'Mr Gilmour, it is not for you to shock your readers into submission. That, young man, is a sure passage to obscurity. Without the public you have no book. Remember that.'

From the *Cornhill* offices he went to those of *Macmillan's*, and there spoke to the editor, George Grove. He came directly to the point, and explained the reasons his novel had been rejected by the *Cornhill*. Grove was a music scholar, and a religious man; he was also a businessman, and he saw Adam Gilmour as a good commercial prospect, and if the *Cornhill* had rejected him, it was only advantageous to him.

'I shall consider it,' he said pleasantly enough. But the non-committal reply was enough to throw Adam into a turmoil of self-doubt which endured until he received Grove's letter of acceptance almost a month later.

He went back and forth to Macmillan's offices; to the Circle Club; to Geoffrey Gray-Courtney's offices – and met the illustrator of his book, a humorous middle-aged man with child-like eyes, by the name of Arthur Williams. Williams was, by coincidence, a friend of Edward Lear, and the pair spent a happy half-hour discussing their mutual friend, now living in San Remo.

Then, on October 3rd, *The Farmer's Son* was published. There it was on the shelves of shops, bound in maroon and green marbled card and embossed with gold – at one shilling and ninepence a copy. Within a week the printing was almost sold out, and there was a second – this time with a run of eight thousand. Adam did the rounds of bookshops, introduced himself to booksellers, signed copies – and made sure that *The Farmer's Son* was displayed to best advantage. Sales continued to flow, and Adam found himself a sought-after figure. He received invitations to dinners and soirées, exhibitions and the theatre. Women flirted with him, and men asked his opinions. The people he mixed with were intellectual, enlightened and free-thinking – with a tendency towards self-absorption and egotism. But he was too impressed by them to see their failings. He himself remained modest, treating his new glory with caution. He was aware only too well of the inconstancies of human nature. The reviews which were rapturous today could revile him tomorrow.

At the end of the month the first three chapters of his new novel were published in *Macmillan's Magazine*, taking the story up to the point where Alicia Manson begged her husband to hit her.

Adam waited – as did George Grove – for the cries of protest from outraged moralists; but instead, congratulatory letters arrived in the magazine's offices – to be forwarded to the author, amongst them letters from Swinburne, George Eliot, Bulwer-Lytton and George Meredith. Adam was euphoric. He even received letters, some amorous, from women who identified with the protagonist.

'I was right all along,' he thought. 'Sometimes one has to take risks in order to advance . . . I must trust my instincts.'

The lone voice to condemn him was Arnold Chesterfield's, and his notice in the *Quarterly Review* was typically spiteful. But Adam was in high spirits, and Chesterfield's antagonism was ceasing to bother him. He joked that the journalist had probably made an effigy of him and stuck pins into it twice daily; and he perfectly imitated the man's high-pitched voice and nervous hand movements.

He wondered how Stephen felt, knowing he had misjudged his readers and also lost an author; whether he regretted his decision; whether their working relations were destroyed, or could at any time be resumed. If Alice Mason read *Macmillan's* then her voice was silent.

But the book had yet to be finished, and he worked manically into the early hours, inspired to complete it by his success. *The Farmer's Son* was gone from his mind; it was as if he had never written it. It was like an affair which at the time seemed all important, and then years later one could not remember the woman's name. Alicia Manson took him over and developed, and he became fascinated by her, and strove to understand her better.

In January 1872, he presented the manuscript to Geoffrey Gray-Courtney, and a month later they exchanged contracts. This time he was paid an advance on royalties of seven hundred guineas, and the initial printing was eight thousand copies. He celebrated with Claud and Leah, Sarah and – inevitably – Jonathan.

For the last few months Adam had been following their progress with a detached and rather morbid curiosity; he noticed the changes for the better in his brother, and for the worse in Sarah; and he thought perhaps one day all these tangled lives could be incorporated into a novel.

Chapter Thirteen

THE BROTHER-IN-LAW

Jonathan Gilmour and Sarah Lowenstein were married on Tuesday, August 27th, 1872, at 11.30 a.m., in Henley-on-Thames town hall. The registrar who performed the ceremony was, in his normal day's work, a pig-farmer, and his fingernails were rimmed with black.

The assorted guests clustered in the characterless room – all family now, through this unusual union. Strangers thrust together with little in common except suspicion.

Adam was best man. He had been astounded when Jonathan had asked him, and his first thought was that his brother's cruel humour had prompted the suggestion; but he quickly realized it was simply that his brother liked to do the right thing. So he read up on his duties and prepared a speech, and as the day approached he thought that never in his life had he so dreaded anything.

He was not the only person dreading it. Lady Elizabeth could not recover from the shock that her son – her only son, as far as she was concerned – was marrying a Jewess. She had tried everything in her power to force him to change his mind; she had wept, lost her temper, drunk bottles of sherry, threatened suicide, threatened to evict him from the house – forgetting that he would be leaving anyway once he was married. Jonathan was firm. He was polite towards his mother but for the first time she saw through the veneer; how cold he was, how hard. When she accused him of these traits, he replied: 'We are two of a kind, Mama.'

Lady Elizabeth was devastated.

Adam said to Jonathan one evening, when they were alone in his mother's drawing-room, 'Well I admire your courage in the face of Mama's opposition. She wouldn't have cared if it were me. She hates me anyway. But you . . .'

Jonathan gave him that tolerant look which was specifically reserved for him. 'But I have always done exactly what I wanted and never anything else.'

'At least you are honest . . .' And then awkwardly: 'I hope you will be happy.'

'I'm certain of it,' his brother said confidently. 'She's a beautiful, splendid girl. And of course her father with his banking connections will be most useful to my career.'

Adam stepped back, stricken, and Jonathan laughed. 'My goodness, don't look so shocked. I only mentioned it by-the-by.'

But the idea was firmly fixed now in Adam's mind that his brother was marrying Sarah for ulterior reasons. 'You can't marry her if you don't love her.'

'Who said anything about not loving her?' asked Jonathan impatiently.

Adam felt ridiculous then, aware that all he had done was expose his own sentiments. 'I only meant that it is important to value her,' he said lamely.

Nobody would value her as he would, respect her as he would; nobody could know or understand her better than he. Such wasted knowledge.

Jonathan became exasperated. 'Really, Adam, you speak out of turn. I think you've said sufficient on the matter of *my* relationship.'

'Just one thing – what about her religion?'

'What about it? For God's sake, I'm marrying one woman, not her whole bloody tribe.'

Adam's worries kept him awake at night. He became hot and itchy; his head would ache. He would get up to have a drink of water or to write a sentence, and the candle beside his bed would be blown out and relit a dozen times. And what if he was wrong? When had he been an expert on women?

But he watched Sarah become quieter, more cautious in expressing her views. What did Jonathan care about her interests or innermost thoughts? What did he care about the 'I' that looked out from within her, and made her Sarah?

He thought of a verse from Swinburne's 'The Triumph of Time':

There will be no man do for your sake I think,
What I would have done for the least word said.
I had wrung life dry for your lips to drink,
Broken it up for your daily bread:
Body for body and blood for blood,
As the flow of the full sea risen to flood
That yearns and trembles before it sink,
I had given, and lain down for you, glad and dead.

He confided in Leah and found that she too was concerned. But she said, 'What can we do? She is a grown woman in love. She must discover for herself. And maybe we are being unjust and disloyal to our brother.'

So, that August 27th they gathered to watch Jonathan and Sarah become husband and wife, united by a pig-farmer with a soft country voice. Lady Elizabeth sobbed audibly throughout, supported on her left by Adam and on her right by Mr Lowenstein, who stared unblinkingly ahead. Mrs Lowenstein was tranquil; she was anxious about this match her daughter was making, but her view was the same as Leah's, and she stood serenely beside her other two daughters, her arm reaching around both. Beside the youngest was Aunt Mary; she had lost her hair overnight a few months previously, and now wore an ill-fitting wig which kept slipping beneath her hat. Every so often, when she thought no one was watching, she adjusted it quickly, and scratched her burning ears beneath.

Adam went up to hand Jonathan the ring. He could scarcely bear to look at Sarah – fragile and unearthly in white organdie and silk. Her exquisiteness hurt him; her happiness hurt him because he was convinced it would be short-lived.

'I now proclaim you man and wife . . .'

That was it then. And his hands were clenched so tightly that his nails left deep pink indentations in his palms. Beside him Lady Elizabeth swayed.

The reception was held at Brambleden Hall – which Lady Elizabeth thought tactless – and she had to force herself to go through the familiar front door and into the house where she had played hostess for twenty or more years. She blamed her ruination on her husband. And yet – wasn't that their little kitchenmaid hovering in the hallway, elevated to the position of upper housemaid? And the butler – what was his name? Was that not he? A tear crept to the corner of her eye, and her hand shook as she took two glasses of sherry from the tray proffered by a footman. 'One is for my sister,' she lied – and then immediately drank both when he had moved on. Such tiny glasses anyway . . .

The two hundred guests gathered on the terrace and in the garden, the men wearing top hats and frock coats, except for a few estate managers who wore their best loose-fitting jackets and bowlers and remained shyly together. Women trailed about in delicate muslins and pastel silks, twirling parasols and scanning the heads to see who was who. Many of the guests were dark and obviously Jewish – as Lady Elizabeth observed disdainfully to her sister. Mr Lowenstein passed at the moment she made her comment, and she blushed and smiled ingratiatingly. She saw her daughter laughing with that dreadful man whom she had hired to teach her French. Her fiancé apparently. And her elder son, whom she had to admit had achieved considerable success, but was still no better endeared to her, relating some anecdote to them. It would serve them right if she were to suffer a heart attack and die on the spot. That would destroy their day . . . She saw her sister-in-law Jennifer Robinson in the distance, waving at her, and she turned her back. After all, it was she who had introduced a Jewess to the Gilmours in the first place.

'Lady Gilmour, you must come and meet my sister – after all, we are one family now.' Mrs Lowenstein took her gently by the arm.

One family . . . one family. Humiliated, weeping within her, the thin, embittered woman allowed herself to be led across the lawn – where once she had played croquet – to meet her new family.

Adam and Leah watched her. 'Poor Mama,' Leah said. 'It is just too much for her.'

'You are too generous-hearted, my littlest mouse,' Claud told her. He looked magnificent in his silver-grey suit, and attracted many glances. 'She is only suffering because she wishes to. Here she is, being offered friendship by charming, cultured people, and yet she thinks herself too superior to accept their offer. And there is nothing to stop her coming to live in Henley again, if she misses it. Property is cheaper than in London . . . No. Her suffering is of her own making, and she wallows in it. She deserves no pity.'

'All suffering deserves pity,' Adam said, 'however self-inflicted. And you see, the trouble is she would not see that she has imposed it upon herself. She would say that her behaviour has always been beyond reproach, and everyone else is to blame for her misery.'

'And what of the bridal pair?' Claud said, emphasizing the last two words with faint derision. 'Let us hope there will be no misery there.'

'Let us hope,' Adam echoed him, feeling he would have liked to add an 'amen'.

The guests began to mingle, the little orchestra – grouped just beside the rockery – struck up, and the buffet lunch – displayed on long trestle tables outside – was served. Sarah flitted from person to person, and was joined by Jonathan who put his arm round her possessively. Who knew the mechanisms of his mind? Adam wondered, watching as his brother shook hands or smiled or stooped to hear better what someone said. He tried to imagine himself in the same position. In his imagination Sarah was his bride and he was Jonathan . . . But he would be too ecstatic to be composed or suave; he would be almost insane with happiness.

. . . And instead, as best man, he had to wish that ecstasy upon his brother. The prospect of his speech terrified him, and during luncheon, seated between Jennifer Robinson and Leah, he was silent as he mentally rehearsed it yet again. Belatedly he realized there were far too many superlatives about Sarah, and too few about his brother . . .

Mr Lowenstein spoke first – unashamedly emotional as he praised his daughter. He said little about his new son-in-law, except that he trusted his daughter's judgement, and whomever she loved – he would try to love also.

'Huh! We shall see about that,' Adam whispered to Leah.

'Ssh!' she said, nudging.

He went up to take Mr Lowenstein's place, exchanged smiles with him – and was stunned when the man whispered in his ear, 'I wish it were you.'

'I must have misheard him,' Adam thought as he shuffled his

pages together and cleared his throat. 'It is surely what I *wished* to hear.'

He commenced. 'Ladies and G-gen-gentlemen –' He forced the word out, and felt everyone's eyes upon him in sympathy. 'As you s-see, my brother is fortunate to be blessed with good looks. He also happens to be clever. But the cleverest thing he has yet done has been to m-m-marry this wonderful young woman who sits at his side now as his wife . . .' And as he paused, turning to Sarah with adoration in his expression, there was a startled silence. Then someone said, 'Hear, hear,' and others took up the refrain, and the awkward moment passed . . .

He took his seat once more, heard the beginning of Jonathan's speech – 'I cannot hope to emulate an author's eloquence, but what I can do is speak from the heart . . .' – and poured himself several successive glasses of wine.

When the reception was over, Adam, Lady Elizabeth, Leah and Claud returned to the Red Lion Hotel where they were staying. Lady Elizabeth went to the room she was sharing with Leah, suffering from one of her headaches, and immediately lost herself in a bottle of sherry; her daughter went directly to Claud's room, where she lost herself in another kind of pleasure; and her son went to his room and wrote in his diary:

' "Thou shalt not covet thy neighbour's wife." So God said to Moses. Sarah believes in God. I believe in Sarah. And I covet not my neighbour's wife, but my *brother's*.

'Well, now they are married and my grand statements about being a brother to her are ironically true. I fear I shall not be able to live up to my word.'

He left the hotel – passing Claud's room from which he heard the sound of bedsprings – and went out into Hart Street. The early evening had clouded over, and a thick pale haze blurred into the river without definition. Adam crossed the bridge to the Little Angel at Remenham, and thought of his uncle. 'Whatever happened, I'd not do what he did. There's surely some purpose to life . . .'

The Little Angel was intimate and beamed, and he was immediately enveloped in its atmosphere. He ordered a jug of wine and sat on a stool at the bar, beside a bald man whose large head slumped over the tumbler of whisky clasped in his hands. He looked up at Adam blearily.

'Come and join the ranks of the disillusioned,' he said, with a humourless laugh; and was about to sink his chin once more when he raised it abruptly and his eyes narrowed. 'I know you. You're Adam Gilmour.'

And at the same moment Adam recognized him as an old school colleague. 'John Clark!'

'Lost a bit of hair, I'm afraid,' John Clark said ruefully, running his hands over his naked scalp. 'One of those unfair things. Why I chose my profession – wear a wig in court. Wish I could wear one in bed. Bloody bed. Bloody sexual organs. Cause of all life's problems.'

Adam chortled. John Clark was one of the few pupils he had liked at Wrokfield College, and he smiled delightedly at the insignificant-looking, half-drunk man. 'You're a barrister, I take it. What do you specialize in?'

'Whatever I can get, old chap. Criminal mostly. Libel. That sort of shit.' He burped. 'Sorry, old chap. Not quite myself. I had a really good woman, and who went and wrecked it?' He smacked his own hand, and the glass wobbled, shooting whisky into the air. 'Mind you – she should have understood. Women should understand these things.' He gave another burp. 'I'm going to order another drink.'

'Have some of my wine.'

'Oh well, if you insist . . . I read about you the other day, in fact I always seem to be reading about you. Can't profess to have read your books, though. Don't read many novels. Are you offended?'

'No, of course not.'

'Lost your stammer as well as your eye, I see.'

'Ha-ha!'

'Sorry old chap . . . Not quite myself, eh?'

'No offence taken.' Adam leaned his elbows on the bar.

'I'm an outdoor man myself, really. No time for books – except legal stuff. Bloody good barrister, though I say it myself.' He began to pick at one of his stained teeth. 'I say, do you happen to have a toothpick?'

Adam fished a small silver one from his pocket. It was attached to a chain with various other trinkets which he loved to collect.

Frowning, he watched as John prodded round his mouth with the treasured toothpick.

'Still as intense as ever, aren't you? You had a great sense of humour, though. Remember that – oh, and those brilliant cartoons!' He finished with Adam's toothpick, and absently put the entire chain in his pocket.

'Hey, John, that's mine!'

'What is? Oh, sorry old chap . . . Not quite myself. Not a thief, you know. Prosecute a few of those from time to time. No – feeling a bit low, to tell the truth. Here for the weekend and it's all rebounded on me.'

He told Adam the saga of his complex relationship with a woman who was leaving her husband for him – in between wine and more whisky, while Adam filled and refilled his own glass from the dwindling bottle. After a couple of hours the pair swore undying friendship, and they sang lustily as they stumbled from the Little Angel, and shouted obscene words at the tops of their voices, giggling helplessly.

Then, without warning, Adam was sick. He stood in the centre of the bridge, where his uncle had taken his fatal leap, and vomited over the side.

'I don't feel too good,' he kept repeating, in between attacks, and gripped by waves of pain.

And the other, rocking on his feet, held his nose and said, 'Sorry, old chap, don't know what to do. Don't fall in, will you?'

Eventually, when the worst was over, they parted company.

'Where do you live?' Adam called out.

'Bloomsbury,' the other shouted back. 'Doesn't everyone? Most intellectual whores in London, in Bloomsbury.' He gave a hoot, and disappeared into the night.

Adam ran his tongue round his foul-tasting mouth and held his arm to his tender stomach. The bridge spun. The water beneath it spun. He saw David Robinson. And he made his way carefully back to the Red Lion, and to his room, where he lay rotating like a leg of mutton on the spit.

Jonathan and Sarah spent a month travelling in France and Italy, and returned at the end of September to live in their new home on the Embankment, towards Westminster Bridge. This house – a narrow, three-storey, white-painted building – was their first experience of having to compromise and had caused them much friction. As was traditional in affluent Jewish families, it was paid for by the bride's father, and whilst on the one hand this was welcomed by Jonathan, on the other it meant he could not have exactly what he wanted without sounding ungrateful. What he would have liked was to have lived in the City in something grander – where he could have walked to work; but Sarah had wanted to be in Chelsea or St John's Wood, and to have a garden. They viewed property after property, becoming increasingly despondent and disenchanted with one another – accusing each other of selfishness, which in both cases was true. Then Mr Lowenstein heard of the house on the Embankment – and with the purchase their earlier passion was rekindled.

For the first months of her marriage Sarah was immersed in the pleasurable task of decorating the house to her taste, and this took her into December, which itself was a busy month with her first Christmas in her new home. Unlike more religious Jewish families who celebrated Chanukah instead, the Lowensteins had always thrown themselves into the Christmas festivities with gusto. For them it was an excuse to be extravagant and lavish, and it was incidental that December 25th commemorated Christ's birth. But they were criticized by many of their friends.

Sarah festooned the rooms with entwined holly, mistletoe and red ribbons. She hung up the Christmas cards, brought back pine-cones and ferns from Brambleden which she arranged with beech leaves and branches . . . She filled bowls with dried figs and sugared almonds, raisins and Turkish delight; and did not once touch her harp – transferred from Brambleden Hall to their own drawing-room – or write a line of poetry. She was indulging her 'nesting instincts', she told Leah; but in reality she was enjoying the novelty of being a wife. All her previous ideals and opinions were forgotten in the excitement of choosing fabrics for curtains, and choosing food for meals which she discussed with the cook. And when her husband returned at between half-past five and seven o'clock, Monday to Friday, she made sure she was always freshly groomed and wearing a dress which pleased him – for she was so lost in her passion for him that her own tastes and pursuits ceased to matter. He was of prime importance, and her happiness revolved around him. She was proud of herself; at nearly twenty-four she felt a mature, wise woman. And had her old self met her new self at some social occasion, she would have spared her no time, and made her excuses in order to speak with someone more stimulating.

Her husband was delighted with his choice of wife, and was the envy of his colleagues – he had few friends. He grew stouter and developed that complacent look of a contentedly married man. He treated his wife exemplarily, remembering to bring her flowers once a week, to take her to the theatre once a fortnight, and to kiss her on the cheek, whatever his mood, when he returned from work. She was free to go to Brambleden whenever she wished, to see whom she pleased, and to do whatever she wished during the day. He asked only for a peaceful life.

But February came – bitterly cold and endlessly raining, and water leaked through the roof into the hallway, destroying the new decorations. Jonathan remarked he had never liked the wallpaper she had chosen, and they quarrelled . . .

Sarah discovered a harshness in her husband she had not suspected, and which frightened her. Within a couple of days the quarrel was repaired and another wallpaper selected, but she was conscious of trembling as she showed him samples, of perspiring under her arms as she waited for him to come to the sample she wanted – longing to cry out, 'That is the one I want . . .' And the deflation when he passed it – that pretty light design – and chose instead the sort of gloomy one his mother might have picked.

She thought perhaps the ensuing effect could be lightened with a mirror, and spent an entire day, perfectionist that she was, hunting for a suitable one. Eventually, in an antique shop, she found a large Regency gilt-framed mirror that was perfect, and she bargained with the man to reduce the price.

'Proper little Jew, aren't you, Mrs Gilmour?' he said laughing, as they finally came to an agreement, and she gasped, shocked. She was about to tell him that her name had once been Lowenstein and she wished to cancel the deal, when she thought better of it. 'I want the wretched mirror, that's the trouble.'

But the day was destroyed, and throughout the cab journey home, the mirror padded and wrapped beside her, she berated herself for her cowardice. 'I could have at least said *something*. I could have still bought it, but said – with dignity of course – "I happen to be Jewish, you know." Even as I left the shop I could have said it . . .'

She looked intermittently at the large package and knew that under the circumstances she would never be happy with it.

But this didn't excuse Jonathan for disliking it; he was not aware of the story attached to its purchase.

'It is the wrong shape. And it is common to have a mirror in a hallway.'

'It is *not* common . . .' They quarrelled again, and this second quarrel was far worse than the first, because there were more dissatisfactions to air, more petty resentments, more differences – and more familiarity.

She cried in bed. Jonathan hated tears. He was glad in a way that she cried, because it was a demonstration of her contrition; that once more he had the upper hand. But once this was established, he wished she would stop. The sound grated on him; her unhappiness grated on him . . . He would go away at the weekend, hire a horse, go hunting – it had been ages since he had been, and he needed to vent a certain restless, brutal energy that had been pent up in him this last month.

She lay beside him with a misery greater than the quarrel merited, and after he had reached out to caress her fleetingly before sexually fulfilling himself, her misery was greater still. She could not say precisely what it was.

To compensate for her growing fears, she threw herself even more wholeheartedly into her marriage. She would not admit to herself that anything was amiss; yet something was gone – from within their relationship, within her husband, and within herself, and she further subjugated herself in an effort to restore whatever it was that was lost.

And there was another problem too shameful to admit to – which concerned her own sexuality. She was, she had discovered, a passionate woman, and she needed satisfaction for herself, without knowing its full meaning. The act between her husband and herself left her throbbing between her legs and with a resentment she couldn't comprehend.

In early spring Sarah became pregnant and miscarried, and a faint line appeared, which ran from her left nostril to the corner of her mouth. She saw it in the mirror and thought with terror, 'I'll be old and nothing will have happened in my life . . .'

An image flashed before her of Adam's face – his unmatched eyes, one serious and beautiful as a girl's, the other vacant of expression and partially hidden by his hair. He was smiling – his tender, teasing smile. She heard his voice – he had a particularly deep and soothing voice – saying, 'You *are* capable of anything.'

'I haven't seen him for so long . . .' She tried to recapture the image as it faded. 'Why doesn't he visit?'

Adam's second novel, published again by Gray-Courtney, was selling as well as the first, and he moved now in exalted circles. He had become friendly with Algernon Charles Swinburne – who at thirty-seven, and with a reputation for paganism, alcoholism and sexual perversion, was not perhaps the best companion he could have chosen. Swinburne showed Adam the darker side of life. They visited various haunts and shows in seedy side-streets, where scraps of humanity slept like animals in doorways or beneath benches. They were accosted a dozen times in as many yards, and rich men with cigars leaned out of monogrammed carriages to take their pick. Once they went to the notorious Cider Cellars in Leicester Square, where sex-scenes were enacted, and virtually nude girls posed, another time to the Argyle Rooms in Great Windmill Street . . .

Adam went to these places out of curiosity, because of his appetite for experience in whatever sphere. These more sordid aspects of life existed, and therefore it was right he should know about them. For his part, Swinburne was delighted to accompany him wherever he wished to go.

In a particularly vicious attack by Arnold Chesterfield, they were nicknamed the Perverted Pair, and Adam, who had never indulged in any kind of perversion, was livid.

'This time I've had enough,' he said furiously to Swinburne, when the latter showed him the article. They were having morning coffee at Mrs Elton's tiny coffee shop in Chenies Street, just round the corner from Swinburne's North Crescent home.

'My dear fellow,' the poet said in his Eton drawl. 'I think it most amusing. And it is all publicity – which is never bad.'

'It's nothing short of libel. I don't know how you can be so complacent.'

His companion laughed. 'The whisky helps.' He poured some more from the bottle into his coffee. The high roundness of his forehead with its receding hairline, the bony nose, were exaggerated as he bent forward.

'I wish I didn't care what people thought of me,' Adam said. 'I have this inherent need to be liked, to be popular.'

'I don't care what people think,' the other said. 'I care about my poetry. Their opinions matter to me, then. But not on a personal level. If you are an original thinker, then you cannot possibly be acclaimed by everyone.'

Like Adam, Swinburne was from an aristocratic family and was radical in his outlook. His passion for those 'dead languages' that Adam had so loathed at school led him to Balliol College, Oxford – from which he emerged a genius, but with the disgrace of no degree. Friend to Dante Gabriel Rossetti and his clan, and also of George Meredith, he fell into an unconventional way of life, and was either liked or despised, admired for his brilliance or hated for his decadence and preoccupation with sin and death. He was a paradox of a man whose deep eyes revealed nothing, but seemed only assessing.

He said, 'I've been accused by many – even my friends – of writing thoughtless poetry. What do you think?'

'That's not a fair question,' Adam answered. 'Besides – I am not a poet. Claud would be a better judge.'

'But I want you to tell me,' said Swinburne aggressively.

Adam reflected a moment. 'Maybe they are too literary, and therefore to some might appear effortless and cold. And there again, their allegorical references might not be understood by everyone.'

'I am not trying to appeal to *everyone*, and I cannot agree that my poetry is cold. I consider it romantic and symbolic. So much the better if it forces people to use their minds when they read it. Take

"Laus Veneris" for example. Surely it cannot be called "thoughtless":

> "Would God my blood were dew to feed the grass,
> Mine ears made deaf and mine eyes blind as glass,
> My body broken as a turning wheel,
> And my mouth stricken ere it saith Alas." '

'You have omitted to recite the other hundred and five verses,' Adam teased.

Swinburne looked impressed. 'You've counted! Well, at least it shows you've read it.'

'It's one of my favourite poems.'

Swinburne looked cheered and they fell silent. Adam thought how similar all writers were – himself included – with their inability to accept criticism.

'As for Chesterfield,' Swinburne said after a moment, 'pity him. He is only bitter that he has not discovered the joys of Venus for himself. Have you ever seen his wife? Truly the gods bestowed on her a hideousness beyond compare.' He laughed loudly and his complexion grew mottled from the wine.

By early afternoon he was drunk, and Adam walked with him to North Crescent and then made the journey back to Hampstead. But not directly home. Instead he had a late lunch in the Flask Tavern, and sat in a dark corner making intermittent notes in the small book he always had with him. He observed the other customers, their expressions and gestures, eavesdropped on snippets of conversation, noted mannerisms and the way a man's clothes hung on him. He watched how the young serving girl responded to men's advances, and jotted down their lewd remarks . . . These observations were for his third novel, which he was about a quarter of the way through. *The Man in the Tunnel*, he had provisionally entitled it; and he was relieved to be writing once more, after a long fallow period when he had not had an idea in his head, and it had seemed to him that his mind was composed of molasses.

After the wedding he had stayed in most nights, refusing invitations, reading or sketching to pass the time, bickering with Claud over a game of backgammon, having supper with Mr Levy. He had decided he would become celibate. He reached this decision seriously, and, as he saw it, logically. But for all his assurances that he would be a 'brother' to Sarah, he could not visit her. And from time to time, when necessarily their paths crossed, he was constrained with her. It hurt him, also, to see the changes in her – her lack of individual thought or conversation, the way she glanced constantly at her husband as though seeking his approval. A sadness in her eyes.

He became irritable and brooding, liable to become annoyed by the least thing, so that his mood would be affected for the rest of the day. He read of an earthquake which killed thousands, reported on the same page as man-induced wars, and was sickened; went to a restaurant with friends for the first time in weeks – and became infuriated by the meaningless act of social kissing between women. He was impatient with his sister – blaming her for making Claud wait for so long before she would marry him.

'It is *my* choice, Adam,' she had said, hurt. 'It is *my* life.'

'It is also *his* choice and *his* life.'

He hated his own inertia and was frightened by it; and he fought against his sexual urges when he lay in bed, helplessly erect.

And then one day, for no reason – he thought perhaps he had had a pleasant dream, but could not recall it – he awoke feeling better. That evening he went with Claud and Leah to see a performance of *Hamlet*, and afterwards went backstage to meet the actress who had played Ophelia. He took her to a new restaurant owned by a hugely fat Frenchman and had, for the first time, Pâté de Grenouilles.

'Is it an aphrodisiac, do you think?' she asked, wide-eyed.

'I don't know – shall we see?' he answered, staring back at her.

He went with her to her lodgings – a shabby room in Soho – and stayed with her for a week, until she went on tour. She was an actress who soon faded into obscurity, and years later he couldn't remember her name, or find any note of it in his diary. But the affair, passionate and short-lived, was what he needed, and he was hauled from his lethargy and despondency. He decided he was not meant to be celibate. And for whose sake, anyway?

The idea for his third novel came on the train journey to Henley to visit his aunt. They came to a tunnel, and as the train was plunged into darkness, and the rhythmical sounds of its passage resounded with a deeper echo, his imagination was fired, and he pictured a man waiting at the end of the tunnel, unable to make his legs move.

'The man could be lying in bed,' he thought suddenly, as the train surfaced into brightness again and all was friendly once more. He delved in his pocket for his notepad, and began scribbling:

> A man falls from his bed into a pit. There is a rail track, and a tunnel ahead. He could perhaps be dreaming, or there again perhaps he is not . . . Unimportant. Have various stopping-points in the tunnel, and at each an incident from his past. He will have been a violent criminal, a blackmailer, an unfaithful husband, etc. . . . And at intervals there will be his parents and himself as an unhappy child. In between each 'incident' he hears a train approaching, and mumbles, 'I have to escape. There's a train coming.' The last incident will be one that has not yet happened – where his victims have their revenge on him, and attack him. He hears the train, and sees himself as a child beckoning him to return to bed, his parents standing like sentries either side. But he cannot move . . .

He stopped writing. 'God, it's an original idea. Too original? Gray-Courtney will take it, I think, but not George Grove. Maybe this time Stephen would be interested . . . I'll write a résumé and a chapter, and see what he thinks.'

Stephen would not take it. 'It has no appeal. It is not topical, and readers certainly won't be able to identify. It is simply too – too – bizarre,' he said finally. 'If you would do another novel like your first – or even your second –' he conceded sheepishly, 'I would take it directly. But this is just too experimental. The public are not ready for it. It is, as the French say, *avant-garde*.'

Gray-Courtney immediately accepted it, and agreed to publish it without previous serialization.

'It's exciting,' he said. 'A combination of reality and the abstract. And of course deeply psychological. Most interesting. But don't expect it to be a big seller. No –' and he gave one of his jaw-jerks, and banged his hands together, '– I think we shall treat this differently; sell it as a limited edition of fifteen hundred, with a leather binding. If it goes well, then we'll bring it out in ordinary form . . . But meanwhile, Mr Gilmour, keep Stephen on your side. Write an article or two for the *Cornhill*. He is a useful man.' And he looked shrewdly at Adam, who nodded in assent.

Preoccupied with this third novel, with his social life re-established, and women to take to bed, Adam existed within a spurious and fragile contentment. Spring and then summer came . . .

Saturday, August 10th, 1873

'This afternoon I went to the fair with Leah, and the little fair-ground, nestling at the foot of hills, was vibrant with colour and shouting, tents crammed beside one another, hurdy-gurdies and stalls . . . We jostled with the crowds, and went from one place to another. There were fairlings for sale or to win; ice-cream sellers; coconut-shies; a trained chimp; chickens flapping loose and rabbits escaped from cages; tethered goats and piebald ponies . . . Barrel organs vied with a brass band and the sun streamed down. Punch thwacked poor Judy, and there was the odd fight between youths.

' "Stay with me," I told my sister. "For God's sake, stay close." And I made certain her arm was tightly linked in mine.

'I watched her whirling on a horse, while behind her I sat on a gaudy rooster, as the merry-go-round span faster and faster; and her face, her mouth – wide in laughter and shrieking – was a blur, as she turned to look at me.

'We dismounted, wobbly on our feet and still laughing, caught up in the vividness of it all, inhaling the smells of the fairground – onions and ices, machinery and animals.

'Leah spotted the gypsy tent. "She tells fortunes," she exclaimed, and insisted on going inside.

'When Leah reappeared, she was bubbling with excitement. "I don't know how she does it," she said. "She got almost everything right."

' "Quick analyses and an ability to surmise," I replied.

'But she would have none of it, and pushed me forward. "You go in, and then we'll compare notes."

'I protested, but was, of course, curious what, for a shilling, I could learn of my future – or indeed my past. So, I found myself in a gypsy's tent, in another world, from which even the sounds directly outside seemed remote. The daylight filtering in was scant, and the old hag turned as I entered; her eyes were opaque.

'"You're a tall gentleman," she said directly, in a coarse voice. "Sit down." And she pointed with a turgid finger, rings embedded in it, to the chair facing her. "Give me your hands," she commanded – and felt them all over with a swift and thorough touch. "Now your face." She repeated the procedure until she was satisfied, the strong garlic on her breath making me feel quite sick.

'I felt a strange and thrilling sense of the unknown being cooped up in there with her, curiously trusting; then she told me to say a few words, and I said the first thing I could think of – God knows why: "I had a dog once, but it died." I felt a fool afterwards.

'But the old woman was unmoved. It was her turn to speak, and this is what she said, as near as I can remember:

'"You are in your middle twenties. An artist of some kind . . . No, something with words. There are words all around you . . . You worry a lot, don't you? About everything. You take it all to heart. You're not married, are you? But there's a woman. She's strong in your heart. There's a shadow across her – she's not yours to love is she? You've a sister, or a brother, or maybe both, I can't tell. And colour all about you. I know colours – I've only been blind these last ten years; there's mixed colours around you, some good, some bad . . . I see some illness along the way. And travel. Hills. I see countryside, proper countryside – water, I think. You'll marry. I think you'll have a son, just one child. There are things I don't understand – to do with your work. More colours. Rich colours. Yours is a life with changes in it. You're not settled, are you? Don't know what you want . . . The woman you marry – she'll be dark-haired. But there's someone before her – I can't see her. She's not really important . . . Come forward, dearie, let me feel your face again . . ." I smelled her breath once more as she leaned towards me and touched my eyelids.

'"Why – your right eye is as blind as both of mine," she said.

'I gave her a florin, and escaped into the daylight again, quite shaken. When Leah compared notes, it transpired the old woman had been as uncannily accurate with her as she had with me, and I must say the experience has quite stirred me. I realize how limited Knowledge is, and how infinite what lies beyond it.

'And what of the gypsy who forecast Sarah's future at Hampstead fair? Was she the same woman? When – when? – *when* I see Sarah, I must ask if she was blind. As, for sure, Sarah is not married to a farmer, and living down west . . .'

Chapter Fourteen

BROWNSTONES

Leah's first exhibition chanced to coincide with Sarah and Jonathan's first anniversary, and the evening beforehand they quarrelled. Sarah wanted to join the small party at a restaurant after the exhibition, while Jonathan wanted to go to dinner with another couple, an influential businessman and his wife.

'Your sister is more important than a pair of strangers,' she protested.

'Now look, old thing –' he had taken to calling her this, and she detested it, '– be reasonable. We can make it up to Leah another time. There will be a dozen of them – why should they miss us? But this meeting could be really significant for me.'

'But this man – whoever he is – could also make it another time.'

'He is going to Italy for a fortnight. It's a case of getting in there at the opportune moment. Striking while the iron's hot, so to speak.'

She thought, 'Why must he always resort to clichés?' Out loud, she said, 'I believe family should come before a *possible* client.' She emphasized the word 'possible', her voice brittle. She had been looking forward to the event, to mixing with stimulating people again; to an entire evening with Leah. And Adam.

'Well it is arranged now,' Jonathan said conclusively.

Sarah sucked her finger hard and bit on it. Her anger remained frozen inside her, and, after giving her husband a hard stare she went from the room without another word.

Later, in bed, his feet edged towards her; she knew the signs. She was still tense, her mind distracted, and she felt distant from him. Her body did not feel inclined to give itself in love.

Yet – 'Do you love me?' she asked, her voice childlike and small in the darkness.

'What a question,' he replied, his voice sounding irritable, and his feet stopping in their tracks. 'I'm your husband, aren't I?'

When she said nothing in return, he obviously felt remiss. His hand stretched out to stroke her shoulder. 'Come on, old thing –' she gritted her teeth, '– what's wrong, heh?'

'I asked you a question,' she answered flatly; although she herself could not have answered that same question had it been put to her.

'Oh for goodness' sake.' He rolled back to his side of the bed once more, with an exaggerated sigh. And she panicked that she had provoked him too far; that perhaps she was to blame. She felt alone and neglected.

'Jonathan? Well, do you? Love me, I mean.'

And in a weary voice he said, 'Oh, of course I do.' But from his intonation she knew he had only said it to have some peace.

She drifted into sleep – and was awakened by his hand on her buttock.

'Sarah? Heh, old thing. I do love you.'

She clung to him in relief, tears flowing from her eyes . . . But: 'What's wrong?' he asked. And her relief changed; she was instantly chilled at his lack of sensitivity.

'Christ, Sarah – I tell you I love you. What more do you want?'

'Nothing,' she murmured, turning away to try and sleep once more.

He pulled her back, and taking her hand put it on his hard penis and moved himself up and down.

'Jonathan, I'm sleepy.'

'Ssh.' He twined her fingers round him. 'Press more firmly. It won't take a minute.'

But it took longer that it ever did when he was inside her. Her fingers ached; her head ached; her soul ached.

'Thank you, old thing.' He lay still.

After a few seconds she said, 'I'm not an "old thing".' But her husband was asleep; while for her, sleep didn't return for a long time.

The next morning – their anniversary – Jonathan presented her with his gift: a lady's workbox in satinwood, an exquisite piece she immediately loved, and which he must have known she would. She was touched by his thoughtfulness, and filled with a rush of guilt – that she was ungrateful and spoiled, her expectations too high. And later, when flowers arrived while he was at the office, she felt worse still. Her problem was, she realized, that she had become idle. She had too much time to brood. She must find something in which to involve herself.

The exhibition was in Joshua's studio – especially cleared for the occasion – and about a hundred and fifty guests drifted in and out at intervals during the course of the evening, when as much wine was drunk as attention paid to art. A couple of art critics with superior expressions busied themselves, looking minutely at the displayed works, scrutinizing from all angles – standing closely and then at a distance.

'And what gives them the right to criticize?' Leah thought. 'They who've never chipped a piece of stone, or coated their hands with clay, or burned their wrists with molten wax. What do they know of the precision of measuring with a plumb-line and frame, or of the attention to detail entailed in using a pointing machine?' But she knew she was only defending herself in advance from the inevitable criticism. Possessive, antagonistic, she watched as people wandered about touching, and longed to cry, 'Don't. That's *mine*!'

She drooped in her corner, and picked at a tiny sandwich on a platter by her. The horse she had been so proud of; the nude – herself revealed in all her imperfections, and which Claud had been reluctant to part with for an evening; a child's head; a weeping mother . . . She could see all their faults as never before, and wished that she might stick the lot in a raging hot furnace. And on a table were her carefully executed preliminary sketches, drawn with love: amateurish, she decided now . . .

Her hair was severely pulled back, as though to make herself look as insignificant as possible, and she shrank further into her corner.

Joshua came up to her affectionately. 'My dear girl, you mustn't hide in this corner, it's too absurd. People are saying nice things, if only you would dare listen.'

'You are just comforting me.'

'No, I'm not – go and soften up some critics, eh? And loosen your hair, for God's sake . . .' He pulled at her pins and she tried to ward him off.

'*Don't*.'

'You're a pretty girl. But you look like an old maid.'

'I don't care.'

'Yes you do.'

'Phooee.'

'You're such a child! Anyway, now it's a mess and I'll have to take the rest of the pins out. Stand still, will you. You are becoming more beautiful by the second.'

She stood docilely, half laughing – and saw Adam, Claud and Swinburne arrive together.

'What *are* you doing?' Claud approached on his own and embraced Leah smiling; he had ceased to be jealous of Joshua.

'She looked like an old maid.'

'Oh, you are hopeless,' Leah said exasperated, still laughing, nonetheless.

Plied with drink, encouraged by the odd compliment, and the sale of two of her works, she began to feel buoyant. She flitted from person to person, watched by her fiancé, whose eyes were quite damp with pride. In a couple of days' time he was going to France to find them a home, to build it, if necessary, with his own hands. He stood on his own, dreaming a little, smiling his beatific smile, as he imagined her in the country, happy and free, barefooted, pursuing her art during the day, while he wrote his books . . . and in the evening, they would sit together at a scrubbed table over a simple French meal and a bottle of wine . . . What an idyll.

Adam had seen all the works exhibited, so did not need to take his eyes from the door – which he stared at steadfastly, intent on not missing Sarah arrive. He had not seen her for several months, and heard her news vicariously through Leah. But the snippets which came his way were unsatisfactory – and anyway, he had tried to put her from his mind.

When she arrived with Jonathan he immediately noticed her tension, and also that she was overdressed for such a bohemian occasion. Her wild black hair was in its usual style, and emphasized the pallor of her skin. Beside him he thought he heard a gasp from someone, and he knew that the eyes of everyone in the room were drawn to this beautiful woman. And he would be the first to kiss her, to speak with her. It was his prerogative.

He was unprepared for her reaction – the flinging of her arms about his neck, as she said, 'Oh Addi – I'm so *glad* to see you.'

'It's good to see you, too,' he replied, relishing the embrace – while Jonathan looked on in amusement.

Sarah drew back, as though confused. Adam said, 'Happy anniversary to you both.' He grasped his brother's hand, and was surprised at how small and compact it was in his own.

'Thank you.' Jonathan moved away as he spoke, his eyes busy wandering over the faces of the guests. 'Who's-rich-spotting,' Adam called this tendency.

Recalling why he was there, Jonathan said, 'I suppose we had better take a look at our sister's efforts. Are you coming, old thing?'

Old thing? At first Adam could not think Jonathan referred to his wife, but when Sarah hung back and answered hesitantly, 'In a moment,' he looked disbelievingly from one to the other. His sister-in-law chewed on her finger that hovered by her lips.

Left alone, the pair were momentarily shy. Adam rubbed his right eye, then fingered the buttons of his waistcoat. Sarah asked, 'Why do you never come and see us, Addi?' And he was surprised by the reproach in her voice.

He gazed at her, his expression so blatant, that for the first time she realized, 'He cares for me.' But her happiness at this realization was gone swiftly, and in her mind she denounced her own stupidity. 'How conceited I am. He's simply like a brother . . .'

Perceptive towards the least change in her, he had caught her look, but it was so fleeting, that he, like her, dismissed it as his imagination. He became jocular, and pointing an accusatory finger at her said, 'But *you* could equally have visited *me*.'

'That isn't fair.' Her face relaxed.

'And why not?'

'Well – I don't like to disturb you from your writing, for one thing.'

'That's a poor excuse. And it would be a welcome disturbance. What is the other thing? It'll have to be better than the first.'

'It's for you to come to us.'

'I don't see why. And I don't like to disturb *you*. You might be busy.'

'Me?' She gave a self-deprecating little laugh and said bitterly,

'I'm not busy. I waste my days doing absolutely nothing of consequence. I don't know what's wrong with me . . .' Her voice trailed off, choked, and he realized she was trying not to cry. He reached for her hand, and finding it clenched, unclenched the fingers gently.

'Dear Sarah – what is it?'

She averted her eyes. 'I am hopeless. There is nothing I can do any more. I can't explain it. And I am truly so happy . . .'

Her misery, her lying to herself, upset him. He held her hand more tightly and felt a tear fall on to his wrist. He looked down. There it was glistening. And very deliberately he put the index finger of his free hand to it and then to his lips, making a kissing sound.

'I'm magicking them away.'

This made her smile. 'How stupid I am. Forgive me. I am only tired – I had a bad night. And I am so happy,' she repeated. Then, on an anxious note, 'But you will come and see us?'

'I promise.'

'Next week? One day next week?'

'Very well,' he answered laughing, feeling reckless.

'Let's have a pact that we see each other once a week. After all – I do with my sister-in-law, why not you?'

Why not, indeed.

Jonathan reappeared and found his brother and wife in good spirits. 'If you are going to inspect Leah's work, you must hurry,' he said. 'We have to go shortly, old thing.'

'Aren't you coming on afterwards with us all?' Adam asked, frowning.

'No,' Jonathan answered shortly, to preclude further discussion of the matter. 'We are having dinner with some important potential clients.'

A closed look came over Sarah's face, and as Adam watched them walk away he could see her back was rigid.

She was thinking, 'I must tell him not to call me "old thing". It's too degrading, even if he does mean it affectionately.'

By autumn their visits were a weekly routine which each looked forward to for days beforehand. All the things Sarah could not discuss with her husband, she could with Adam. Most importantly, he had restored her faith in herself. And he made her laugh.

Sometimes his visits overlapped with his brother's return from work, but Jonathan was not concerned that Adam spent so much time with his wife and was clearly infatuated; he regarded the matter as rather a joke. His confidence in himself was unshakeable, and he was jealous of nobody, least of all Adam, whom he had never taken seriously, and saw no reason to now. Recently he had changed his job, and moved to his father-in-law's company; and this new arrangement, coupled with his wife's restored humour, meant that life was constantly pleasant for him.

He would return home, invariably pour himself a glass of wine – never sherry: it reminded him of his mother – sit before the fire and read the newspaper. Over dinner he would satisfy his wife by telling her just enough about his day, then politely enquire about hers. He was adept now at giving the appearance of listening, while projecting his mind forward to other issues – a business trip, the start of the hunting season, an important luncheon. After dinner they'd retire to the drawing-room, where sometimes he would request she play the harp – he would find the music soothing, and often drifted into sleep. Later, in the big double bed, she was his to have as he pleased. She rarely refused him, and he had only to stroke her strong thighs briefly, before he was fully aroused. Jonathan – growing ever stouter and smugger – was an uncomplicated, contented man.

Meanwhile Leah was on her own with her mother in the Knightsbridge house, and Lady Gilmour was becoming increasingly demanding and dependent. At fifty-two years old she was prematurely old, with her raddled liver and stiff arthritic hips, her discontent and few happy memories. She took to spending more and more time in bed, complained continually of headaches, and was so finicky with her food that there was hardly anything she would eat. Her shoulder and collar bones stuck out, her cheekbones jutted, and Leah felt herself being dragged down by her and was unable to run to Claud, who was now in France. The trouble was that her mother was beginning to realize just how alone she was, and was terrified. She used every excuse she could to detain Leah – questioning her, nagging her, commanding her, in order that she would not be left on her own with her thoughts. Leah felt as though she were being consumed. Then she had a letter from Claud:

My dearest, darling littlest mouse,

I hope you are still missing me as much as I miss you. Do you know – last night I sat on the bed in my room, strumming the old lute, and I had such a clear picture of you flash before me, it was as if you were there in the room. It was seven o'clock, our time, six, yours. Were you perhaps thinking of me then, so that there was some sort of telepathy between us? I miss you snuggled up like a questionmark against me; I miss being inside you: your lovely hospitable body . . .

But news! My littlest mouse, I have found us a house! (Apologies for that less than brilliant verse.) But I truly have, and am quite insane with excitement. It is on the edge of the quaintest village between Les Eyzies and La Roque Gageac, and surrounded by magnificent countryside and vistas all around. The garden backs on to a large field – included in the sale – and the field itself is bounded by a tributary of the Dordogne River – such a glorious stretch – with hills forming a backcloth, and other villages nestling in their folds. I am euphoric. I can see us there, with our children; I smell the hay being cut, and damp in the air, and fresh trout cooking over a fire; I imagine us shopping at the market . . . And guess what! There is even a little shaded square where local men play *boules*. We shall be so happy, my littlest mouse.

That is the good news. The bad is that the reason I can afford it is that the building is in a severe state of dilapidation, and to have it ready in time for the beginning of April, I must remain here for some while longer to organize builders and work on it myself. It should have plenty of room, ultimately, if we want to take paying guests and make it into an *auberge*, and the dining-room is huge.

I wish you were with me. I long to say to you – what do you think of this, or should such-and-such be done in a particular way; but we know each other well enough by now, and I think you can trust my judgement. Suffice to say, everything I do and think is with you in mind.

It is late – and very cold. Mid-France at this time of year is barely warmer than England. I am actually half lying in bed as I write this by candlelight, and I have just splodged ink on the counterpane! *Tant pis*. My eyelids are drooping. But what a good day I have had; I shall sleep the sleep of the virtuous . . . And in the morning awaken with a massive erection for you!

I trust your mother will not read this letter. If she does, then it serves her right. I send much love to my favourite littlest mouse in the whole world. Be happy, for I am, despite missing you,

Your Claud

At twenty-seven, Adam was now a well-known figure in the literary world – albeit on the fringes; but this was by his choice. During the past year he had kept himself out of trouble, and the articles he wrote were powerful, but muted in tone. People started to pay attention to him and he daydreamed of founding some sort of boys' club. He envisaged it – a sanctuary for deprived children where they would learn the meaning of pride and hope. The more he contemplated it, the more positive he became of its viability – and who better than Sarah to assist him?

'It's a wonderful idea,' she said, when he broached it. 'I'd love to help . . .'

She read anything she could on the subject of underprivileged children, visited slum areas with Adam, made lists of potential patrons . . . She was convinced she was on the brink of something important, and it had only needed a suggestion like this to inspire her; something with which to concern herself, where she could be of use. Her days took on a new meaning, and she was tireless in her enthusiasm; she thought of herself as a pioneer.

Meanwhile, Adam tried to raise money and to find a large property he could buy or rent at an impossibly low price. He visited businessmen, government officials, property owners, hospitals, archdeacons and mayors, to enlist their help. He looked at disused churches, warehouses, factories, tumbledown mansions, hotels – and eventually found a pair of adjoining Georgian houses in Islington. They belonged to the Church and were due to be pulled down; but Adam was allowed to buy them for a low sum.

After he signed the deal he went directly to see Sarah. It was December, and when he arrived she was on her knees wrapping presents. He went down on his knees facing her.

'Grr,' he greeted her.

'Silly – get up!' she said laughing, standing up herself and pressing her hand to the small of her back. She rang for the maid and ordered tea, then sat beside him on the sofa. He scanned her face and was relieved that she looked happy, and she stared back, repressing a smile.

'What's funny?'

'You! The first thing you do when you see me is check whether or not I'm happy. Only when you're satisfied that I am, do you relax. You really are very sweet.'

'I don't want to be sweet. Who wants to be sweet?'

'You know what I mean. Well, this is a lovely surprise, having only seen you yesterday.'

'I've got the house.' And as he said it, and imagined them working together, he was jubilant.

'You got it? You *got* it!' She gave a little scream, and hugged him. He hugged her back – and felt something change: an awareness, a moth-like touch on the neck, a silence, the sound of their breathing – and then they broke apart.

Sarah licked dry lips. Her body felt burning hot. 'So –' she tried to sound normal, '– what next? I mean – what are our plans for this marvellous house?'

Adam wondered, 'Did I imagine her reaction?' He cleared his throat and said brightly, 'I thought the boys themselves could start on the place – all help knock down walls, convert it into one house, decorate it . . . They'll feel involved – and earn whilst doing it.' He had only just thought of the idea. The awkwardness passed and they began chatting normally again.

That night, when Jonathan rolled her on to her back and made love to her, it was not his face Sarah saw in shadowy outline, but Adam's.

However, such unguarded moments were best forgotten – besides, there was much to do; and they threw themselves into their tasks. By March 1874, there were a hundred and seventy-two boys on their growing list, and seven benefactors, including Mr Lowenstein and the new Lord Brambleden. Letters poured in daily for both Adam and Sarah at their respective homes.

He said, 'It's hopeless under two roofs.'

And from her expression he could have sworn she was thinking the same as he was – that if they lived together they would be so happy, with their shared interests and ideals.

He said firmly, 'We must make an office out of one of the rooms at Brownstones.' This was the name of the house. She nodded in agreement and lowered her gaze, and he thought, 'I must stop imagining things.'

Saturday, March 28th, 1874

'Today, the day before Leah's twenty-fifth birthday, she married Claud at last. Never did a pair look better contented, and as a willing best man this time, I confess to a great lump of emotion in my throat as I watched them exchange vows. My sister was a tiny white smiling creature beside her giant of a bridegroom . . . And Claud's incredible light-blue eyes were swimming with tears as he stooped to kiss her.

'How I shall miss them. I feel quite dreadful thinking I cannot simply call on Claud for a moan or a chat, or even to pick a quarrel . . . And those games of backgammon: win, lose, win – no matter in the end. And little Leah beavering away in Joshua's studio. Evenings without the pair of them: two such rare people. How dismal.

'I tell myself, as each of them has told me in turn, I am fortunate to do work I enjoy, instead of having to endure toiling in some office; that I have my new project, and that – yes – I do have numerous friends whom I could see every day of the week if I chose. But no friend so close as Claud. Inimitable Claud, with his lute and hat, prophetic expression and bellowing laugh. They tell me I must visit them, and of course I shall; never to have been abroad is absurd. But it's not the same as knowing that the two people closest to you are a coach ride away.

'But to revert to the wedding itself: the ceremony was in a small church in Knightsbridge, and only the closest friends and family were invited. This time Mama did not sob, but stood beside me, tight-lipped and white-haired and shrunken – and reeking of sherry. Does she know she's addicted to the stuff?

'The reception, paid for by Claud, was at Morley's Hotel, and everybody was very jolly and noisy. I sat at the 'family' table, and from the one behind us could be heard the uproarious behaviour of Joshua and Algernon amongst others, and there was much fist-banging, singing and swearing. I could almost feel Aunt Mary's ears smouldering beneath her wig, and her pink-rimmed eyes bulged.

'There was dancing throughout the meal, and caught up in the mood of gaiety, I stretched my hand across the table and asked Sarah to dance. On the little floor we were immediately swallowed up by the other dancers, and kept being jostled, so that her body would be pressed against mine. We came together and parted, and came together again, and I wished it might not end . . . But end it did, and I escorted her back to the table, to her husband – who himself straight away asked her to dance.

'Algernon became dreadfully drunk, and was at his most shocking, talking at the top of his voice about flagellation and death, while Leah kept trying to cover his mouth with her hand; the afternoon degenerated generally and was most amusing. Leah and Claud stayed behind in the hotel, and tomorrow will travel to France, and their new life . . .

'I must have flopped on to the bed and fallen asleep; and when I woke I couldn't think where I was – lying fully clothed, darkness all round. A wave of isolation swept through me when I recovered my senses: I visualize myself in the years to come, still in this same place, breakfasting with Mr Levy, who will be smaller, plumper and greyer; a confirmed bachelor going to social events and returning home to nobody. And still hankering after my brother's wife.'

Over a year passed. Brownstones Boys' Club was flourishing, and in February Adam's third novel had been published. But instead of the expected rush to buy the limited edition advertised in the national papers and displayed on the shelves of the specialist bookshops, there was a disheartening lack of interest. The chief reason for this was undoubtedly the reviews. They were unanimously bad.

Despondently, Adam recalled Stephen's comments: '. . . It's

simply too bizarre . . . too experimental. The public are not ready for it . . .'

Yet he was still certain he had written a profound book. He felt frustrated and misunderstood – and in an interview for the *Athenaeum*, told the reporter that the public were no better than a bunch of gorillas with their ignorant preconceptions and limited imaginations.

This remark was not well received, and an angry Gray-Courtney summoned Adam to his office and said that he was doing neither of them any favours with such a display of arrogance. But he was no longer talking to the same person. The malleable boy had become worldly. He was a prominent figure now, entirely of his own making.

'One has to admire him,' the intense dark man thought, nevertheless casting his mind back with some wistfulness to their first meeting.

But Adam had relied on the book doing well, and needed money for Brownstones. He had become passionate about the place, and the boys were his boys, their problems his. He was their godfather and their saviour; and they trusted him. Too proud to enlist the help of his brother or Mr Lowenstein, he had the idea of creating a series featuring weekly happenings at Brownstones, stories which were amusing and sad and which he would illustrate himself. Leslie Stephen thought the notion delightful, and paid Adam £250 in advance.

He was back in favour once more, and more important, Brownstones became a household name with which readers identified. Generous contributions arrived every day, and the merry sounds of hammering as improvements were made echoed throughout the building and mingled with the children's laughter . . .

But Adam was restless. He said to Swinburne, 'A novelist without a novel to write, and his last one a failure, is an aimless person.'

'Everybody is aimless,' mumbled the poet into his glass – they were sitting in a tavern garden.

'Surely not everybody.'

'Aimless in love. Aimless out of love. Self-doubting . . .' Swinburne took another gulp of wine. 'Only unintelligent people are totally satisfied.'

'I can't agree.'

Swinburne shrugged, not bothered.

'Much help you are when I look for a bit of cheering.'

'Sorry, I can't oblige.'

His mind was increasingly befuddled with alcohol. Yet the brilliance was still there, and he was in the midst of working on a new set of poems with a Greek theme . . .

He laid his hand on Adam's arm which rested on the table, then briefly stroked his wrist. 'A manly wrist,' he commented. 'And quite marvellous hands . . .' Then, abruptly: 'You worry too much, you know. Look at that sparrow there.' He gestured with his head to the bird by the table. 'It doesn't worry where the next worm is coming from. My dear fellow – let things happen, and for sure they will.'

He sank his chin into his beard and quoted, ' "Yea, wise is the world and mighty, with years to give, And years to promise; but how long now shall it live?" '

With Claud and Leah blissful in the Dordogne, and letters a poor substitute, it was natural the friendship between Adam and Sarah should develop. Jonathan remained unperturbed by their closeness. Occasionally, when he noticed some sign of his brother's passion, he chuckled inwardly from his secure pinnacle.

'He's like an overgrown puppy,' he thought once – and hid behind the financial pages of the newspaper again, giving no further consideration to the matter. Nor did he give consideration to the fact he was rapidly losing his hair, developing a jowl and a paunch, and scarcely resembled the hero Sarah had married.

He could not know, either, of his wife's terrified thought: that she had married the wrong brother.

Chapter Fifteen

OLD LETTERS

Towards the end of June, Jonathan was away on business, and Adam took Sarah to the opera. While he waited for her to come downstairs – her time-keeping was as unreliable as his – he examined the photographs grouped on a table, and picked up a faded one of her as a serious-faced child.

Sarah stood for a moment watching him, and, feeling her eyes on him, he set down the photograph carefully, and turned.

'I didn't hear you.'

'Papa always said I'd have made a good thief, I was so silent on my feet,' she said, coming up to him.

Unusually, her hair was swept completely back, revealing her fine bone structure. She wore an emerald taffeta dress and emerald jewellery which contrasted with her ivory-toned skin.

'You look beautiful, he said, his kiss landing on her eye.

'And you look handsome.'

He was a man who became better-looking as he grew older; there was strength in his features now, and the odd, characterful line, and in his black tail-coat and tight-fitting trousers, he looked quite distinguished.

Every so often, in the coach, they were thrown together. They each felt rather shy, for despite seeing one another almost every day, a formal evening together seemed to hold other connotations.

When the coachman dropped them off at Covent Garden, the first bell had already sounded and people were rapidly evacuating the foyer and bar. Hurriedly, Adam bought a programme and they went to find their places in the stalls.

'Marvellous seats,' commented Sarah, brushing past feet, to annoyed tutting.

'There's no point otherwise,' he said. 'To appreciate opera fully, it must be a complete experience.' The conductor appeared amidst loud applause, and there was a burst of coughing, a rustle of programmes, and then a hush as he lifted his baton in readiness for the overture to *The Marriage of Figaro*.

Throughout the performance Adam was conscious of Sarah – engrossed beside him. He glanced at her profile and saw that her lips were parted; and the music, the atmosphere, Sarah's proximity combined to fill him with a sensuous pleasure, which engulfed him.

Afterwards they went to a nearby restaurant where they sat facing each other, a flickering candle between them, and discussed the performance – barely noticing what they ate, and taking so long over the first course that the waiter returned several times before they were ready for him to remove their plates.

She said, 'I hadn't been to the opera for ages. The theatre is as much as Jonathan can stand.' Then she looked guilty and added, 'Of course opera is *not* to everyone's liking.'

'No, but it ought to be,' Adam said.

'I'm so pleased you invited me.'

'It's *my* pleasure,' he answered, beckoning the waiter to refill their glasses.

'How sad to have died a pauper,' she said, referring to Mozart. 'And in an unmarked grave. And now his music gives pleasure to thousands.'

'He was of unparalleled genius.'

'I wish I were talented. You have no idea how I envy talented people. You are truly fortunate.'

'But you are talented,' he said. 'Look at the way you play the harp. And your poems –'

She tossed her head impatiently, and he noticed the way the candlelight caught the slant of her cheekbone. 'My harp-playing is mediocre, and I haven't shown you my poems, so you cannot know. They are childish,' she said dismissively. She looked down, and taking a small piece of the roll on her side-plate, crumbled it in her fingers.

The waiter wheeled a trolley laden with desserts towards them and asked Adam, 'Would your wife like to choose something, sir?'

And they both became flustered, and chose desserts neither

particularly liked. The words rebounded, 'Your wife, your wife . . .'

Later he saw her back to her house. The cab driver waited beside his placid horse, civilly staring ahead.

'You could stay,' she suggested, 'and leave in the morning. It's awfully late – and he will charge you the earth.' She lowered her voice to a whisper.

'I don't think I will,' he said uncertainly.

'But why not?'

It was simpler to agree to her proposal than to explain.

The servants were long in bed, and the house was quiet. Adam stood at the window and parted the curtains to look at the river. He was joined by Sarah.

'Shades of Henley?' she asked.

'Yes, that was what I was thinking.' Absently he put his arm around her. 'We even read each other's minds,' he said.

'I have had such a special evening,' she said quietly.

He made no reply, but turned and tilted her chin towards him.

'Addi . . .'

Kissing her was such a relief; feeling her respond, such joy. But it was fleeting, and she broke away, her expression distraught.

'What are we *doing*? Oh *God*, Addi.'

'Ssh.' He put his arm about her and led her over to the sofa. He wanted her so badly; but somehow the situation must be salvaged.

'We have a great – fondness – for one another,' he said carefully, retaining her hand in his. 'A very great friendship. What happened was simply a natural thing after a beautiful evening. There's no need to upset yourself.'

She relaxed next to him, and they began talking almost naturally again, until eventually, yawning, she said, 'I'm tired,' and he pulled her to her feet. He had the room next to hers, and outside her door she hesitated, before kissing him chastely on the cheek; it was her way of showing him nothing had happened.

In his room, Adam undressed quickly and turned off the gaslight. Dawn would break soon. He heard the clanging and tinkling of the river barges . . . He heard sounds of Sarah next door – a wardrobe opening and closing; a drawer; a window being shut. And then he heard the spring of the bed as she climbed in. He imagined her lying there, her hair fanned out. Or perhaps she lay on her stomach; he thought she probably would. Her lips had felt beautiful . . . her breath had tasted sweet . . . her hands had caressed his neck . . . These memories would have to suffice him.

In September Lady Elizabeth Gilmour fell ill. Her liver was no longer functioning properly, her kidneys had seized up and her heart was weakened. She was dying – but not subdued.

Adam went to stay with her in the Knightsbridge Morgue, as he called it. It was the first time he'd been back for three months, and he found that since Leah had gone, the maids had become slacker than ever. Cobwebs festooned corners and pipes, and dust formed layers on windowsills and mantelpieces. The place smelt stale and musty, and vases of dead flowers stank of foul water . . . Furious, Adam lined up the sour-faced threesome and gave them a severe lecture, and within twenty-four hours, the place was at least clean again, if not appealing. Dutifully, Adam would go and sit by his ailing mother, and the hired nurse would leave them alone together.

'You are only staying because you want my money,' Lady Elizabeth, ever hateful, hissed. But she was too weak, and in too much pain, to say a great deal, and Adam was too kind to remind her there *was* no money; that the house was in reality his, by virtue of the fact he should have inherited Brambleden Hall.

'You have all let me down,' she said, one afternoon, when the rain beat against the window, and outside it was as if it were night. 'There has only been one person in my entire life who loved me . . .'

And she fell back on to the pillow, her vengeful face clouding over with some sweet reminiscence. Her eyes became soft and youthful. 'Ah,' she sighed – a girl sighing in love. And the sigh became an exhalation of expiry, and was the last sound she uttered.

Leah returned without Claud for the funeral, which was held in the church where she had been married. She stood between her two tall brothers and tried to feel sad. What she felt was pity – that her mother should never have known happiness. She herself was happier than she had imagined possible, living in France with Claud. She was rosy with health, softer than she had been.

The vicar muttered a prayer for the dead, and glanced every so often over the rims of his glasses at the little cluster of mourners –

eight in all. He hated a small turnout: it made life seem so lonely.

Adam was pensive. 'What did she mean, only one person loved her? . . . Poor Mama. The original matriarch . . . And me as a child craving her affection . . . How she hated me . . . And what'll become of Aunt Mary? . . .'

He looked at his aunt, who was next to Aunt Jennifer and Mrs Lowenstein. She was the only person crying, and the tears crept under her wig. He cast a quick, surreptitious look at his brother beside him; the one who had been loved, worshipped almost. Did he feel any sorrow? But Jonathan's face was as smooth as a stone made sleek by the tide.

Adam thought, 'If he were dead, according to the old Levirate law I could marry Sarah. It would be my duty as her brother-in-law . . . God forgive me. What am I thinking? . . .'

Leah and Adam sorted out their mother's personal possessions – in her will she had left her jewellery to Leah, and furniture to Jonathan. The house was Adam's.

'Any dresses you want?' he asked Leah, who was going through a drawerful of letters, photographs and other souvenirs.

'Are you joking?'

'What shall we do with them?'

'Give them to the maids? Aunt Mary? Burn them?'

'Poor Mama.'

'That's what I thought at the funeral. I wanted to be sad. To know that I should miss her. But all I could think was, poor Mama.'

'I'm going to the attic to fetch a trunk. It's best to put the dresses away for the time being . . . God, here's *another* hidden empty sherry bottle. And packets of snuff . . .'

He returned a few minutes later, dragging a large trunk.

'I can hear something sliding about inside.' He opened the trunk and immediately saw a thin bundle of letters tied up with ribbon. There was also a crumbling dried rose hanging on to its brittle stalk. Slowly he lifted out the letters; the envelopes were yellow with age, and the writing pale. Leah came over and knelt next to Adam.

' "Miss Elizabeth Longman",' she read . . . 'They're from before she was married. Perhaps they're from Papa.'

'It's not his writing.'

'No, of course not.'

'I feel like an interloper looking.'

'Well I don't,' his sister said briskly, and took the first letter from the pile:

The Vicarage,
Rushington Brook,
Near Taunton,
Somerset
April 10th, 1842

My darling Elizabeth,

It is impossible to believe that tomorrow I am setting off for another world. I keep thinking that something will occur to prevent it. As I gaze round my room, at everything that is familiar, and then through the window – at the blossom raining down from the tree outside, at the well-tended lawn and fields beyond, I confess to a most unsoldierly fear at the prospect of leaving it all. And of course at leaving you, my love, so many thousands of miles behind. I console myself by saying it is only for nine months – but then, I think nine months is an eternity. Nine months ago I did not even know of your existence. However, when I return, perhaps your father will not be so antagonistic towards a mere vicar's son. Perhaps India will be kind to me, and I can show off some medals to impress him. I am enclosing a lock of my hair, and have already wrapped yours in tissue paper and placed it in a pocket of my writing box. I shall unwrap it each day and study its lustrous gold, and think of you, your beauty and sweetness . . .

The letter was signed, 'Jonathan'.

'I don't believe it,' Adam said.

'Jonathan!' exclaimed Leah.

From the other letters they could piece together the story: the 22-year-old lieutenant attached to the Somerset Light Infantry who had been sent to India to the Afghanistan border . . .

His hair, according to the lock they found wrapped in velvet, was thick and light brown, and he must have been tall, for he wrote of her head reaching his shoulder; he suffered badly in the sun with his fair skin, and he was pitifully homesick. The letters were nostalgic, amusing and informative, and that he loved her deeply was obvious.

On September 17th he was shot and wounded in a skirmish on the Khyber Pass, and he died on September 20th at their camp. This news was relayed to her in a letter from his friend, who said that Jonathan had been the most popular of all the men, and he enclosed his signet ring . . .

Leah passed the ring to Adam. It bore the initials J.S.B. Their brother's second initial was also S, for Sebastian.

They looked at one another, tears in their eyes.

'I can't bear it,' Leah said. 'It's too terrible. So much we didn't know . . .'

'What about the date he died?' Adam felt suddenly chilled.

'Good heavens – it is the same date Mama died.'

She became ashen, and he put his arm around her. He tried to imagine his mother as a nineteen-year-old girl. Had she married her lover, would she have been different? Did disappointment form her character? He remembered the soft expression in his mother's eyes as she died, the drawn out 'Ah –', and thought, 'How she suffered. And how, as a result, she made everyone else suffer.'

Adam decided to keep the Knightsbridge house. It was more convenient for Brownstones. Brownstones and its boys had become his life, and his charitable work was recognized and acknowledged by everyone. He had never dared hope his venture would succeed on such a scale, and the organization now employed several people.

He stripped the house of its gloom, dismissed the three poker-faced maids, and started again.

'Light,' he told Sarah. 'I just want it to be light.'

She helped him select fabrics and colours, and instructed builders, and together they watched the house being transformed. He moved in just before Christmas, to the sorrow of Mr Levy.

'You will come and visit.'

'Of course.' Adam clasped the tailor's hand. 'You have been a true friend to me over the years. I shall miss our chats and meals together.'

'Not half as much as I.'

'But you'll visit me too?'

'Nothing would give me greater pleasure.'

Adam stood for a moment in the doorway of the little shop. At the corner of the street were four horses and a van full of his belongings.

Mr Levy embraced him. 'Find yourself a wife, Adam. Someone worthy of you. It's high time . . . Now go, or else I shall let myself down and start to cry . . .'

One day in the new year, 1876, Sarah remarked to him, 'It is the women's turn now. It's time something was done for them. All these boys have mothers. What of them?'

'Do you want to launch another charity for them?'

'It's not so much a charity women need. It's support for our rights.'

'Well you could start campaigning.'

'It is not a – good – time, Addi.'

'Why's that?'

And she faltered as she told him, 'I'm expecting a baby.'

'Oh –' He was shocked, struck mute at first, reminded of the impossibility of his situation. 'It's w-wonderful n-new-news,' he said finally, stammering for the first time in ages.

'I long to have a child, Addi,' she said quietly.

'Then I am truly glad for you,' he told her, and kissed her gently on both cheeks. He remembered the wicked thought which had occurred to him at his mother's funeral; but the Levirate ruling would not now apply.

It was time to write another book. It would be based on his own mother's story; the sad tale of her love. It would surely not incite any controversy.

Spring again. And Adam witnessed a new loveliness in Sarah as she swelled with her child. 'You mustn't work so hard,' he told her anxiously, as she threw herself into her various tasks at Brownstones.

'Don't take my enjoyment from me, Addi.'

'I only worry for your health.'

'You have no need. And you're very dear.'

She wished that her husband were as attentive; but in the last year

Jonathan and she had drifted further apart as their different interests took them in divergent directions. She suspected her husband was being unfaithful, but preferred not to know for certain; it would have been too much of an admission of failure, quite apart from the insult to her pride.

Meanwhile, Adam himself was having an affair with a twenty-year-old ballerina who reminded him of Sarah with her pale skin and dark hair. It was the most serious relationship he had had for a long while. He worked well during this period, and Leslie Stephen was delighted with the first two chapters of the new novel.

'This is better,' the powerfully-built man exclaimed, clapping Adam on the back, when they met at the Circle Club. 'At last you are writing what people want to read.'

'If my mother but knew,' Adam thought.

He dallied with the idea of marrying Helena; but then he began to discover missing items: money, a couple of pairs of cuff-links, studs, an ornament or two, a silver inkwell . . .

Tactfully, he enquired of the three new maidservants, but believed them when they denied all knowledge. There was only one person left, and Adam dreaded facing her. With a sickness in the pit of his stomach, he searched yet again in case he himself – he was incurably untidy – had mislaid the articles. But they could not be found, and when she left him one morning, and he found a further five pounds missing from his trouser pocket, where he had deliberately placed it the evening before, he knew for certain, and was shattered.

That evening, over dinner in his dining-room, he quietly told Helena that he'd discovered her thefts.

'How dare you,' she cried angrily. 'I shan't listen to such accusations.' And she muffled her ears with her hands.

'Oh, but you shall listen to them.' He tried to wrench her hands away from her head.

'No, take your hands from me.'

'I shall if you stop resisting. Let us go into my study. I have no wish for the servants to hear.'

'But I do! Let them hear what you accuse me of. The man who thinks he's a saint.'

'That is untrue,' he said angrily, and managed at last to pinion her hands. 'Come with me and tell me what you have to say. You have taken advantage of me, cheated me – and *I* shan't have it.'

Her pretty little face became pink, and then crumpled, and he led her into the study – a room completely lined with books – and sat her down on a leather chesterfield.

'Why?' he asked. 'And don't, *please*, try and sell me the sick mother story. Credit me with some intelligence.'

'I want to go to Paris to study. I couldn't afford it.'

This was the girl who only a night ago had told him she had never loved anyone as she had loved him, and that without him her days had no meaning; fool that he was, he had almost believed her, she had been so convincing.

He ran his hand through his hair; his skin felt taut round his mouth and across his cheeks. He said, 'I would have lent you – given you – the money. You know that.'

'I didn't like to ask.'

'So you preferred to pretend to me that you cared for me –' he smiled sadly, '– and to steal. And very clumsily, too, if I might say.'

Her lips trembled. 'It isn't in my nature.'

'Well, I'm glad of that at least.'

'I'm – sorry.' She looked at him, ashamed, and he thought of their recent cavortings in the bedroom.

'I am too. I had come to – be fond of you. What now?'

'I don't know.'

His anger dissipated. She was so young. 'What have you done with my bits and pieces?'

'I – pawned them.'

'Then I can at least reclaim them. Most of those items were of sentimental value, you know. They belonged to my father. But of course sentiment would not mean anything to you . . . And the money?'

'I have it. I was saving it.' She was close to tears again. There was nobody she could turn to for help. Paris retreated from her vision.

'Then I shall add to it, so you can go to Paris.'

'You mean it?' Her face lit up with joy.

'Yes. On condition you let me know how you get on, and that you never resort to dishonesty again.'

'Oh you are wonderful.' She wrapped her long thin arms round his neck and tried to kiss him. But he held her away.

Her deceit had hurt him, and his role was no longer that of a lover or potential husband (the thought of that made him laugh inwardly), but as a kind benefactor.

He told Sarah, and she said, 'I never liked her anyway.'

'Why?' he asked.

'Oh,' she said vaguely. 'An instinct, I suppose. Women have an instinct about these things.'

But the truth was she had been unreasonably jealous of the closeness of the relationship.

Jonathan and Sarah's baby was born early in the morning of July 15th, but Jonathan was away at the time, and so Adam saw the little girl, his goddaughter, before the father did, rushing round in the afternoon as soon as he received the message by courier.

Sarah half lay, half sat in the bed, her face tiny and pale, and her hair emphatically black against several pillows, and asleep on top of her, scarlet and wrinkled like a raisin, was her baby.

Adam had to turn away when he first saw them, to hide his emotion, but she called to him, 'Addi, dearest, come and see her,' and he composed himself and went up to them, smiling and brandishing his unwrapped present of a white shawl.

'Thank you, it's beautiful.' She lifted her weary face for a kiss, then lay back again.

'You're beautiful,' he wanted to say, but asked, 'Was it bad?'

'I don't know. I mean – I've nothing to compare it to. The midwife said it was normal, so I suppose it must have been. But it felt bad to me. I'm not very brave with pain. It comes of being spoiled.'

Adam sat carefully on the edge of the bed and very lightly touched the spiky down on the sleeping baby's head. 'It's like a dandelion when it's gone to fluffy seed,' he said.

'I can't believe I've had her. That she has come from me.'

'Well she has. And I think you'll be an excellent mother.'

'I pray so . . .' She looked fretful. 'What time is it? I've lost all sense of time.'

He took his watch from his pocket. 'Almost three o'clock.'

'Don't you think he could have put off going away just this once? He knew the baby was due.'

Adam leaned forward and stroked her hair. 'I daresay Jonathan just couldn't avoid it. I am not a businessman, but I know sometimes things happen which cannot be deferred.'

'I'm sorry. He is your brother.'

'And he's your husband. You have every right to say what you feel.'

'I would have thought he'd want to be here to see his child.'

'When is he due back?'

'Tomorrow morning.'

'Well then – he probably didn't count on the baby being born on time. It is unusual, I gather . . . Have you named her yet, by the way?'

'Well, I want to call her Rebecca.'

'It's a lovely name.'

'Jonathan doesn't like it.'

'Why not?'

'He says it's too Jewish.'

Shocked, Adam stared at her. She stared back, then gave a resentful laugh. 'But he cannot take away one fact.'

'What is that?'

'The baby *is* Jewish. According to Jewish law the child takes the mother's religion.'

The months passed, and in January 1877 Leah wrote to say she was pregnant, and that her baby would be born in August. Adam decided that when the time came he would travel to France to visit them. All these babies, he thought, and none of his own; no wife in sight. Just his book, and a hundred and fifty boys in need. He consoled himself they were all his children; and he took them in groups to visit castles and museums, on picnics, and walks, to the seaside . . . He tried to help them with their problems, read stories to them, drew cartoons of them, gave them odd jobs and paid them, and taught them the meaning of pride. They were his reward. And he was theirs. They called him Uncle Addi, and thought he was quite old.

Chapter Sixteen

BEAKY

Adam stood on the steamship deck, facing the rugged coastline and white cliffs. Overhead, seagulls wheeled and howled – then swooped on to the water to bob there, before soaring into the sky again. The sea was calm – for which he was grateful – and after several noisy blasts from the funnel, and the sounds of heavy chains being pulled, he felt the vibration of the immense paddle, and they were moving. The gap between boat and quay widened, and widened further, the cliffs became diminished, and then there was only the sea, steely and endless . . .

Several hours later they arrived at Calais and disembarked. The port smelled of fish and oil, and reverberated with loud French voices. Burly, tanned men in open shirts mended nets or oiled chains, or lugged cargo from a boat . . .

Adam was childlike in his excitement. He thought, 'How stupid not to have travelled abroad before – it's really not complicated at all.' And he headed for the station, and the train for Paris . . .

Monday, August 16th, 1877, Paris
'What a marvellous city this is – and vibrant in a way London is not. Tables and chairs line crowded pavements; waiters sing; people shout and gesticulate; street musicians abound, and artists pitch their easels wherever they find space. There is constant activity.

'I wandered about for a couple of hours or so with a street map, asking directions in French I haven't used since leaving school – then to a small bar where I am now, near my hotel. A pretty young girl brings me my delicious-smelling croissant and coffee, looks at me boldly, then leaves me with a wiggle to her hips . . .

'I love the symmetry of the buildings here, and the elegance of the streets, the *boulevards* with their wide-leafed trees, and the little roads, arterial like, leading off. Helena is somewhere in this city. But I couldn't see her, even should I wish to, for, predictably, she never wrote to me with her address. A consummate actress, besides ballerina. She used me utterly, and I was a fool. I'll always be a fool where women are concerned.

'Spent hours in the Louvre, and walked afterwards in the Tuileries; then went into a couple of bookshops and – guess what – saw *The Farmer's Son* tucked away in one of them, translated into French! That certainly fed my *amour-propre*! Bought *Le Figaro*, and read it on the omnibus which I took from left to right bank, crossing at Pont Neuf. Beginning to feel like a native!

Evening
'Just returned from a concert, having walked all the way back to my hotel, which is in a quiet cul-de-sac. My feet were quite swollen by the time I got back, and hurt rather, but my mind was alive, and I felt intoxicated by everything – and then literally so, when the genial proprietor and his wife brought me a huge brandy, and remained to talk with me in the courtyard, while in the background the fountain splashed.'

That night he dreamed of Helena, that she had in fact loved him, and when he woke he felt bereft. What was a city, after all? Or buildings or streets? He was weary of his own company, thought that surely out there was someone who could find something in him to love, to share his joy at beauty and all that was good . . .

From Paris, he boarded the train for Toulouse. The day was hot, and the compartment already stuffy, and he immediately opened the window and sat beside it, his jacket and waistcoat unbuttoned. After Fontainebleau he went to the dining-car for a light lunch, returned to the compartment, dozed – and woke with a start to find they were crossing the magnificent Loire at Orléans.

The countryside was flat and expansive and dotted with houses with shuttered windows and peeling paint; vineyards were interspersed with pastures where cattle grazed, undisturbed by the great beast streaking through their meadows . . . Through small, depressed towns – and the flatness gave way to hills and huge vistas; maize-fields, more vineyards and fields of sunflowers – tall and almost human with their faces upturned to the sun. Such luscious richness everywhere, and Adam wished he might pluck it all . . . They were alongside a river, and he could see bathers – nude – splashing about, hear their shrieks – and then they were past.

He was met at Brive-la-Gaillarde by Claud with a pony and cart, and they hugged each other emotionally. It was over two years since they'd seen each other, and against his ruddy tan, Claud's light eyes seemed more extraordinary than ever, the pupils defined black dots.

'You look disgustingly healthy,' Adam said, punching him lightly in his huge stomach.

'Except for this,' he said, glancing down at himself ruefully, and then grinning. '*Tant pis* . . . Meet Florence.'

'Florence?'

'My mare.'

Laughing, Adam stroked the bay pony's muzzle, and hoisted his luggage into the cart.

It was still light when they drove through the village of St-Paul-de-Boulez, a pretty little place with its tall-steepled church in a small square, enclosed by the crumbling remains of ramparts. Houses leaned towards one another, linked by trailing bougainvillaea, wrought-iron railings, and washing, their peeling shutters flung wide . . . A little alleyway led to the grander houses – where lived the chemist, a prosperous man who could cure everything from rheumatism to toothache, the undertaker, and a lawyer. Another lane, behind the church, led to a long driveway up the hill – and a small château surrounded by its own vineyard.

Outside the bar two old men waved at Claud – and stared at Adam, sitting on his case in the cart. Four more men – younger – played *boules* in the tree-sheltered square; a young woman sluiced down her doorstep then disappeared inside again. Another woman chased a cat outside, screaming shrilly; a couple of chickens scuffled in the dust; a rabbit in a cage outside the bar scratched itself . . .

'Well, this is where it all happens,' said Claud, as Florence plodded placidly through the village, her feet echoing on the cobbles, and the wheels rattling. 'This is life for Leah and myself now. We love it.'

'I can see why,' Adam said.

Just outside St-Paul-de-Boulez was an unmade track to the right, across farmland, and the pony took this path without any directions from Claud, her ears keenly forward, her pace quickening.

'Well, she knows where she's going,' commented Adam, amused.

'It's greed. Her field is full of clover, and I'm sure she has this fixed picture of it in her mind as we head for home.'

'Home, what a good word,' Adam murmured. 'I use it so rarely.'

Ahead of them was the house. Surrounded by big sky and fields, it was a long honeyed-stone building with white-painted shutters and a steeply-pitched clay-tiled roof, down which, according to Claud, the rain poured in the winter. The front door was open, and Leah rushed out, licking her fingers. She was plump still, after her pregnancy, radiant.

'I was helping the cook. I didn't expect you yet . . . I thought you'd stop for a drink . . . Oh how lovely . . .' She reached up to kiss him, and Adam embraced her, tears momentarily blurring his eyes. He wiped them away and said shakily, 'Let me look at my sister.'

She stood back. She wore a simple peasant-style blouse tucked into a skirt with a bright petticoat beneath – no crinolette or dress-improver, or other concessions to fashion; and with her glowing brown skin, clear eyes and shining curls caught in a ribbon, she could have passed for a pretty French village girl.

'I've never seen you look lovelier,' he said.

'Phooee. Now come in . . .'

Inside it was cool, with a flagstone floor, a rug, and white walls. Leah suddenly began to giggle.

'What is it?' Adam asked, perplexed, as Claud began to join in, holding his stomach and rocking.

'You'll see,' said Leah, still laughing, and dancing slightly from one bare foot to another. Putting her finger to her lips in a gesture intended to silence both her brother and her husband, she tiptoed up the wooden staircase, into a large room.

It was their bedroom, and beside the double bed was a cot. Adam peered inside, holding his breath without being aware of it. Beside him, Leah hopped agitatedly.

'I don't believe it!' he gasped, and then was overcome by laughter himself, despite Leah's frantic 'hushing' signs – for the cot contained not one baby boy, but twins.

It was an evening of rare intimacy and talk, with each of them continually interrupting the other. Supper was by candlelight in a simply-furnished dining-room, where Claud's mother's samovar had pride of place on the sideboard, and Louise, the cook-cum-housekeeper, kept appearing with food: a terrine, followed by cold roast pork, salad tossed in garlic and herbs, and hot buttered new potatoes. She was a large, amiable woman with a jutting jaw, and given to laughing a lot – revealing her hideous brown teeth. Her voice was rasping, and she had such a strong dialect that Adam could barely decipher it, and marvelled at the way Leah coped.

Claud brimmed with well-being. He had everything he desired, and could ask for no more, he told Adam, his eyes ready, as ever, with sentimental tears after too much wine, his well-remembered hat sliding forward comically. It was a sentimental evening altogether, as they spoke softly on the terrace, drinking liqueurs and listening to the crickets – and then the peace was shattered by simultaneous wails which rent the air, and Leah ran upstairs to gather her babies to her.

She returned with one over each shoulder, and passed them – still bawling – to Claud, before unselfconsciously baring herself.

As Claud settled them one at a time against her breasts, they instantly stopped crying and began to suck.

'That used to be my prerogative!' he joked.

'And it will be again,' Leah said, giving him a long look. She was replete with love – for her babies, for her husband, her home – and now her brother was with them.

Adam watched. He felt profoundly moved. 'They're like wallabies the way they cling,' he said. Turning his face to the stars, he sat back, and their companionable silence was broken only by the whirring of the crickets and the sucking noises of the babies, who eventually fell asleep against their mother.

'They're so lucky,' he thought. And within him he yearned, ached, for such a fulfilment as theirs.

Hot days followed one into the next. Leah seemed effortlessly to combine motherhood and running a home with her sculpting; while Claud could apparently turn his hand to anything – be it fixing a shelf, taking a cutting of a plant, or bathing the boys.

'It's only a question of reading,' he told Adam airily. 'Forget intellectualism. My book selection nowadays comprises manuals on gardening and building. Practicality is the essence of life, I have decided. A peasant understands true philosophy far better than most academics.'

But he himself was rapidly gaining respect as an academic and historian, besides as a poet, and had just had published a slender volume of descriptive poems in French which had been highly acclaimed.

They drove to nearby towns – Les Eyzies with the Vezère meandering through it, and its hidden caves; La Roque Gageac with its sheer cliffs and the church perched on a rock, and beneath, the Dordogne – peaceful and flat, reflecting the towering grandeur; medieval Sarlat with its maze of tiny streets, alleyways and squares . . . None of these towns seemed changed by the advancement of time, and many of the inhabitants existed much as their ancestors had done.

They swam naked in the river; went fishing; saw friends from neighbouring villages – two of whom were artists – and talked every night until late, sitting outside, while Claud sang quietly and strummed on his lute, and Leah closed her eyes, smiling a happy woman's smile, and in the background the insects hummed. Adam found himself becoming drawn closer into their lives. He walked about bare-chested, helped Claud in the garden and Leah with the babies. He drove the pony and cart to market himself and bargained for fresh vegetables at the best price . . . And he was immersed in their idyll, happier than he had been for a long while, healthy and fit.

Then, one evening, when Leah was alone with Adam, she mentioned Sarah, and it all rushed back: his hopeless passion; Brownstones; his boys; his book he hadn't touched since he'd arrived. This idyll belonged to others, and he was merely a guest.

Not noticing the change in his expression Leah said, 'Sarah wrote that she'd like to come and stay with us in a few months' time – with Rebecca of course. Do you think Jonathan would let her?'

'Oh, I should think so,' he replied vaguely.

'I long to see her . . . She's a different person since Brownstones, you know. I can tell, from her letters.'

'She seems happier,' Adam agreed evasively.

Leah was about to say that she believed another of the reasons for Sarah's happiness was her friendship with Adam – when he changed the subject so pointedly that she could not revert to it.

Another few days passed, and he became restless, dissatisfied, kept thinking about things which needed doing; and at the end of a month he decided it was time to return to England.

'You could come back and live with us,' Claud said at the station, pressing his friend to him. 'Please consider it.'

Adam shook his head. 'It wouldn't work.'

'You know it would make us really happy, Addi.' Leah, too, had reverted to his childhood pet-name, and he was glad to reclaim it.

'I know that, Leah. Little Leah. But *you* know I have to discover my own purpose.'

'. . . And the trouble is,' Leah remarked to Claud much later, when her brother was on the train back to Paris, solitary and brooding, 'that his purpose is Sarah. He's obsessive in his passions. He was always single-minded as a child. It is his strength and his weakness.'

Eighteen months passed. Adam's fourth novel, *Estelle*, escalated him back to popularity as a novelist; his mother's tragic love affair had furnished him with a plot which captured every reader's imagination, and in its first six months of publication, *Estelle* had been reprinted twice. At thirty-two, he was handsome, rich and famous; there were few people who hadn't heard of Adam Gilmour, or did not respect him for his literary achievements and his charitable work. Yet the boy-Adam was not greatly changed. The insecure stammerer lurked not far behind the façade, and after dinner parties, where he amused fellow-guests with his dry wit, and ability to draw caricatures in a flash, he returned home alone, exhausted from the effort of being entertaining.

Algernon Swinburne had faded from his life: the poet had degenerated rapidly during the past year with his addiction to alcohol, and the friendship had petered out. There was no other man with whom he was close, and he longed for Claud's weekly letters, which came as bursts of light, reminders that there was always an escape.

The problem, he knew, was that he needed a woman – and there were plenty to choose from nowadays, who flirted with him and sought him out. But he had been a bachelor on his own for too long; he had become too exacting, and had set such high standards for comparison. Who, in the end, could match Sarah's beauty, intelligence and generosity? Who else would so perfectly comprehend his fears and insecurities, obsessions and hopes?

One February morning in 1879, Adam took a hansom to Islington as usual and went up the steps to the imposing, freshly-painted door, which was always open during the day. Within was a smell of polish and wax. The murmur of a man's voice came from one of the rooms. He was newly employed and was explaining to three youths about the need to learn a skill, and how Brownstones would help to finance them.

Several other boys appeared when they heard Adam arrive; they worked in a textile factory, and this was their day-off-a-month which Adam had negotiated with their employer.

'Uncle Addi . . .' Boisterously they tackled his waist and butted their heads at him by way of greeting. At thirteen and fourteen years old, they were too old to kiss or hug.

He clapped each one on the back briefly, his face alight with pleasure at seeing them. 'Hallo lads . . .' He asked for their news. Later he would take the little group to the British Museum for their 'cultural' morning, and then to St James's Park where they would play football.

One of the boys was nicknamed Beaky because of his nose, a title he accepted good-naturedly. Tall and talkative, he was this morning unusually forthcoming.

'Is anything up, Beaky?' Adam asked when the child lingered after the others had disappeared.

Beaky was about to answer, then looked silently at the floor, scratching his mop of fair hair.

Of them all he was the toughest; or pretended to be; and Adam was astonished when he saw a tear fall to the ground.

'Beaky?' he enquired kindly. Tentatively he touched his shoulder, and the boy hurled himself at Adam, sobbing. Adam led him into his office that he shared with Sarah. She was there already, working with the latest typing machine she had taught herself to use. She looked up as they came in, her smile dying as she saw the crying boy. 'Hallo Addi . . . Beaky dear – what's happened?'

He shook his head, refusing to say anything, and stared at the floor, still giving broken sobs. Sarah glanced hopelessly at Adam and mouthed, 'Do you want me to leave?' pointing to herself. 'No,' he mouthed back.

'Beaky – now take a seat,' said Adam, in a man-to-man voice, and the boy hauled himself obediently into a chair, which Adam knelt beside. He stared directly into Beaky's eyes and Beaky suddenly giggled through his tears.

'What is it?' Adam asked, smiling.

'I can't remember which eye I have to look into!'

Adam roared with laughter and ruffled his hair. 'The left, Beaky – though when you're this close it doesn't make much odds.'

'Does it hurt you, your eye, I mean?' Beaky asked curiously, momentarily forgetting his unhappiness.

'No. It is my good eye which gives me problems. It becomes strained, having to do the work of two . . .' He looked at Beaky shrewdly, and confided, 'My secret dread is that something will happen to this eye and that I'll be competely blind.'

He waited; and sure enough, this confidence elicited from Beaky his own problem: 'Me Dad's upped and left us, and me Mum's on her own with no money and six of us. Littlest's only three months, and next one up's two . . . She can't get no work 'cause of them. All she does is cry all day. She's going mad with it all.'

'I don't blame her,' Sarah said tightly. 'It's a mad system.' Her eyes blazed. Adam had never seen her so furious.

'Beaky – dear – please don't worry.' She got up and went over to where he sat, and knelt beside Adam. She took his hand, and the boy looked at it, elegant and slender surrounding his own rough one. 'Please will you tell her to come and see me here? *Will* you?' she entreated.

And he nodded silently, his eyes welling again, as he continued to gaze down at the beautiful, pale hand.

The mother – Irene Black was her name – a submissive, worn-out looking woman, visited the next day, and sat nervously on the edge of her seat, alone with Sarah in the office.

'Would you like some tea, Mrs Black?' Sarah asked.

'If it ain't too much trouble, Ma'am,' the other answered almost inaudibly, twisting and wringing her hands constantly.

'It's no trouble at all, I assure you. And I should like some, too,' Sarah reassured her, and got up to fill the tea-kettle, light the burner and take out two cups and saucers.

The woman stared at her as Sarah busied herself, graceful in her movements. She had never seen such a beautiful lady; kind as well . . . The kindness shone from her face. She herself had been pretty years ago – oh so long ago, it seemed now, before she had become worn-out; when she had laughed and flirted, and had had the odd nice dress handed on to her by the mistress when she'd wearied of it . . .

Now she worried she would spill her tea when it came to drinking it, for her hands trembled so much sometimes that on occasions she became frightened she would drop the baby. *He* had done it to her; made her like this.

But the young woman standing next to her was sensitive to her anxieties. She set the cup of tea carefully on the desk beside Irene, and said, 'It's very hot. Just sip it when you want to . . . I know how you must be feeling.'

Did she? How could she know – a woman like that? But the dark eyes with their hazel flecks were full of compassion, and Irene blurted out, 'Beaky – he told you everything, then?'

'I don't know if it was *everything*, Irene – do you mind if I call you Irene?'

'No – no – I'm glad for you to, Ma'am.'

'And you must call me Sarah. I hate formality . . . Beaky only said your husband had left, and that you were at the end of your tether with all your problems.'

'He's a good lad.'

'He's a *very* good lad,' agreed Sarah.

'Oh, and you're ever so kind to him. He tells me about you and the gentleman. Proper angels, he says you are. Both of you.'

Sarah blushed, and chewed on her finger. 'We *care*,' she said passionately. 'That's all. We're not angels, Irene. Far from it. We only *care* . . .'

She sighed, calmed herself and took a large gulp from her cup of tea. She felt nervous herself, and was anxious not to seem patronizing, or as though she were prying.

Encouraged, Irene also sipped her tea, and her fingers didn't tremble, nor did a drop of tea spill. Her confidence crept back.

'Bastard's left us with scarce a penny. Gone to some little strumpet he'll soon wear out same as he done to me. Let her see what he's like when she's lost *her* looks after doing all his washing and cleaning and cooking and bearing his children – doing the same for them – and taking in laundry and sewing. Let's see how long he stays before quitting to go to the next one, and making an old hag of her . . .'

She was shaking, crying with the injustice of it all . . . And the tea was going everywhere. Gently, Sarah took the cup and saucer from her and set them on the desk again. Her own eyes watered with sorrow and rage. She moved her chair close to the other woman's.

'What about your children now?' she asked.

'Beaky's at the factory. The others are at home. The two next oldest are girls – ever so good really, I'm lucky like that – they're looking after the little ones.'

'I'd love you to tell me about them.'

'Well – Nancy – next one to Beaky – she's twelve, and ever so grown-up. Lorna's nine and a half – the quiet type you know. Next one's a boy. Tom. Proper tearaway, he is. A bit like his dad I suppose . . . He's coming up seven – There were another boy after him, Albert – after the Queen's poor husband, you know – but he died last year; only three, poor little mite . . . Little Mary's just two, and then there's the baby . . .' She reddened.

'What's its name?' Sarah asked, propping her chin on her left hand.

'You'll laugh.'

'But of course I shan't!'

'Well, Beaky – he's known "Uncle Addi" this past year or so, and he's so taken with him we thought . . . Well, the baby's called Adam. Addi for short.' Her face was scarlet, her hands busily twisting.

Sarah leaned forward and embraced the other woman. 'I am so

touched,' she said huskily. 'I cannot tell you just how touched. And how touched Mr Gilmour – Adam – will be when he hears.'

Irene looked pleased. 'Beaky says you've a little girl.'

'Yes, she'll be four in July.'

'You've plenty of help with her I dare say,' Irene commented without bitterness.

'Yes, I'm very fortunate. I have a lovely young nanny. However, I do try and look after Rebecca a great deal myself, and I only come into Brownstones three days a week now. The rest of the time I work at home.'

'You've a good husband?'

'. . . Yes . . . I'm very lucky.'

'It's no more'n you deserve. A beautiful, kind lady like you.'

'Thank you.'

There was a brief, comfortable silence between them, and then, very cautiously, Sarah said, 'Irene, I'd like to help you. I've had a good idea.'

The other was immediately suspicious. She had not come here to beg.

'No – don't look like that. We're friends now, I hope. Listen to what I say. Please?'

'Yes – yes of course,' Irene whispered, humbly.

'You see this machine on the desk?'

'Yes.' Irene looked at it dubiously.

'You know what it is?'

'It's one of them new machines as makes letters.'

'That's it. A typewriting machine. And it's ever so simple to use.'

'Is it really?' She became interested.

'Yes. Look –' And Sarah got up and demonstrated. Irene peered over her shoulder.

'It don't seem too hard,' she admitted. 'I mean, not once you know how.'

'Can you read and write, Irene?'

'Oh yes.' She laughed. 'I went to school till I was almost eleven. I were quite good at writing really.'

'Well I think you should learn to type.'

'What? Me?' She looked horrified.

'Yes,' Sarah said firmly. 'I taught myself.'

'But I ain't like you.' Irene's voice quavered and rose.

'Irene – you are an important person. Everyone is an important person. Only, not everyone is made to feel like it. Why *should* you just be a drudge and struggle to earn a pittance – and maybe have to give up your baby? Women have to learn to *value* themselves. If you could type, you could find a decent job as soon as little Adam's weaned. And meanwhile I'll help you.'

'I can't take money from you.'

'We'll work it out. I have a two-year scheme. I'm going to buy you a machine – no please listen – and you can learn to use it. You can repay me, and practise at the same time, by typing letters for me – that would be most useful. I will pay you by the hour, so you will be earning. But you must become expert on that machine and learn to spell properly from a dictionary. Don't you see – this machine offers you a chance of a different life?'

Her fervour had communicated itself to Irene, whose face was transformed from the strained expression of before: it held hope now. She sat upright, and her mouth parted in a smile.

'It were God put you in our path,' she said, shaking her head, staring at Sarah. 'And bless Beaky for making me come today . . . It were surely God.'

Weary from a long day of *serious* work, as he told his wife, Jonathan sat across the dinner table from her, glaring.

'Why must you involve yourself with waifs and strays?' he said. 'Brownstones is one thing, and is of course most commendable, but when it begins to intrude on our home life, that is another issue.'

'It's not intruding on –'

'Of course it is. Why should we pay for a typewriting machine for this woman, and then pay her weekly wages? She'll be coming here, begging, the whole time. You'll never be rid of her. She can get help if she needs it – there are charities who would help her. Or she could stay in a poorhouse . . . Better still, take a few brats off her hands. These women shouldn't keep breeding like rabbits.'

'Jonathan, I can't bear this.' Sarah stood up abruptly, paling, and gripped the edge of the table.

'Oh, for goodness' sake sit down. How do you think I feel, coming home after a hard day, to *this*? I don't see why this woman should cadge from us. There are thousands more where she came from. What are you going to do? Educate them all? Buy machines for them all? Pay for all their multitudinous children?'

'Yes Jonathan,' answered Sarah very softly. 'That is my aim, and my desire.'

She pressed her fingertips into the polished surface of the table, then, with great dignity, trembling within her and feeling faintly sick, she left the room.

She lay rigidly when he came to bed, feigned sleep, but his icy feet brushed hers and made her snatch hers away with the shock of the cold.

'Hey, old thing,' came his voice in the darkness. 'I know you mean well.'

She said nothing. He smelled of wine. He stroked her body.

'Jonathan – I'm tired.'

'Well, I'm tired too. And I'm getting up at dawn. I'm hunting in Hertfordshire tomorrow.'

'Go to sleep then.'

'Don't be a bad sport – heh?'

She had noticed over the years that he always became sexually aroused after a quarrel, and this seemed a kind of perversion to her; a travesty of what the act should have meant. She felt a wave of antagonism – against him and all men, with the exception of Adam. The interview with Irene Black had disturbed her, and Sarah had taken her problems and grudges on to her own shoulders. Irene Black became representative of every woman who had ever suffered.

Jonathan's fingers moved between her legs. 'No!' she shouted, the first time she had ever raised her voice to him. '*No*. Don't you understand? I don't *want* to. That is my *right*, not to want to. It's *my* body. And please don't call me "old thing". I hate it.'

Weeping, she stumbled from the bed and rushed from the room, into the one next door, where once Adam had slept. She locked the door and, shivering, climbed into bed, where she lay awake and troubled for most of the night – finally to doze in the early hours. She awoke again at dawn to hear her husband getting ready; and then his footsteps downstairs, the front door – and the sound of the horse and carriage taking him away . . .

Throughout the day she was alternately elated by her own behaviour, and appalled. Nervously, she kept ringing the maid to bring yet another pot of coffee. She kept Rebecca downstairs with her for the entire afternoon to try to take her mind off the confusion and anger there, and then the child became tired, and went upstairs to rest. Calmer by now, Sarah sat at the little desk in the sitting-room and began to make notes on her ideas for helping women in need. Outside it grew dark and a strong wind blew; but within it was cosy, with the fire and the gaslights. Sarah continued to write, increasingly excited by her plans.

She was still writing when the front-door bell rang, and a sober-faced man she had never met before was shown into the room, to tell her that her husband had been killed in a hunting accident.

Chapter Seventeen

ADAM AND SARAH

On Wednesday, February 26th, at just after eight o'clock in the evening, the same man who had earlier called on Sarah to inform her of her husband's death visited Adam in Knightsbridge. Bad tidings didn't sit well on him: as the Hunt Master, he was a fanatic, a bachelor with little thought for anything unconnected with his sport, an emotionless, blustering man. He had not known Jonathan Gilmour well, and himself had not seen the accident – only the body afterwards, lying in a distorted position, but otherwise unremarkable. The sight had left him unmoved.

Death had been instantaneous, he told the new widow, and now the brother, assuming an appropriate expression of commiseration, which settled rather like a sneer on his round, red face. He had, of course, heard of Adam Gilmour, and as someone who more than anything enjoyed dropping names, he made a mental note of the room into which he had been shown – a cosy pine-panelled place with books flanking one complete wall.

'He made me most welcome in his study,' he would tell colleagues at a later stage. 'Frightfully cut up about his brother, of course . . .'

In reality, Adam couldn't wait for the man to leave, wanting to be alone with his thoughts, but clearly the fellow expected a drink for his trouble, lingering with that false expression of sympathy stuck like a clown's nose on his moon of a face; Adam disliked everything he represented, but courtesy prevailed, and politely he enquired what the other would like.

'A whisky wouldn't go amiss, if it's all right with you. Bit shaken myself, y'know.'

'Yes, I'm sure,' Adam murmured, pouring whisky into two glasses.

'Dreadful thing to happen. Quite dreadful. But like I say – instantaneous. Wouldn't have known a damn thing. Hmph.'

'No.'

'Excellent whisky.'

'It was kind of you to go to so much trouble.'

'Not at all. I knew your brother well. Excellent sort.'

When he eventually left, Adam went over to the chaise-longue by the window and lay down, staring unseeingly ahead, his hands tightly clenched into fists. Within him was turmoil, and his heart raced. At first he had been stunned and disbelieving at hearing the news, and he tried to cling to these sentiments as the proper ones, to concentrate on his shock, and convince himself of his own sense of loss. But intrusive, like snide little stabs, were other thoughts – invidious at such a time – that he could not prevent, and for which he was horrified at himself. He got up again and poured himself another small whisky, before putting on his overcoat and hat, and leaving the house.

As he waited for a cab to come by, he stamped his feet to try to keep warm. It was trying to snow – fragmented flakes landing on him, on the ground. What pleasure did people get in this freezing weather chasing over muddy ground after a fox? he wondered. What thoughts occurred to Jonathan, the second he fell? Were they of Sarah? Sarah, Sarah, Sarah . . .

A hansom approached and halted next to him, and he climbed inside, rubbing his hands together – he had forgotten to bring gloves – trying to still his churning mind.

She was in bed when he arrived, and a doctor was there, having just given her a draught which would act as a sedative.

'She is beside herself,' the doctor told him. 'I would suggest you just sit quietly with her and let her talk or sleep, as she feels like it. The draught will have a soporific effect. It is unfortunate her mother is not in London at present, and the father is abroad, I gather. I think, if it's at all possible, you should stay with your sister-in-law until the mother comes. Mrs Gilmour is incapable of making arrangements, she is in far too bad a state . . . And please accept my condolences over your own tragedy . . .'

Adam tiptoed upstairs. Into her room. There Sarah lay, on her side, her hair tangled and half-hiding her tear-streaked face. Her grief hurt him more than anything. Her eyes were half-closed, their lids puffed; they flickered and opened properly as he came and sat on the stool by the bed.

'Addi? . . . Oh Addi . . .' She extended her hand limply and he took it, holding it first to his lips, then to his cheek for a moment, closing his eyes.

'Dearest Addi . . .' Fresh tears slid down her cheek, and she gave little animal-like moans. The draught had made her mouth dry and ill-tasting, and she continually sucked on her lips and swallowed. He wanted to kiss her, to fill her mouth with moisture. Her dishevelled state did not repulse him in the least; it only served to make her more real to him, more loved.

'I shall fetch you some water to drink.'

'Don't leave me,' she cried, panicked.

'Only for an instant, my darling. I am only filling the tumbler from the pitcher.'

She was half-asleep barely a minute later when he sat by her again, and set the glass of water on the little table beside her. Once more her eyes opened, and he passed her the water and propped up her head.

'What shall I do?' she said plaintively, when she had finished sipping. 'I don't know what I am to do.'

'About what, my sweetest?'

'Anything. About anything. The funeral . . . Afterwards . . . He was such a good man.'

'I know,' Adam, the hypocrite, said.

'And I'm wicked, *wicked*.' She thumped the bedclothes weakly with her free hand, in self-directed anger.

'You're not wicked,' he assured her tenderly. 'No one could be less wicked than you.'

'I am,' she insisted brokenly, and drifted into sleep, while he continued to sit by her, holding her drooping right hand, stroking it, chilled by the possibility that she meant she had been having an affair.

That night, in the library of his sister-in-law's house, he had the idea for a new novel: *Aaron*.

'Aaron was the first-born brother,' he began, 'so named by his father because A was the first, the most important letter of all alphabets . . .'

He looked out of the window on to the little garden, patchily illuminated by the moon and the settling snow. It all seemed very tranquil out there. He thought of his brother sitting in this room, his legs stretched out, his face buried behind the paper. He could muster up no grief, only a rather tired resentment which had not quite run its course.

'Perhaps I should move to the country again,' he thought. 'I could travel to London weekly, to Brownstones. The paperwork could be done at home . . . the boys could visit, stay with me . . . I've had enough of London . . . If she'd only come with . . . Perhaps. Patience . . . Oh God, how wearisome patience is . . . And such thoughts on the eve of my brother's death . . .'

He stared again at the sentence he had written, and felt a surge of that old eagerness which always took hold of him at the onset of a novel: first, the bones of an idea, and then the substance, the flesh . . . ideas springing from here and there willy-nilly, coming together, linked by some incident as yet undreamed of. Writing, for him, initially provided enormous relief; but as a work progressed, the struggle would commence; the sentences did not flow as they should, or the apt words leap to mind. Although his fingers might itch to write, that mind might have become frustratingly barren. And for every word he wrote, Adam crossed out another. He strove for precision.

Aaron would be the story of an artist of aristocratic birth, and would be partly autobiographical. He himself was, of course, Aaron, the subjugated older brother to Jocelyn, just as in the Bible the character had been dominated by his younger brother, Moses. Aaron would be in love with his sister-in-law, Celia, a Jewess; a beautiful, intelligent woman confused by her own passionate nature . . .

He had no thought, as he made notes, of disloyalty to the woman he loved. It was simply a book he had to write, and it would, he knew, be his best yet.

Wet spring, and the young widow was trying to adapt to the changes in her life.

'Perhaps I might move,' she told Adam one day. 'I never really liked the house. It was our first major compromise, you know.' She gave a little laugh. She had become too thin, lavished endless energy on everything she did, but devoted no time to anything for herself. She seemed to despise herself, and Adam knew she was troubled by a problem she wouldn't confide to him. He ceased to worry she was having an affair, and was shocked at himself for ever having supposed such a thing.

'Sarah – why not go and stay with Leah and Claud for a while? They would so love to see you, and it would do you good.'

'Oh I am far too busy,' she said, brushing aside the suggestion. There was a pile of letters in front of her – all rejections from high-ranking men refusing to help her found a women's charity. Bitterly, she read one after the other, and then she rolled the lot into a ball and threw them disgustedly into the waste-bin. 'That,' she said, 'is what I think of them.'

'Sarah, you are *not* too busy.'

'Oh Addi, I *am*.' She looked at him properly then, and the misery in her face dismayed him.

He got up from his desk and went to stand by her, cupping her chin in his hands. 'Please, Sarah dear. For me. Go with little Rebecca to France. It would do you *such* good.'

'I do not deserve goodness.' Her chin quivered and he touched it affectionately with his index finger.

'Why are you feeling guilty? Will you not tell me, dearest? You seem so confused.'

She broke down then, in a fit of weeping, and he held her. 'You cry . . . Cry . . .'

'Oh, you're too kind to me.' She stamped her foot feebly.

'And why shouldn't I be?' He held her away slightly, and smiled at her.

'Addi –' She took a deep breath as though to tell him something, then decided against it. It was too shameful. 'No, I cannot,' she said. 'I'm sorry.'

'Would you confide in Leah?'

'Perhaps,' she answered hesitantly.

'I hate to see you suffer. I long only to help you.'

'I know. You do so much for me, and I do nothing in return.'

'Of course you do. Anyway, you have no need. But you could do me *one* small favour.'

'Anything.'

'Good. Then I should like you to go to France for a while.'

'Cheat! That is not fair.'

'It is absolutely fair!' Her smile, the laughter in her eyes, delighted him.

She said, 'You know – that reminds me of the first time you came back to Brambleden Hall, and met my mother, and you made me play the harp. How long ago it seems.'

'It *is* a long time ago.'

'How glad I am to have you as a friend.'

'And I you . . . So you will go?'

'Yes, I shall. But what about Irene?'

'Irene will be fine. I'll give her plenty of letters to type, lend her books to read, and generally make sure she is looked after.'

'I have had an idea for starting an organization where mothers may take turns looking after each other's small children, enabling them to find part-time work. A centre for mothers and children really.'

'It's an excellent idea.'

'Would it work, do you think?'

'When you return, we shall plan it and *make* it work.'

She hugged him. Her face was damp against his, and her lips only an inch or so away. He had only to move a little . . . But he would not.

A week later he saw Sarah and Rebecca off at the station – ran alongside them on the platform as the train gathered speed and their faces blurred, and their waving hands were pale flashes. Then they were gone, and he felt as empty as a vessel from which the wine has been drunk.

Sarah's first letter arrived. Boyishly excited, Adam saw it amongst the other letters on the lobby floor. The envelope was addressed 'Monsieur Adam Gilmour', in her firm round handwriting, and he carried it like a prize, apart from the rest, resisting opening it until he could sit in solitary comfort at the breakfast table with a pot of coffee and a plate of kippers before him. Then he tore it open. It was dated June 3rd.

Dearest Adam [and what implication might he draw from that?],

So – we have arrived safely, which during the boat crossing I doubted we would, for the sea was like a wrathful god, and passengers were vomiting and fainting as the boat plunged and rose like an insignificant plaything. In the cabin, Rebecca lay on her bed *giggling*, would you believe, treating the whole thing as a joke, whilst I felt myself turning more ashen by the minute, and fought continually against retching . . . However, as you gather, we finally reached Calais, and travelled thence to Paris, where upon your recommendation we stayed for two nights at L'Hôtel Blanc. Monsieur and Madame Blanc made us most welcome, and Madame Blanc kindly looked after Rebecca for a few hours while I made a tour of the city. But apart from that I have had my daughter to myself, and am so pleased I did not bring Eileen with me, and was firm with her when she begged to come, for I have grown really close to my daughter in a way one cannot with a nanny around.

And now I am here with darling Leah and Claud and the twins – and after their initial hesitation the children play together beautifully, running around everywhere semi-nude, like primitives. What a fit Eileen, with her liking for orderliness, would have. What a fit my Jonathan would have had. I sometimes think he would have been happier with more disorder in his life. It is a healthy thing, I realize. You – as surely the untidiest man on this planet – would understand that!

What a paradise this place is. After five days I feel quite at home, and have already visited Sarlat and Domme and different parts of the countryside. We pile – and I mean pile – into the cart; our belongings go too, including Claud's lute. Claud sits perched on the driving seat like a weather-beaten farmer with his old hat pulled down over his bleached hair, and shielding his mariner's eyes.

They are so happy here, and in their own ways successful,

for which I am glad, as a rural idyll could perhaps pall for two such intelligent people as they, without some sort of mental stimulation in addition.

Everything is just as you told me: the house, the setting, the village, the people. You were right to persuade me to come here. Although of course I still think about everything – it is so short a time ago, after all – I can feel my strength returning, as though I were being replenished. Naturally it has helped, as you said it would (how well you understand me, dear Adam), to talk to Leah, and she has been a great support since I confided in her. Please do not be insulted that I could not confide in you, but despite our special closeness, you are a man, and there are certain issues I could not discuss with you . . .

Adam broke off from reading and gazed unseeingly at his plate of cooling, part-eaten kippers. He could hear Sarah's low, lilting voice, see her before him, unwittingly sexual; he could caress her, kiss her, undress her – and she stood there, naked, slender, but full-breasted, her nipples darkened and larger after having borne a child, and he bent his head and took one in his mouth . . .

'Oh God . . .' He got up, and walked round the table. He had become hard, and he ached with it – longing for her with a fierceness which made him beat his fist against his thigh in frustration. He returned to the table, his cold breakfast, and resumed reading:

It is evening now. Delicious food smells drift from the house; Jasper, Mark and Rebecca roll over and over on the lawn, screaming with joy and playing with the new puppy; a nearby frog gives intermittent hiccoughs (I did not know what it was until Claud told me). Leah is in her studio working on a great chunk of marble; Claud is in a far corner of the garden, miraculously lost in his writing (earlier, he finished building a raft); and I sit here writing to you, letting the end-of-day's pleasant tiredness wash over me, the sweet evening warmth seep into my body, while a gentle breeze lifts up the edges of my skirts and cools my legs.

I realize I have asked you nothing of yourself, and written entirely of me. Please forgive me, especially since your welfare is very dear to me. I hope you are well, and that you are coping with all the trials and tribulations of Brownstones. Brownstones seems a long way away – but not you, Adam. I think often of you. I hope your book is going well – this mystery novel you will not speak of! Strange man! Take care of yourself, and I send you my love – and of course, also from your goddaughter.
Sarah

Adam did not go to Brownstones that day, and after breakfast went into his study, where he shut himself in, to work on his 'mysterious' novel. It was beginning to possess him, as writing it became an outlet for his emotions . . .

He had jumped four chapters, and he wrote feverishly. First came Celia's disappointment in her husband, and her refusal to acknowledge a failed marriage, then her growing attraction to her brother-in-law, whom she had thought she loved only as a friend. He wrote of 'Celia's' efforts to establish herself as a person with her own identity, described her involvement with a cause, and resultant estrangement from her husband . . . She became pregnant, and he wrote of her joy, and later, the birth of her daughter. Her husband was not there afterwards, but he – Aaron – was. He was always there. He loved her to the point of obsession, this shy, stammering man, whose artistic talent was just becoming recognized. But his younger brother taunted him and regarded him as a failure, just as his mother had done . . .

And then Jocelyn was killed in a ballooning accident (it would not do to keep every sequence identical to his own life), and Celia was free . . .

Adam wrote a long passage in which he described Celia's thoughts and fantasies, her developing love for her brother-in-law, while in his own fantasies Celia and Sarah became indistinguishable, and he was Aaron.

He broke off writing, breathing hard. His mouth was parched, his eye watering. He felt enclosed by the room suddenly, and had to go from it, outside, into the long narrow garden where he had sat with Leah and Jonathan, and Jonathan's latest young lady friend, as their mother twitched and did her embroidery on the terrace.

In July he took his incomplete and unedited manuscript to Gray-Courtney. 'I have no copy,' he said, protectively clasping his work to him, 'and it is very precious to me.'

'You will have it back in three days,' Gray-Courtney promised, intrigued.

'Be careful of it,' Adam begged, agonized.

He returned to the publisher's office on the appointed day. 'What do you think?' he demanded, standing, hands clenched, while the other sat calmly behind his desk.

'I think it's a risk,' that man said, and watched Adam's face tumble. 'But,' he continued, smiling, 'I am prepared to take that risk if you are.'

Adam released an exhalation of breath.

'There is no chance, of course,' Gray-Courtney added, 'of having it serialized.'

'No, I didn't think there would be, which is why I brought it directly to you.'

'We could both be in trouble for it.'

'In France nobody would blink an eyelash.'

'We are not in France, Mr Gilmour.'

'No . . .' Adam paused, then said. 'I have a request to make.'

'And what might that be?' Gray-Courtney asked, smiling genially.

'I must take a pseudonym.'

'No – that cannot be permitted.' He stood up abruptly and banged his fists together.

'Then the book cannot be published.'

'The readership would be halved. And without serialization beforehand . . . No, it would be a disastrous move. I cannot agree.'

'Then *I* cannot agree to publication,' Adam said quietly, his face set stubbornly.

Gray-Courtney sat down again, leaned his elbows on the table, and placed his fingertips together. His eyes narrowed behind their spectacles. 'The risks increase,' he said meditatively.

Adam sat down also, and bit his lower lip. 'It is n-not, of course, for m-m-me to tell you about m-mar-marketing,' he said.

The other man laughed for the first time. 'My, you have a nerve. And what would you do – advertise your book as "The sensational new novel written by a famous author under a pseudonym"?'

'It could work.' Adam raised an eyebrow consideringly.

Gray-Courtney sat back and said slowly, 'I shall have to think about it.'

'I am prepared to have it published myself, if you will not,' Adam told him pleasantly.

'Mr Gilmour, I have said I shall think about it.'

Just four days later Adam received a letter from Geoffrey Gray-Courtney:

> Dear Mr Gilmour,
>
> It is a risk in more ways than one, but I believe in what you have written. Gray-Courtney are happy to offer you an advance sum of twelve hundred guineas for *Aaron*, with a view to publication in May 1880.
>
> Sincerely, G.G.C.
>
> P.S. You have just four months left to complete it, therefore, so shut yourself away!

On a hot August evening Adam went to meet Sarah and Rebecca at Victoria Station. He scanned the passengers as they disembarked from the train, dreading that he might miss them, for Sarah was not expecting him to be there. And then he saw her: a distinguished-looking man was assisting her down the little steps as she clung tightly to her daughter's hand. A porter carried her luggage. Adam felt a surge of jealousy as he watched the man bend to kiss her hand suavely, and raise his hat in a sweeping gesture, before walking off in the opposite direction; his elation at the prospect of seeing her withered and he was momentarily stricken. He was about to slip away, holding the flowers he had bought, when she spotted him, and called at the top of her voice, so that everyone turned, 'Addi? Addi!' And ran towards him, pulling along her daughter, and followed by the puffing, elderly porter.

The distinguished-looking man had only sat in her compartment for the last half-hour, she assured him, sitting pressed beside him in the hansom, with Rebecca on her lap dozing and snoring very slightly. He had talked endlessly of his wife and children, and she in turn had spoken of Brownstones and her famous brother-in-law.

Adam's jealousy ebbed. Now all he wanted to do was stare at her, listen to her voice – as she chattered away while he scarcely heard what she said. He shook his head, still hardly believing she had returned.

'You look wonderful. So well. Wonderful,' he repeated, taking her hand. She left it in his, and he could feel the pulse in her wrist throbbing.

Brownstones had become an important and nationally recognized charity, receiving patronage from some of the wealthiest and most respected names in Britain. Numerous staff were employed, and at last Adam and Sarah could delegate some of their responsibilities . . . There was a heatwave that August and September. They would sit on a rug spread out in the garden – Adam, Sarah and Rebecca, and Adam would relate stories to the child:

'Once upon a time there was a fat king –'

'Was he *very* fat?' the little girl interrupted, her expression serious.

'Hugely fat.' Adam extended his arms as wide as he could. 'So fat he had to have doors made especially large in order to go through them.'

'Oh Addi,' said Sarah, laughing. Her eyes glinted gold in the sun.

'Anyway, this hugely fat king sat on his extra huge throne and ruled his empire from there, telling people what to do all day. He could do nothing himself, because he was too fat to move far. The furthest he ever went was to the great dining-room, where the immense table was permanently laid for him . . .'

The months passed, and his relationship with Sarah seemed no further advanced. The dry spell ended and autumn arrived. Adam was behind schedule with his novel, and Geoffrey Gray-Courtney frequently nagged at him.

Sarah asked him once, 'What is this enigmatic book?'

'Oh, it's not worth discussing,' he replied vaguely. 'It will take years to write. I may even start on another . . .'

She herself was keeping busy with her new charity – visiting women in factories, poorhouses, prisons, in their own homes . . . And the more she explored, the angrier she became at the outrages she saw everywhere. Her energy was impelled by a growing fury as, daily, she uncovered fresh horror-stories: beaten women compelled to remain with their husbands; women toiling endless hours like a pony on the treadmill; women dying prematurely, ignorant of how to get help; women forced to resort to prostitution because the options were worse; women like Irene had been, bound by numerous children, unable to take jobs . . . And such jobs as there were, were inevitably demeaning or menial, and did not allow for a woman's intelligence which, Sarah heatedly told Adam, at least *matched* a man's, if not was superior.

'We are quite simply not recognized or acknowledged as people in our own right. Mere ornaments or drudges, depending on which end of the social scale we come from – that is how we are regarded.'

Aaron was almost finished. It had a happy ending; Celia became Aaron's wife, they moved to the country, and he helped her realize her aims, at the same time achieving success for himself as an artist . . . But there was an entire chapter missing.

Then, in the beginning of November an incident happened to change things. Sarah was at Adam's house – he had invited her to dinner – and they were sitting companionably together in the study after their meal, when there came a crashing noise from the far end of the room, making them start. Adam put his hand on her arm and they went to investigate: two pictures – matching prints of a courting couple – had fallen simultaneously from the wall, and the glass had smashed. They had been a present from Sarah.

'How horrible.' She leaned against him. 'It makes me shiver.'

'It's rather sinister,' he agreed, and bent to pick up one of the pictures.

'Careful of the broken glass,' she warned, as he examined it.

'The picture is undamaged at least,' he said. 'Did you know the woman looked a little like you?'

'No. How funny. One never knows what oneself looks like. But the *man* reminded me of *you*.'

'Really?' He gave a self-deprecating smile. 'The half-blind hero with too many grey hairs.'

'They suit you. I love your hair,' she said tenderly, and reached up to stroke it.

He caught her hands. 'And I love you.' He said the words at last, after so many years of wanting to, after endless patience and vacillating hopes. And before she could answer, he tilted her chin towards him and kissed her. He sucked her lips with his, ravelled her tongue with his, drew on her warm breath . . . and her arms wound round his neck, her body was against his, her back curved towards him. Their breathing became rapid, and he felt the heat radiating from her, little sighs vibrating against his lips, quivers running through her. He moved away and looked enquiringly into her eyes. They had become almost black; her cheeks were flushed, and her hair awry. He held out his hand towards her, and she took it, and wordlessly they went up the stairs to his bedroom.

In there he kissed her again, and she responded immediately, seemingly lost in the strength of her feelings. With his mouth still on hers, he unbuttoned the front of her blouse, fumbling a little, and her fingers found his to help him. She undid her skirt herself . . . After that came the paraphernalia of her underclothes – and then she stood there as he had imagined her so often, naked in *his* room, by *his* bed, her belly firm and rounded, her breasts more voluptuous than he'd realized – and her strong long legs smooth-skinned and sleek-thighed. The V between them was liberally covered with black hair, and he crouched and kissed her there, his tongue finding her folds through the dense curls.

'Addi – no.'

He looked up briefly. 'Hush. It is normal. Natural. And I *love* you. This is part of it.'

Her eyes glazed, and she stood there rocking over his head, giving little groans.

He undressed himself hurriedly, throwing his clothes on to the floor where they mingled in an untidy heap with hers. Sarah did not take her eyes from him.

'I never realized a man's body could be so beautiful,' she said softly, and tentatively ran her fingers over his chest and belly, stopping, shyly, at his erect penis.

Very gently he pushed her on to the bed, and for some while, as in slow motion, they kissed and caressed one another, savouring every sensuous feeling – the smoothness of skin on skin, hair on hair, tongue on tongue. When, at last, he probed with himself between her legs and felt her open for him, take him in, he was surrounded by glorious warmth, and softness and quivering muscles . . .

'Oh God, you feel exquisite,' he murmured, as he sank deeper into her. And one arm tightened around his neck, while the other hand stroked and pressed his buttocks.

He held still in her. 'I have wanted you for so long . . . I don't know how long I can go on for,' he said in her ear.

'It doesn't matter,' she whispered tightly, her body gyrating, feeling on the brink of some extraordinary crest. He placed his hands under her and brought her leg over his so that she was slightly on her side. He stared into her eyes, felt as though he were drowning in them, felt the tingling in him spread to his toes. Her breathing came more and more quickly, and he felt her muscles grip him tightly. She screwed up her face and put her hand in her mouth as though in pain – and then gave a sharp cry, which she foreshortened in a series of broken gasps, just as he himself reached his climax.

Afterwards, she lay cocooned by his body, her thighs sticky, her eyes wet from weeping.

'I didn't know,' she said. 'I didn't know . . .'

He got up to switch off the gaslights and returned to the bed. Her arms opened for him, and, entwined, they fell asleep. He awoke a couple of hours later to find her searching in the dark for her clothes.

'What are you doing?'

'Dearest – I cannot stay. It would not be right, with the servants.'

'We are free to do as we wish. It is no business of the servants.' Dismayed, he got up, switched on the lights. Sarah began to dress, picking her clothes from the untidy pile, symbolic of their earlier impatience.

He went over to her – she was busily searching for a garter – and embraced her, kissed her neck, her hair, her mouth.

She responded – but only briefly. 'Dearest, I have to go. I am expected at home. Rebecca may need me in the night or early morning. She has been waking recently.'

This seemed reasonable, and reluctantly he helped her sort out her clothes, and lovingly fastened the tiny buttons of her blouse; then he dressed himself. He looked at his watch: it was gone midnight.

'I hate the idea of you taking a hansom alone at night.'

'I shall be fine.' She gave a small tug to the laces of her short boots. 'You worry too much.'

'Only because I care,' he said, hurt.

'I know.' She looked up at him quickly then, with an expression of absolute love.

He walked with her until they found a cab, drew the collar of her coat up to keep her warm, kept his arm protectively around her, fiddled once with a wisp of hair that fell over her forehead into her eyes . . . Every one of his gestures demonstrated his adoration of her, and within her, Sarah wept.

'Sarah – darling – it was beautiful being inside you. I could never have believed such joy possible.'

She stopped walking, and grabbing his hand, held it to her cheek. She hesitated, then said softly, 'Neither could I have imagined such a feeling.'

'And it gets better. The more we learn about one another, the better it will become.'

She made no reply, and almost with relief cried, 'There is a cab,' and hailed it. Adam paid the driver in advance.

'See you tomorrow, my dearest,' he said softly, and she kissed him passionately, hugging him as though in despair – before the coachman lifted his whip and the horse trotted off smartly.

Back home, Adam stayed up for the remainder of the night and wrote the entire missing chapter of his book. He fell asleep at his desk just before his maidservant came to wake him for the day . . .

Sarah did not sleep either. Her body was still alive, every nerve tense and quivering. She should have been ecstatic, but she was desolate. What she had done was terrible, unthinkable, contrary to every code of morality: she was in mourning, widowed not yet nine *months*; Adam was her brother-in-law. She had denied her husband, on the last night they had had together, what she had just freely given to his brother; and the pleasure she had derived with Adam, she had never known with him. And what of the act itself, which should be confined to married partners? . . . What had she done? She was consumed with remorse, appalled at herself (Adam she regarded as blameless) – and despairing of this great love she bore which must not be expressed again, and which she knew to be the most real kind of love, born as it was of the deepest friendship.

She sobbed for the entire night at the hopelessness of it all, at the dreadfulness of her behaviour, and prayed, for the first time in months; said the Shema, in Hebrew: 'Hear oh Israel, the Lord our God, the Lord is One . . .' Her mother had said it every night with her as a child. She wished she were a child again. She wished her Mama and Papa were there to cosset her. How old he had looked when she had last seen her father. When had it happened?

She felt suddenly on her own – her parents would die, she was husbandless, her best friend lived abroad, and everything would be changed between Adam and herself. She would devote herself to her child and her new cause. She cried – and cradled her own head, which just a few hours ago Adam had cradled. 'Oh Addi . . .'

Adam, having no inkling of these sentiments, hummed as he washed and dressed and prepared for the day. He put his manuscript under his arm, and walked briskly all the way to Gray-Courtney's new office in Piccadilly.

'I shall marry her,' was all he could think. 'As soon as a respectable time has elapsed, we'll marry . . .'

And when he strode into Geoffrey Gray-Courtney's office, to triumphantly hand over his novel, he looked so utterly happy that the publisher remarked, 'You look like a man who has inherited the earth.'

Chapter Eighteen

A CASE FOR PROSECUTION

November 8th, 1879. Thursday evening.
'From yesterday night's supreme joy I have plunged into despair. Sarah has said that what happened must never be repeated; the episode has become convoluted in her mind, and she has attached all kinds of complexities to it, to do, I think, with her guilt over Jonathan. She will simply not discuss the matter, and I confess I lost my temper with her for the first time. I cannot comprehend her decision. How can she deny what happened, what we both felt? I just don't know what to do . . . In addition I fear I am about to have one of my attacks – I have been having breathing problems since this afternoon . . .'

His illness was short and not severe, and it had the effect of lessening the tension between them, for Sarah spent most of the week by his bedside. By the time he was recovered, their friendship was almost on its old footing. No allusion was made to that one night, and although each was guarded with the other, the mundaneness of working together further eased the strain. Adam resigned himself to another period of patience.

He wrote letters on her behalf to patrons of Brownstones, persuading them to support her new charity, had a meeting with her father about financial help from his bank, wrote articles highlighting their aims; and gradually they had some response, and the funds accumulated. Then, in February 1880, they found suitable premises to rent for the new organization – round the corner from Brownstones Boys' Club.

'What shall we call it?' she asked, going from one empty cobweb-adorned room to another, her voice echoing.

'What about Brownstones Women's Club?'

'Of course. What an obvious idea!' For a moment she looked sad.

'What's wrong?' he asked.

She shook her head. 'Nothing.'

But she was thinking of her husband, the anniversary of whose death would be in a few days' time. A year already. How impatient Jonathan would have been with her new plans.

Adam didn't press her to confide, and the moment passed. She ran from one part of the building to another . . . 'Here will be the office, here a dormitory, here a place for children . . . A perfect recreation room . . . I shall put Irene in charge as supervisor . . . The whole place is wonderfully light. That is most important . . .'

He watched her tolerantly, sadly. He had no way of knowing any more what she felt for him. He sometimes longed for those evenings in past times, when they had been more selfish, and spoken of other things than Brownstones, when she had played her harp to him – curved over it, transported.

They left the building, and again he noticed that wistful expression. He linked her arm in his. Their breath made huff which mingled in the air. Dragons' breath, he remembered, he had called it as a child.

'Sarah – you know you haven't played the harp to me for ages. I miss it.'

'How funny – I was just thinking of that.' And fractionally their gaze held – before she lowered hers and changed the subject.

On February 26th, although she was not religious, Sarah kept Yahrtzeit – lit the memorial candle, and went to synagogue in memory of her husband – who would no doubt have been horrified at this Jewish ritual. She sat in the drawing-room alone for most of the day – a room she rarely used, but which Jonathan had liked – and tried to concentrate her thoughts on him.

Staring at the wavering flame of the candle, she conjured up his face. It came and went, and came and went. And when it was there she felt no great hankering, and when it was gone, no great sense of loss. A year. And he was remote from her, almost as though they had never been married. For the first time she acknowledged to herself that their marriage had been a sham, her love for him shallow, and her husband not a particularly pleasant person.

Shocked, she stood up abruptly and paced a few steps. And then she became calm. 'Why am I so shocked? Is it my fault he was as he was? I made every effort I could to make the marriage work . . . It was simply a mistake – an error of judgement . . . Why am I so ashamed?'

These thoughts were a revelation, and she felt a great relief and sense of freedom. She could look ahead again, consider a future for herself. She thought of Adam. 'How patient he's been . . . But then he's a remarkable man . . . I love him . . . And we've no secrets from one another . . .'

Friday, February 27th
'As the date of publication for my book draws closer, I am more than ever bothered. Rashly, I put pen to paper in an attempt to exorcize my own passions, and I begin to fear the consequences . . .'

Aaron was published on Tuesday, May 4th. On the Thursday Adam took Sarah to the theatre, then dinner at a nearby restaurant in Leicester Square, where they both drank rather too much. Their hands rested on the table, and every so often their fingers crept towards each other, and touched lingeringly – before backing away, spider-like. Beneath the table their feet brushed, as if accidentally.

'It's become a game,' Adam thought, unable to keep the smile from his face. There was a tantalizing shyness between them, the atmosphere charged with sexuality. She sucked on her finger, as she always did when she was flustered, while he kept running his hands through his hair; and each recognized these familiar traits in the other for what they were.

He was about to broach the subject of his book, when she said, 'I keep seeing this new novel, *Aaron*, being advertised. Do you know about it?'

The timing of her question, the candour in her eyes, caught him off guard, so that he found he could not tell her after all. Stammering he answered, 'N-no doubt it is so-some insignificant writer giving himself airs, and trying to achieve m-m-maximum publicity.'

He consoled himself that this was not a lie, and gestured to the waiter to remove their plates.

Back at her house she played the harp for him; he lay on the floor beside her, his eyes shut, but seeing her still in his mind.

'You play beautifully,' he said when she had finished and was taking the sheet of music from the stand.

'I don't play enough nowadays,' she said dismissively, 'I am rather out of practice. I think it is this room. I just cannot like it. You know how it is – some rooms, some houses, feel right, and others do not.'

'Yes I know.'

'I really must do something about moving.'

'I, too. My mother haunts the Knightsbridge house, I swear! It has never felt like home, despite all your wonderful redecoration. I still see it as it was . . .'

His voice trailed off. Sarah bit her lip. Each was aware of the other's thoughts: that they could choose somewhere together. They moved towards each other simultaneously.

'I love you.'

'And I love you.' There were tears in her eyes.

'It's up to you now. I have no wish to force anything.'

And tenderly she clasped his face and kissed him. 'You taste so good,' she murmured against his mouth, tracing his lips with a slender finger.

'*You* taste so good,' he answered.

'Do I have to invite you? Beg you?'

'What for?' he teased.

'Oh you *are* mean.'

'Why are you embarrassed to say it?' He held her away from him, looking searchingly at her.

'Convention, I suppose.' She tried to press herself to him, but he continued to hold her away.

'I *want* to hear you say it. I *want* it to come from you.'

She looked at him shyly. 'Addi, I want us to make love.'

This time they undressed slowly, very tidily, and in between each movement, came together for an embrace.

'I have been so muddled,' she said.

'I know you have.'

'And now I am better. I want to give – give – *give* myself to you. I want you to do whatever you want, to me. I simply want to *give* . . .'

He stayed the night with her, and during it they would awaken with delight at being beside one another, and reach out yet again. They could not believe it – such mutual pleasure, where each was so aware of the other – mind and soul and body. And when finally their bodies were satiated, and dawn slid through the curtains, they locked their hands together, fingers interlaced, and made plans . . .

He bought *The Times* on the way to Brownstones, but did not open it until he arrived. Then, seated at his desk, still euphoric, he opened it leisurely. The headline of an inside column leaped out at him: 'Outrage at Scandalous Novel by Mystery Author'.

He read:

> The publication of a new book by Gray-Courtney Publishers on Tuesday, May 4th, has just come to the notice of a horrified general public. Written under the pseudonym of Paul A. Osborne, the true identity of the author of this explicit novel remains an enigma. But it seems likely that it will be shortly revealed.
>
> The writer and critic Arnold Chesterfield said yesterday, 'This kind of thing cannot be permitted. It is an affront to public morals. I have a hunch who is behind this – there is a ring of familiarity about the style of this pornographer – but as yet I shall say nothing, for fear of slander. Rest assured that when I do know for certain, I shall do my utmost to ensure that charges are pressed. Such filth should be confined to the gutter, and not masquerade under the guise of literature.'
>
> The book, which tells of an artist with an obsessive love for his sister-in-law, describes his fantasies concerning her, and is likely to cause considerable offence. It has, however, been selling fast and furiously. Geoffrey Gray-Courtney was unavailable for comment today.

'Oh no . . .'

Beaky's cheerful face appeared round the door. 'Message for you, Addi –' He had dropped the 'Uncle' since he'd been working full-time at Brownstones. '– Courier just come with it . . . Blimey, you look glum.'

'So would you, Beaky.'

'What's 'appened, then?' The boy perched himself on Adam's vast and cluttered desk.

'I think it could be said that my life is about to be shattered.'

Adam rubbed his hands over his face, then seeing the boy's concern, assumed a cheerful tone: 'I'm only teasing you, Beaky. Now run off. You are in charge of the group today.'

'Won't you be coming?'

'No – I've things to do.'

The message was from Gray-Courtney, and Adam hurriedly shuffled a few papers into a semblance of order, then made his way to his publisher's. He felt heavy-hearted sitting in the hansom, while in front the driver whistled and sang as though a day had never seemed more optimistic.

Geoffrey Gray-Courtney looked grim when Adam arrived. He gestured for Adam to sit down, and poured him a sherry, as he always did. For a few seconds he was silent, then said, 'I want you to know I have no regrets. It is part of my job to be forward-thinking in my selecting of authors and books. There are too many namby-pamby publishers around, too many syrupy novels . . .' He gave one of his jaw-jerks and continued, 'You have written a brilliant book, the most exciting I have read in years. It is true literature, and those who criticize it are bone-heads!'

His reaction, his fervour, took Adam by surprise, and he grasped the other man's hand across the table. 'Thank you,' he said emotionally. 'Thank you for your support. I did hope that what I had written was a fine book; but one does begin to doubt oneself.'

'Never do that, Mr Gilmour . . . However, I hope you are feeling rich and ready for battle.'

Adam smiled. 'Never the former. But have I an option for the second?'

'None. I have already spoken to the firm's solicitor in anticipation – a friend of mine – and he will be here shortly. Can you wait?'

'Yes.'

'We have to know where we stand. This is literature we are discussing. Pornography, indeed. I could wring that man's puny little neck. Where is the pornography in a woman's naked breast, I ask you?'

'Naked breasts have featured in painting and art since time immemorial. Take the *Venus de Milo*, for instance,' said Adam.

'Exactly. And that is a good point to make.'

There came a knock on his door. 'That is probably him now,' Gray-Courtney said, and called, 'Please come in.'

And in ambled a familiar figure – as shabby as ever, more stooping, and fifteen years older.

'Mr Baker!' Adam exclaimed. 'I don't believe it!'

'Well, well, well,' said his ex-employer, with his dry-humoured laugh. 'What have you been getting up to? Perhaps you'd have been better to have remained a clerk.'

He wore the same sickly-smelling hair ointment, still twisted his pliable mouth, still had halitosis, and when they shook hands gladly, Adam noticed his fingernails bitten to the quick.

'It is likely you will both be prosecuted,' said Baker briskly. 'However, I think, having read the book – I'll have you know I stayed up for the best part of the night reading it – I think we stand a reasonable chance of winning the case. You, Geoffrey, will be charged with libel as a criminal offence, as the publisher of a book calculated to outrage public feeling or morality, and you, Mr Gilmour, will be charged under your *own* name, as the writer of such material.

'The case will probably end up at the Old Bailey, and will be brought by the Crown. I suggest we prepare ourselves fully, and that I brief counsel –'

Adam suddenly remembered his old school friend. 'Do you know a barrister called John Clark?' he asked.

'Yes I do. An excellent man – when you catch him sober. He's a member of a well-regarded set of chambers in the Temple.'

'Could we use him? We were at school together.'

'I don't see why not. He specializes in criminal law. What do you think, Geoffrey?'

'I defer to your judgement,' the latter said.

Adam leaned back in his chair with a sense of unreality. He was overwhelmed by premature sorrow – had never envisaged that events could come to this. His beautiful, sensitively-written book was being debased, and as a result of it he feared he would lose Sarah.

*

'I've something to tell you . . .'

A hundred times he almost spoke the words, but at the last second was unable to. He was desolate. He clutched at his dreams, talked of their future together, and all the time knew their plans were no more likely to come to fruition than an acorn would grow into an elm.

Then one day she announced, 'I have bought that book, *Aaron*. I wanted to see what all the furore is about . . .'

I have something to tell you . . . But he could not tell her, and instead stared, dumbfounded.

'Addi – what is it?'

Her concern struck him as ironic.

'Nothing,' he said dispiritedly. 'Let her read it first,' he thought. 'Then I'll tell her.'

But the next day almost everyone in Britain knew, for it was on the front page of every newspaper, and somewhere in London Arnold Chesterfield gloated. Adam went to visit Sarah.

'Madam is not in, sir,' the maid answered mechanically, as she had been instructed to.

'Please – I must see her.'

'But she isn't here, sir.' The maid blushed as she lied.

'Then perhaps you would allow me to wait.'

'Oh no, sir. I don't think that would be right.'

Sarah's face appeared over the banister. 'Thank you, Josephine, I am sorry you have had to be discomforted.' The maid blushed further, bobbed, and fled into the servants' quarters.

Sarah came slowly down the stairs, as though in physical pain. 'Why did you do that – embarrass my maid?'

'I wanted to see you.'

'*I* have no wish to see *you*.'

He was stunned. He had prepared himself for her anger, but the actuality of confronting it was another matter. The coldness – hatred – in her expression shocked him.

'Dearest, I have to explain.'

'You have betrayed me – privately and publicly; stripped me of my dignity. Please will you go.' Her voice wavered, and tears rushed from her eyes. Her lips were pale in a white face.

He tried to touch her, but she recoiled and screamed at him, 'For God's sake , leave me alone! What do *you* know about a woman's mind or her fantasies, Adam? What gives you the right to degrade someone because the urge takes you to write?'

'I *love* you,' he said, not moving, crying himself.

'Get out, get *out*!' she screamed again, in that same mad tone. 'You *sicken* me.'

And he stumbled from the house.

A few days later a summons arrived for him to appear alongside Geoffrey Gray-Courtney, in Bow Street Magistrates' Court on June 2nd, charged with Criminal Libel – leave having already been given by the High Court. He tried in vain to see Sarah, but time after time she refused, and he would go away again, defeated.

He sent her flowers, but on the day they arrived there was a cartoon in the *Daily Telegraph*; entitled 'The Perils of a Pseudonymous Author', it depicted Sarah standing behind Adam whilst he wrote at his desk. Her hand was on his shoulder, and the caption read, 'I am only offering you sisterly help.'

She was the laughing-stock of everyone, the butt of every society joke, the target of the basest gossip. Who did not know of the voluptuousness of her breasts, the shape of her nipples, the smallness of her waist, and the roundness of her belly? Who did not know of the imagined fancies accredited to her by Adam? She had become public property, and this humiliating invasion of her privacy was unbearable. That her disgrace should have been caused by Adam, of all people, whom she had elevated above all men and loved in the truest sense, was the most wounding thing of all. He had exploited her, and she was devastated.

She threw his flowers away, tore the cartoon into pieces, and shut herself in her room where she lay on the bed, sobbing. Irene came to see her. Irene never read the papers, and only snippets of gossip had reached her ears. She paid little attention. To her Adam was god-like, and Sarah a goddess, and she couldn't think of them in lesser terms. Her future was bound up with them both.

She was shown into Sarah's room, and found the young woman, composed now, and red-eyed.

'Irene, dear, I have to go away for a while. Everything will just have to tick over for a bit. I'll give you an address, and you can forward the mail to me twice weekly. I am going to leave you a cheque for Brownstones Women's Club, and one to cover your own expenses and salary . . . Will you cope?'

She looked pleadingly at the other woman, and Irene, who had at first been seized with alarm at hearing the news, mustered up her confidence, and said, 'You leave it t'me, my duck. It's the least I can do.' She shook her head in sympathy for Sarah's unhappiness, and for the untrustworthiness of men.

. . . Six children, and in charge of Browstones Women's Club; the baby barely weaned, and the three-year-old round her ankles . . . But Irene Black was filled with pride, and she drew herself up, ready to face the challenge . . .

Meanwhile, indignant letters poured in – the outraged howls of moralists intimidated by the least hint of sexuality. Adam was shaken by the vindictiveness of these letters, the threats and curses. Yet these harsh disciplinarians masquerading as Christians were probably more decadent than anyone, Adam thought. Sexually repressed, they would, given the chance, be guilty of every kind of depravity. His book – if indeed they had read it – had titillated them, and reminded them of their lusts; and for this, they despised him. They spoke of filth, obscenity, perversion, and he knew that these things existed only in their minds.

But amongst the letters of condemnation were ones of praise; they came from such illustrious names as George Meredith, who mentioned the scandal of his own book, *The Ordeal of Richard Feverel*; Thomas Hardy, whose *Return of the Native* had been much criticized; his old supporter, Edward Lear, himself a saddened man after years of personal disillusion. Lear wrote that the whole thing was nothing but a rumpus stirred up by men with inflated heads and deflated hearts – and that he would be in London in a month or so's time. He heard, too, from Algernon Swinburne, now recovered and rehabilitated with Theodore Watts, who had plucked him from self-destruction, and restored his pride. The poet's letter was wise and sympathetic – and congratulated Adam on prose he himself would have been glad to have written . . .

On June 2nd, Adam met Geoffrey Gray-Courtney at his office, and they took a cab to Bow Street. The publisher said, 'The latest I heard was that Chesterfield was prepared to bring a private prosecution, had the Director of Public Prosecutions not taken up the case.'

'The bastard,' came Adam's vehement comment. He had slept atrociously, was haggard and pale, his eye sore. He saw his carefully constructed life in shreds; much-needed patronage was already being withdrawn from Brownstones – as if the boys were to blame for his 'misdemeanours'. In order to punish him, they punished innocent children. It was they who were the sinners, with their distorted values.

'God, I hope we don't find John Clark suffering from the after-effects of drink when we arrive,' he said.

Gray-Courtney said nothing; he was envisaging the possible collapse of his business. They sat on, in silence, as the hansom rattled along at a brisk pace, weaving in and out of traffic, the driver shouting energetically at his horse.

When they arrived, Alan Baker and John Clark were outside the courtroom, in addition to a police sergeant, the Chief Inspector, and various members of the press – who immediately besieged the two defendants.

'Please could you leave us,' Adam said tiredly. 'We wish to speak between ourselves.'

'When you wrote the book, did you set out to shock the public, sir?' one of them shouted.

'What a stupid question,' he replied angrily, and was nudged by Gray-Courtney.

'How will this case affect your future?' another asked.

'I suggest you consult a clairvoyant,' Adam answered acidly.

Eventually they were left in peace, and John Clark, sober, and respectable in his gown, told them, 'I doubt the case will take more than a couple of hours. It will be referred.'

'Can you be sure of that?' Adam asked.

'Ninety-nine per cent,' his old friend answered. 'It has become of national interest. Today is a token gesture.'

Adam sighed hugely. 'I feel so *angry*.'

'Well, that at least is a positive sentiment,' said the stout little man. 'We shall ultimately *win* this case. I have every intention of doing so.' His eyes were alight with the excitement of battle, and both Adam and Gray-Courtney gazed at him like two dependent children seeking reassurance.

Shortly after their arrival, Arnold Chesterfield arrived on his own. He ignored them, and faced the reporters jostling each other, their notepads and pencils poised.

'I have this to say –' he struck a theatrical pose, '– that I have every confidence the British public will do its duty, and that this man –' he turned his fox-face in Adam's direction, disregarding Gray-Courtney, 'will be punished accordingly, for misusing his position as a distinguished author and disseminating pornography.'

And his look was so vitriolic that Adam was appalled. He began to perspire, and his collar rubbed his neck. 'I mustn't be intimidated,' he thought. 'His hatred isn't based on reason . . .'

They were called into the courtroom, and the charges were read by the barrister representing the Attorney-General, after which they had to state their names.

'Are you, Sir Adam Malcolm Gilmour, the author of the work entitled *Aaron*, written under the pseudonym of Paul A. Osborne?' Adam was asked by the Clerk to the Court.

'I am.'

'You have heard the charges. How do you wish to plead?'

'Not guilty.'

The clerk turned to the publisher. 'And are you, Geoffrey Robert Gray-Courtney, the publisher of that same book?'

'I am.'

'How do you wish to plead?'

'Not guilty.'

'Be seated.'

The hearing lasted barely two hours – during which both the Chief Inspector and Arnold Chesterfield answered questions put to them by the barrister, in evidence against the two defendants. At the end of the hearing, the magistrate, Sir Peter Barwell, predictably announced, 'I am satisfied there is a case to answer – in my opinion this is a fit case to be committed to trial at the Old Bailey. You will be notified in due course when this will be; meanwhile bail is granted.'

'So it goes on,' Adam said dispiritedly, as they left the courthouse.

'Look on it as a challenge, old boy,' John Clark said, his good-humoured face and bald head, now that he'd removed his wig, giving him the air of an overgrown baby.

'Let's go to a tavern and have a bite,' suggested Baker, whose stomach was making loud rumbling noises.

'And more to the point – a little drink,' said Clark . . .

Adam wrote to Sarah at Brambleden – he knew she was there from Irene, who had passed him the information reluctantly. Her wariness hurt him; but he understood her loyalty to Sarah. The letter was, he believed, his last chance; and across the top of the page he wrote, '*Please* read this,' then began:

My darling Sarah,

Perhaps this endearment makes you cringe, and I can well understand if it is the case; however, to me you always have been 'my darling', since the day I first met you, and you always will be.

I know you are feeling resentful and bitter at the moment – justifiably – for what you regard as my maltreatment of you. You said that I had betrayed you, and that I sickened you. But you must know that nothing I did was with intent to hurt you; how could I wish to hurt someone who is more precious to me than life itself?

In mitigation I can only say that my passion for you inspired me to write that book; it was my homage to you, if you like; and by using a pseudonym I thought you would be protected. I realize now I should have thought more of the possible consequences, but at the time I was only excited by the knowledge I was writing a beautiful book – and to this day I maintain that *Aaron* is a beautiful book. There is nothing in it that is offensive or sordid, and the female character is, I believe, portrayed with great sensitivity.

My chief fault is, perhaps, to love you too much. But I think I have, during the years, been a good friend to you. We have shared many special moments, and our ideals, our dreams have been the same; how often one of us could turn to the other and know what he or she was thinking.

Will you not understand, despite your fury, that I did not

deliberately set out to exploit you or debase your good name? That my desire was simply to write a book which I knew would be my best so far, and which almost compelled me to write it. I still have faith in that book, and to deny it would be a lie.

However, to have injured you is to have injured myself. And do you think that I am not possessive over you – that I did not want to guard your body's wonders to myself? I had no inkling that matters would be blown out of such proportion.

Can you no longer see in me those qualities you once admired? Do you so despise me for letting you down that you can never forgive me?

If I receive no reply to this letter, then I shall know this is indeed so, and I shall not trouble you again. I shall say only that I am desolate for the pain I have caused you, desolate that I have deprived us of a future together, and desolate for the loss of a treasured and unique friendship.

For what it is worth, I adore you. But it seems *Aaron* was my Burned Offering.

Adam

He addressed the envelope with disguised handwriting so she would at least open it, and went out into the drizzle to the post.

Every day he awaited a reply, but none came, and on June 11th he was notified that he was to appear at the Old Bailey for ten o'clock on Thursday, July 8th.

Chapter Nineteen

JUSTICE

July 8th was a sweltering day, when London seemed to be steeped in dust and lethargy. At half-past nine in the morning Adam and Geoffrey Gray-Courtney sat in a hansom, perspiring, loosening their collars and neckties. The horse pulling the carriage hung his head, his ears back, his tail – mercifully not docked – swishing continually at flies.

'How do you feel?' Adam asked the other man – whom circumstances had made into a friend.

'No doubt much the same as you – angry it should have come to this. Prepared to fight – but lacking in faith when it comes to public support.'

Adam nodded and sighed. 'And this infernal heat . . .' He left the sentence to dangle, and looked out – they were turning into High Holborn.

'I must say,' he murmured, 'prison has little appeal as the possibility of it draws nearer.'

'Good fodder for your next novel.'

'Hah!'

'However, prison is unlikely,' Gray-Courtney mused. 'A fine, I should think. Depending on the judge.'

'Everything hinges on the sensibilities of others. Twelve small-minded men condemn us because they do not recognize literature.'

'Hang on. We are not yet condemned.'

They turned into the Old Bailey, and drew to a halt outside the Central Court where a crowd was gathered, and police were trying to establish some kind of order.

'Good luck, Mr Gilmour.'

'Scum!'

'You've got my backing, sir.'

'Decadence! That's what it is. Decadence!'

Someone spat, and the spittle landed on his cheek. Cheers and jeers vied. A fight broke out, and two men were arrested . . .

A barrage of reporters surrounded them, some whom Adam knew. They slapped him and Gray-Courtney on the back. 'We're all on your side, sir,' one, a very young man, said, his expression that of someone face to face with his hero.

'Thank you. It's very kind and encouraging of you,' Adam said humbly.

And then John Clark appeared, again in wig and gown, face gleaming with perspiration. He hustled them up the steps and into the building.

'I never dreamed one day I'd be standing trial here,' Adam said, gazing about the imposing building with its guarded doors. 'I suppose it's just another day's work for you, John,' he said wryly to the barrister.

'No, old boy. This is a special case. And what is more – we're going to win it.' His lips came together in a determined line.

'I wish you were right,' Gray-Courtney said nervously – removing his glasses for the umpteenth time, and rubbing the sides of his nose where the wires had pressed.

'Incidentally, Mr Justice Thornton is the judge for the case,' John Clark informed them. 'He has a reputation for being hard. But he's also fair –'

'And has a penchant for French literature, so I heard,' interrupted Alan Baker, who had joined them, and was looking uncomfortable and clammy-skinned in the heat. 'I happened to read an article he wrote a while back. It was entitled something like, "In defence of Flaubert".'

'Well, that does augur well.' Adam looked cheered.

Arnold Chesterfield appeared, flanked by a chief inspector. Other police, various wigged gentlemen, messengers and the press hovered around.

'Looking forward to your fate, gentlemen?' Chesterfield asked spitefully.

'You are the dregs, Chesterfield,' Adam said scathingly, as reporters busily scribbled.

Chesterfield whitened. 'It is you who are the dregs, sir, you and your depraved and disgusting book.'

They were summoned inside the courtroom by a nervous-looking clerk, and shown to their places. Overhead, in the public gallery, a hush, then a giant murmur went round, some shouting; one person threw flowers, which scattered over Adam. He thought, 'This can't be happening . . . it isn't real.'

He stared about him – at the table where sat several bewigged men, their features apparently alike; at the judge on the bench, sitting riffling through some papers, whispering to the recorder on one side of him; at Chesterfield, expressionless and immaculate . . . And then above, at the crowd, all dressed up for the occasion. He scanned the faces. Perhaps Sarah would be there. Her presence, even if she were antagonistic, would bring him luck. He searched in vain, and dropped his eyes once more; ran his finger round the inside of his collar to stop it sticking to his neck; felt a nervous, griping pain in his stomach.

Beside him, Baker picked his nose then recalled where he was, and looked round to see if anyone had noticed. Geoffrey Gray-Courtney had removed his glasses again, and kept clearing his throat. From his table, John Clark winked gleefully at them.

The jury of twelve was sworn in and called into the jury box, but two unsuitables were immediately objected to by Clark, and replaced. The chattering in the gallery increased, and a woman shouted, 'Well done, Adam. We all love you, ducks!'

'Silence please,' thundered the judge's sonorous voice, and silence duly fell.

The Attorney-General stood up. 'If Your Lordship pleases, members of the jury – I am appearing with my learned friend Mr Alfred Lewis. The defence are represented by Mr John Clark and Mr Edward Martin.' He sat down again – a heavy, pompous figure, with several satisfied chins.

The Clerk to the Court called: 'Put up Sir Adam Malcolm Gilmour.'

Adam stood, scuffling his feet awkwardly, aware of craned necks, and every eye focused on him. He longed suddenly to answer nature's call; felt his bowels weaken.

The clerk read: 'On the fourth day of May, 1880, the novel

entitled *Aaron* was published. Are you the true author?'

'I-I-I am.' He ran his hand shamedly through his hair, as a rustle of embarrassment went round the room at his stutter.

'How do you plead?'

'Not g-g-guilty.'

'Please be seated.'

'Put up Mr Geoffrey Gray-Courtney . . .'

The publisher stood up, enunciated his piece and sat down again quickly. His glasses were back on; spotless. The heat in the room grew more sweltering. Brightness flooded through the windows. It made Adam catch his breath, as he remembered Brambleden Hall, and he was a child on his father's knee and all this was undreamed of.

The Attorney-General read the indictment to the jury, and then the first witness was called, and Chesterfield went forward purposefully. His voice, as he swore to tell the whole truth, was strong and nasal.

The Attorney-General questioned him. 'Mr Chesterfield – you have known the two defendants for some time; would you kindly tell us in what capacity this is.'

Chesterfield gave a small cough. 'I have known Mr Gray-Courtney over the years slightly. As a writer, one inevitably mixes in an environment of writers and publishers.'

'Quite so.'

'I have always regarded him as rather undiscriminating in his selection of authors.'

'Why is that? Would you say that in order to gain business he was selecting authors whose works would gain readers by appealing to their baser instincts?'

'Objection!' Clark sprang up. 'Prosecution is leading the witness.'

'Sustained,' the judge said. His heavy-lidded eyes looked down his nose.

'Would you say that Gray-Courtney Publishers are well-respected?'

'On the whole. Though not by everyone.'

'Would this be because lately the company has been publishing books of a controversial nature –'

'Objection!' Up sprang Clark again. 'The charge relates to one book, not every other book which has been written and published.'

'If you please, My Lord, I am trying to establish a background,' the Attorney-General said.

The judge considered first the one of them, then the other. 'Objection overruled. You may continue . . .'

Gray-Courtney consulted Baker anxiously, and the solicitor whispered back, 'It is too early on in proceedings to worry about that kind of thing.' He was sucking discreetly on a peppermint, and Adam wondered if at last someone had ventured to tell him of his problem.

The questions, the answers, the objections continued for a few more minutes, and then his turn came for attack.

'Would you tell the jury –' the Attorney-General asked, 'in what capacity you met Sir Adam Gilmour.'

'Yes sir –' he paused significantly. 'I do not know him *socially*. But his name first came to my notice several years ago, when as an anti-Christian Radical he incited public violence –'

'Objection!'

'And he was distributing filthy leaflets –'

'Objection!' called the defence again, furiously. 'These inaccurate snippets have absolutely nothing to do with the case.'

'Sustained.'

Adam wiped his forehead with the palm of his hand. He listened to the Attorney-General's laden questions, and Chesterfield's smug replies as he vented his personal hatred and jealousy; even Brownstones was dismissed simply as a place from within whose fortifications the defendant could write his pornography and indulge his fantasies: the headquarters of evil masquerading as a charitable organization . . .

Adam could not bear to listen; could not stand to hear the distorting of truth, the clever turns of phrase, the snide innuendoes. He felt helpless; and that he and Gray-Courtney, as defendants, were not allowed to speak, further frustrated him . . . The journalists frantically scribbled, and the silence in the public gallery was such that the women could be heard fanning themselves.

And then it was John Clark's turn to interrogate.

'*Mister* Chesterfield,' he commenced, in his high, amused voice, his sweaty baby-face at its most genial. 'Has it ever occurred to you that to draw attention to a cause inevitably means drawing attention to oneself?'

'Yes of course.'

'Has it occurred to you that Mr Adam Gilmour – I call him that, My Lord, out of respect to my client, since that is how he prefers to be known – that Mr Gilmour, with his stammer and partial sight and shy nature, is the least likely person to wish for personal attention? Please answer a straight yes or no.'

'. . . No.'

'And did it never occur to you that for a man in his early twenties – the time which you earlier referred to – a man from a privileged background such as his, his selfless preoccupation with the impecunious and deprived, his determination –'

'Objection – the defence is leading the witness.'

'Overruled. Continue please.'

'– his determination to fight for their cause as a spokesman, his personal financial contribution, were quite remarkable?'

'As far as I was concerned, he was just one of many trouble-makers out for self-publicity, mindless of law and order and the proper way to go about things . . .'

The witness was in the box for twenty minutes, and defence finished by saying, 'I venture to suggest you are jealous of Mr Gilmour's background, and of his professional success –' he gave his brightest smile, '– I venture to suggest that your obvious personal dislike of him stems from some feeling of inadequacy on your part.'

'I venture to say you are insulting,' said Chesterfield furiously.

'I have no more questions,' Clark said, grinning round the room.

A rustle went through the court, a burst of murmuring and chatter and shifting of position, and then the book was produced, and the Chief Inspector was called to the stand. He was asked if he had read it.

'I have,' he answered, 'and I was utterly disgusted, sir.'

'Would you tell us what you found disgusting about it?'

'There were certain pages, sir, where the woman's – anatomy – was described . . . and certain actions took place, the couple being unmarried, sir. And another incident where she is thinking – rude thoughts.'

A cheer went round the public gallery, and the judge called for silence. The Attorney-General sank into his chins, and holding the book with a distasteful expression said, 'If I read a few extracts, would you tell me if those were some of the passages you found disagreeable?'

'Yes sir.'

He bent his head and read, ' "Her final garment slid to the floor – the last vestige of modesty – and she stood naked and shy before him, as for so long he had tried to imagine her . . ." ' He stopped. 'And another: "She lay naked, partially concealed by the long grass, felt the sun's warmth seep into her flesh, the breeze flutter across her nipples . . ." '

He continued to read, in a voice which removed all the loveliness from the prose, and instead ridiculed it: and in his seat Adam cringed, and gnawed on his lip in impotent anger.

Then came John Clark's turn. He began, 'In a world increasingly obsessed with material goods and achieving wealth, it is easy for the layman to sneer at the arts, to be suspicious of them, to forget the controversies by which they have always been surrounded . . . Tell me, Chief Inspector, do you read much?'

'Well, I don't get a great deal of time, sir,' he answered in an aggressive tone.

'No, no, I can appreciate that,' said John Clark pleasantly. 'So in other words you have not read too many books. You have not read the translation of a French book called *Madame Bovary*, for instance?'

'No, sir, I can't say as I have.'

'That is a pity. The book concerns a woman's infidelities to her husband, and goes into some detail. The author, Flaubert, was tried and acquitted, on a –'

'Objection,' roared the Attorney-General. 'This is of no relevance to the case we are hearing today.'

'Sustained. The jury will disregard the remark.'

Unruffled, John Clark continued. 'And what about painting, Chief Inspector – it takes less time to look at pictures than to read a book: do you sometimes look at pictures – either in books or galleries?'

'Sometimes.'

'Perhaps you admire some of the Greek sculptures you might have seen in pictures?'

'Well, yes I do – I mean they're ancient, aren't they?'

'Precisely. Tell me – are some of those sculptures of nude women and men?'

'Yes, sir.'

'Do they shock you?'

'No, sir.'

'Why do they not shock you?'

'Well it's art, isn't it, sir?'

'Of course,' said Clark in the tone of one who has just been enlightened. 'And so is literature one of the arts. Why is it that it is perfectly acceptable for your eyes to confront a realistic image of nudity – often in explicit detail – but the written word, where it is much harder to conjure up that image, is insulting?'

Confused, blustering, the big man could not answer.

'You cannot answer,' persisted John Clark triumphantly, 'because there is no *logic* behind your reasoning . . .'

The case continued throughout the day, with an hour's break for lunch, and the room grew ever hotter, and buzzed with flies. One minute Adam thought that victory was within their grasp, and the next, he was certain they would lose, and he was gloomy again. All day his hopes were like a pendulum swinging from one extreme to the other as he listened to damning evidence, and from the witness box Chesterfield eked out his hatred; and his book was metaphorically torn to shreds.

Then, virtually at the end of the proceedings, John Clark asked Chesterfield, in his deceptively benign voice, 'Mr Chesterfield, would it be fair to say you have a liking for prostitutes?'

'Objection!' called the Attorney-General. 'The defence has no right to question in this outrageous vein.'

'I don't know what you mean!' shouted Chesterfield, visibly paling, and clutching at the rail, as the spectators gasped, and there was an outbreak of chatter.

'My Lord, I was trying to establish a link between certain aspects of the witness's character, and his antipathy towards the book *Aaron*.'

'Mr Clark, you will kindly refrain from such questioning,' the judge reprimanded him coldly. 'Objection sustained. The jury must disregard the remark as having no foundation whatsoever.'

'I have *no* more questions,' chirped the irrepressible John Clark.

The Attorney-General and the defence said their final pieces, and the judge carefully summed up. He spoke of the gravity of the charges; the powerful influence of the written word, especially by a popular figure such as Adam Gilmour whose attitude to society should set an example; the responsibilities of a publisher to the unsuspecting public . . . And he spoke of literature as an art: was Sir Adam Gilmour's novel, as the prosecution had stated, merely a thinly-veiled autobiography in which the author had indulged his most erotic fantasies? Or was it, as the defence suggested, a novel of exquisite prose; comparable to a painting by Rembrandt? Was *Aaron* suggestive, or pornographic, written with intent to shock, or a piece of serious literature? It was for the jury to decide . . .

The jury listened attentively, and Adam studied each one – upright citizens, all of them. 'Who were they? Who knew whether or not in the privacy of their homes they beat their wives or drank too much, or what other sins they might be guilty of? Who were they to decide what constituted literature? Yet his fate depended on them.

They retired to debate, and a messenger went to fetch refreshments.

'What do you think, Clark?' asked Alan Baker.

'Good chance, old boy.'

'How did you know about Chesterfield?' Adam asked admiringly.

'A hunch – then had him followed.'

'It was a good ploy to bring up Flaubert, under the circumstances,' Gray-Courtney said.

'Too heaven-sent to miss . . .'

The jury returned after two hours – a period which seemed interminable to the four. The foreman stood – a pale, ginger-haired man who looked the most intellectual amongst them.

'Have you reached your decision?' the judge asked, in his booming voice.

'Yes, My Lord.'

'Would you please tell the court whether you find the two defendants guilty or not guilty.'

Adam's heart thumped; he could feel it pumping beneath his shirt.

'Not guilty, My Lord.'

A roar of delight, interspersed by angry jeers, resounded from the public gallery, where everybody now stood up, and Adam and Gray-Courtney hugged each other joyfully. Baker, still chewing on mints, said wryly, 'Well, I suppose the increased sales will cover my bill!'

'Cheek of it,' Adam protested, laughing. He glanced upwards – saw little Mr Levy amongst the crowd suddenly, and further back, Beaky.

'I must go and talk to them,' he told the others. He made his way out, and found his path blocked by Chesterfield, his expression malevolent.

'This is not the last,' he said, tight-lipped, into Adam's ear.

'And what does that mean?'

'Just that.' He pushed Adam aside violently and disappeared.

The hall was crowded, and people kept coming up to him, congratulating him as though he were an old friend; reporters harangued him; and then Mr Levy appeared. He kissed Adam on both cheeks.

'You deserve your success,' he said. 'Every bit of it.' He dabbed at the corners of his eyes. 'I could have killed that man Chesterfield. Yes, happily I could have done so.'

Adam was touched by his loyalty. 'How are *you*? You cancelled our last dinner arrangement.'

'I am well now. But then I had palpitations. I am not so young.'

'Of course you are. Don't talk like that. But you must take care . . .' He spotted someone else he knew approaching him. 'Reverend Hibbert!'

'Adam.' The old rector clasped his hand. 'Well done. I am too, too delighted.'

Adam introduced him to the tailor, and the three chatted; then he left them and went up to Beaky, who was hovering awkwardly nearby.

'Hallo there young man.' He ruffled the boy's hair. 'It was nice of you to come.'

'I wanted to . . . I'm ever so glad you got off, Addi.'

'That makes two of us.' He smiled wearily.

'Me mum don't know I'm 'ere.'

'No. I don't suppose she'd approve.' Beaky had stopped coming to Brownstones under instructions from Irene.

'Addi, can I come back? In secret? She don't 'ave to know.'

'I'm not sure that would be wise, Beaky.'

'Don't you want me to, then?' he asked, hurt.

'Of course I do. I just don't want to stand in the way of your mother and yourself.'

'I wouldn't tell her.'

'I don't know how you would keep it a secret.'

'She'll just think I've a job somewhere else. She's too busy to look into it.'

'It does seem wrong. But I'll admit I miss having you around.'

'Can I then, Addi?'

'The decision's got to be yours, Beaky.'

'Then, yes – I'll come back.' He wiped his huge nose, which was running, and his eyes. 'You never know – now this is all over, you might all be friends again,' he said hopefully.

Adam joined the others at a tavern to celebrate their victory, and John Clark ordered champagne – but had a couple of large whiskies first. He quickly became drunk – and steered the conversation towards the pleasures and perils of women. Gray-Courtney, who was happily married, became sentimental, and Alan Baker confided he had just become engaged. Hence the peppermints, Adam thought. He himself was quiet. He should have been jubilant, but his earlier elation had waned, and he was numb. He had lost more than he had gained.

He made an excuse that he was tired, and left them. Gray-Courtney grabbed his arm as he departed. 'We've been through it together, friend,' he said, slurring the words.

It was growing dark already, and Adam was still at Brownstones. There was so much to do; amongst other things were letters to write to all those who had withdrawn their patronage, in the hope that since his acquittal two days previously, they might renew their support. Beaky was with him, addressing envelopes.

The building was quiet: the half-dozen or so resident boys were asleep; the servants and supervisor in their respective rooms. Adam was tired and depressed. He stretched, yawned – and then sniffed. There was a smell of smoke.

'Can you smell it, Beaky?' he asked.

'No – but then I've got a cold.'

Adam opened the door – the hall, staircase and galleried landing were full of smoke. Small flames were already running along the floor and licking the walls.

'Oh God . . . Beaky – grab what you can – the box of records, files – and go outside. Do as I ask, please . . .'

Coughing, he raced upstairs, yelling, 'Fire, fire . . .' And as the various doors opened to the rooms, so the fire spread. Further intensified by an open window, the flames sprang into terrifying life, and people began to scream.

'Don't panic,' shouted Adam, holding his hand to his mouth; and he gathered up a crying child in his arms, and carried him downstairs.

They were all safe outside; he told one of the servants to notify the fire brigade, and she ran off thankfully. A crowd had gathered, agog at the scene, and Adam watched, stricken, as window after window was lit by flames. Beside him, incredulous, Beaky was mute. Several other boys sobbed.

Then, in horror, Beaky exclaimed, 'The cat – it's still inside. I shut it in the top room because there were mice in there.'

'You can't do anything about it, Beaky,' Adam told him gently.

'I *can*. It were *my* fault. He'll *die*.'

'He probably already has – *Beaky!* . . .' The boy had broken away, and was haring towards the blazing house. Adam chased after him.

'Beaky, *Beaky!*'

The boy was up the staircase. 'I'm all right,' he called. 'Don't come after me, Addi.'

The heat in the hallway was tremendous. The flames were closing in.

'Come *down*.' He began to choke, watched the boy sprinting along the galleried landing, eerily illuminated, and was about to go after him – just as there came an almighty crashing and rending of timber, and the staircase collapsed.

'Beaky!' he bellowed. 'Jump. For God's sake.'

But Beaky was not to be seen. Adam sank to his knees – then felt himself hauled to his feet, and was dragged from the hall by two policemen.

'Come on, sir . . . It's all right , sir . . . come on . . .' As though he were a child.

He fought against them. He struggled to escape their grip. A third man had to help restrain him. He thought he would go mad. 'Let me *go*,' he roared repeatedly. He wanted to be inside, to go down with Brownstones, to die.

The crowd was enormous now, and the spectacle had become a theatre for voyeurs; the buzz of excited conversation filled the air; smoke ballooned into the sky . . . And then, the clanging of bells as the fire brigade arrived.

Too late, the men connected the pipes and turned the water on to the building. But the flames were erupting all over the place – the roof, the chimneys, the gables.

Brownstones burned well into the night, and by the time the fire was under control, the building was reduced to a smouldering shell. And somewhere in its embers were the corpses of a boy and a cat.

Chapter Twenty

MATTERS CONCLUDED

The police informed Irene Black of her son's death that same night, and the following morning Adam called on her; she lived in two rooms in Islington.

'It were *your* fault,' she turned on him, when he was barely through the doorway. 'He died because of you.'

'That's not so,' he told her gently. 'I tried to dissuade him. I went after him –'

'Where are your burns then? You're not even marked,' she spat derisively, close to hysterics. 'It were your fault. If you hadn't lured him to Brownstones –'

'I didn't lure him. He *wanted* to come back. I tried to stop him.'

But that wasn't strictly true.

There was no point in staying. She did not want his comfort. Turning to go, he said simply, 'I loved Beaky.'

'I wish you'd died instead of him!' she screamed. 'I *wish* it.'

'I wish it, too.'

'Oh, you're a fine one with words, you are. Well, they don't trick me, no more. And to think my baby's blighted with your name . . .' She pushed the door firmly shut against him, and he heard her sobbing inside.

He had no one to talk to. He was isolated in his unhappiness and guilt. At night he dreamed of better times – and then awoke to find himself still in the Knightsbridge house with his problems. He longed for news of Sarah; and recalled Beaky's optimistic remark: 'Now this is all over, you might all be friends again . . .' But the boy's death had made that an impossibility. Sarah would not write.

Adam became haunted by the idea that the fire had been started deliberately, and that Chesterfield had been behind it. He kept hearing Chesterfield's words: 'This is not the last.'

The more he thought about it, the more it seemed likely, and he went to the police. But he had not endeared himself to them in the past, and they told him that arson would be impossible to prove.

'This man is a murderer,' Adam told the inspector heatedly.

'I'd be careful whom I said that to, if I was you,' cautioned the inspector. 'You could be accused of slander.'

He wrote to the Attorney-General – that man of many chins – who replied that his accusations were defamatory and dangerous, and best forgotten. He wrote to Chesterfield himself – who showed the letter to the police. They immediately visited him and reiterated their warning that he could be prosecuted for slander . . . His dreams gave way to a limbo-like state midway between sleep and wakefulness; a listless, dark unreality in whose depths he floated. He longed for mornings so he could legitimately get up from his bed.

The venture in which he had wholeheartedly immersed himself, and for which he had had such hopes, had ended in tragedy; and daily he was reminded of it as he dealt with insurers, wrote letters, and wound up the affairs of Brownstones. He had nothing to look forward to, could make no plans, and it meant little to him that his book was selling in large numbers, or that those critics previously afraid to speak out were now lavish with their praise. He blamed them as well as Chesterfield. They were too late.

Edward Lear called on him unexpectedly. Absorbed by his problems, Adam had forgotten he was in England, and when he saw his father's old friend his thin face lit up.

'I don't believe it – I just don't *believe* it,' he kept repeating delightedly.

'It has been many years indeed, young Adam.'

'Well, you will *bury* yourself in far-off places.'

'Never far enough. Never deep enough,' Lear said.

'Now what does *that* mean?' asked Adam, leading him by the elbow to the most comfortable chair.

He was sixty-nine now; a tall, stooping figure whose mild eyes behind the round spectacles had a permanently bewildered air. He sat down, arranging his baggy trousers around his knees.

'I was terribly sad to hear the news about Brownstones,' he said. 'And so sorry for you. You worked hard to establish it.'

Adam said, 'A boy was killed in the fire. Did you know that?'

'No. How frightful.'

'I am convinced the fire was started deliberately . . .' He told Lear about Chesterfield, and the other shook his head slowly as Adam spoke.

'There is nothing you can do about it. That is the damnable thing.'

'It's disgraceful. They bring charges over an inconsequential book, and yet they won't take the trouble to investigate a possible murder.'

'The trouble is there is no way of saying for sure how a fire started.'

Adam sighed and sat back. He was forever weary. Closing his eyes he said, 'I can't sleep. I can't think logically . . . I am wrecked, Mr Lear.'

'You have had a dreadful time of it, but now it is over, and you must look ahead.'

'What *to*?'

'Ah,' said the old man, understandingly.

He was staying in Hyde Park with his friend Frank Lushington, and since he had been in England, he informed Adam, had been to a Gilbert and Sullivan operetta, and out to dinner a few times – and was now pining for Italy.

'I shall return in a couple of weeks,' he said. 'I've little patience for things English nowadays. London imprisons me.'

'And yet you were born in Holloway.'

'That is probably why!'

'There's an underground station in the Holloway Road now.'

'Is there?' Lear was unimpressed. 'Better there was some sunshine or an attractive view . . . I have abandoned my old home in San Remo, you know.'

'Why's that?'

'Some unthinking person erected the most awful hotel in front of it, entirely blocking my view! However I have bought a plot along the hillside – my friends have all been most generous with loans – by the sea. I intend to make it *identical* to the other villa so that my cat, Foss, will be tricked into believing himself in the same place! He is really a most amiable cat . . . He has part of his tail missing, you know . . .'

Tea arrived, and the maid poured it into the cups, then served cake from the old silver dish they had used at Brambleden Hall. As Edward Lear ate, he shed crumbs down his beard, which he didn't notice. They passed the afternoon reminiscing, talking about religion – Lear believed unquestioningly in God – and chatting generally.

'I must go,' he said finally, consulting his watch. 'I have a dinner engagement later, and must take a nap first, otherwise I am likely to become irritable and disagreeable. At least, that is what I am told. Now Adam, will you please stop wallowing in your misfortunes and blaming yourself for what might or might not have been. The chains of events set in motion by ourselves or others are unavoidable, quite simply because as human beings we are erratic. You love a woman. Do you truly credit this fairy-tale creature with such perfection that you can attach *no* blame to her behaviour? Come, come, Adam, that is unlikely. Where is that sense of challenge which helped you to combat your eye problem all those years ago?'

Adam smiled. 'You were so kind to me then. Your letter after my illness gave me strength when I felt devastated.'

'And now you are devastated again, and will find similar strength from your own resources . . . Now I must go.'

As they clasped hands, Adam realized he might never see Lear again.

He received a telegraph from Claud saying, 'Come and visit us. C.' And he sent one in return: 'Arriving on August 17th. A.'

After he left the post office there was the barest shifting of the heaviness within him, and he went directly to a local firm of estate agents. 'I should like to sell my house,' he announced – and felt the heaviness shift still further . . .

It seemed that for his first week with Leah and Claud he could do little except sleep, and they cosseted him as though he were an invalid. They did not persuade him to talk, or to join them in outings, but spoke softly to him and filled him with good food.

Where the river ran through their field, it formed a small inlet, and he would sit on the shingle watching the ripples chase one another, sparkling in the sun; hearing the 'plip' they made against the large stones which lay on the little shore like beached seals. In the background the hills changed colour according to the light, and shadows made endless patterns. He would strip naked and lie down – let the sun's warmth stroke his body and penetrate his skin, while his mind emptied of thought. His eyelids would close, and he would be drifting . . .

One afternoon he was startled from his doze by a sound, and awoke to find his nephews standing by him. They giggled as his eyes opened.

'You are always asleep,' Jasper said.

'I am always tired,' he answered, sitting up and stretching mightily, licking his dry lips and blinking in the sun. He could tell the boys apart easily now that they were older.

'May we undress too?' asked Mark politely.

'I don't see why not.'

They both giggled again, and came to lie beside him, having lined the pebbles with their clothes as he had done.

'You looked like an ogre when you yawned just now,' Jasper, the more fanciful of the pair, said. He was smaller, elfin-looking. Both resembled Leah rather than Claud, and she said that Jasper in particular was like Adam as a child.

'Do you believe in ogres?' Adam asked.

'No!' they shouted in terrified unison.

'And neither do I. They definitely do *not* exist,' he soothed them. He lifted both boys closer to him and put an arm round each of their brown little bodies. 'However, I could tell you a story about a very sleepy giant, who once gave such a colossal yawn that accidentally he swallowed a whole palace with the royal family and servants inside. Would you like me to tell you that story?'

'Yes.'

He paused, gazed ahead, then began. 'Once upon a time, in a land of rivers and mountains, there was a magnificent white palace. It had pinnacles and towers, turrets and chimneys, taller than anywhere in the world. Its hundreds of windows sparkled in the sunlight like crystal glass, and its great arched doors were so heavy they took ten strong men to open them. Around its spiked walls ran a moat which separated the palace from the rest of the kingdom, and just on the other side of the moat was an immense, dense forest. It was here in the forest that Lorn, the giant, lived . . .'

Leah stood watching them from the picket-gate. Her throat caught at the sight of the three naked, golden-brown figures huddled together – her two babies, as she thought of them still, and her brother. Their voices drifted over:

'. . . The biggest hands you could ever imagine – the size of my entire body –'

'But was he a *kind* giant?'

'Be quiet, Jasper. You always interrupt.'

'Yes, he was essentially kind. Although he was inclined to be short-tempered.'

'Like Papa . . .'

She went away again. It was their moment, and she did not want to disturb them.

She herself had been feeling confused recently. She believed that Adam should not have written his novel, *Aaron*. She had read it, and whilst she could see that it was a fine and beautifully-written book, the central characters were plainly Adam himself and Sarah. He had had no right to exploit Sarah. As a woman, Leah felt very strongly that this was what he had done, and as a close friend of Sarah's she resented this exploitation. But as Adam's sister, knowing him as she did, she realized that he hadn't deliberately intended to do this, and her anger against him was tempered with pity for his suffering. She had mentioned nothing to him yet, but she felt great bitterness on behalf of her friend, whose life was shattered, and who had vented her anguish in a ten-page letter to Leah.

She and Claud had quarrelled over the matter, for Claud took an entirely one-sided view and supported Adam, dismissing Sarah's feelings as 'hysterical'.

'Adam has caused so much trouble,' she thought – and then had gone in search of him to tell him this; to bring her sentiments into the open, as she had always done with him when they were children. But then she came upon him with her sons, and her anger had dissipated and become a wave of love . . .

That night Adam dreamed of Beaky: he was scaling a wall as though he were a fly – higher, until he was in the open, on top of a roof. He held a box of files in his arms, and Arnold Chesterfield was trying to take it from him. 'Jew,' he called Beaky, whose nose had become obscenely long. Beaky ignored him and tossed the files one after the other into the air, where they became balls of fire. As he did so Chesterfield's face changed into Irene's, and Beaky was a cat winding its tail around her legs, in the office at Brownstones . . . Getting up from his desk, Adam went over to the cat and bit off its head. 'It's the kindest thing,' he explained to the weeping mother. 'You must understand. Look at my charred knuckles – now you see why I had to do it . . .'

Holding a candle, Claud bent over Adam and shook him. 'Wake up – come on, Adam – you're *dreaming*.'

He had been shouting in his sleep. Now he sat up, drenched with sweat and breathing heavily.

'Oh God.' He stared briefly at Claud and then lay back once more, his eyes fixed on the ceiling.

'I shall never get over it, you know,' he said flatly. 'It was the most awful thing . . .'

Claud waited. He sat at the bottom of the bed in his rumpled nightshirt, his face creased with sleep, and lined from the sun. He was forty now, and looked more.

'. . . Watching a place you have built from nothing, a place in which you've invested your *soul* – watching it go up like a bonfire. And Beaky . . . I know I could have stopped him. I *know* it . . . You see it *is* my fault. But Chesterfield started it. I know he was behind the fire in the first place. But I could have saved Beaky. I could have stopped him going back. So it's *my* fault, you see . . .' he finished in the same flat voice.

Claud laid his massive hand on his friend's forehead. 'It could not be helped. By all accounts, according to the papers, you were heroic. You could have done no more than you did.'

'I could have *stopped* him,' he said, agonized.

'Guilt is a terrible thing,' murmured Claud.

'Murder is worse,' replied Adam. But he fell asleep again quickly, with Claud's golden-haired hand still on his forehead; and the following day he was brighter, and appeared not to remember his nightmare or their conversation.

*

Weeks passed, and Adam's improvement was perceptible. Leah finally dared broach her feelings.

'You should not have written it.'

'The mistake was not in writing it. I am proud to have written something which in years to come will be recognized as a work of true literature,' he said with an immodesty which surprised her. 'The mistake was that my identity was discovered – and therefore Sarah's also.'

'That is an *arrogant* outlook.'

'But it is *not*. It was a book written from love, written with love. Where is the arrogance in that?'

It became obvious that despite his sorrow over Sarah he couldn't repent the book itself – only the outcome; and she knew it would be a subject on which they would always disagree.

. . . Through the remainder of August, and into September. In the evenings men played *boules* in the square until the light failed, and Adam and Claud joined in; it was a serious game. Old women with missing teeth and black dresses sat on chairs outside their front doors, crocheting. Chickens scuffled in the dust. Dirty-faced children played with balls – or skinned rabbits for the evening's casserole. From the bar came the raised voices of the dentist and undertaker having a friendly argument . . . The flies still buzzed; the crickets still whirred; but the days grew shorter and the skies heavier.

Adam saw a peasant woman force-feeding a goose in her back yard – pinioning the bird, straddling it and pumping food into it. Horrified, he vowed he would never touch pâté de fois gras again.

'But it couldn't go to a more caring home,' Claud said innocently, patting his belly.

'You are perfectly vile,' Adam said.

In the mornings he would fling open his shutters and gaze out of the window – at the kitchen garden with its rich brown earth and mysterious green tufts; at the unkempt lawn dotted with toys, and with chickens scratching around; the vineyard which adjoined Leah and Claud's field, with its grapes in the midst of being harvested; the river, with Claud's raft tied to the willow, just visible; and beyond – the hills, often shrouded by the early mist . . .

On Tuesdays he accompanied his sister to the market. '*C'est mon frère*,' Leah assured curious women, until they knew him – in case the story was put about that she had a lover. In her clogs and shawl, she looked like one of them.

It was a bustling little market with a vegetable stall, haberdashery, charcuterie, butcher, second-hand clothes stall, the local vineyard owner with his wines, and a man who sold everything from carbolic soap and tooth powder to pots and pans. Geese, ducks, chickens and rabbits squawked and quacked and honked and scratched in cages. Sometimes goats would be tethered under the pollarded branches of the plane tree . . . The shopkeepers were sour-faced on Tuesdays, because it meant they did no business.

They breakfasted late, haphazardly: there were few rules in the household, the only one being that at some time during the day Leah gave the boys an hour's reading lesson. Apart from that, everyone did as he or she wished. But the twins had discovered their uncle's capacity for storytelling. It was apparently limitless – despite his teasing of them when he would place his finger on his forehead and pretend to look perplexed for a moment as he strove for inspiration. And then his brow would clear: 'Ah,' he would say. 'I have it . . .'

This little act delighted them every time. They loved the suspense, the feeling of uncertainty. The disappointment which crossed their faces was only half feigned. And then would come that delicious relief when he smiled, and they would shiver, and rub their knees in anticipation . . .

The evenings of sitting outside were almost over, and this night promised to be cold and windy. Claud had lit the first fire of the season in the sitting-room, and momentarily Adam's expression had registered panic; he was standing outside Brownstones watching it being demolished by flames . . . Beaky was breaking away from his grip . . . The image faded. The backgammon lay on a small table between him and Claud, the pieces set out, ready; a flask of wine was open; the inadequate gaslamps and the firelight cast shadows on the white rough-cast walls. Adam thought about the letter he had seen on that same table in the morning; it had been in Sarah's handwriting – addressed to Leah. He had thought Leah seemed odd throughout the day; curt and abrupt with him: something in the letter had turned her against him. But then her sisterly affection had reasserted itself, and she had mellowed again, and was now assisting the cook with the dinner. The smell of some sort of stew drifted from the kitchen. Outside, the wind began to howl.

Claud shook a dice. 'Six. Beat that.'

Adam shook his, 'Likewise.'

'Two. Blast.'

'Four.'

'You sod.'

Adam's mouth twitched in acknowledgement as he made the classic move.

Claud did not immediately shake his dice. 'You should write a book of children's stories, you know.'

'What – as penance for my other, you mean?' Adam said, smiling wryly.

'Not at all. I am actually serious. You relate excellent children's stories. The boys have become addicted to them.'

'What's this?' Leah returned and sank into an armchair. 'Supper is ready, by the way.'

'I told Adam he should write a book of children's stories – that Jasper and Mark are addicted to them.'

'They are lovely boys,' Adam said. 'You are both very fortunate. Brownstones was my family. *They* were my boys . . .'

There was a ridge in his throat. His grief threatened to overtake him. He turned away. 'I am very weak, very unmanly sometimes,' he apologized, ashamed. 'I cannot help myself. I see you both . . . Jasper, Mark. Then I see myself, and it's just that: my – self. As much as I helped the boys at Brownstones, they helped me more. I loved to hear their laughter. Without Sarah, it's bad enough. Without Brownstones and the boys, with Beaky dead . . . I don't know what to do . . .'

He put his head in his arms and wept, and they both immediately came to him.

'You must start again,' Leah said. 'Another Brownstones.'

'No.' He rubbed his eyes. With his hair awry he looked a young boy himself.

Leah was about to say something else, hesitated, then changed her mind, shaking her head decisively.

'Why not?' Claud asked gently.

'I've had enough of London.'

'Stay in France!' they said in unison – and laughed at each other.

Adam smiled – sniffing to clear his nostrils. 'Fool that I am,' he said. 'No – I can't stay in France. I'll look for somewhere in England. Maybe the West Country. Maybe I'll buy a small farm . . . I apologize for my stupidity just now. I hate the idea of seeming pathetic. It is only that I'm rather low right now.'

'And so would anyone be under the circumstances,' Claud told him stoutly. 'You've barely spoken of anything. You *need* to.'

'In my mind I go over and over each incident, until my head feels it will explode.'

Leah said, 'Addi – please stay with us until you're fit again. There will be no pressure on you. At least here you can feel loved and needed. When your strength is regained – then is the time to return to England, and find your farm, or whatever it is you wish to buy.'

He mused, 'I remember persuading Sarah to visit you. I used all the same arguments you are using now.'

'Then you know their worth,' Leah said briskly. 'Now, you have no time for backgammon. Supper is ready. You will have to gamble your souls away afterwards.'

The following morning when he opened the shutters as usual, he was greeted by the sight of driving rain. The view was obscured by greyness, and the air was fresh and damp against his face. He closed the window. Claud had thoughtfully put a writing table beneath it, and Adam took out a new pad of paper from his writing box. He regarded the greyness outside for a few seconds and fingered his pen abstractedly, then he dipped it in ink and wrote a title: 'The Invisible City'. He underlined it heavily, and began, as he began all his children's stories, ' Once upon a time . . . Long before your great, great, great, great-grandfathers were born, there existed a unique city. The reason it was unique is that it was visible from only one secret point in the world. For years explorers set out to find this concealed city, leaving as young men and returning – if indeed they returned at all – with white beards which reached their travel-weary toes . . .'

He tested his stories on his nephews. Sucking their thumbs, they sat – one on each knee – listening enraptured to their uncle's deep voice as it related tales so fantastic that one scene after another of vivid imagery flashed before their eyes.

Leah said, 'I am reprieved. I have time again for myself! Do you realize that, thanks to you, I have at least half an hour a day when I can do my sculpting without interruption!'

Claud, too, had resumed his work and was busy writing again. He no longer felt the need to play host.

Adam did his own illustrations for his book, watercolours of intricate detail, which again he showed to his nephews for approval. They were helpful and critical.

'I thought the giant would be taller than the building,' one might say, disappointed, and accordingly, he would alter his picture.

'Her hair isn't yellow enough.' And he would make the princess's hair more yellow.

'The king should be smiling.' And the king smiled . . .

The weather became cold, and the rain streamed down the steeply pitched roof. In December he finished the book.

'But you will stay until after Christmas,' Leah persuaded him. 'It goes without saying, you will . . .'

He posted his manuscript with its illustrations to Geoffrey Gray-Courtney with a scrawled note saying, 'Merry Christmas. No, I have not gone mad.' And then he and Claud drove Florence to bustling Sarlat, where they spent the day perusing and shopping amongst the tiny streets, and being wildly extravagant. They took the backgammon set with them, and gambled on a litre of wine in a dark bar, and did not return until evening.

Loaded with parcels, and smelling of drink, they half fell out of the cart – to be greeted by a distraught Leah: a fox had just beheaded every one of their treasured *Poulets-Noirs*, and also consumed Miss Greedy, the twins' pet white rabbit.

'What will I tell them?' she asked.

'We'll buy them another, tomorrow. There's a woman in the village who breeds rabbits. The boys will never know the difference.' Claud swayed on his feet. 'The old sod took five games and a litre of wine off me,' he said, gesturing with his head to Adam, and putting his arm round his wife.

'Serves you right. You said you would check the pens ages ago.'

'Nag. Don't nag.'

'Why is it nagging because I remind you of what you said you were going to do?'

The next day the two men returned with a grown white rabbit, personally selected by Adam. 'There you are,' he announced. 'A new Miss Greedy.' Claud busied himself making the pen secure, and Leah lifted the rabbit from its box. It was complacent, but enormous. She examined it carefully – and burst out laughing.

'What is it?' Adam asked.

'Miss Greedy has the biggest testicles you've ever seen.'

In early February 1881, amongst the letters Adam received was one from Geoffrey Gray-Courtney:

> . . . Are you a permanent exile? Will you return to England to sign your part of the contract, or shall I post it to you? I have shown the manuscript to Dr Macleod, the editor of *Good Words*, as you requested, and they have agreed to serialize it, so you should hear from him any day. Incidentally, I confess I was quite as enthralled by your stories as my seven-year-old daughter, and expect this will be so with many adults – a useful bonus, since it is the adults who select their children's books . . .

A second letter from the estate agents informed him a buyer had, at last, been found for his house, and wanted to move in as soon as possible; and a third letter was from the insurance company handling his claim for Brownstones: matters had finally been concluded, and they were posting him a cheque for damages. As agreed, they would have first option on purchasing the site . . .

'I have to go back,' he told his sister and brother-in-law. 'I have things to do, matters to conclude.' Unconsciously, he repeated the insurance broker's words.

'Couldn't you wait until spring?' Leah said. 'I hate the idea of you travelling in such dreadful weather. Your health . . .' She didn't finish the sentence. He disliked being reminded of his health.

He shook his head. 'No. These are all important things to be dealt with.'

'When you have dealt with them, will you come back?' Claud

asked gruffly. He was on his knees, repairing a broken drawer. From the set of his shoulders, Leah could tell he was upset.

Adam picked at the leaf of a rubber-plant on the *torchère*. 'No, I must find somewhere of my own. It's time to move on to the next stage. I have to learn to live with myself again.'

'Oh Addi.'

'What?' he asked his sister.

'Just – "oh Addi". I want you to be happy.'

'I want me to be happy too,' he said, smiling with false gaiety.

It was a bitterly cold day when he left. Claud drove him to the station. 'You've become part of our household,' he said as they waited on the platform. His light eyes regarded Adam seriously. 'We shall miss you.'

'And I, you. I don't know how I'd have coped without you. But now I must make a fresh start.'

'Yes.'

'I shall go to the theatre when I return. I read that Ellen Terry is performing at the Lyric in *The Merchant of Venice*. I shall re-establish contacts at the Circle Club . . . When I move I'll have friends to stay. And I'll come to London frequently . . . Just one thing, Claud – does Leah ever mention Sarah to you?'

'Sometimes. But I have no patience for such talk. Women think differently. Or we do to them. A man would not take such offence.'

'But I wronged her.' But there was doubt in his eyes when he said it.

'Perhaps. I cannot say. What I *can* say is that you wrote a bloody good book, and I'd have been proud to have featured in it, in whatever context!'

Adam punched him affectionately. 'Tell me, though – is she well, does Leah say?'

'I believe she is well.'

'I hate to think that she's suffering. I think of her constantly, and it grows worse. I miss *caring* for someone. *Being* cared for. We were so close. Such friends . . . I can consider no one else.'

'But consider you must. No man can live without a woman. You will have to compromise.'

'It's easy for *you* to say that.'

'Yes. I am blessed.'

'Do you ever grow bored here?'

'Never. Truthfully, never.'

The train for Paris arrived, and the two men hugged. Then Adam held Claud away and regarded him gravely. 'You are the most valuable friend a man could wish for,' he said – and climbed hurriedly on to the train.

His last view of Claud was of him smacking his gloved hands together to keep warm. The journey promised to be long and uncomfortable and cold.

Chapter Twenty-one

SHEEPSFORD MANOR FARM

Adam found his farmhouse in the spring. He heard of it through a fellow writer at the Circle Club, whose uncle it belonged to. The man was a recent widower, and with his four daughters grown and married, he no longer had the heart to go on living there.

'I recollect visits there as a child,' the writer said. 'It was always a happy place. That's important, because the aura of a house very much depends on who has previously lived in it.'

'Is it huge?'

'Not at all. It always seemed rather small to us lot.'

'How much land?'

'That I couldn't say. I haven't a clue. Best go and visit . . .'

It was in a small village called Sheepsford, three and a half miles to the east of Dorchester, in Dorset, and rested in a small, verdant valley through which ran the Frome River. The 'T' of the village was intersected by a ford, near which was a thatched inn owned by a widow known as Old Martha, who ruled her customers with the strictness of a schoolteacher.

Adam stopped there to ask the way, and she glared at him, a stranger, daring to intrude on territory well-trodden by locals. His smile disarmed her, and when he had complimented her on her raspberry liqueur, she was won over.

'A fresh face wouldn't go amiss round 'ere,' Old Martha said, smoothing down her apron with stained, leathery hands as she stood, lopsided and lame, to see him off. 'The Manor'd just suit a young man like yourself . . .'

The ford was fairly deep, and fast-running, and the horse balked at it at first – leaping forward as the driver brandished his whip.

'Gerd-on with 'ee then.'

Adam leaned out of the window, his spirits rising by the minute, with every jolt of the carriage, or glimpse of a view – the way the hills folded and unfolded, or animals grazed peacefully, or corn waved . . . This was the place, he knew it. This was the place.

Behind the church with its little graveyard was the driveway to Sheepsford Manor Farm, sweeping into a wide gravel expanse when it came to the house. Staddle-stones separated it from the lawn, and to the left was a coaching-barn with a dovecote. A pair of doves were sitting on the roof as Adam arrived, and he thought immediately of his father. The house itself was a small Georgian building, with one large window either side of a porticoed door to the lower floor, and three, evenly spaced and shuttered, to the upper. Three further windows were set into the roof. Wisteria, just in flower, made a purple splash over the stone façade, and behind an adjoining wall were visible traditional farm-buildings. In the background the hills rose gently from the valley . . .

An elderly butler answered Adam's ring, and showed him inside to a flagstoned hallway which smelt strongly of wax polish and tobacco. The light came through the low-silled window in a broad shaft, and shone on the highly-polished Carmarthen chest and pair of tall-backed Carolean chairs. Adam heard the sound of uneven footsteps on the landing above, and of someone clearing his throat; and then down the stairs, limping and using a stick, came the owner of the house.

'Mr Gilmour, Mr Gilmour!' He was a tall, white-haired man, informally dressed in tweed, with trembling, veined hands, both of which he extended now towards Adam in greeting.

'Mr Alistair – I have heard much about you from your nephew. What a lovely place.' And as Adam scanned the room again, a warmth filled him. He felt at home here.

'It is indeed. And I have lived here for forty years. But I am going to inflict myself upon my eldest daughter who lives near Bridport. It makes more sense . . . Now come into the drawing-room and I shall tell you about the place. And then, if you don't mind, my butler will show you around, as my legs are not what they were.'

Adam followed his host into the drawing-room, an elegant pale-yellow room, with french doors leading to a conservatory, which in turn led to the terrace and a vine-clad pergola. The garden stretched from a wide lawn with topiary around the rosebeds, to a wild area which bordered a small lake. He imagined himself writing on the terrace, or drifting into a light sleep by the lake. It was a place for children. And why not? He would look for a wife once he was settled . . .

Sheepsford Manor was a mixed farm of two hundred and fifty acres, and Mr Alistair explained that fifty acres were in grass, which was mown for hay, fifty in wheat, and the remainder put to grazing. Livestock consisted of two hundred Dorset Down sheep, ten cows, seven horses and nine young cattle. The land was irrigated by a brook, a tributary of the Frome.

'But I leave the running of the place to the bailiff – a quite excellent chap about your age, I imagine,' Alistair said. 'He has been with us for ten years and would be happy to stay on. He and his family live in one of the tied cottages. The farmworkers live in another cottage. And in the third live the butler and the head gardener – he's fairly new, and unmarried.'

'It all sounds very well organized,' commented Adam.

'It is. And as you are a writer you'll need that. Farming is a tricky business. Disheartening sometimes, when you see your harvest ruined by our wondrous weather . . .'

A month later, at the beginning of June, amidst much upheaval, he moved in. He hadn't realized how his possessions had accumulated during the years, and being incurably untidy and such a hoarder had not helped. Odd boxes, half filled with things he never used, or which were broken or forgotten, travelled from London to Dorset, where he vowed he would sort them. But this never happened, and the boxes were simply incorporated into the amalgam of chaos.

So he arrived in his new home, excited, nervous, not yet able to believe this was all his: a grand house, a working farm, and servants who needed paying. With the exception of the butler, they had all remained behind, and his apprehension as he was welcomed by each of his staff in turn was far greater than theirs. They saw a tall, slim young man with a bewildered look and gentle smile. He was, if they had but known, trying not to stammer, and this made his speech stilted, so that afterwards he worried, 'They'll think me the most fearful snob.'

But Mrs Roberts, the housekeeper, had read the full serialization of *Estelle* in the *Cornhill*, and had told the others about it, so that they were all delighted by the prospect of working for a Famous Man. Amongst the smiling country faces, only the young gardener's was hostile . . .

Adam picked the rooms he wished to use, where he intended to make his mark, and summoned the sevants separately to chat to them in the one he had made into his study. Sitting in his new wing chair, he interviewed each of them for about half an hour in an effort to get to know them, that they might trust him – he was aware of the suspiciousness lodged deep in country folk. Real acceptance would take time. And the silent head-gardener bothered him.

The bailiff was called Tom Jarvis, a short, powerfully-built man with a clean-shaven square jaw, ruddy complexion and steady blue eyes. He spoke slowly and softly, with the same West Country burr as everyone from these parts. There was a dignity about him, without a trace of arrogance, and his deference to his new master was without servility.

The two men took an instant liking to each other, and Adam confided to him, 'I am entirely in your hands, you know. I understand nothing of farming, or the laws of the land . . . I should very much like to learn, to be part of what I now own. Will you teach me?'

'I'll do my utmost, sir. You can rely on that.'

'Tell me about yourself, your family.'

'Well, sir,' the bailiff looked proud, 'I've a wife of ten years now and three littl'uns. All girls they be. Nothin' but trouble in store, my wife says. We came here when we was first married . . . It's our home.'

'And so it shall always be,' Adam assured him.

It was a long day, but he went to bed contented and slept deeply. Towards morning, when his sleep was lighter, he dreamed of a child with his features. The child was laughing delightedly, and the laughter filled Adam's ears. When he awoke his eyes were wet and he felt a nameless longing within him.

He went for a walk before breakfast that morning – crossing his own fields where his own sheep grazed, and over the hay field which in a few days would be mown. The long grass was damp and wrapped itself round his calves, but the air was already warm, and he felt invigorated. His mind raced with plans – things to do, places to visit, people to meet, books to write . . . Then suddenly an image of Sarah intruded upon his thoughts, and with it a searing pain. He banished the image. This was his life now. Here in Dorset, where he would find himself a suitable wife and have a child – a son? – whom he would rock on his knee as his father had done with him until his mother had put an end to it. He would tell his child stories, teach him about nature, and the meaning of fairness and kindness and laughter . . .

He walked a large square, and returned via the church and graveyard. Out of curiosity he stopped to look at the graves; at least half of them seemed to be marked with the name Tandy, going back generations. Cousins had married cousins and produced prolifically, and there were several infant mortalities. He was pondering over the Tandys, when he was surprised by the crunch of footsteps near him, and turned fully to see the vicar approaching. A man in his early fifties, with bushy dundrearies, short, wiry hair and walrus moustache, his lively eyes gleamed with pleasure at the sight of Adam.

'No, don't tell me – I know exactly who you are, sir, and I was going to call on you today anyway, but what chance to see you like this! Beaver's my name. Austin Beaver. And you are, of course, Sir Adam Gilmour.'

His voice was as jolly as his face, and he spoke in a rapid burst, taking a great gulp of air when he had finished. They shook hands warmly, and Adam said, 'Come and breakfast with me, or have you already eaten?'

'No, no. I should be delighted to, thank you.'

Back at the house, Adam felt a glow of pleasure as he informed Mrs Roberts that the table should be laid for two: this was his first guest in his new home.

'The Tandys,' explained the vicar, who talked with his mouth full as he demolished the devilled kidneys, 'have been around for ever. Masons, labourers, ladies' maids, farmworkers, factory workers – you name it. And it is a Mrs Tandy who owns the post office and stores. She organizes the church choir. The rest of the family – not many now, I am afraid – have scattered: Weymouth, Bridport, Bournemouth, Salisbury – gone to seek mythical fortunes. My sermon this Sunday is going to be about that: the need to retain the simple values. Shall we have the pleasure of seeing you in church on Sunday, Sir Adam?'

'*Mr* Gilmour, please . . . I'm afraid I'm not much of a church-goer,' Adam apologized.

The other laughed. 'And how many genuinely are, I ask you, Mr Gilmour? No, in rural areas with small parishes, church is merely the instrument to unite people, a social occasion, if you like. Sure enough, there is some godliness mixed with it, but there is far more concern with, will the braces stay up, or the bonnet-bow tied!'

'What a realist *you* are,' Adam said, laughing with him.

They were in the parlour, a small cream-painted room with a huge fireplace, and being close to the kitchen, it always smelt of cooking. On the small gateleg table, arranged round a jug of Sweet Williams, were the dishes of food Mrs Roberts tempted Adam with daily. He offered the vicar more kidneys.

'Oh I think not, Mr Gilmour . . . Oh well, why not indeed?' he said, as Adam was about to pull the dish away. 'Just two . . . You know, you are in good company in these parts.'

'Oh? How's that?' Adam sat back in his chair, unable to help smiling at the sight of the genial vicar with the huge napkin tucked into his dog collar, and some sauce glistening on his moustache.

'You did not know that Thomas Hardy hails from just a couple of miles away?'

Adam was immediately interested. 'Of course, I knew he was from Dorset, but whereabouts, I was not sure. I have long admired his writing, and in fact, I once had a letter from him . . .' He didn't finish; the letter had been sent in circumstances he preferred to forget.

'He has just moved back to Dorset, I was hearing, after three years in London. To Wimborne. But his parents still live in Higher Bockhampton, and he often visits . . . Oh, Mr Gilmour, you have fed me too well. I shall have to go for a gruelling walk as punishment. Really, I am becoming too rotund.'

'You are my first guest,' Adam told him.

'And I am honoured indeed. Where was I? Ah – Hardy. He is a rather odd fish, to tell the truth, though it is not for me to say. He is aloof, shy rather; almost secretive. My favourite literary person is old William Barnes. He is a quite splendid character.'

'I confess his name means little to me,' Adam said.

'He is eighty now – as remarkable to look at as he is in character. He grew up around Sturminster Newton and started out as a solicitor's clerk –'

'That sounds familiar,' interrupted Adam.

Austin Beaver looked at him keenly. 'Were you one yourself?'

'Yes.'

'But not at aged thirteen, I'll wager.'

'Goodness, no.'

'Well, it was so in Barnes's case, but he had a voracious appetite for learning – science, history, archaeology, philology – you name it. It is said he speaks seventeen languages and has some knowledge of seventy-two! Anyway, he started a school which he moved to Dorchester, and is responsible for the founding of the town museum. He has written hundreds of poems – filled with that great love he bears his countryside and fellow men. Some are written in dialect! He has also written text books. And during all this, he found time to take a Cambridge degree in divinity, and when his adored wife died, about twenty years ago, he became rector at Winterborne Came Church. He walks around in the oddest clothes – a kind of cassock, tied with cord, breeches and black silk stockings fastened at the knees with buckles . . . You know, the best thing for me to do would be to make a party! I could invite an excellent mix of people, and you would meet everyone from the locality.'

'Oh no, that's too much to expect of you,' Adam protested, gesticulating – so that the coffee pot almost fell, and the other man just caught it.

'But you didn't expect it,' he corrected Adam. 'I offered. And the more I think of it, the more delightful I think it will be. Not a lot happens round here you know. It will be a good opportunity for a merry evening. Yes – when I go home I shall draw up a guest list with my wife . . . Goodness, but I am already looking forward to it. When should we have it, do you think?'

'What about three weeks from this Saturday?' suggested Adam, flinging his hands again, his reluctance dispelled by the vicar's infectious enthusiasm.

'Excellent.'

'And I shall of course pay for all the wine and food, and have my servants assist yours, if you would permit?'

'Well –'

'It is the least I can do. You must allow me,' he insisted, looking stubborn, and the vicar smiled, and getting up, patted him on the back.

'Well, I daresay some sort of compromise might be reached.'

'I look forward to seeing you soon. Call any time.'

'Thank you. I shall. Most kind. However, I shall see you on Sunday.'

'Sunday?' Adam asked, puzzled.

'Yes,' the other said in a benign tone. 'In church . . .'

When Austin Beaver had gone, Adam fetched his diary and went outside, on to the terrace.

'I feel better than I have for a long while,' he wrote. 'Of course S. is still constantly in my thoughts, and always will be; however, I find myself looking forward to my future, and believing in it. This place is already home. I must establish a routine – start on a new book, explore what is to be explored in the locality. Suddenly there is much to occupy my mind! I cannot think I shall miss London in the least . . . But I shall become fat if I'm not careful. Mrs Roberts is insistent on feeding me huge meals three, if not four, times a day! I shall become as rotund as the amiable vicar. And as I write, I think – why should I not help the men in the fields after the mowing? I could help with the carting and rick building. What exercise it would be. And what pleasure, working my *own* land . . .'

Later in the day he asked his bailiff if he knew where a calm, sturdy horse could be bought for him to hack out quietly, and which could also be driven.

'Why, I know just the man,' Tom Jarvis said. 'He's got this cob he bought for hunting – ever so good-tempered it be, but it don't like to jump.'

'Neither do I,' said Adam drily. 'I think you should introduce us, Tom.'

He rode his new cob back from West Stafford that evening – plodding quietly along the lanes; the first time he had ridden since his accident all those years ago. And his heart swelled at the goodness of it all.

He took to riding everywhere on his little grey horse, and people came to recognize him and would wave. In Old Martha's inn he drank amongst the farmworkers in their smocks, or with anyone else who happened to be there; on his second Sunday in church nobody stared at him as they had the Sunday before; Austin Beaver visited him regularly, and his own bailiff often sat and chatted to him while he breakfasted. Adam confided in him that he wanted to find a wife.

'There aren't too many of your kind round these parts, sir,' Tom Jarvis said dubiously.

'I think I'll marry a country girl, Tom.'

'Now, sir, that wouldn't be doing.' He laughed, showing white, strong teeth.

'Why not, tell me?'

And Tom looked flummoxed, and only repeated, 'It just wouldn't be doing.'

The field was mowed. It had rained hard the latter part of the previous week, and cutting had been postponed.

'Will it be ruined?' he had asked. And the other had smiled kindly at his anxiety, and said, 'Now it won't do to be fretting, sir. There's a good chance the weather'll turn again. And if it don't – well, the hay'll be like most other years – unexceptional.'

Then the rain held off for two days, and Tom announced, 'Well, today's the day, sir.'

The mowing machine, an Albion, was drawn by two horses, and had a sprung seat which projected to the rear. Its wheels were large and wide apart. Tom explained the parts of the machine to Adam, and how it had to be constantly maintained, rarely lasting more than three seasons without a substantial overhaul.

'The blade and bar are the important part,' he said, pointing to the structure. 'And the fingers, or spikes if you like, move up to the next bit then back again when the machine's in gear. If these are blunt you get an imperfect cut, and too much grass left on the knife . . . And the machine must always be kept greased.'

A farmworker appeared leading two Shire horses, and began the intricate task of harnessing them and fixing the pole gear, finishing by carefully checking the height of the cutting bar. He held the horses as Tom climbed into the saddle. Adam watched enviously.

'I'd love to try it.'

'Well, you could do a strip in the middle,' Tom said. He sounded reluctant, but Adam leaped at the opportunity. 'I'll follow you on foot, and you can explain what you are doing.'

'It'll be hard going, sir.'

'No matter. I have to learn.'

The day became hotter. The horses plodded up and down dutifully, and beside them, puffing and sweating and determined, Adam kept abreast, watching every move – the way the bailiff manoeuvred the horse and cumbersome machinery, pivoting expertly before commencing the next line, in order not to strain the bar . . .

The morning wore on, and they broke for lunch. Tom was about to return to his cottage, but hesitated, and said shyly, 'You're welcome to join us, sir. There's plenty.'

'I'd very much like that, Tom,' Adam said, laying his arm on the shorter man's shoulder, and accompanied him back.

His home was a small thatched place, and the roof in need of some repair, Adam noticed.

'Does it leak?' he asked.

'Sometimes.'

'I'll get hold of a thatcher . . . No, you do it. I don't know who to use. Just go ahead and organize it.'

'Thank you, sir.'

His wife was a plump woman with bright red hair and freckled skin. Adam had seen her a few times, and she was always laughing. She welcomed him into their cottage – which was cool and dark inside – and apologized that it was untidy; she hadn't expected such an important guest.

'I should have hated you to have stood on ceremony,' he said, glancing appreciatively around the homely place. 'Besides, I see very little evidence of untidiness.'

'My wife – she's a fiend for housework.'

'I'm not, Tom. That's not true.' She pushed him fondly.

'Mr Gilmour was saying we could have the thatch done.'

'Oh sir, that'd be ever so welcome. It do leak sometimes.' Her accent was broader than her husband's; Adam loved that Dorset roll – as full and luscious as the countryside itself.

He watched how the husband and wife were together – their easy informality, the unashamed love they showed before their daughters, who hung back shyly before him. But then he delighted everyone by telling a story he invented on the spot . . . As lunch extended into the afternoon, so he became determined that he would marry out of his class; and a picture fixed itself before him.

Replete with food and a mugful of cider each, the two men traipsed back to the field, and removed their shirts again. Overhead, a bird with a huge wingspan hovered. 'A hawk,' Adam exclaimed. 'No – it's too big.'

'It be a buzzard,' his companion corrected him, looking upwards, and creasing his eyes against the sun's glare. 'You get plenty of them in these parts.'

They both stopped to watch the magnificent, silent bird, and then it circled and flew off.

The horses had been rested, but were now harnessed once more. 'My turn,' said Adam. And again the bailiff looked doubtful.

'I'll be careful,' he promised, and looked so much like a happy, excited child that the other smiled.

'Well, leave it to them, then. They know what to do,' he said, referring to the horses.

Adam climbed into the saddle, and moved himself about until he was comfortable; then gathering the long reins in his hands, he clicked his teeth, and they were off. He felt disconcertingly precarious in the saddle with nothing substantial about him, and the wheels bounced on the uneven ground . . . But he grew used to the motion, and began to enjoy himself. In front of him were the great bay hindquarters of the horses, their docked tails swishing against flies in vain. The two animals kept perfect instinctive pace with one another, their huge hooves making a soft thudding sound to the accompaniment of the swishing of the long grass and the rattle and creaking of the machinery.

Adam's thoughts wandered . . . Then he realized they were nearing the end of the line already, and began to panic. From the other end Tom Jarvis watched, but Adam could not see his expression. He drew to a halt, ensuring that the bar was a good distance in front, and made the horses pivot. Then he looked down to ensure everything was in the correct position, and set off again.

He did three lines in all, and was triumphant when he climbed down from the saddle. After that he was content to lie back and watch Tom Jarvis doing the work. A slight breeze came up, and it cooled the sweat on his body. Listening to the sounds of the mowing, the occasional blowing down their nostrils by the horses, the mysterious rustlings in the hedgerows, Adam thought that now he truly belonged. He had worked his own land – and felt ludicrously proud of his accomplishment.

He went to bed early that night, but just before sleep came, he went through in his mind everything that he had to do. In a few days' time it would be Austin Beaver's party – and he wondered whom he would meet. His eyelids closed. Fortunately he did not hear the rain that fell that night, wetting his precious hay; and by morning the sun was shining again, and continued to do so for the next two days, when he helped gather it from the ground and into the four-wheeled box-wagons for stacking.

Chapter Twenty-two

AMABEL

On the evening of Austin Beaver's party, Adam began to feel apprehensive. All his old shyness returned at the prospect of meeting so many new people, and as a newcomer to the area, he would be on display. What did one wear for such an occasion? He looked again through his wardrobe, and at the clothes heaped on the floor, and eventually selected a light beige summer-weight 'lounge-suit' which was narrow cut and closely buttoned.

He surveyed himself in the cheval mirror as critically as a girl going to her first ball, and his reflection stared back sombrely – his thin, suntanned face, without the moustache now; full-lipped mouth with a faint line at either corner; dark soft brown brows above the grey eyes – one so expressive, the other fixed. And his hair flopping over his forehead as usual, but with as much grey in it as brown . . . How did others see him? He drew back his shoulders – and noticed that in doing so he grew another inch – and left the room with all its chaos of clothes and boxes and tissue paper, shoes and books . . .

When he arrived at the vicarage the voices – the buzz of chatter, bursts of laughter – could be heard outside. The front door was open, and Adam wandered hesitantly inside to find the party in full swing. Amelia Beaver, Austin's wife, saw him and drew him into the small group in the hallway. One of his own maids offered him a drink of fruit cup from a salver, and he smiled at her and took it gratefully. He was introduced to each of the group, who were all from a neighbouring village: a doctor and his wife, an elderly solicitor, and a farmer – with whom Adam had an enthusiastic discussion about the hay crop. Then through the doorway came Austin Beaver, who, after welcoming him, almost dragged him into the small drawing-room, which seemed packed with people. At first

Adam thought that conversation stopped and everyone was looking at him, but in fact it was not so, and he quickly recognized several people he already knew, who shook hands and seemed pleased to see him.

Tom Jarvis was there, talking to an attractive, dark-haired young woman, dressed in the latest fashion. She had bought the tight-bodiced dress with its beribboned bustle from the second-hand clothes stall at Dorchester market, as soon as she had heard about the party, and had thought of little else but this evening for the past three weeks. Her name was Amabel, and she was Tom Jarvis's youngest sister.

The bailiff introduced her to his employer, and Adam, in his curiosity about her, didn't notice the reserve in Tom's voice.

'I've heard ever so much about you,' the girl said, looking up at Adam with flattering admiration in her blue eyes. 'My brother speaks ever so well of you, sir.' And she smiled, showing the same strong white teeth as her brother's. Her face, too, was broad like his, and high-coloured.

'I think well of your brother, too,' Adam replied, articulating his words carefully in order not to stutter. 'But I confess I have heard no mention of you, Miss Jarvis.'

'I teach at the infants' school in Dorchester.'

'Amabel,' her brother growled warningly, implying she was being too forward.

'I were only saying, Tom.'

'Well, you don't *teach* there. You *help*.'

'It's all the same thing,' she said lightly, waving her hand dismissively in the air. A square, tanned hand, Adam noticed. Her lips were very red and she licked them often. He wondered if their colouring was natural, decided it was, and was even more drawn to her earthy attractiveness.

'Most importantly, do you enjoy your job?' he asked her.

'Oh yes, sir. I do like working with young children – listening to their chatter and laughter.'

And he stared at her, caught in a spasm of emotion at her words.

'I too love children,' he said softly. 'Nothing gives me greater joy than to hear the sounds of their happiness . . .'

Tom's face was expressionless as they talked on, and then his wife appeared, and said that someone wanted to speak with him, and Amabel and Adam were left together. Out of the corner of her eye she saw the vicar approaching, and knew that now was her chance, or perhaps not at all; she had planned some of her conversation in advance.

'Do you know what Amabel means?' she asked quickly.

'No,' he answered, laughing.

'It means lovable. Do you think me lovable, sir?' She gazed at him, deliberately coquettish, and he gazed back – and answered a throaty 'yes'. A moment later Austin Beaver cornered him and took him off to meet Thomas Hardy and William Barnes. Alone, Amabel smiled a secret smile of satisfaction.

Thomas Hardy was six years older than Adam, a short man of slight build, with brown receding hair, and a yellowish moustache blending into his clipped beard. Thick eyebrows shielded grey eyes that were both piercing and pensive, and his Roman nose jutted prominently from a round, flattish face.

They shook hands, and Adam said, 'I have long admired your work.'

'The admiration is mutual,' replied Hardy, in a voice which was precise and without a trace of Dorset inflection.

Adam then turned to the old poet. 'Your name is legendary round these parts, sir,' he said.

William Barnes smiled and joked, 'Legends have a habit of fading into oblivion.'

'I am certain yours will not,' Adam said, immensely struck by the man's appearance – his expression of almost spiritual goodness, the nobility of his face, silver hair flowing from a bald crown, and a white beard tumbling to his barrel chest. His clothes were as Austin Beaver had described them, and he looked, Adam thought, half priest, half sorcerer.

Adam had bought a book of his poems from Dorchester, and now, confronted by the man himself, he could discuss them with at least some knowledge. The three talked amongst themselves, until dinner was announced in the dining-room, and Hardy's wife, Emma, a large, fair and heavy-jawed woman, appeared. Their group separated, and he found himself beside Amabel once more . . .

At about midnight people began leaving, and Adam prepared to go.

'Come and visit us at Wimborne,' Hardy said. 'It's yet another furnished house, I'm afraid. We are accused by relatives of wandering about like tramps, because we're constantly on the move! But Llanherne – that is the name of the house – has a lovely garden full of flowers and ripening fruit, and the avenue is newly planted with lime trees.'

'I should be glad to call on you. Is there a railway station at Wimborne?'

'Yes. It is on one of the main lines between London and Dorchester. So you have no excuse.'

'And I shall not look for one,' Adam said, briefly touching the other's arm – and noticing how he flinched; Hardy had a dislike of physical contact. 'But you must also visit me, whenever you are at Bockhampton. It would give me pleasure to show you round the farm.'

'A writer who is a farmer,' mused Hardy.

'I am not writing at the moment, so it is rather the other way, I fear,' he said.

Barnes and Adam exchanged invitations as well, and finally, after various other farewells, the only person left to say goodbye to was Amabel Jarvis.

'I be staying with my brother the night,' she informed him, moving close. 'It be too far to return to Dorchester at this hour.'

'Very wise,' he said, feeling himself becoming aroused by her nearness.

'And t'morrow being Sunday and no school, I'll probably stay around. I daresay I'll see you in church.' Her soft voice slid upwards in question, and she tilted her chin, so that he could see she had a short, strong throat.

'I daresay you will,' he echoed, raising an eyebrow. She actually blushed, and some of the boldness went from her eyes as she fiddled with a tendril of hair which had come loose from one of the coils on top of her head.

Tom Jarvis came between them, and looking coldly at his sister, smiled at his employer and asked, 'Are you leaving then, sir?'

'Yes, Tom.'

'And you're on foot?'

'Yes. It wasn't worth driving.'

'I've a lamp if you need one.'

'No Tom – I already have one, thank you.'

'Well, that's fine then. Good night sir.'

'Good night Tom.'

As a result of the vicar's party, invitations began to arrive, which adorned his study mantelpiece. A couple were from parents keen to introduce their daughters; but Adam, unaware of their intentions, would not have been interested. He had decided, after just a fortnight, to marry Amabel.

He had not yet said anything to his bailiff, who he knew would disapprove, or even to the girl herself, whom he had met several times since the party; but the more he saw of her, the more sure he was she would make him an ideal wife. She was practical, attractive and uncomplicated, and she seemed fond of him. He could tell, not only from the way she flirted with him, but also by little things she said or did. On the fourth meeting, during a walk across the magnificent and bleak Blackdown heathland – he had fetched and driven her there himself, tethering the cob to a tree – she had said, 'I don't know what you do see in me, sir. I'm not clever in the least.'

'Yes you are. Only in a different way. Your own way.'

'Oh? And what way might that be, then?' she asked sharply, smiling and showing her strong teeth. And he had kissed her by way of reply, under the shadow of the great grey tower built to commemorate Admiral Sir Thomas Masterman Hardy. While the wind whistled around them, he stood with his arm about her, surveying the vista – heathland and wide plains, the extraordinary, long line of Chesil Bank to where it met Portland, the coast and views across the sea as far as Bournemouth . . .

'On a clear day you can see Dartmoor to the west, and the Isle of Wight to the east,' Amabel said, nestling close to him.

'It is spectacular. Quite spectacular,' Adam said. He felt surprisingly emotional – stirred by the magnificence around him, and the girl leaning against him, within the protection of his arm. It didn't occur to him that he might be idealizing her, or that he was naïve with his romantic concept of a country girl. He tasted their kiss still, and when she said, 'I like being with you, sir,' almost proposed to her on the spot.

'Amabel – call me Adam.'

'Oh no, sir I couldn't do that. Not *yet*, anyrate.'

And he didn't press her, but respected her all the more. He did not see the cunning in her lowered eyes . . .

He started another novel that night – about a Scotsman who moved from Edinburgh to buy a Lowland farm, and fell in love with a local girl, who was not what she appeared to be, and set about destroying him.

The weeks passed, and he was busier than he had ever been in London. He read avidly still, wrote his book, explored the countryside on his horse, sometimes stopping at inns for the night; there were farm matters to attend to . . . And he had never been so sociable. He began to feel as though he had lived in Sheepsford all his life. People dropped in from neighbouring villages, although his most regular visitor was still Austin Beaver. Adam had visited William Barnes a couple of times in his thatched rectory – sat with him in the cluttered parlour listening to the poet reading aloud his own poems in a melodic voice. Barnes had told him about his six grown children and many grandchildren, how he liked to dig in the garden, and that sometimes he walked for miles, whatever the weather, in order to visit someone sick . . .

And there was Dorchester, with its Roman remains and museum, the Antelope Hotel in Cornhill where the Bloody Assize, presided over by Judge Jeffreys in 1685, was said to have taken place; the site of the old gallows in Ison Way . . . He might have a drink at the King's Arms in High East Street, or tea in the Admiral Hardy Tea Rooms; or he would stroll down West Walks to Borough Gardens to listen to the band playing. Wednesday was market day, and then he would mingle with the locals as they jostled for bargains, while from the Eldridge Pope brewery opposite wafted the smell of malt.

So Adam spent his time; but all was not perfect. There was poverty not only in the rural villages, but in Dorchester itself, to rival some of the worst he had seen. Mill Street in the Fordington area by the river was overpopulated, and disease was rife, and Adam was horrified by the living conditions. He had the idea of doing a series of articles for the *Cornhill Magazine* depicting local life, and contributing the money he earned from it to the poor of Dorchester.

'I cannot believe how quickly you have settled in,' Austin Beaver remarked to him one day in early August. He had found Adam sitting on a stool amongst the trees and shrubs, painting a view of the lake. The branches of a weeping willow fell into the water, and leaves were strewn on the surface, like silver fish.

'I am thinking of marrying,' he answered.

'Good heavens, man!' exclaimed the vicar.

'Does good heavens constitute swearing?' asked Adam mildly.

'I don't believe so . . . My goodness, but this is a surprise.' He pulled at his moustache and sat cross-legged on the grass beside Adam.

'I don't see why it should be. After all, I am nearly thirty-five.'

'Are you? I presumed you to be younger. However, that is not what I meant. No – it is only that I was unaware you had a young lady-friend.'

'I didn't until I came here.' Adam put his brush in a jar and watched the water turn a shade of purple.

'So she is a local girl then . . . I must say this is all most exciting! Give me a clue.'

'It is Tom Jarvis's sister, Amabel. Although I haven't broached the subject with her yet.'

'Good heavens above! Amabel Jarvis! You can't be serious, Adam.'

'Why not?' he demanded. 'Why shouldn't I marry her?'

'But of course. If that is your choice. I just would not imagine a man like you . . . a woman like her . . . Ah well – of course it is your choice,' he repeated.

Adam laughed. 'Come now, Austin – stop pretending. Look at you with your hands twisted around your knees in your anguish! What are your objections?'

'No, no. It's not my business,' the vicar said hurriedly.

'That may be true,' Adam said, 'but I'd still like to hear what you have to say.' He swivelled on his stool, and laughed again at his friend. 'I've never seen you look so serious. So lost for words.'

'Well, marriage is a serious business. Have you thought about this properly, Adam?'

'I believe so.'

'It is only that you are regarded now in the village as having some standing. You are invited to the smartest houses . . . Like it or not, you *are* titled. The lower classes respect you and the upper station likes you. You risk being ostracized socially. I have to tell you this.'

'Would you ostracize me?'

'Of course not, man.'

'Well then. You'll see – people will accept it in the end. And if they do not – then they're not the kind I desire as friends in the first place . . . No, I feared you were going to say something disparaging about Amabel.'

'I have heard she is – flighty.'

'High spirits, that's all.'

'Adam, there are at least two marriageable young ladies within the locality, who are of your own background, and not at all bad-looking.'

'I want to marry a country girl, Austin.'

'Ah, so that's it. That is false reasoning. You are fostering that curious illusion about country-folk which is typical of an urbane –'

'I grew up in the country.'

'You told me your adult years have been spent in London. As a child, what did you learn about country girls?'

'Not a great deal, I suppose,' he said, thinking of Ethel, and recalling Miss Tinley's silence over her mysterious fate.

'They can be as wily as the most sophisticated socialite. And much looser in their morals.'

'What a fuddy-duddy you are, Austin! Well, I am going to propose to Amabel.'

'Oh dear, oh dear,' Austin Beaver sighed – then stood up to inspect Adam's half-finished watercolour, and the subject was changed.

Adam sat in the parlour waiting for Tom Jarvis to arrive. He was not looking forward to the meeting. From the corner came the comforting ticking of the mahogany longcase clock, and by his feet was curled the lurcher puppy he had just acquired from a neighbouring farmer. It had one ear, the other having been bitten off by one of its siblings.

'What a pair,' he thought, glancing down fondly as it slept. 'A one-eyed owner with a one-eared dog!'

Outside, the day was drab – he thought it had a prematurely autumnal feel about it. He saw the bailiff hurrying up the drive, and turned quickly away from the window in case it should seem he had been anxiously waiting. He sat further back in his chair, stretching out his legs and waking the puppy. It was a skinny, beige, long-tailed and long-nosed creature, and now it sprang on to Adam's lap. He knew he should discourage it, but had not the heart: he already loved it.

'Good boy. Good Rags.' The dog tried to clamber on to his shoulders, and smothered him with urgent licks – then it heard the bailiff's feet crunching on the gravel and the subsequent knock on the front door, and leaped down, and shot, barking, from the room.

Tom Jarvis was shown in. By now they had a mutual liking and respect, and Adam hoped that his news would not affect Tom's attitude towards him. The bailiff sat down. He emanated calm and honesty. He enjoyed working for Adam, because the latter had ambitions for the farm – to expand, acquire more land, enlarge the dairy side, improve their sheep strain by buying some prize rams, and the pair had spent many hours making plans for the future. Tom was proud to be working for such a man as Adam Gilmour, who had been the talk of the district since his arrival. He was always considerate, that was why Tom liked him; he always had time; was always concerned . . .

'Tom, I wanted to ch-chat to you about something in particular.' Adam sat on the edge of his chair, tense, and ran his hand several times over his right eye, while the bailiff looked at him expectantly, trustingly.

'A while back I mentioned to you that I wanted to marry . . . Do you recollect that discussion?'

'Yes sir, I do,' and he smiled, the same white-toothed smile as his sister's.

'Tom – what would you say if I told you I wanted to marry Amabel?'

The other's smile disappeared. 'Amabel? *Am*abel? Oh no, sir – you're having me on now, aren't you?'

'No Tom, I'm not,' answered Adam quietly, looking him directly in the eye.

Tom slumped, speechless, in his chair, and Adam reached over and anxiously touched his shoulder. 'Please – say something.'

'I'm too – flabbergasted – sir,' Tom said finally.

'I've been seeing her for a month now. She's a lovely girl. I'm convinced it's the right thing.'

'Well I'm not, sir,' Tom burst out vehemently, jumping to his feet. 'I don't see as it's the right thing at all. You don't *know* her, sir, and it's not *right* – a man like you marrying a girl like her. She's not of your kind. Why – she's not even educated. She only helps out in the school –'

'She is naturally intelligent,' Adam interrupted. 'And she says she longs to learn to further her knowledge.'

Tom wanted to say that it was merely part of her act, that she was impatient of anything she could not immediately grasp; that she was the spoiled youngest child . . . But she *was* his sister, and loyalty prevailed.

Seeing his confusion, watching the range of expressions crossing his face, Adam was about to make some comforting remark, when Tom said almost petulantly, 'And what about *me*? How will it be for me?'

'But Tom, it won't affect you. Why would it?'

'You'll be my *brother*-in-law, sir,' he said, sounding so distressed that Adam laughed and asked gently, 'And would that be terrible, Tom?'

'No, sir. I wasn't meaning that. You know I wasn't. But I'm a servant in your employ, and Amabel – well she'll be *Lady* Gilmour.'

'She'll not,' Adam corrected him sharply. 'I don't use my title.'

'You mightn't. But you just try stopping her using hers.'

For the first time Adam felt a twinge of doubt – and then the bucolic little scene reappeared before him in his imagination, and he said, 'Tom, you are too busy putting obstacles in the way. It will all work out satisfactorily. You'll see. Besides, I have not yet proposed. Amabel may not accept me.'

'She will,' her brother said gloomily.

*

Adam Gilmour and Amabel Jarvis were married one Saturday at the beginning of December 1881, and over a hundred and twenty people crowded into the fourteenth-century Sheepsford Parish Church. It was the most talked-about event for years, and the division between friends and relatives of the bride, all bedecked in their finery, and those of the groom could not have been more clearly marked. The local gentry sat on one side and the labourers on the other – every so often glancing pointedly at one another and whispering behind their hands.

Among the guests were Leah and Claud – they had left the twins in France – and the pair sat together in the front row, taciturn, as they waited for Amabel to arrive. Everything there was to say had been said – the attempts at dissuasion, the reasoning, the accusing, and then the accepting . . . Adam had been stubborn all his life, and he remained intractable.

Leah was thirty-two now, but looked five years younger with her smooth olive skin like her brother's and her bouncing curls. She had become plumper over the years, but it suited her, added to her radiance, and Claud still called her 'his littlest mouse'. Adam, in seeking an idyll like theirs, saw Amabel as his only answer.

'I never thought I would have to accuse you of snobbery,' Adam said reproachfully to them after an argument two nights before the wedding.

'It is *not* snobbery,' Leah said furiously. 'But the girl has no conversation. She's frivolous. That's what I object to. If she were from a wealthy background you wouldn't look at her.'

Adam set his jaw and made no reply.

But the night before his marriage he had asked his sister about Sarah. 'Do you still hear from her?'

'Yes, often.'

'How is she?'

'The same,' Leah replied enigmatically; then, seeing her brother's stricken expression, softened and added, 'She is making a life for herself. She's involved with the women's movement, and with her Women's Club.'

'Is it still called Brownstones?'

'Yes.'

He turned away for a moment.

'Addi –'

She touched his hand and he turned back. Relieved, she saw that he was composed. 'You know that in the end we're behind you, whatever you do,' she said.

'Yes, I know.'

'It's only you have had so much unhappiness, and we want you to be happy.'

'I'm sure I shall be.'

'The house is lovely.' Leah looked appreciatively round the drawing-room. 'You were right to move here. I'm sure of that.'

'I'm very busy,' he told her. 'The serialization of my children's stories has done well, and I have started a new novel.'

'What is it about?'

'A Scottish aristocrat who opts for the rural life, and marries a simple country girl.'

'That sounds faintly familiar! Oh Addi, you are incorrigible,' she said, laughing.

'Ah – but wait. What our hero does not know is that his simple country girl has married him out of revenge on another rich but untitled man who wouldn't marry her because he thought her beneath him. She then, from her position of security, proceeds to wreck both men's lives, playing one off against the other.'

'I don't know how you dream up your ideas,' she said.

They lapsed into companionable silence, which he broke when he asked suddenly, 'Have you seen her since you came to England?'

Realizing he referred to Sarah, Leah answered, 'Yes. On our first night.'

'Is she still beautiful?'

'More so.'

'Oh God.'

And then Claud came in, brandishing the backgammon, and Adam fetched the brandy and glasses, and they all became rather drunk . . .

From the pulpit Austin Beaver looked down at the kneeling couple – at Amabel, her dark head crowned with ivory silk and a little garland of flowers. Her navy eyes met his, challenging, unwavering, and he averted his gaze. After that he was more than ever convinced he should not be performing this ceremony or giving his blessing.

The reception was back at Sheepsford Manor, and as in church, the party was divided. Adam spoke to as many guests as he could, but he noticed a new constraint amongst those who only a couple of months ago had welcomed him into their homes and accepted him into the hierarchy of Dorset society.

He heard someonc laughing raucously and turned. It was Amabel. She was talking with a middle-aged squire from nearby West Stafford. Adam had never really heard her laugh before, and it came as a shock to him. She sounded like a chicken squawking.

Chapter Twenty-three

WEDDED BLISS

The newly-wedded couple spent Christmas in Italy and returned to snowy Dorset in the middle of January 1882.

It had been a honeymoon of mixed moods. The first few days – in Paris – were mostly spent in bed. Adam had not had a woman since Sarah and he delighted in Amabel's body; their pleasure in each other was uninhibited and Adam rediscovered the sensuous joy of simple touch. He loved to tease her, to caress her to the point of frenzy before finally entering her. And then her arms would wind round his back, her nails dig into him, and her gasps became short cries. After an hour or so's nap they had only to reach across to begin all over again.

And there had been the pleasure of showing her Paris, and seeing her childlike wonderment at everything. She had hung on to his arm as they walked along the Champs-Élysées, and looked admiringly at him when he had spoken to a cab driver in perfect French. And she could not stop thanking him when, after she had gazed longingly at an expensive dress, he had insisted on buying it for her . . .

But in Rome it rained continually and was bitterly cold. She grew bored with the endless sightseeing, and thought if another beggar-child came up to them with huge pleading eyes, she would slap it across the face. Adam could not speak Italian, and in Italy, like her, he was merely another tourist without status. His enthusiasm for everything began to infuriate her. She was tired. This was supposed to be a holiday. She wanted to sleep.

At first he felt guilty, believed that it was his fault she was so obviously bored, and remained with her at the hotel, reading in one of the elegant drawing-rooms; or he window-shopped with her in one of the covered arcades. But this was not what he had come to

Rome to do, and he felt repressed, then irritated, and finally lost even his sexual interest in her.

Eventually he thought, 'This is absurd. We are each trying to do things to please the other, and ending by dissatisfying ourselves.' So he confronted her and asked if she minded his going out on his own.

'Not at all, my sweet,' she replied in her soft voice. 'Not if it be what you want.'

She was combing her long thick hair in their bedroom, and he went up to her – stroked her hair, then her naked back. She leaned against him.

'I'm sorry,' he said. 'I know I've been irritable.'

'Tell me of a man without a bad temper,' she said brightly, 'and I'll show you where his bones lie.'

Adam laughed. 'Did you make that up?'

'No. My nan used to say it. I'm not clever enough to think up things like that.'

'You *are* clever,' he said emphatically, wanting her to be.

'Well, to tell the truth I'm not much caring whether I am or no, my sweet.'

And something jolted within him.

Sometimes, after dinner in the evenings, he would recite simple poetry to her or read aloud passages from *Far from the Madding Crowd*, and at first she listened attentively. But when it came to discussing the pieces afterwards, it would transpire she had absorbed little, and had simply enjoyed listening to his voice for its comforting sound.

He thought that when they returned home, and she was back in her own environment, everything would be better: he had plucked a country girl from her native soil and once he took her back there she would thrive again and have plenty of time in which to show her common sense and practicality. He stopped trying to educate her, let her do as she pleased, and bought her another dress . . .

It was a quiet period on the farm, and Adam would shut himself away in his study to write. Bored, Amabel wandered about desultorily. Once she had spent her days helping in the school and her evenings – when she was not out with some young man –

making herself dresses and taking in other people's sewing. But there was no need for that now. As Lady Gilmour she must be well-mannered and do nothing but a little discreet needlepoint. And where were the parties she had envisaged, the smart functions she had imagined herself attending? She would interrupt Adam a dozen times in a morning over inconsequentialities, and eventually he would become angry.

'I am trying to *write*, Amabel, for goodness' sake.'

'But you are *always* writing.'

'It's my work. My job.'

'Well, why do you need a job? You're titled. Most titled people don't have jobs.'

'What rubbish you do talk,' he said impatiently. 'Of course they do. One has to have money to live.'

'I thought you were rich.' She fiddled with the edge of a book on his desk.

'Well I'm not.'

'Oh,' she said, looking crestfallen. And then a hardness came into her eyes. 'Oh,' she repeated, and left the room.

'Amabel –' he called after her, aware he had been offhand.

'Yes?' Her face reappeared round the door.

'It is only I am busy, and I must concentrate when I write or my thoughts go from me . . . Forgive me . . . Why not take Rags for a walk? Wrap up warm. It would do you good.'

'Oh all right then,' she said grudgingly. She hesitated, then asked, 'Adam, you're not poor though, are you?'

'No, my love. I'm not poor.'

'Only I was hearing the other day how you give ever so much money away to charities. You do keep some for – us – don't you?'

He smiled. She was not yet twenty-four and such a child.

'We'll not starve. Oh come here.' He stood up as she came to him, and when he held open his arms she nestled in them as she had used to.

The months passed. Austin Beaver still visited regularly; Tom Jarvis still insisted on calling him 'sir', and apparently felt that by doing so nothing had changed. William Barnes passed by occasionally, and a couple of times Thomas Hardy, when he was at Bockhampton.

But few invitations came his way nowadays, and on Sundays, after the church service, no one lingered to chat with him as before. Adam was sorry, for he had liked many of those who now ignored him; he felt let down, and some of his enchantment with the village evaporated.

Amabel, too, was disappointed. She had had her own aspirations, and now knew they would come to nothing. She had deliberately severed her ties with many of her family and old friends – but with nobody to replace them she felt lonely. Her husband told her she should have a hobby. Such as what? she asked him. She had no one to see, had never learned to ride, could not play an instrument, do needlepoint, or read complicated books. All she did was walk the one-eared lurcher and annoy Mrs Roberts by interfering with the running of the house. Amabel would get rid of her; *she* would be the housekeeper in her own home.

'We *can't*,' Adam said, horrified.

'I can keep house just as well as her. Don't you think I can?' Amabel asked, pouting.

'Of course. I know you can. It isn't that. But she has worked in this house for twelve years. It wouldn't be fair.'

'Then she's more important than me – your wife.'

'Don't be silly.'

'Well then.'

'Oh Amabel, Amabel.'

She had won. 'Please let me try,' she wheedled. 'I do so want to be a good wife, my sweet . . .'

In the end he told Mrs Roberts himself, but not before he had found her a new post.

For a few months – into the summer – Amabel kept her word, and did her utmost as a wife, and their marriage lived up to Adam's ideal of nuptial bliss. The farm was busy, and he helped with the harvesting, drinking ale with the men in the fields from the cool stone bowls, becoming fitter and more muscular every day. His health was better than it had been for years, and contentment settled comfortably within him . . .

He would stroll with Tom Jarvis to check the sheep, carrying with him his own thistle 'spitter' – an implement like a walking stick with a chisel-type blade used for taking out weeds; or he and

Amabel and the lurcher would go for long walks, across heathland and water-meadows. He always held her hand, massaging her knuckles from time to time as a reminder he was there.

'Happy?'

'Yes, my sweet.'

Her skin was ruddy and brown and her hair flowing, and seeing her like that, he was happy, too. She picked flowers and grasses from the hedgerows and took them home – she never went anywhere without her pannier – and every room in the house smelt sweetly of the bundles of flowers hanging upside down to dry. Chairs and sofas were adorned with cushions she had made, and patchwork covers were draped over beds . . . She was forever busy, making the place daily more comfortable.

And she began to take an interest in the garden.

Wednesday, August 17th, 1882

'I am already three-quarters of the way through my novel, and believe I am writing better than ever before. The calm of marriage, now that we have settled and grown accustomed to one another's ways, has provided me with the stability I have long needed, and I am constantly aware that there is someone else to care for, and who, in return, cares for me.

'It doesn't matter in the least that intellectually we may be at variance, for there are many other things to share. So – despite everyone's fears, I was right in my decision to marry. All that is missing now is a child, but in time that will surely happen. And meanwhile, we have each other, do we not, Amabel, my lovable one?'

Towards the end of August Adam was in the conservatory writing his column for the *Cornhill*, when he heard the raucous pealing of his wife's laughter coming from the garden. He glanced out and saw her with the gardener standing in a provocative and rather slatternly pose, with her hands on her thrust-forward hips. Her head was thrown back. He saw the gardener's lips move in conversation, and there came again that ugly laughter. Thoughtfully Adam shut his notebook. He could no longer concentrate, and felt a wave of annoyance. He went over to the doorway to the garden and stood watching them for a moment, before calling, 'Amabel,' in a rather authoritative tone.

They both stared at him; he thought the gardener's expression held contempt, while Amabel looked resentful. Then she came tripping lightly towards him. 'What is it, my sweet?' And for the first time he detected a falseness in the endearment.

'I'd like to talk with you a moment . . . Amabel, you're too familiar with that gardener.' Then he realized how old and pompous he sounded, and bit his lip.

'He was only telling a little joke. I can laugh at a joke, can't I?'

'Yes, of course,' he said lamely, beginning to feel disadvantaged.

'*You* never tell jokes.'

He remembered how as a child he had always made his sister laugh. 'I'm sorry,' he said stiffly, hurt. 'Forget the whole thing.' And gathering his bits and pieces, he went into his study.

The post had arrived and was on his desk. Amabel always put it there for him to look at. The very last letter he opened was an invitation from Thomas Hardy, to visit them in Wimborne in ten days' time.

Excitedly, Adam rushed from the room. 'Amabel,' he called '*Ama*bel.'

And she appeared quickly, her sulkiness apparently over. Her eyes sparkled, and in his own mood of excitement he thought how intolerant he had been with her. He kissed her, and lifting her into the air, whirled her round.

'What is it?' she asked, laughing, kicking her feet so that her shoes fell off.

'We've had an invitation to the Hardys' at Wimborne.'

'What – *Thomas* Hardy?' she asked slowly, as he put her down.

'Yes.'

'Oh Adam. Oh, I couldn't go.' He had never seen her look so troubled, so uncertain. 'I shouldn't be knowing what to talk about.'

He cupped her chin, and felt a fierce protectiveness towards her. 'You must not say things like that. You mustn't feel inferior. Why – you talk to *me*.'

'You're my husband,' she said giggling. 'It's different.'

'But before I was your husband – you talked then.'

She looked fleetingly wistful. 'You made it easy for me,' she said softly. And she ran a finger over his forehead, smoothing out a worried line. He captured her finger and kissed it.

'Please come with me?'

'I'd be awful *bored*, Adam.'

Who was this girl he had married? He thought he saw again that taunting look in her eyes of earlier, heard her shriek of laughter with the gardener.

'You must do as you wish,' he said.

'Thank you . . . Oh Adam, my sweet, there was this really darlin' dress and hat I saw in Dorchester yesterday –'

'Yes, of course. You must have them.'

'Oh thank you, my sweet . . .'

He took the train from Dorchester and at midday arrived at Wimborne station where he was met by Thomas Hardy. They grasped hands, but only for a brief moment before Hardy jerkily withdrew his, recoiling as always from physical contact. They walked side by side, Hardy quickening his step to match Adam's stride. A good head shorter than Adam, he had to peer up from under the brim of his hat as he enquired, 'I trust your journey was good?'

'Most comfortable – and speedy,' answered Adam. 'Really, the rail service is very efficient.'

'We're delighted you could come. Emma and I often speak of you.'

Wimborne was an attractive small market town on the Hampshire borders, dominated by the magnificent Minster. Little was left of its medieval origins, but fine eighteenth-century streets led from the square, and it was a wealthy place with substantial houses on its northern slopes. The house the Hardys had rented, in The Avenue, was in a low-lying part near the station and river, and the lime trees Hardy had described to Adam when he'd first moved there were in fact barely established.

Llanherne was a new, detached villa which was modest but comfortable, and had an old-fashioned quality to it with its conservatory, vine on the wall and orchard. But Hardy confided to Adam that he missed Dorchester.

'It has done wonders for my health being back in Dorset,' he said as they settled themselves in an informal sitting-room, 'but I long to return to the Dorchester area, where I grew up. I know that to do my best work I must move back there, and have decided to look for a plot of land on which to build. In fact, I have just written to the Earl of Ilchester's agent about a plot on Stinsford Hill.'

'We would be neighbours,' said Adam.

'And that would be a pleasure indeed.'

'But he mopes still for London!' His wife, Emma, appeared – stouter and taller than Adam remembered her, her jaw heavier than ever. She said brightly, 'We were delighted you could come. What a pity your wife was unable to accompany you.'

Without intending to sound disloyal, Adam explained truthfully, 'She said she would feel awkward – would not know what to talk to you about.'

'Oh, but she mustn't feel awkward with us, must she, dear?' Emma turned to her husband who looked small beside her. 'After all, we're not exactly grand or intimidating,' she added.

Her husband grunted. Besides being a shy person he was self-conscious about his origins. As the son of a servant and a mason – albeit a mason who had become a fairly successful builder – he longed to belong to the upper echelons of society and preferred to forget where he had come from; guiltily he purged himself on paper, inventing working-class heroes with whom he could identify.

He said, 'You took a risk marrying an uneducated country girl.'

'But it is working well,' Adam said.

And Emma, herself from a more genteel background, said, 'Dear, I don't think it is for us to comment on Adam's marriage.'

'I only spoke my mind. But I am glad all is satisfactory. And what of your writing?'

'My children's stories are being published in book form next month, and Leslie Stephen has just accepted my uncompleted novel for serialization.'

'Good old Leslie! He is a great friend of mine. But I do dislike the whole procedure of serialization. It cramps one's style, and at the same time puts one under such pressure to have the next chapter written.'

'And then one is criticized at the end of one's arduous work!' Adam said ruefully.

'My soul seems to shrivel when I read a bad review,' Hardy sighed. 'It is utterly discouraging . . . One is either elated or despairing as a writer. In the case of *Two on a Tower*, for instance, I was accused of immorality, and irreverence to the Church. The reviewers would have one remain with a single safe topic, and never deviate from it. Sometimes I think I'd have done better to have stuck to architecture!'

He had been an architect until his writing had brought him success with the publication of *Under the Greenwood Tree*, and then *Far from the Madding Crowd*. But prior to the recognition and acclaim there had been rejections and heartache, and even now he was still sensitive to harsh criticism, and was disappointed his poetry was not better received.

Over lunch, Emma Hardy told Adam about their proposed trip to Paris, and about life in Wimborne. She described their few friends, and her husband joked about the local Shakespeare Reading Society, which held its meetings at various private homes.

'It attracted me for a while,' he said, 'but I have to admit now that the amateurish performances amuse me.'

'You have become too sophisticated since London, dear,' teased his wife. 'That is your problem.'

'I think that hardly true,' he answered seriously. 'You know I never really fitted in, in London – except for my love of the theatre. I always felt as though I were an observer on the fringe of everything.'

'But that is exactly how I always felt,' Adam said – and for the remainder of lunch the pair compared their experiences and views, arguing in a friendly way where their opinions differed.

In the afternoon they visited the Minster, and so the day passed. That evening Adam stood by the window in his room, which overlooked the large garden with its profusion of shrubs and flowers, and he thought, guiltily, 'I'm glad Amabel isn't with me. The conversation wouldn't have been nearly so stimulating. She was right – she'd have been bored . . .' And then: 'How different it would have been with Sarah. How she would have enjoyed this weekend, contributed to it . . . Oh God, what did I destroy? The dreams we were hatching, the hopes we shared, and all my years of patient waiting. I wrecked everything. What is she doing now? Where living? . . . What am I thinking?' he castigated himself. 'I've a lovely wife, a good wife. What point hankering after what can never be?'

There was someting different about Amabel when he returned. When he went to embrace her she tensed and held herself aloof, yet she was garrulous. Her cheeks, too, were flushed.

'You are not ill?' he asked anxiously, pleased to see her despite his disloyal thoughts of the weekend.

'No. Why do you ask?' Nor did she look at him properly, and began rearranging in a vase flowers that were already perfectly arranged.

'I don't know –' he made a gesture of vagueness with his hands. 'You seem different.'

'How silly you are, my sweet! I'm not different. You writers – too much imagination by far, that's your trouble. Now come see the new dress and hat I bought. I'll go and slip them on for you.'

'I had a most enjoyable time at the Hardys,' he said, following her upstairs – followed in turn by the lurcher, who was beside himself with excitement at Adam's return.

'Oh I forgot to ask,' she said, turning.

'We missed you,' he lied.

'You never,' she retorted, laughing her squawk laugh.

Sitting on the edge of their double bed, he watched her undress and dress again, marvelled at the complications and paraphernalia involved in the procedure. She was by the long window, haloed in the light, putting on a great show, revealing her profile with its large breasts pushed out and waist held in . . . Aroused, he got up and went over to her, thinking it would be fun to pull her on to the bed, half-clothed – and she moved quickly away from the window. But not before he caught sight of the gardener standing beneath.

Furious, Adam shouted, 'That was all for him, that little act, wasn't it?'

'What do you mean, my sweet?' she asked, stammering slightly.

'You *know* what I mean,' he answered, icily now, driving his fist into the other palm.

'No. But I truly do not.'

'Oh forget it. Just forget it,' He began to doubt himself again, as he always did when he reacted hastily.

The weeks passed, and he could not ignore the changes: she found excuses not to make love, and when they did, she lay frozen beneath him; she no longer hummed as she went about her day and the house ceased to be orderly and well cared for . . .

'It can't be the gardener,' he thought. 'Amabel's become a snob. She wouldn't be unfaithful with the gardener.' Perhaps she wasn't having an affair at all. Perhaps there was some other problem she would not talk about, and he had been remiss in not trying to discover it.

One autumn afternoon, sitting before the crackling fire, he asked, 'Amabel, are you sad? Is there something bothering you?'

'No, my sweet. I'm right as rain.'

'I feel that we don't seem to speak any more . . . Perhaps we ought to take a holiday.'

'Oh no – I don't want to travel,' she said hurriedly.

'Why not? You enjoyed it last time.'

'Oh I like being at home, Adam. I feel – safe – here. B'sides, I don't like the boat crossing.'

'But you loved it on our honeymoon.'

'I only said I did to please you. I didn't really. And there's so much needs doing at home. I've let things slide recently.'

'I *care* about you, you know,' he said, looking sadly at her bright face.

'I know,' she answered kindly, but said nothing in return about caring for him.

Later on, when he was in his study writing, he heard the front door close – it was impossible to shut without banging – and glancing out of the window he saw Amabel running down the drive, her cloak flying . . .

'What did you do this afternoon?' he would ask her, and she'd answer, 'It were my turn t'do the flowers in the church,' or, 'I went to Tom's cottage to chat with my sister-in-law,' or 'I went black-berrying but all the hedgerows are bare now . . .' And any reply she gave, would, he knew, be a lie.

Adam was nearing the completion of his book. He wrote: 'Roger had long suspected his wife of deviousness, but had not wanted to admit to himself that her behaviour did not tally with his image of her as a simple country girl . . .' And he lost himself in his writing.

A couple of hours later he heard the front door bang again and footsteps in the hall, then running up several stairs. She was back. His study door was open. 'Did you have a good time?' he called to her invisible figure.

The footsteps stopped, and her voice, confused, called down, 'Yes – I only had to go out for a bit.'

'But whatever it was went well?' He walked slowly down the passageway, towards the stairs, and saw her standing hesitantly there like a cornered animal.

'Oh yes. I – I – the flowers had to be done in the church.'

He smiled knowingly at her, and she fled upstairs.

He wrote in his diary, 'Amabel is having an affair with the gardener. If I tackle her on the subject, she will deny it – and laugh with him behind my back, and so I have no choice but to ignore it, although I shall dismiss the gardener. I am more disappointed than heartbroken, sad rather than angry. And I think: well, this is what it is about. Life. Nobody ever said it was supposed to be constantly pleasant or easy. When was life either of those things for the boys who came to Brownstones? And I am just another contender caught in its apparently pointless barbed circle.

'I am as solitary now, despite all my striving not to be, as when I was a child . . .'

Austin Beaver visited Adam the next morning. 'Adam, I think you should know –' he began.

'I do,' Adam interrupted. 'Amabel is having an affair with my gardener.'

The vicar slumped in his chair. 'Oh dear. I am sorry.'

Adam shrugged. 'At least you're not saying, "I told you so".'

'She is appallingly blatant. Everyone is chit-chatting about it . . . And wherever she goes, she calls herself Lady Gilmour . . . I thought you ought to know.'

'Thank you, Austin.' Adam tried to smile. But he felt lost; deadened inside. 'Just tell me one thing. Are people laughing at me? I couldn't stand that.'

'No. Most certainly not. People are indignant on your behalf. You are very well liked.'

'Thank you,' Adam said again. 'You are a true friend.'

'Yes, I am that,' the odd-looking man said gruffly. 'That is honestly how I have come to regard you.'

Adam did two things that morning, the first of which was to dismiss the gardener. The young man stood sulkily before him without saying a word. He was gangling and waxy-skinned, and Adam wondered what Amabel saw in him – was vaguely insulted that her infidelity was not with someone more prepossessing. Or perhaps his taciturnity appealed to her. Perhaps she was sexually drawn by his indifference.

'You know why I am dismissing you,' Adam said.

'Yes sir.'

'Good. I'm glad that neither of us has to pretend on that score. Your work is good. I am prepared to give you a reference and a month's pay as long as your next job is not in this vicinity.'

The other nodded slightly in acknowledgement, and the interview was over.

'Fair unto the last,' Adam thought bitterly about himself.

The second thing he did was to saddle his cob and ride into Dorchester. On the way he was greeted by several people he knew, and he thought, gratefully surprised, 'Austin's right, I *am* liked. That's something, at least.' He felt strangely resigned as he rode through Whitcombe, past the thatched cottages and the church. In Dorchester he went into three dress-shops he knew his wife to frequent, and told the proprietresses that from now on he would not be responsible for paying her bills should she decide to place an order. Then he rode home – stopping first at the water-meadows at Lower Bockhampton, where he sat by the stream and let his horse graze.

'I had hoped for so much more. I always hope for so much more . . .'

The peacefulness of his surroundings, the undemanding beauty, caused the hardness in him to dissolve, and a wave of sorrow came over him. He buried his head in his arms and quietly cried.

Chapter Twenty-four

EXIT AMABEL

It was about a week after this that Adam saw the newspaper article. He was having breakfast with Amabel – she had been withdrawn and resentful since the gardener left – when he suddenly exclaimed, 'Good God!'

'What is it, my sweet?' She still called him that, but it was from habit, and the ease and thoughtlessness with which she said it annoyed him.

'Nothing. Just something in the paper.'

'Oh.' Uninterestedly she went back to munching on her toast. Newspapers were boring.

He read:

> Mrs Sarah Gilmour, who is the sister-in-law of novelist Sir Adam Gilmour, was arrested yesterday and held overnight in Westminster Police Station for 'disturbing the peace'. Mrs Gilmour, who is a widow, was the subject of much speculation two and a half years ago when she found herself at the centre of a scandal concerning Sir Adam's book, *Aaron*, written under a pseudonym, whose heroine was reputedly modelled on her. Shortly after this she established Brownstones Women's Club, which supports and campaigns for deprived women. However, due to lack of funds, the home is in danger of closing, so yesterday, following family tradition (you may recall Sir Adam Gilmour's activities some years back), Mrs Gilmour led a demonstration outside No. 10, Downing Street with several other women. When asked politely to advise the women to disperse, she equally politely refused, and after several further requests by the police, and her continuing refusal – by which time her refined manners had deserted her – she was forcibly and noisily dragged away . . .

'Oh, *Sarah*.'

'What's that? What's that, my sweet?'

'Oh for heaven's sake.' He glared at her and, pushing roughly by her chair, left the room.

Amabel, who as a child had often been reprimanded for her fiery temper, and now found it bothersome trying to keep it in check all the time, was glad of his anger. A spiteful expression came into her face: if he wanted to treat her miserably, she was fully justified in retaliating. She picked up the newspaper he had left behind, but could make little sense of the article.

Petulantly she put it down again. Then she took another bite of her toast and got up from the table. She would have the Welsh cob harnessed, and drive into Dorchester where she would treat herself to a couple of new dresses. And then she would go in search of some excitement . . .

Adam, too, decided to go into Dorchester; he had his own plans. Amabel had already left by the time he went into the yard to saddle up his horse, and he rode directly to the bank and did not see his wife. When he had completed his business he had a couple of mugs of beer in the Ship Inn, in High West Street. He felt elated, purposeful, and afterwards, when he went to untether his horse, he hugged its thick neck impulsively.

Amabel was not in such good humour. She had just endured the embarrassment of having her custom refused in three shops.

'Why?' she had demanded, outraged. 'I am *Lady* Gilmour.'

And when told the reason, she had felt her cheeks grow scarlet, and tears of humiliation prick her eyes.

'I'll kill him . . . I'll murder him, I will. What right does he have? Oh I hate him, the mean bastard . . .' These were her thoughts as she climbed back into the governess cart and shook the reins. But then as the journey progressed, she grew calm, and that sly look came into her eyes.

'Well, I'll find someone who *can* buy me pretty dresses then, and take me dancing.'

Adam arrived home about half an hour later. His wife was sitting in the rocking chair – rocking back and forth, absently twining some strands of corn into a design. He felt remiss suddenly. He hadn't tried to understand her; didn't consider her needs. Perhaps it was *his* fault she had strayed.

'Hallo,' he said awkwardly.

'Hallo.' She didn't glance up from playing with her strands of corn, and he stood there uncertainly for a moment longer, before abruptly turning and going into his study. At his desk he took a couple of sheets of writing paper, and began a letter to his sister:

My dearest Leah –

How are you? Having written only a few days ago I have not much news, so shall come straight to the point of this letter: this morning I read the most disturbing article in the *Telegraph*; it concerned Sarah! She was held overnight in a police cell (shades of familiarity?) for campaigning outside No. 10, Downing Street on behalf of her Women's Club, which, it seems, is in desperate financial straits. Why did you not *tell* me of this? You must have realized I would have wished to know, and I cannot believe Sarah has not confided in you. Also, why does not her father, with all his contacts, help her? I have arranged for an anonymous contribution to be sent to her monthly, and hope it will be sufficient to save the place from ruin, if not bring it the success it and she deserve. Call it reparation, if you like. I trust you'll not tell Sarah who her benefactor is, for if she knew she would certainly reject the money. She is so proud . . .

Ten days later he received Leah's reply. She had written by return of post.

Addi dearest,

Thank you for your letter. Yes, I did know of Sarah's plight, but it was that very pride to which you referred which made her insist I mention nothing to you. She longs to succeed in her venture, and to be seen to do so. As to her father – the reason he does not help is that sadly he died seven or eight months ago. His bank had been doing badly due, I believe, to the dishonesty of his partner, and the stress caused him to have a heart attack – he had a weakness anyway.

Brambleden Hall has been sold on yet again – our poor lovely home – and Mrs Lowenstein lives at the Belgravia apartment . . .

The months passed and it was almost Christmastime. Adam had been married a year and he had to concede it had been a disastrous mistake. Nor was there any sign of Amabel becoming pregnant, and his dream of having a large family, of children filling his home, withered. He changed the ending of his book. It was to have been happy, but he saw now that it would have been implausible. The first four chapters had already been serialized in the *Cornhill*, but the reviews were poor and Adam was disheartened and resentful, convinced that the critics were reacting negatively because of a general wariness after *Aaron*.

'They are like sheep,' he thought disgustedly. 'Only less original.'

But a report in *The Times* made him happy. It said:

Brownstones Women's Club, run by Mrs Sarah Gilmour, the widowed sister-in-law of writer Sir Adam Gilmour ['How that must gall her,' he thought, 'the constant reference to me as though she had no identity of her own'], has been saved at the eleventh hour by an anonymous benefactor who has been making sizeable donations.

Commented Mrs Gilmour, 'I am very relieved, and shall be eternally grateful to this unknown person for his or her support at a time when I was beginning to despair. I hope whoever it is realizes the gladness these gifts have brought not just to me, but to the many women who have come to regard the Club as a sanctuary, the only place where they can salvage their pride and their hopes. I wish I could thank this generous and selfless person myself.'

Amabel's next affair was with an unmarried schoolmaster from Dorchester, and this time it was her brother Tom who told Adam. They had been discussing plans for the farm for the new year – purchasing extra land and buying more dairy cows, when the bailiff had become red and bothered, and suddenly banged both fists hard on his muscular thighs.

'Damn me sir – Adam – you ought t'know. It be my duty t'tell you, even though she be my sister . . . Amabel's up to no good, sir.' Miserably he stared at Adam – who felt himself grow cold.

'I assume you mean she's having another affair,' he said.

'Yes,' mumbled Tom, embarrassed and torn in his loyalties.

'Poor Tom.' Adam smiled at him gently. 'What a pr-pre-dicament for you. It must have been hard for you to tell me s-such a thing.' He crossed and uncrossed his legs, and Tom felt a rush of pity for him.

'I kn-know Ama-bel now, Tom. She isn't really a b-bad girl – just gree-greedy for li-life. She wants a b-big life. Th-thrills . . . Oh God, l-listen to me stuttering l-l-like an imbecile . . .' He hunched forward and put his head in his hands.

'I'm ever so sorry, sir.'

Adam sighed and gave a shrug. The last fortnight had been better between them, he had thought. They had resumed making love; she had seemed happy and had been bustling around once more, making the place homely. He felt surprisingly sad now that he realized it had all been an act on her part.

Tom broke the silence. 'Well, I says she *is* bad, sir. I'll have nothing t'do with her, I want you t'know. And nor'll my wife.'

'It explains why the locals have been rather awkward with me lately,' Adam said, his stammering fit over. 'Perhaps I ought to wear a placard announcing, "Do not worry, I know about my wife's affair." Would that be a good idea, do you think? Is everyone talking about it, Tom?'

'Well, sir, it's on a few lips.'

'Bother her.' Adam got up abruptly. He imagined himself as the butt of gossip. 'I'm going to say something to her. It's all very well trying to be reasonable . . .'

Much later that evening, after Adam and Amabel had quarrelled and gone into different rooms, he wondered if he was not, in his way, as unfaithful as she, as he mentally paid homage to Sarah – thinking about her, dreaming about her, giving money to her cause. If Sarah came to him now, would he have spared Amabel a thought?

He visited the schoolmaster. He was hardly more than a boy. A beautiful-looking young boy.

'I love your wife, sir,' he told Adam defensively.

'Then I feel sorry for you,' Adam replied.

The other flushed. 'I wish to marry her.'

Adam glanced round the shabby room of the terraced cottage. 'Please,' he said kindly, 'please believe me, she wants nothing from you but one thing, and that will bore her in another month or so.'

'I cannot believe you. I'm sorry, sir . . . I am really sorry to have disrupted your marriage.'

This incensed Adam. 'You haven't disrupted my marriage,' he said scornfully.

'She says you don't understand her.'

'I daresay I understand her as well as anyone,' answered Adam, suddenly weary. 'I understand that she needs constant excitement and is highly ambitious and that she uses the sexual act as compensation.'

'But she is not like that!' protested the beautiful young man passionately.

'But she is,' Adam said, and left.

Spring came. Adam watched his fields changing colour, his stock fattening. Amabel had grown bored with her second lover and was back in her husband's bed.

'It'll never happen again, I promise, my sweet,' she said, snuggling up to him after a particularly energetic bout of love-making. 'Trust me? I know I was wrong.'

Adam smiled in the darkness and tweaked her cheek. Her activities did not hurt him, and her promises were a waste of breath.

Every so often they went to London – to the theatre, to concerts, to see old acquaintances – but his wife was uncomfortable with Adam's friends, and after the first time or two he tended to see them on his own. She enjoyed going to the music hall, or listening to a brass band, visiting Regent's Park Zoo – which he thought cruel – or going to restaurants. And she loved to window-shop quite as much as she loved to spend money . . . He still found her naïve excitement appealing, could see in her then what had first drawn him to her.

'You should have married a rich merchant or a factory owner,' he teased once.

'Why?' she asked, puzzled.

'Someone like that would not be so fuddy-duddy as me. He would not care about books, only about making money and having fun.'

Amabel stared at him. A change came over her face, and he realized she had taken him seriously. She saw the faint mockery about his mouth and knew he had guessed her thoughts; touching his cheek lightly, she said, 'I only want you, my sweet . . .'

From time to time Adam read about Sarah in the paper – an incident at Brownstones, her involvement with the women's movement, her constant efforts to raise money; and he would cut out the articles and lay them lovingly in a box on top of her long-ago letters. He increased his monthly donations to the Club . . .

He had also founded a charity for the poor in Dorset, and was now a known figure wherever he went; a young man still at thirty-six, with that same uncertain look, that refined aestheticism, and the old shyness despite his fame. His novel was due to be published shortly in book form, but he had no inclination to start another. He felt strangely distanced from himself, and increasingly obsessed with Sarah.

He had discovered from Leah that she had a house in St John's Wood, and tried to picture it – it was probably a small, semi-detached place, he thought. He tried to imagine Sarah and her daughter there – his goddaughter – and recalled the summer after Jonathan had died when he had sat with them on the lawn and told stories . . . He spent long periods immersed in his memories now . . .

The lurcher took to bringing a dead rabbit home regularly and the cook would skin it and make it into stew or pie or pâté, until Amabel screamed that she was bored with rabbit; the cat had a litter of ten kittens which Amabel was about to drown in the lake, when Adam, livid, stopped her; doves nested in the roof and the hatched offspring kept Adam and Amabel awake half the night; the calves and lambs were sold at market; the hay was mown and summer was there, the men, naked to the waist and brown-bodied working in the fields – Adam amongst them – and the heavy horses trudging laboriously back and forth towing farm machinery. Swallows skimmed over the lake, landing briefly and flying up again with insects in their beaks; dragonflies, drawn by the nettles, hovered over the water, Red Admiral butterflies rested on lilies . . . Amabel spent hours bathing herself and oiling herself and coiffing herself, and Adam knew she had found a new lover . . . And he had a letter from Sarah.

It was amongst a pile of other letters, all of which he read beforehand, and when he opened the envelope at leisure he could not have imagined the contents. There at the top of the page was printed: Brownstones Women's Club, Hillcrest Road, Islington. His heart racing, Adam began to read:

Dear Adam,

This is not an easy letter to write, after what happened three years ago. However, yesterday it came to my notice who the mysterious benefactor to Brownstones Women's Club has been, for the last ten months. It seems that your bank has a new member of staff who did not realize that your payments were supposed to be anonymous, and when the latest contribution arrived your name was revealed.

I was, needless to say, stunned, and have felt very confused since. My first reaction was overwhelming gratitude for your generosity, but my second that I wanted to take nothing from you. But I must, in all honesty, say that without your donations Brownstones Women's Club would not have survived, and it is only now, thanks to your help, that it is finally beginning to succeed.

So I find myself in the position of having to thank someone whom I never wanted to hear of again; and yet such ungracious thanks seem an inadequate reward for your kindness. Nevertheless, I feel it would be wrong for you to continue with your donations, not because of my pride or any animosity I might bear you, but because they are too generous: I had imagined all this time that my benefactor was someone exceedingly wealthy. The monthly contributions must be a considerable financial strain for you; it would be unreasonable of me, especially as Brownstones is no longer threatened with closure, to continue to accept them.

Yours,

Sarah

Her ending was so abrupt that he imagined her toying with her pen, uncertain how to finish, before just signing her name hurriedly and putting the letter in its envelope. His heart was still racing, and he ran his hands vigorously through his hair and over his eye.

He sat down to write his reply. 'Dearest Sarah, I love, love you, love you . . .' He laughed out loud and wrote instead:

Dear Sarah,

Thank you for your letter. And how do you know I have not become exceedingly wealthy? I am sorry that you had to discover my 'identity', but glad that for the past few months my contributions have helped your Club.

You intimated that it was your concern for my financial well-being and not personal antagonism which made you disinclined to accept further contributions, but surely that is my affair? I am certainly able to afford the amounts I have been donating, and should very much like to continue giving to your worthy cause.

I hope you are keeping well, and must congratulate you on your achievements with Brownstones Women's Club. You should be very proud of yourself. I would also like to say how sorry I was to learn of your father's death, and send you my deepest sympathy. He was a kind, erudite man.

Yours ever,
Adam

Her second letter arrived after a few days.

Dear Adam,

Thank you for your letter in answer to mine. Can we come to an arrangement? Whilst I am extremely grateful to you for your proposal to continue with your donations, I think I should feel a great deal happier if they were halved; these lesser contributions would still be enormously helpful to Brownstones, believe me, and I myself would feel better about accepting them.

Thank you for your kind words about my poor father. I miss him terribly, even now, and cannot quite realize I shall never see him again. The wonderful thing about him as a father was that he never judged and always gave one room to be *oneself*. I must tell you that I read Rebecca your children's stories every night before she went to sleep, and she and I laughed and cried our way through them together. They were truly enchanting.

I trust you are in good health.

Yours,

Sarah

A friendly letter! Adam danced with it around the room, oblivious to the sight of his wife dressed up and perfumed on her way out to 'visit her mother'.

He went out himself to choose a birthday present for his goddaughter who would be eight on July 15th. Did she like dolls? he wondered anxiously, recalling his sister's antipathy to them as a child; or spinning tops, or paintboxes . . . In the end he found a musical box which combined puppet figures of Pierrot and the man-in-the-moon. He had it especially wrapped and mailed to Rebecca, care of Brownstones . . .

Several weeks passed and Adam's life was becoming inextricably bound with Sarah's again, as he donated to her cause, and wrote articles to leading newspapers promoting Brownstones and the women's movement; but he made no attempt to see her and gave his love to her the only way he could – by respecting her from a distance and supporting her ideals.

She had written twice since that last time, once to thank him for Rebecca's present – also enclosing a letter from Rebecca herself – and once to thank him for his journalistic efforts, which were beginning to have an impact. She had ended the last letter 'yours ever' (as he always did), instead of just 'yours'.

Meanwhile Thomas and Emma Hardy had moved back to Dorchester, into yet another rented house – a dark, narrow building named Shire Hall Place, which had once belonged to the headmaster of the Dorset County School. It stood on the west side of Shire Hall Lane near the top of the town, and Adam often called there. But he never mentioned Sarah to Hardy, or discussed his marriage, nor did Hardy confide about his boredom with Emma. They were both private men, and theirs was a more cerebral friendship. It became a weekly ritual that on a Thursday they would breakfast late, then go to the new museum together and sit in different parts of the reading-room.

'I should be writing, thinking of a plot for a new book,' Adam wrote in his diary. 'But my mind is full of Sarah, nothing but Sarah. Thank God for Tom Jarvis running the farm, as for sure in my hands at the moment it would be falling into ruin! His sister, my wife, is another story. She flounces about in new dresses bought by someone else, and a hairdo which is in the latest Parisian style and hardly apt for a rural Dorset hamlet. Lovable one! Hah – her heart has as much love in it as the paperweight on my desk. However, she is no guiltier than I . . .'

Amabel announced that she was leaving towards the end of September when the stubble fields had been burned, and the horses with their ploughs were busy all day, and children scoured the hedgerows for blackberries.

Adam had just returned from Old Martha's to find her frantically packing her things. He had known this was inevitable, but the actual shock was greater than he had envisaged, and he was surprised at himself. Or was it fear of being on his own again, with no chance of children, living for Sarah's occasional letters, and becoming increasingly dominated by his one-sided, obsessive love? Amabel had been an anchor for him. The farm, the house, Dorset, his work – all those things which he had built upon after the demise of Brownstones and the scandal of *Aaron* were meaningless if he was to be on his own. He was to blame. He had ignored Amabel, he realized – had claimed to understand her, but done nothing about that understanding . . .

'Please don't go, Amabel.'

'I have to, Adam.'

'Who is he?' he asked dully, sitting cross-legged on the floor. And for a moment she seemed to soften towards him, as she saw him looking so handsome and vulnerable.

'Oh, my sweet –' She bent as if to stroke his hair, then remembered her lover, he with the small round bald head lost in the fatness of his body, and a purse ten times as fat as himself . . . Resolutely she straightened again.

'I have to go, Adam. I'm sorry. It's not your fault.'

‘Can’t we try again? I’ll take you out to places. I won’t spend so much time reading, or being silent, not asking about *you* . . .’

‘You’re a good man,’ she said, shutting the case with a final click. ‘But I feel like a prisoner here. I don’t laugh any more.’ Her squawking raucous laugh which had so grated on him.

‘I never imprisoned you,’ he said defensively. ‘That isn’t fair.’

‘No, you didn’t. But your friends wouldn’t accept me. Him that I’m going with, he’s more my kind. He were from an ordinary home like me, but he struck it lucky.’

‘Well, I hope you’re happy,’ Adam said tersely, untangling his legs and getting up.

‘He’s not like you, he’s ugly,’ she said softly, putting her arms around him.

Adam pressed himself against her, held her hard to him. ‘Don’t go. You don’t *know* what you want, Amabel.’ He undid a button at her neck.

‘And nor do you, my sweet.’

He pushed her away, and she left with her two cases, her cape over her shoulders, ridiculous little hat perched forward on her elaborate hairdo, and not a backward glance.

Chapter Twenty-five

A FARM DOWN WEST

Tom Jarvis sat facing Adam in the conservatory, his face set in a scowl.

'The trollop,' he said. 'She needs a good hiding. She's spoiled, that's her trouble.'

Adam was tired. He had lain awake all night, mulling over everything, and had come to the conclusion that he was weak and easily tricked, that he was a poor judge of women. He was disappointed in himself.

'The trouble is,' he thought, 'that we all have this fixed, idealized picture of how life should be. I was determined to make mine real at any cost.'

He had yearned for the perfect life, and the knowledge that it would never happen made him sorrow as though someone had died.

Disturbed by Adam's silence, Tom said, 'Sir – she's not worth your distress. You be better off without her.'

'Maybe.' Adam sat back and closed his eyes, became aware of the birdsong outside and the smell of jasmine in the conservatory. 'Maybe,' he repeated.

'Sir – I want to say, I shan't be speaking to her no more. I gave her the chance once before. She's gone for good this time so far as me and my family's concerned.'

'Tom, she's your sister. I won't hold it against *you* if you see her. And I daresay I'm partly to blame,' he added.

'That may or mayn't be, sir. But you're principled and she's not. She's dead as far's I'm concerned. Now sir – presuming you want me to stay on, that is – we've the drilling to discuss . . .'

*

'I must be the most famous cuckold in the county!' Adam said to Austin Beaver several weeks later when they were out for a walk together one damp morning, and had stopped for a breather.

'You wait,' the vicar said, 'the invitations will soon start pouring in again, mark my words.'

'I'm not certain I want those kind of invitations, Austin.'

'Adam, let me tell you about the people round here. They are mostly decent. You mustn't blame them for not knowing how to react when you married Amabel. Look at it from their point of view – they had nothing in common with her, nothing to say at the dinner-table . . . Why, man, even you confided to me once that you were glad she did not accompany you to the Hardys at Wimborne.'

'I know, I know. I am full of contradictions. I try to be tolerant, pride myself that I am, and now realize I am not.'

'I think you are being too harsh on yourself. You are really not at all a bad chap to have as a friend.'

Adam elbowed him lightly in the ribs. 'And for a country parson, you are really quite enlightened.'

Still he could not think of an idea for a new novel; and he was disheartened, too, by the reaction to *A Simple Country Girl*. The reviews at best had been tepid, and at worst, harsh. The *Athenaeum* had accused him of having an implausible plot which 'the author seemed uncertain how to direct', while the *Examiner* had called it 'an ill-orchestrated piece of writing . . .' Thomas Hardy commiserated with him and tried to offer encouragement. 'That book is past now. Posterity will judge its real worth. As for commencing another – how can you expect your mind to be fertile so soon after all that you have undergone? First you must try to replenish your soul, in order that your mind be nourished . . .'

Claud wrote to say that he and Leah would be coming to England with the twins in December, as there was a sculpture exhibition in London Leah wanted to attend, and that they would like to spend Christmas in Dorset with Adam.

Adam wrote back: 'You have no idea how already I long for your arrival . . .'

He felt buoyant again – looked around the house and realized how unkempt it was. He had heard that Mrs Roberts was unhappy in her new job, and wrote asking to meet her.

Humbly he said to her, 'Would you consider coming back? I never wanted you to be dismissed, you know.'

'Bless you, sir. Of course I know that. And it'd make me the happiest woman in Dorset to come and work for you again.' Tears bulged in her round eyes and trickled over the creases beneath. 'Bless you, sir,' she said again, beaming through her tears. 'We'll soon have everything to rights again. You'll see.' And she got up and, clasping his head impulsively, kissed his hair.

The time approached for their arrival, and Adam worked himself into a frenzy of anticipation. He went to London to shop, and returned laden with parcels and boxes. He bought a huge Christmas tree and decorated it – decorated every room in the house – festively; he wrote a story for each of the boys and was once more full of purpose. He did not dare think beyond Christmas to the flatness which would follow. The servants caught his mood of gaiety, and the house was alive with excitement.

Then, the day before his sister, brother-in-law and nephews were due to arrive, Adam fell ill. It had been brewing for a couple of days, but he had been so busy, and was longing so intensely for their arrival, that he had paid no heed to the symptoms.

On December 23rd he awoke early, shivering, drenched in sweat and gasping for breath. He thought he would choke with his need for air, and heard the sounds he was making with a curious deatachment. Forcing himself to sit up, he wrapped his arms tightly around his diaphragm, pressing with his thumbtips in the hollow beneath his breastbones, and trying to push against the pressure.

'Breathe . . . Breathe . . .' But his body wouldn't respond, and he became panicky, the perspiration running down his face from his forehead. He was going to choke, suffocate, die. And then he sneezed and with the sneeze his breath was released in great wheezing gasps, and he gulped greedily . . .

He needed to use the privy, and tried to get out of bed, but his legs felt molten and he made several attempts before he was finally able to stand and take a few tremulous steps – grasping the bed, then the wall, the door . . . Into the corridor – like a drunk, he thought; for his mind was still lucid and he continued to regard this out-of-control creature who was himself as though from a distance. But he could not impose his will on his limbs, nor prevent the sudden bodily lightness which overtook him . . .

The two housemaids were just setting about their day and both heard the thud. Soon the whole house was roused, and Mrs Roberts, the cook and the two girls lifted Adam and carried him back to bed.

'Poor boy,' wept Mrs Roberts, bending over to stroke his forehead. 'Why, he be nothing but a boy.' Then she ran downstairs and out of the house to alert Tom Jarvis, and have him ride in search of a doctor.

The doctor came from nearby West Knighton and knew Adam slightly. Alone in the room with him, he felt his pulse, put the stethoscope to his chest, and took his temperature. There was an ominous rattle in the breathing, and the doctor thought, 'I'll not bleed him. There's no point.'

From his bag he took out two bottles of a draught he made up himself, and filled a dropper with the medicine. This he squeezed down his patient's throat. Some dribbled from the corner of Adam's mouth, and the doctor wiped it with his own handkerchief. He shook his head pityingly. 'What a waste of a great talent so early on . . .' And he left the room.

Outside Mrs Roberts waited anxiously, and again the doctor shook his head – at the same time handing her the medicine and dropper.

'Just in case, give him the medicine four times daily.'

'Will he –' She couldn't finish the sentence.

'It seems probable.'

'It were all *her* fault, going off like that.'

'A wicked world, Mrs Roberts. A wicked one indeed.' He had heard, of course, about the wife. Everyone had.

Pain raged in Adam, and light flooded his head. He had been dimly aware of someone else, a tangible presence, but then it had gone, and now alone, outwardly in a coma, he knew only his agony and the immense weight bearing down on him.

Time, meaningless, passed and he emerged from his state of unconsciousness and heard voices reverberating around him, while hideous gargoyles glared down from corners of the ceiling and leaped out from the floor and from under his pillow. He had not the strength to avoid them, could only roll his eyes in horror, and cringe. His whiteness was emphasized by the dark three-day stubble on his face, and his lips seemed to have disappeared; his hair was lank and damp, and his skin glistened, fish-like. Up and down rose the bedclothes with his rapid, rasping breathing which allowed scarcely any air into his lungs . . .

Leah sat by his side, hopeless, her handkerchief, screwed into a wet ball, gripped in her left hand. Claud sat on the window-seat bowed like an old man, his eyes swollen and red. He felt useless – would intermittently leave the room, go to his sons and play with them for a while, then shout at them over some tiny thing, and return to the sick room, with its smells of body odour and medicament. The air outside was too cold for the window to be opened. Christmas Day – and who was in festive spirits?

'But he is out of his coma at least,' Leah said on a note of optimism. 'Perhaps there is a chance, after all.'

'Rubbish, woman,' snapped Claud. 'He's going to die. You know he is. So why the hell can't it be quick. Why can't this sodding God who this poor soul's fool enough to believe in make it quick?'

'Adam doesn't believe in God,' Leah said, surprised.

'He told me that "on balance" he thought he did last time we met. That was how he put it, looking frightfully intense as he said it. Stupid bastard,' he said, his voice cracking. And he broke down again. 'I love him . . .' He buried his great head in his hands, and his wife went to him and supported his head with its tired gold hair and thinning patch.

The doctor called later. 'How is he?'

'Dreadful,' Leah said.

'But conscious?'

'Sometimes.'

'I think I should bleed him.'

'No!' The voice, weak but distinct, came from Adam, and they all turned, startled, to see him recoiling beneath the bedclothes, his face terror-struck. 'Don't murder me . . .' He had a fit of coughing and spat blood, then began to cry.

'Hush, Addi. Addi, it's me – Leah.' She sat beside him again and pressed his hand to her cheek, but he snatched it away.

'Don't *murder* me,' he tried to shout, thought he shouted, but he barely whispered the words.

'Goodness me,' said the doctor, who had drunk too much port. 'Well, I think it would only distress him further if I released blood. Perhaps it is for the best to leave him after all. Keep on with the draught. And some broth. Merry Christmas to you.' And he was gone.

He left the door open, and fresh air filled the room. In the hall, just near the foot of the stairs, the twins had grown bored with waiting to open their presents and begun on their own. The sounds of their excitement reached upstairs, and Adam's eyes opened.

'Beaky? *Bea*-ky?' he murmured. A tear trickled down his cheek. 'Children's laughter,' he sighed. He slept, and dreamed that old dream of a child with his features. But now the child swam in his lake and jumped up every so often to try to grasp a dragonfly – which became a snake that entwined itself around the child's neck, and the child was him, and his life was being pressed out of him . . .

Days passed, unnoticed. Death was imminent, and then receded, and then came close again. The images and voices – real and hallucinatory – the past and present, were all intermingled. He emerged from his delirium and knew with a sense of relieved resignation that he was dying.

'Leah?'

'Addi – are you better again?' Leah gently pressed a cool damp flannel to his forehead. She was alone; Claud was with the twins.

'Leah. Don't be sad for me.'

'You will be *well*,' she said, crushing his hand to her mouth, muffling her sobs with it.

'Little Leah.' He imagined he flew over rooftops, and his eyes closed. Dying was simple.

'Addi. *Please* . . .'

'Little, little Leah . . .'

'*No*, Addi.' She jumped up, her voice shrill. 'No.' And Adam's eyes flickered open, surprised.

'You'll *not* die.'

'I want to.' He had a coughing fit, and his face became purple with the effort.

When it was over his sister said, 'Addi – listen to me. Are you listening?'

He tried to smile. 'Bossy little thing . . . Joshua said that, didn't he?'

'Yes.' Leah smiled through her tears. 'Addi, you *are* going to be better. And there are two people arriving shortly to see you. Can you hear me?' With each word she jolted his hand up and down in hers.

'. . . Yes . . .' The preliminary to sleep was beautiful in its variety of colour and sounds in the air, he thought; patterns forming like strange maps, then dispersing.

'Addi – Sarah is coming to see you. *Sarah*.'

'Sarah?' His eyes flickered open.

Leah nodded and fought against crying again. 'Sarah is coming. And your son. Addi, you have a *son*.'

'A *son*?' His eyes widened, and then he shut them once more. Voices were in his head. Mocking him. A son. Sarah. My sweet, my sweet.

'Don't mock me . . . I'll not be pitied . . . Go away . . .'

'Sarah and your son are coming, Addi. They are. They *are*.'

'Don't cry, little Leah.' He tried to stroke her face, but his fingers were wisps of hay. He longed to sleep, but she forced him to remain awake. It was something she had said which prevented him from sleeping . . .

She stayed by him, talking, willing him not to sleep, glancing every few moments at the little carriage clock to see how many minutes had ticked by, wishing Sarah would arrive. The room grew darker. Already mid-afternoon; and Adam was sleeping again, looking more like a waxwork than a human being.

'It's no good,' his sister thought. 'This time nothing will work . . .' And she began to reproach herself for not having told him about his son earlier, although she had promised Sarah not to. How easy things were, with hindsight. One would do this – or not; behave in a certain way . . . She heard the sounds of a carriage coming down the lane, a horse trotting at a brisk pace, and held her breath in case it would not turn up the driveway, but it did, and when she ran to the window the carriage was drawing up, and inside it – Sarah and a little boy.

'Thank heaven.'

Claud was outside, hugging Sarah, lifting up the child, and the twins appeared, their raised voices drifting upwards so that even with the windows shut Leah could hear them. She tapped on the window and beckoned frantically, and they all glanced towards her, saw her gesticulating and mouthing, 'Hurry . . .' And disappeared inside.

When she returned to his bedside, Adam's eyes were open again and Leah knew an overwhelming sense of relief. She knelt down next to him. 'Addi?'

'. . . Yes.' He felt at peace. His pain had subsided to a great heaviness which was pulling him away. Leah . . . Claud . . . His mouth moved slightly in a smile. What else? So many things, all confused . . . And an unbearable sadness as he remembered Sarah . . .

'Sarah . . .'

'Addi. She's here. She's coming any second now. With your *son*.'

His mind was a merry-go-round whirling at nightmare speed. He shut his eyes tight and reopened them, and said lucidly, 'I have no son.'

'Yes you have, my dearest.'

That voice. That lovely, low voice. And there, moving swiftly from the doorway to his side, was Sarah. Leah left them alone, tiptoeing from the room, unable to suppress her sobs.

Sarah sat on the edge of his bed. His Sarah. His beautiful Sarah. But of course it was not her. He turned his face away and tears slid from beneath his eyelids.

She brushed away her own tears, and said softly, 'Aren't you pleased to see me? You might at least say hallo!'

He turned back to her, and tried to focus on the woman sitting on the edge of his bed. Tremulously, he reached out to stroke the black waving hair, and she caught his hand and held it against her cheek, and then leaned forward and kissed him – his eyes, his parched lips, sunken cheeks . . . He lay perfectly still, unsure whether or not he was hallucinating, whether this was some wonderful preliminary to death. Her hair brushed his nose, tickled his nostrils. He could smell it . . . He stared into the gold-flecked dark eyes hovering over his, and she saw the recognition in his expression.

'I'm here, darling . . . I *love* you.' Her voice quavered. 'Oh God forgive me.'

'Sarah? *Sar*ah?'

She nodded, biting her lips, tears pouring down her face, and she lay beside him on top of the bed, as close as she could get to him.

The fuzziness within him lessened, but the pain returned to replace it, the terrible constriction across his chest.

'I – am – in – such – pain,' he whispered.

'I know, darling. But it will pass.'

He shook his head from side to side sorrowfully.

'It *will*,' she repeated vehemently. 'You *will* live – for my sake and our son's.'

'You are – as – bossy as – Leah.' He smiled feebly, felt her shape curved into his, her face close to his, her hair like a scarf about his head. Such pain. Such happiness. He slept.

When he awoke hours later, she was still there, asleep beside him. He had not, after all, dreamed it, and he lay watching her, her face illuminated in the strange glow of the gaslight. Her gentle breathing contrasted with his own wheezing sounds and he concentrated on trying to emulate the rhythm of her breathing, to force himself to be in time with her. He slept again.

This time when he awoke the room was dark, and he could feel she was no longer lying next to him, and knew a moment's panic. 'Sarah?' Adam said, in a voice made strong with fear.

And her voice came back in the darkness. 'I'm here, my love. In the chair by the window.'

Relief swept through him. 'Lie with me again. Please.'

'I thought I was crushing you, that was the only reason I moved.'

He heard her getting up as she spoke, stumbling and feeling her way over to the bed. He began to cough and retch, and she was there, supporting his neck until the fit was over, and he lay back once more, exhausted.

There was the rustling of her clothes, and she climbed into bed with him, wearing only a chemise. Her skin was on his skin, her heart beating against his arm. It was as though life itself were being pumped into his body.

*

'What is his name?'

'Andrew. It was Beaky's real name. Did you know?'

'No.' He squeezed her hand, and Sarah saw that his eyes were watering. Her throat tightened.

She had had plenty of time during the past week to reflect – and to ponder upon her own shortcomings. And while Adam lay upstairs hovering between life and death, she had gone from room to room in his beautiful house, trying to imagine how his life had been . . . Here he had placed a Minton ornament of a greyhound, here an ugly Toby jug, here a miniature of his father, and beside it a bowl of polished pebbles; on a 'whatnot' was his entire collection of antique writing implements. There was the usual chaos on his desk in the study no one dared touch . . .

And the servants behaved as though one of their own family was dying, and even the dog lay constantly outside Adam's bedroom door . . . Donning stout shoes and cloak, Sarah took Adam's usual route across the fields with Tom Jarvis – whose voice caught as he spoke of his master. And people continually called to enquire after him. She heard only words of admiration and respect for the man she had never ceased to love, whose child she had borne, who had caused her suffering, and whom in return she had caused to suffer . . .

'I long to see him.' Adam spoke with difficulty.

'Then –'

'No. Not like this. He would shrink back at the horrible sight of me. I could not – bear – that. I wish *you* hadn't seen me like it. Without – dignity. Hideous. Smelling foul.'

'I love you. You are none of those things.'

He rolled on to his stomach and could feel his hip bones jutting, digging into the mattress. He had bed-sores on his bottom. 'How much wasted time,' he mumbled into his pillows. And then from downstairs came the peal of a child's laughter, and he fell asleep, smiling.

Stroking Adam's lank hair, feeling him relax into sleep, Sarah's thoughts drifted. She saw them, the four of them – for there was Rebecca, too – a proper family at last, living here at Sheepsford Manor. They would marry as soon as Adam obtained his divorce. She would help with the farm . . . What was it a blind gypsy woman had told her once at Hampstead fair? 'You'll marry a farmer and live down west . . .'

Sarah continued to stroke Adam's hair, willing him to become strong, willing her vigour and health to flow into him. She stared ahead, envisaging their future together: a future enriched with love and companionship; and the sounds of their children's laughter.

EPILOGUE

In 1884 Adam married his Sarah, thus fulfilling a blind hag's prophecy. The wedding took place in France where it was permissible to marry one's sister-in-law. They returned to Sheepsford Manor farm to live, and Adam spent the next two years working on his greatest book, *The Son of the Sun*, a fantasy which appealed to adults and children alike. In 1888, the same year as the death of his father's old friend, Edward Lear, he was elevated to the peerage for his services to charity and his contribution to literature. The honour was too great to decline. Finally he had earned his title.

One day in October 1895, at the age of forty-nine, Lord Adam Gilmour died at Sheepsford Manor after a short illness. His beloved wife was at his bedside, her hand entwined with his.

The Juniper Bush

Audrey Howard

Winner of the 1987
Romantic Novel of the Year Award

The passionate saga of a nineteenth-century Lakeland girl, her search for happiness in a web of conflicting emotions and loyalties.

Lovely Christy Emmerson is the only daughter of an explosives manufacturer and a fine catch for any man. But there is only one man Christy cares about, and when she becomes betrothed to the Squire's son, Robin, it seems that all concerned are happy.

But with only a few weeks to go before the wedding tragedy strikes the community, and the Emmerson family. Apparently abandoned by Robin at a time when she needed him most, Christy, heartbroken and confused, falls into a marriage with a local mine owner, the handsome but arrogant Alex Buchanan. As her family grows, Christy becomes increasingly wrapped up in her new life and almost succeeeds in forgetting Robin. Then, one day, she meets him again and her whole world is thrown into confusion.

Audrey Howard's other bestselling sagas, *The Skylark's Song, The Morning Tide* and *Ambitions*, are also available in Fontana Paperbacks.

FONTANA PAPERBACKS

The Heath
Abigail Frith

Hunger, cold, the humiliation of Poor Relief, and the overshadowing menace of the workhouse are the lot of the Ruddock family in rural Bedfordshire in the hungry 1830s. Fiery John Ruddock and his lively, tough daughter, Sarah, come into conflict as they pursue different ways to escape from suffering and help their family and friends.

John campaigns with the Chartists but Sarah is tempted by the glamour of London and susceptible, rich young men. Ruthlessly exploiting her charms and her unerring sense of style, she contrives to set up as a fashionable dressmaker in the village. Everything goes well – until Francis Vaughan comes along. He is one of the gentry, a man whom John regards as an enemy. Worse still, he is much older than Sarah and he already has a wife . . .

FONTANA PAPERBACKS